4—

The Ghost Who Fell in Love
AND
The Chieftain Without a Heart

BARBARA CARTLAND

*The Ghost
Who Fell in Love*
AND
*The Chieftain
Without a Heart*

E. P. DUTTON & COMPANY, INC.
NEW YORK

The ghost who fell in love

The chieftain without a heart

Printed in the United States of America

*The Ghost
Who Fell in Love*

AUTHOR'S NOTE

The first race was run at Ascot on Saturday, August 11, 1711, under the patronage of Queen Anne. In this novel every description of Royal Ascot in 1822 is correct, including the race-horse owners, the jockeys, and the horses, with the exception of the winner of the Gold Cup. This was actually won by Sir Huldibrand, owned by Mr. Ramsbottom. Today the winner receives a Gold Cup, and twenty-five thousand pounds, which was added in 1975.

The very small enclosure round the Royal Stand, to which only those invited by George IV were admitted, was the beginning of the Royal Enclosure.

Up to the last war this was very exclusive and even today tickets are only obtainable from the Lord Chamberlain.

CHAPTER ONE

"Demelza!"

Demelza raised her head from the book she was reading and listened.

"Demelza! Demelza!"

Hastily she jumped up and ran along the creaking boards of the Picture Gallery to the top of the stair.

Below her in the hall was an extremely elegant figure, his handsome face upturned to hers, his head thrown back, his lips already forming her name again.

"Gerard!" she exclaimed. "I was not expecting you."

"I know you were not, Demmy," he said, using the childish nickname he had given her when he was only four years of age.

She ran down the stairs to throw her arms round her brother's neck.

"Careful!" he said warningly. "Mind my cravat!"

"A new style! Oh, Gerard, it is very smart!"

"That is what I thought," he said complacently. "It is called 'the Mathematical.'"

"It certainly looks difficult to achieve."

"It is!" he agreed. "It took me hours, and over a dozen muslins completely ruined."

"Let me look at you," Demelza said.

She stood back to admire the dashing figure he made in his tight champagne-coloured pantaloons, close-fitting cut-away coat, and elaborate waistcoat.

"Your new tailor does you proud!" she said at length, knowing he was waiting for her verdict. "But I am terrified at what the bill will be!"

"That is what I have come to talk to you about," Sir Gerard Langston replied.

Demelza gave a little cry.

"Gerard! . . . Not the duns?"

"It was almost as bad as that," her brother replied. "But let us talk about it in the Library. And I could do with a drink—the crowds on the roads were ghastly!"

"I can imagine that," Demelza said. "It is always the same before race-week."

The preparations for the Ascot Races always began well in advance of the meeting. The horses usually arrived first, to be installed in numerous stables round the course.

Visitors from the provinces set out on the long journey many days, even weeks, before the date fixed for the meeting, while from London people began to move into the neighbourhood of Ascot during the week before the races actually took place.

As they entered the Library, Gerard looked round him in a manner which surprised his sister, as if he were appraising the room.

Usually when he returned home it was either to collect his clothes which had been washed, ironed, and mended by her and their old Nurse, or else because his pockets were so empty that he had for the moment to give up his expensive lodgings in Half Moon Street.

"What are you looking for?" Demelza asked at last.

Gerard's eyes had wandered over the faded velvet curtains, the carpet, which was threadbare in places, and the arm-chairs, which had needed recovering for the last ten years.

Worn and shabby the room might be, but it still had a dignity and a beauty about it which made her brother say at length with almost a sigh of relief:

"It is not too bad, and after all only parvenues and the new rich have everything too slap-up and shipshape."

"What are you talking about, dearest?" Demelza asked in her sweet voice.

"I have brought you some very exciting news," Gerard replied. "Hold your breath, because it will astonish you."

"What is it?" Demelza asked a little apprehensively.

"I have let the house for the whole of next week!"

There was a pause before Demelza said incredulously:

"Let the house? What can you . . . mean?"

"Exactly what I say," Gerard said, throwing himself down on the sofa, which creaked under his weight.

"But . . . why? What . . . for? To . . . whom?"

The questions tumbled from Demelza's lips and there was a marked silence before her brother answered:

"To the Earl of Trevarnon."

He saw Demelza's eyes widen and added quickly:

"Wait until you hear what he has offered me."

"But why should he want to come . . . here?"

"That is easy to answer," Gerard replied. "The Crown and Feathers at Bracknell was burnt down the night before last."

"Burnt down?" Demelza exclaimed. "How terrible! Was anybody hurt?"

"I have no idea," her brother replied carelessly, "but Trevarnon had taken the whole Inn for race-week."

"So now he has nowhere to go," Demelza said slowly.

"He was desperate," Gerard answered. "You know as well as I do that there is not a room, or even a bed, available in the whole district."

Demelza knew this was true.

Unlike the Epsom Races, which could be easily reached in a day from London, Ascot Race-course was nearly thirty miles from the Capital.

Only a few Corinthians drove there daily at a speed which necessitated a change of horses. For most race-goers it meant a five-day visit, which resulted in the whole neighbourhood being packed to bursting.

If, as she and her brother knew, one was fortunate enough to be a guest at Windsor Castle or at one of the country houses for which astronomical rents were paid, there were no problems.

But otherwise it meant being crammed into the extremely uncomfortable local Inns, which charged exorbitantly for the privilege. In some cases a guest returning from the Heath found he was expected to sleep on a sofa or even roll up on a hearth-rug.

Demelza could imagine, without her brother telling her, what a problem it would cause when one of the better Inns like the Crown and Feathers at Bracknell was burnt down on the Friday before race-week.

Gerard was telling her what had occurred.

"We were drinking in White's Club yesterday evening, when Trevarnon learnt the news, and asked: 'What the devil can I do?'

"No-one answered, and he went on:

" 'I have five horses entered for the meeting, one of them being Crusader! They are already on their way to Bracknell.' "

"Crusader?" Demelza repeated almost under her breath.

It was the horse she had been looking forward to seeing, for he had won a number of races already and every newspaper had published eulogies about his appearance and his pace.

"Exactly—Crusader!" her brother repeated. "And I stand to lose a packet if he does not run!"

"Oh, Gerard, how could you?" Demelza cried. "You know that you promised me you would not bet until you had paid off some of the bills you owe."

"But Crusader is a certainty!" Gerard answered. "The Earl himself has wagered a fortune on him."

"The Earl can afford to," Demelza said quietly.

"And so can I, now that I have let the house."

"You mean," Demelza asked, "that you are really allowing the Earl of Trevarnon and his party to come here?"

"That is what I am trying to tell you, Demmy," her brother replied. "Do not be a nit-wit about it! He is paying through the nose for the privilege, and God knows we need it!"

"How much?"

There was a little tremor in the words.

"One thousand guineas!"

There was an unmistakable note of elation in Gerard's voice, but his sister stared at him as if she could not have heard him aright.

"One thousand guineas?" she repeated after a moment. "It is . . . impossible! You cannot . . . mean it!"

"I tell you he was desperate," Gerard answered. "The Coffee-Room was crowded, and he looked round as if it had struck him that somebody present might have a house in the neighbourhood. Then his eyes fell on me.

" 'I seem to remember, Langston, that you live near Ascot,' he said slowly.

" 'That is true, My Lord,' I replied.

" 'And is your house fully occupied?'

" 'No, My Lord,' I answered, 'but I do not think it would be suitable for your requirements.'

" 'Anything with a roof would be suitable in the circumstances, and I presume you have stables?'

" 'Yes, there are stables,' I replied.

" 'For how many?' "

Gerard Langston threw out his hands.

"I told the truth, Demelza. What else could I do?"

"Go on with the story," his sister pleaded.

" 'About forty, My Lord,' I replied, and the Earl walked across the room and drew me aside.

" 'Have you any particular objection to me as a tenant?' he enquired.

" 'Certainly not, My Lord!'

" 'Then why so much hesitation?'

" 'The house is old, and, as I am seldom at home, there are few servants.'

" 'That is of little consequence,' the Earl replied. 'I will bring my own Chef, my Butler, and any number of footmen that are required.'

"I said nothing and after a moment he said:

"'Would one thousand guineas be acceptable to you as rent for the week?'"

Gerard paused as if he was remembering how his own breath had been taken away at the magnificence of the sum. Then before his sister could speak he said:

"It is all settled, and he is arriving with his party tomorrow. The horses should be here later this evening."

"But, Gerard, how can we cope? There is only Nattie and old Betsy to do everything!"

"If he is uncomfortable the Earl has no-one to blame but himself," Gerard said airily. "And one thousand guineas, Demelza, think of it!"

He glanced at her a little uncomfortably as he said:

"I was just on the point of coming home and spending the rest of the summer here."

That meant, his sister knew, that he was completely broke.

No-one knew better than she did that it would have been impossible for him to refuse such a generous offer, even though she could see innumerable difficulties ahead.

Langston Manor had been in the Langston family since the reign of Henry VIII and the dissolution of the Monasteries.

It had been added to and altered during the years, but it had kept its gabled roof, its twisting chimneys, its diamond-paned windows, and its air of mystery and other-worldliness, which Demelza attributed to the fact that it had originally housed dedicated Cistercian Monks.

The fortunes of the Langstons had fluctuated down the centuries: some members of the family had been immensely rich and Statesmen of great power and prestige, while others had been spend-thrifts who frittered away the family fortune.

Their father and grandfather both had belonged to the latter category, and Gerard in fact had inherited little but the house and a few acres of woodland.

He of course wished to live most of his time in London and associate with the Bucks and Beaux who had made themselves notorious during the Regency.

They were still the core of the sporting world which centred round the newly crowned King George IV.

If Gerard enjoyed himself in London, Demelza was forced to live very quietly at home.

She had never known any other life, so she did not miss the Society whirl to which she would have been entitled had her mother been alive and had there been any money.

She was in fact perfectly content helping their old Nurse keep the house in order, tending the garden, and spending much time reading.

Her real happiness was that she could ride her brother's horses, which, fortunately, he could not afford to stable in London.

He had one race-horse, Firebird, on which he built great hopes. He had left him to be trained by his sister and the old groom, Abbot, who had been at the Manor since they were children.

It was Abbot who had insisted they should enter Firebird in one race at Ascot, to be ridden by his grandson Jem Abbot.

Jem had grown up at the Manor and was just beginning to be noticed amongst the younger jockeys who looked for mounts at every well-known race-meeting.

It was from Jem that Demelza had heard of the unrivalled appearance and outstanding performances of Crusader, but it was from her brother that she had heard of the Earl of Trevarnon.

"All you have to do now," Gerard was saying, "is to leave things as tidy as you can, get in as much help as possible, and find somewhere to stay."

"F-find . . . somewhere to . . . stay?" Demelza repeated in astonishment.

"You can hardly remain here," he answered. "It is a bachelor-party, and anyway, as I have told you often enough, Trevarnon is a man's man. I admire him, but I certainly would not let him come in contact with my sister!"

"But . . . Gerard . . . where can I go?"

"There must be somewhere," he replied carelessly.

"But if I go away, it will be quite impossible for Nattie and Betsy to manage, and old Jacobs will forget to bring in the coal for the kitchen and clean the floors. He gets more senile every day."

"You cannot stay here, and that is the end of it!"

The way Gerard spoke told his sister that he was thinking of the Earl.

"Can he really be so wicked?" she asked.

There was no need for her to explain of whom she was speaking.

"He is the devil himself where women are concerned," her brother replied. "I have never known a man who can ride better, has more knowledge of horses, is a finer shot, and is a sportsman in every possible way—except one."

"You have spoken of him before. I have often thought he was not a . . . good companion for . . . you," Demelza said gently.

"Companion!" Gerard exclaimed. "I can hardly aspire to that! He counts few people as his really intimate friends. He is pleasant to me, includes me in his parties, and I admire him—of course I admire him. He outshines every other Corinthian who was ever born, but God, when it comes to women. . . !"

"He has never married?"

"He *is* married."

"I had no . . . idea. You have . . . never mentioned . . . the Countess."

"She is mad—shut up in a mad-house, and has been for the last twelve years."

"Mad! How terrible! You must feel very . . . sorry for him."

"Sorry for Trevarnon?" Gerard laughed. "That is the last thing anyone would be! He owns more property than any other man in England and is as rich as Croesus. They say he obliged the King when he was Regent with enormous loans which will never be repaid."

"But for his wife to be . . . mad!"

"It does not seem to trouble him, but it is certainly an obstacle to all the women who want to walk him up the aisle."

"Perhaps he would like to be married."

"There is no chance of that as long as he has a wife alive, and I assure you he turns to his advantage the very fact that he is shackled."

Gerard laughed a little bitterly.

"If he leaves a woman weeping and broken-hearted, she can hardly blame him when she knew from the very beginning he could not marry her."

"I can understand . . . that," Demelza said.

"You understand nothing!" her brother snapped. "And I am not having you coming into contact with the Earl, and that is final! You will leave here this evening, and with no more arguments about it."

"But where am I to go? I can hardly undertake the journey to Northumberland to stay with Aunt Elizabeth without anyone to accompany me, and if I take Nattie with me I am sure Betsy will refuse to do anything!"

"Oh, God, you are making unnecessary difficulties!" Gerard cried.

"I am not, I promise you I am not, dearest, but we have to face facts. You know as well as I do that I keep the house going, that I cook your meals when you are here, that I see to the linen, the opening of the rooms, and all the dusting."

"Then pay someone to do it while you are away!" her brother replied in an exasperated tone.

"Pay whom?" Demelza asked. "Every available woman on two legs is already engaged to wait on the visitors to the races."

This was so irrefutably true that Gerard found there was nothing he could say.

"And what is more," Demelza went on after a moment, "I cannot have strange servants spoiling the few things we have left, like the sheets with real lace which Mama always used and the pillow-cases she embroidered so beautifully."

Her brother was about to speak, when she gave a little cry.

"I have thought of it! I know what I can do! I have solved the whole . . . problem."

"Where are you going?"

"To the Priests'-Room!"

"To the Priests'-Room?" he echoed.

"I will sleep there," Demelza said. "No-one will know I am in the house, and when you are at the races I can tidy everything and put things ready for your return."

Gerard looked at her speculatively. Then he said slowly:

"I do not like it. It is too dangerous."

"Dangerous?" Demelza queried.

He was not prepared to explain, but it was as if he saw his sister in a different way for the first time.

He was so used to her that it had not struck him until now how exceedingly lovely she was, with a beauty that was different from that of the women he knew in London.

There was something very young and almost childlike in her small oval face and her huge eyes, which were the colour of a pansy.

It was a characteristic of the Langstons that their eyes looked purple in some lights.

Gerard followed the family tradition but, surprisingly, Demelza, while inheriting her father's eyes, had her mother's hair. It was such a pale gold that it sometimes appeared to be silver.

It was a strange combination, but at the same time it was so arresting and unusual that any man would be fascinated by it.

Demelza was four years younger than her brother, but Gerard thought of her as a child, except that in many ways she looked after him as if she were his mother.

Now he told himself that he had to protect her, especially from a man like the Earl of Trevarnon.

"Why are you staring at me?" Demelza asked.

THE GHOST WHO FELL IN LOVE

He smiled and it made him look attractive and boyish.

"I was thinking that properly gowned you would be the toast of Saint James's."

"I hope not!" Demelza exclaimed. "Mama always said it was very . . . vulgar for ladies to be talked about in Clubs. In fact it meant they were not . . . ladies!"

"Well, you are not going to be, so the question does not arise," Gerard said with a sudden note of authority in his voice. "If I let you stay in the Priests'-Room, do you swear to me that you will not come out of the secret passages as long as Trevarnon or any of his guests is in the house?"

He paused before he added:

"I mean that, Demelza. You will give me your word of honour, or you and Nattie will have to go to Northumberland."

"Of course I promise you," Demelza said disarmingly. "You do not think I wish to meet men like the Earl or any of your other raffish friends? Although it fascinates me to hear you talking about them, I disapprove of most of them and all they do!"

Gerard laughed.

"Of which you know nothing, thank goodness! Well, I trust you. Perhaps I am doing the wrong thing, but I do understand that the whole household depends upon you."

"That is the nicest thing you have said to me," Demelza replied with a smile. "But, Gerard, as you are getting so much money, you will give me some for the wages and for our food when you are not here?"

"Yes, of course I will," her brother answered. "I am a cad to you in a lot of ways, Demelza, but just as you share the bad times, naturally you will share the good."

"Thank you, dearest, I knew you would understand, and I hate owing money to the local tradesmen."

She kissed her brother's cheek as she spoke and he said:

"I have not cashed Trevarnon's cheque yet, but here is a guinea or two to be going on with."

He drew some golden coins out of his pocket and put them into her hand, and Demelza kissed him again.

"Now I must go and get everything ready," she said. "There is very little time if the gentlemen are arriving tomorrow, and you had better go to the stables and tell Abbot to expect the horses. The stalls are all right except for the three at the end, where there are holes in the roof and the rain comes in."

"It does not look as if it is going to rain," Gerard said. "It was terribly hot riding here and both Rolla and I were pretty well done in by the time we reached Windsor."

"You rode Rolla the whole way? Oh, Gerard, how could you?"

"I rested him while I had something to eat and rode him carefully for the last five miles," her brother answered. "I also came across country, which is shorter, as you well know. I cannot afford to have more than one horse in London at the same time."

"Yes, I know that, but it is really too far for him."

"And for me!" Gerard replied. "I suppose there is no chance of a bath?"

"Of course there is, if you do not mind a cold one."

"I should welcome it."

"I will go and get it ready for you," Demelza said, "but you will have to get a bottle of wine for yourself. There is very little in the cellar, but I suppose His Lordship will be bringing his own."

Gerard grinned.

"He will be very thirsty if he survives on what we can provide."

Demelza reached the door.

"You have not told me how many there will be in the party."

"Six with me!"

"And will you be here for dinner?"

Gerard shook his head.

"I am going over to see Dysart at Winkfield to tell him that the Earl will be staying here. He is dining with him on Tuesday after the Grafton Sweep, which the Duke of York is quite convinced he will win because he has drawn Trance."

"I expect he will with Trance," Demelza said reflectively. "Is there a lot of money on him?"

"Thousands!" her brother answered.

The way he spoke made Demelza glance at him sharply.

"How much have you risked?"

"There is no risk where Trance or Moses is concerned, as you well know," he answered.

Demelza, though she wished to argue with him, knew that he spoke the truth.

Trance was an exceptional horse, and the Duke of York had won the Derby with Moses the previous year.

With the exception of Crusader, the latter was the most outstanding animal amongst all the highly bred ones which would be seen at the race-meeting.

As Demelza hurried upstairs to open up the bedrooms, many of which had not been in use for a long time, she was thinking with interest and excitement about the horses she would see in two days' time.

To her they were far more important than the crowds of distinguished people who watched them race, and to think that Crusader would actually be stabled at the Manor was a thrill beyond anything she had known for a long time.

She longed to talk about it with Abbot, but she knew that first she must prepare the house for the Earl and his guests and she only hoped he would not feel that his money had been misspent.

To her the large but low rooms, with ancient carved panelling on the walls and huge four-poster beds whose canopies touched the ceiling, were an enchantment that she loved and which had always been part of her life and her imagination.

Now as she drew back the curtains, many of which were worn, and threw open the diamond-paned windows, she wondered if the Earl, who was so rich, would only see how shabby everything was.

Perhaps he would not notice the mellow beauty of the faded tapestries, the colour of the polished floors, or the soft shades of many of the rugs which lay on them.

To Demelza there was beauty everywhere, just as there was the history of the Langstons in every room, in every picture, and in every piece of furniture.

One blessing, she thought, was that because it had already been such hot weather she had made fresh potpourri and most of the rooms were fragrant with it.

Her mother had taught her the secret recipe which had been handed down from their Elizabethan ancestors, just as there was a special one for the bees'-wax which polished the floor and the furniture.

There were also recipes for cordials, which she gave the villagers when they had an ailment which the doctor from Windsor thought beneath his condescension.

Everything was usually so quiet at the Manor. It stood on the very edge of Windsor Forest, surrounded by trees, and although it was only a little over a mile from the race-course, the noise of the crowds did not encroach upon it.

But now, Demelza thought, it was somehow very exciting that the Manor should be drawn into the thrill of race-week.

She knew it was not only the thought of the house being ill-used which made her fight to stay when Gerard would have sent her away, but also that she could not have borne to miss the races.

She had attended them ever since she was a small child, and she loved every moment of it.

Now she knew that all along the edge of the course the tents and booths were going up, just as they did every year.

There would be every kind of refreshment for hungry and thirsty people; entertainers of all sorts—jugglers, glee-singers, and freaks; and a profusion of gaming tents, which as Demelza knew only too well fleeced all those who were foolish enough to risk their hard-earned savings.

Even Jem had been taken in last year by the thimble-game men, who were always numerous on the Heath. He had lost over a guinea trying to identify the thimble in the game which his grandfather had scornfully denounced as "a mug's game!"

Also arriving in their hordes would be the pickpockets and the thieves.

She and Nattie, who always accompanied her, were still laughing about the gang who, on a hot day such as they were likely to have this week, had made off with seventy great-coats stolen from carriages and stands.

But whatever happened it was all entrancing to Demelza and something to talk about and laugh over during the year which ensued until the next meeting.

"I could not bear to miss it," she said to herself, "and this year I shall not only see Crusader run, but I shall be able to talk to him and touch him when he is here in the stables."

What could be more fortunate, she thought, than that her grandfather, the spend-thrift who had wasted a great deal of money on slow horses and fast women, had also built for the former some very fine stables?

'Perhaps they will all be in use at the same time,' Demelza thought.

Her eyes were shining as she ran to the linen-cupboard to see if there was enough linen for the six beds which would be in use.

The sheets and pillow-cases all had lavender bags packed between them, which she had made the previous year.

She hesitated for a moment as she looked at one pile, separate from the others, which were edged with real lace. These had been her mother's pride and joy.

Then, almost beneath her breath, Demelza said:

"He is paying enough, he deserves them!"

She carried them into the Master bed-room, where the Langstons who owned the Manor had slept since Sir Gerard Langston had been given the Monastery and its grounds by King Henry VIII.

It was where Demelza's father had slept, but when Gerard had inherited he had preferred to keep his own room.

This was filled with all the things he had treasured ever since he was a small boy and the trophies he had won when he was at Oxford and racing his own horses in amateur steeplechases and point-to-points.

The Master bed-room was furnished with dark oak and the huge four-poster had the Langston coat-of-arms emblazoned on red velvet.

The curtains were drawn back and the windows were actually open when Demelza entered the room. She laid the sheets she carried down on the bed.

Because she had loved her father she had kept his things as he had always liked them; his ivory-backed brushes were on top of a high dressing-table and his polished riding-boots still stood in the wardrobe.

'I must move those,' Demelza thought to herself.

She picked them up and was about to carry them to one of the cupboards in the passage when she had a better idea.

She went towards the fireplace. On the right-hand side of it where the panel was exquisitely carved with flowers she put out her hand and pressed one of the petals.

Silently a whole section of the panelling opened.

Inside was a flight of steps.

This was one of the secret staircases which Demelza had spoken of to her brother which led up to the very top of the house, where there was the Priests'-Room.

Used as a Chapel during the reign of Elizabeth, it had also secreted many Priests when the Catholics were persecuted and burnt at the stake, just as the Protestants had been under her sister Mary.

Langston Manor had in fact been one of the most notable secret hiding-places for the Jesuit Priests in the whole of England.

Demelza thought that some of the secret staircases had been built before that time, perhaps by the Monks who wished to keep watch on the novices or perhaps for more-sinister reasons.

But during the reign of Queen Elizabeth the house had become a labyrinth of stairs and narrow passages with doors which opened into almost every main room in the house.

Gerard had been aware, as she was, that once she was sleeping in the Priests'-Room and using the secret staircases, it would be quite impossible for any outsider to have the slightest idea that she was in the house.

'Even if they do see me,' Demelza thought to herself with a smile, 'they will think I am the ghost of the White Lady.'

She told herself that she must remember to tell Gerard to refer laughingly to the Langston ghost, which was locally a famous legend.

The Langstons at the time of Cromwell had openly declared themselves uninterested in the policial fortunes of the country. Cromwellian troops had even, from time to time, been billeted in the house and on the grounds.

But the daughter of the Baronet had fallen in love with a fugitive Royalist and had hidden him in the Priests'-Room.

Unfortunately, one day when she was away from home, he was betrayed by a treacherous servant.

Dragged out by the troops, he had been executed on the spot, his body buried before she returned.

Legend related that, distraught by not knowing what had occurred, the lady had finally died of a broken heart, but her ghost continued to seek her lover.

Demelza had never actually seen the White Lady herself, although she had sometimes imagined that she felt her in the Picture Gallery late at night and heard her footsteps moving behind her on the twisted staircases which led to the Priests'-Room.

But the maids, especially the younger ones, continually shrieked out that they had seen the ghost, and even Nattie had at times admitted to a cold feeling between her shoulder blades and complained that she felt as if a ghost was walking over her future grave.

"I shall feel like a ghost," Demelza told herself, "when they are having a party in the Dining-Room and I am shut outside and cannot take part in it."

Then she laughed, because it did not trouble her in the least that she could not be invited to the parties that the Earl would be giving, while she could be with Crusader and his other horses in the stables.

'Abbot will be able to tell me all about them,' she thought, knowing that in most cases if they had run in any major race she would already know how they were bred and who had sired them.

"Could anything be more thrilling?" she asked aloud.

She looked at the velvet cover on the big bed, which had once been red but had now faded to a lovely shade of pink, thinking that the owner of Crusader would sleep there.

'Tomorrow,' she decided, 'I will pick some of the roses which are exactly the same colour and put them on the dressing-table.'

She wondered if the Earl would notice.

Then she told herself it was very unlikely he would notice any-thing except that the ceiling was stained with damp and one of the gilt handles was lost off the chest-of-drawers.

"Why should we apologise?" Demelza asked herself disdainfully. "He will certainly be more comfortable than he would have been at the Crown and Feathers, and even if he does not like it, there is no-where else he can go."

Some pride within herself made her almost resent the fact that they had to take money from a man who was so rich while they were so poor.

"Our family is as good if not better than his," she said aloud, and lifted her little chin higher.

Then she heard Gerard calling her, his voice echoing up from the hall.

She ran down the corridor to lean over the bannister.

"What is it?" she asked.

"I want to talk to you," he replied. "And what about my bath?"

Demelza started guiltily.

She had forgotten, in her anxiety to open the rooms, that Gerard wished to bathe.

"It will be ready for you in a few minutes," she promised.

She rushed to his room to pull from the cupboard the big circular tin bath in which he bathed when he was at home.

She set it down on the hearth-rug, laid a bath-mat and white towel beside it, and, still running as quickly as she could, went down the back stairs.

Fortunately, at this time of the day old Jacobs thought that most of his chores were done, and so he was sitting, as she expected, in the kitchen, drinking a glass of ale and talking to Nattie.

Demelza burst into the huge kitchen with its flagged floors, and its long beams from which in prosperous days had hung hams, sides of bacon, and strings of onions, but which were now lamentably unen-cumbered.

As she entered, Nattie looked up at her in surprise.

She was only fifty years of age but her hair was streaked with grey. With her clean apron and rather severe face she looked exactly what she had always been, a child's Nurse, loving and tender, but at the same time strict as to discipline.

"What is it, Miss Demelza?" she asked in a surprised tone. "And your hair needs tidying!"

"Sir Gerard has come home, Nattie," Demelza said, and saw the older woman's eyes light up.

If there was one person in the world whom Nattie loved more than Demelza, who had been her baby from the time she was born, it was Gerard.

"Home!" she exclaimed. "I suppose he's on his way to stay with some of his smart friends."

"The Crown and Feathers burnt down last night," Demelza related breathlessly, "which means that all sorts of thrilling things are going to happen here."

"Here?" Nattie questioned.

"Sir Gerard wants a bath, Jacobs," Demelza said.

She knew that the old man, being rather deaf, had not heard her.

"A bath, Jacobs!" she repeated. "Will you take two cans of water upstairs to Sir Gerard's bed-room?"

Jacobs put down his glass.

He was an amenable old man, and reliable as long as he knew exactly what he had to do.

"Two cans, did you say, Miss Demelza?"

"Two cans," Demelza repeated firmly.

He shuffled out of the kitchen, and Demelza, her eyes shining, began to tell Nattie of the excitements which lay ahead.

CHAPTER TWO

"Will you drive me to Windsor Castle tomorrow?"

"No!"

"Why not? I felt sure you would be staying there when I learnt you could not go to Bracknell as you had intended."

"I have made other plans."

"Whatever they are, they must be in the vicinity of Ascot, and surely you can take me to the Castle on your way?"

It was difficult to imagine how any man could refuse Lady Sydel Blackford when she pleaded with him.

Lying back on a *chaise-longue,* she looked exceedingly alluring, wearing nothing but a diaphanous gauze negligee which clung to her perfect body.

She had been told so often that she resembled in face and figure the exquisite Princess Pauline Borghese, sister of Napoleon Bonaparte, who had been sculpted by Canova, that she almost instinctively fell into the same pose as the statue of the Princess.

Her golden hair was caught up on top of her head and her blue eyes looked at the Earl from under long, dark eye-lashes which owed more to artifice than to nature.

Everything about her was in fact slightly artificial, but at the same time there was no doubting her beauty or her sexual allure.

The Earl, however, leaning back in an arm-chair and sipping his glass of brandy, seemed for the moment immune both to her beauty and to the pleading in her eyes.

"Why do you not stay at the Castle?" she asked poutingly. "The King has asked you often enough to be his guest, and you know full well that he likes having you with him."

"I prefer to be on my own," the Earl replied, "especially in race-week, when I want to think about my horses."

"And not about me?" Lady Sydel enquired.

He made no reply and she said almost angrily:

"Why must you always be so irritatingly elusive? I would believe it was a pretence if it were not habitual."

"If I do not please you, there is an obvious answer," the Earl remarked.

Lady Sydel made a helpless gesture with her hands, her long fingers seeming almost too frail for the enormous rings she wore.

"I love you, Valient!" she said. "I love you, as you well know, and I want to be with you!"

"My party, as you are equally well aware, is a bachelor one," the Earl replied.

"And where will it take place now that you cannot go to the Inn at Bracknell as you intended?"

"I have rented Langston's house. It is, I believe, quite near the race-course."

"Langston? Do you mean that handsome boy who I understand has not a penny to bless himself with?"

"I imagine that is a fairly accurate description," the Earl replied dryly.

Lady Sydel laughed.

"In which case you will doubtless find yourself in some crumbling old Manor, extremely uncomfortable, with the rain leaking through holes in the roof and onto your head."

"It would undoubtedly please you if that proves to be the case."

"You had much better come to Windsor Castle with me."

Her voice was very soft and alluring, but the Earl yawned and she said hastily:

"His Majesty is expecting you to dinner on Tuesday."

"I have told him that I will dine with him on Thursday, after I have won the Gold Cup."

"You are very sure of yourself!"

"I am sure of my horse, and that amounts to almost the same thing."

"It is so bad for you, Valient, that you should always win what you desire, whether it is a horse or a woman."

The Earl appeared to consider this for a moment. Then he replied cynically:

"I think the odds are on the latter category."

"I hate you!" Lady Sydel exclaimed. "And if you are thinking of Charis Plymworth, I swear I will scratch her eyes out!"

The Earl did not reply and after a moment Lady Sydel said:

"I think I know why you will not come to the Castle on Tuesday evening. You are dining with John Dysart, and Charis Plymworth is staying with him."

"If you know I am already engaged, why press me to accept another invitation?" the Earl enquired.

"I could hardly believe you would be so treacherous and so abominably cruel to me!"

The Earl raised his eye-brows and took a sip of his brandy before he said:

"My dear Sydel, I have never tied myself to any woman's apron-strings, and let me make it clear, once and for all, I am not tied to yours!"

"But I love you, Valient! We have meant so much to each other, and I believed that you loved me."

There was a break in her voice that was very moving, but the Earl merely rose to his feet and set his glass down on the mantelpiece.

"Dramatics, as you are well aware, bore me, Sydel. I will say good-bye and look forward to seeing you in the Royal Box at Ascot."

He bent to kiss her hand, but she held up her arms to him.

"Kiss me, Valient, kiss me! I cannot bear you to leave me. I want you! I want you desperately! I would kill you rather than let you love another woman!"

The Earl looked down at her, at the passion flaring in her eyes, at her head thrown back at the invitation in her arched, half-naked body.

"You are very beautiful, Sydel," he said in a voice which did not make the words sound particularly complimentary, "but at times your protestations of affection become a bore! I will see you at the races."

He walked without haste towards the door and without looking back left the room.

Alone, Lady Sydel gave a cry of sheer exasperation. Then with her clenched fists she pounded one of the silk cushions on the *chaise-longue* until, exhausted, she flung herself back to stare despairingly at the painted ceiling above her.

Why did the Earl always leave her frustrated and almost desperate?

She told herself that she had in fact been rather stupid with him. She should have known by this time, having had innumerable lovers, that when men are satiated by love-making they want to be soothed and flattered—not engaged in a controversy such as had just taken place.

But her insatiable jealousy made her indulge in scenes and sulks, which, while they had other men on their knees, invariably left the Earl unmoved.

"Curse him!" she exclaimed aloud. "Why should he be different?"

She knew the answer only too clearly: he was different!

Because of it, she had sworn that she would make him as slavishly enamoured of her as she was of him.

Yet it seemed that she had succeeded in making him her lover only when it suited him, and she was not sure that he was any more enamoured of her than he had been of dozens of other women.

Lady Sydel had originally been confident that where she was concerned everything would be different.

Was she not the most acclaimed beauty in the whole of the *Beau Monde?* Had not her looks and her fascination been extolled by every womanizer and roué? Was it not a fact that she had only to snap her fingers to have any man she fancied prostrate at her feet?

Yet she knew indisputably that the Earl eluded her.

Even when he made love to her, she realised, his mind, and certainly his heart, if he had one, was not hers. She now thought despairingly that since Lady Plymworth had appeared on the scene he was not even as attentive as he had been in the past.

"I hate her! God, how I hate her!" Lady Sydel cried.

She had only to think of Charis Plymworth with her dark red hair and slanting green eyes to feel murderous.

"I will kill her, and I will kill him!" she told herself, speaking with a ferocity that meant she was on the verge of one of her temperamental rages, which terrified her household and at times even herself.

Lying on the *chaise-longue,* she tried to imagine herself striking with a sharp knife the smile from Charis Plymworth's enigmatic face, then turning on the Earl.

She wondered what she would feel if she had him lying dead at her feet, the blood oozing from a wound in his heart.

Then she told herself that life without him would be insufferable, and somehow, by some means, she must ensure that he remained her lover.

"Charis Plymworth shall not have him!"

Her voice seemed to ring round the walls of her *Boudoir,* and to mingle with the exotic perfume she always used and the fragrance of the tuberoses with which, since someone had once told her they exuded the scent of passion, she always surrounded herself.

She rose from the *chaise-longue* to walk to a gilt-framed mirror which stood at the end of the room.

She stood in front of it, looking at the curves of her body, which men always described as belonging to a Greek Goddess, at the round white column of her neck, and at the passion which still lingered in her eyes and on her lips.

"He can rouse me as no other man has done before," she told herself. "I cannot lose him. I will not lose him!"

* * *

The Earl, driving himself in his high-perch Phaeton, wondered why women always became abandoned either mentally or physically after they had been unusually passionate during the act of love.

It seemed to release something within them which at other times they kept under control.

He decided that he was already bored with Sydel's clinging possessiveness and almost insane jealousy.

'I was a fool to have become involved with her,' he thought.

He decided that when he returned to London from Ascot he would not call again at her house in Bruton Street, where the gossips said spitefully that the steps were almost worn away with her lovers tramping in and out.

"She is beautiful," he told himself, "but that is not everything."

Knowing that the remark was banal, he smiled as he made it, then asked himself what he did want from a woman.

There had been so many in his life, but always after a very short while he grew bored, as he knew now he was bored with Sydel Blackford.

But Charis Plymworth was waiting for him. She had made that clear at their last meeting, and he would see her on Tuesday night when he dined with Lord Dysart.

It might be rather difficult to say anything very intimate on that occasion, for he had the idea that Dysart rather fancied Charis, and if he did, there was no reason why he should not marry her.

The Earl was aware that Charis, like Sydel, was looking for a husband.

They were both widows, but while Sydel Blackford's aged husband had died of a heart-attack, leaving her exceedingly wealthy, Lord Plymworth had been killed two years ago and Charis was not well off.

The Earl, with a little smile, dwelling on her red hair and green eyes, thought it would be amusing to dress her.

Long experience had made him an expert in what became a woman, and he had paid too many dressmakers' bills for them not to respect his judgement and hastily put his suggestions into operation.

'Green,' he thought. 'And naturally she will desire emeralds to wear with it. Peacock-blue would also be exceedingly effective, and diamonds to glitter in her small ears and against her hair.'

He hoped that when she let it down it would be long, soft, and silky.

Sydel's hair was thick but not particularly soft beneath his hands.

He remembered one woman—what the devil was she called?—who had hair which was like pure silk and which reached below her waist.

"Cleo? Or was it Janice?" He never had been good at names.

With a start the Earl realised that while he had been deep in his thoughts, although he had been driving superbly at the same time, he had reached Trevarnon House in Grosvenor Square.

Large and impressive, he had improved it out of all recognition after he had inherited from his father, and, like the Prince of Wales, he had collected pictures that were the envy and the admiration of a great many connoisseurs.

He had, as it happened, a number of family portraits that were unique in themselves.

There was the first Earl of Trevarnon, painted by Van Dyke, those that followed him by Gainsborough, Reynolds, and a recent one of himself by Lawrence because the Regent had insisted upon it.

The Earl entered the large hall in which stood a number of statues that he had also bought with discrimination.

His Major-Domo hurried forward to take his high-crowned hat and gloves.

"Have you arranged everything for tomorrow, Hunt?" the Earl asked.

"Everything, M'Lord."

"As I told you, there are few servants at Langston Manor, so we shall have to make up any deficiencies."

"I've seen to that, M'Lord. The Chef is bringing two kitchen-boys with him, and the footmen I've chosen are not above giving a hand in the household if necessary."

"Thank you, Hunt. And, as you are coming yourself, there will be no need for me to give the arrangements another thought."

"No, M'Lord. And I've made sure the Chef will bring most of the food he requires for your party. In race-week it'll be difficult to purchase anything locally."

"I am sure it will be," the Earl replied.

As he spoke, he walked away towards his Library, dismissing the problem of Ascot from his mind as he dismissed the thought of Lady Sydel.

Hunt would see to everything. He always did.

Nevertheless, on the following morning the Earl decided that he would arrive early at Langston Manor, before his guests were expected.

Like all born organisers, he could not resist, even with the most experienced servants, Major-Domos, and Comptrollers, checking things for himself.

A perfectionist in many ways, he saw no reason to suffer any discomfort if it was unnecessary.

If during the five days he was to spend at Ascot there was anything lacking he had not thought of, he could send a groom back to London. His Comptroller would see that it was despatched to him immediately.

He prided himself that he had been rather clever in finding at the very last moment an alternative to the Crown and Feathers.

He was well aware that there was not a house in the vicinity of Ascot, from Windsor Castle to those belonging to or hired by his friends, in which he would not be a welcome guest.

But he had long made it a rule that where large race-meetings were concerned he preferred to be with his horses and independent of other people's whims and fancies.

He also found that women were a distraction he could well do without when he wished to concentrate on the racing.

Soon after breakfast, at which he ate sensibly and well, drinking coffee and not alcohol, he set off from London, tooling a team of chestnuts that were the envy of every Corinthian in the whole of Saint James's.

He would have liked to drive six horses as he was accustomed to do in competition with the Prince of Wales, who had been painted in a high-perch Phaeton driving to Ascot, with, of course, an attractive woman beside him.

But the Earl had learnt of old that on the crowded roads round Ascot six horses could be an encumbrance and would restrict the pace at which he travelled rather than add to it.

It was a sunny day and already exceedingly hot, and the road as the Earl had anticipated, was crowded with coaches, tilburies, chaises, carts, and gigs.

As he drew nearer to Ascot, having twice changed horses on the way so as not to slow the pace at which he wished to travel, he was amused to notice slow-moving wagons covered with leafy branches of trees to protect the loads of countryfolk from the heat of the sun.

These vehicles were so overcrowded that the Earl's lips tightened at the thought of the suffering that was being caused to the wretched animals which drew them.

There were a number of Phaetons similar to the Earl's and splendid barouches with painted panels displaying the crests or coats-of-arms of their owners.

There were naturally a number of horses at which the Earl gave a second glance, only to decide that they did not equal his own.

He drew nearer to the course and began to look for the turn which Gerard Langston had told him would lead him to the Manor.

The thick fir trees of Windsor Forest bordered the road on either side until so unexpectedly that he almost missed it, the Earl saw a dusty lane winding into the wood.

He supposed that this was where he was intended to go, and he slowed his team, hoping as he did so that he would not be obliged to turn round, as this appeared to be an impossibility amongst the tree-trunks.

Then in front of him he saw two ancient lodges which appeared to be uninhabited and some iron gates which fortunately were open.

"This must be Langston Manor," the Earl told himself.

He thought that the appearance of the lodges and gates did not auger well for the condition in which he might find the house itself.

If Sydel was right, it would prove to be a crumbling Manor, with holes in the roof and perhaps too small for his party.

For a moment as he drove down the moss-covered drive, the Earl regretted that he had not accepted the King's invitation to Windsor Castle. At least there he would have a comfortable bed.

Then with a twist of his lips he thought that if Sydel had anything to do with it he would not spend much time in it, and he decided that however uncomfortable he was he would rather be on his own.

The drive turned, and suddenly he saw in front of him Langston Manor.

It was not in the least what he had expected and was indeed far more attractive than he had imagined possible.

It stood surrounded by trees and he saw at a glance that it was not only very old but also larger than he had thought it would be.

Spread out in front of him, the sun glinting on its diamond-paned windows and the pigeons sitting on its gabled roof, it seemed to the Earl as if it were something that had stepped out of a fairy-story.

He almost expected it would vanish and he would find himself staring at the ruins of what had once stood there.

But he knew he was being imaginative and it was in fact real, although it seemed impossible that he had been coming to Ascot all these years and had never been aware of its existence.

He thought too that it was very quiet and peaceful as there appeared to be nobody about.

He remembered how at other places he had stayed there had invariably been the noise of carriages, grooms, and ostlers hurrying and scurrying, their voices shouting as he appeared.

Driving slowly so that he could take in the house and its surroundings, the Earl finally drew his team to a standstill outside the front door.

His groom jumped down from the back of the Phaeton and as he went to the leader's head the Earl said:

"We must find someone, Jim, to direct us to the stables."

"Oi thinks they be over there, M'Lord," Jim replied.

He pointed as he spoke and the Earl could see now a roof a little beyond the house.

"I will ask," he said.

He walked in and found himself in a hall with a carved staircase curving up to the first floor.

It was very attractive and the Earl was instantly aware of the fragrance of flowers and saw that they came from a bowl of red and white roses arranged on a table at the bottom of the stairs.

It encouraged him to see that the house was as attractive inside as was its outer appearance. It struck him that it was a home, and he wondered if young Langston had a mother.

He walked across the hall and looked into what he saw was the Drawing-Room.

Again there were flowers arranged on tables, and through the open French windows he could see a garden which was a riot of colour with great banks of crimson rhododendrons interspersed with bushes of syringa and white lilac.

The Earl's eyes came back to the room.

He saw that it was shabby, but at the same time everything in it was in perfect taste.

The pictures on the panelled walls needed cleaning, but he had a feeling that they would be interesting to look at more closely later.

Retracing his steps he found himself in the Library and knew instantly that this was the room he would make exclusively his own.

He liked the comfortable leather arm-chairs and the big flat-topped desk which stood in exactly the right place for the light.

There was still nobody about, and, because he was curious about the rest of the house, he did not go towards the kitchen-quarters where he was certain he would find what servants there were.

Instead, he walked up the staircase, noting that each oak pillar had originally been surmounted by a carved figure, although some were missing or damaged.

At the same time he appreciated its age and the way the wood had mellowed.

There were also pictures on the stairs, and as they were mostly portraits he guessed they represented Langston's ancestors, and he thought he recognised a resemblance in some of them to Gerard's handsome features.

At the top of the staircase he had the choice of going right or left. He chose the left, and moving down the low-ceilinged, narrow corridor saw in front of him a long Gallery.

It was the type of Gallery which Elizabethans had always built in their houses and into which on the long cold winters they moved their four-poster beds clustering them round the great fireplace and pulling their curtains for privacy.

In one of the houses he owned the Earl had a Gallery rather like it and he would often visualise the householders encamped there, the most important being nearest the fire.

He reached the door of the Gallery and saw that the sun was glinting golden through the windows on the polished floor.

Then at the far end he saw a woman in a white gown and thought he had at last found someone to tell him what he wished to know.

He moved forward, but even as he did so he realised that she had vanished!

He thought for a moment that, not having heard his approach, she must have sat down on a chair or sofa. Then as he walked farther down the Gallery he saw that it was in fact empty.

"I must have been dreaming," he told himself.

As he stood near the place where she had seemed to be standing, he heard a voice behind him say:

"Good-afternoon, Sir."

He turned round and saw an elderly woman wearing a grey dress and over it a white apron.

As he looked at her she curtseyed and said:

"I think you, M'Lord, must be the Earl of Trevarnon, who has taken the Manor for race-week. Sir Gerard told me to expect Your Lordship, but you are earlier than we anticipated."

"I hope that will not inconvenience you," the Earl said, "but I came ahead of my party to see that everything was in order."

"I hope it'll be, M'Lord," Nattie replied, "but we're very short-handed, as doubtless Sir Gerard informed you."

"He did," the Earl answered. "But my Major-Domo is on his way with a large number of servants to do everything that will be required."

"Thank you, M'Lord. And would Your Lordship like to see the bed-rooms?"

"I would!" the Earl replied.

Nattie led him along the corridor, in the opposite direction from which he had come, to the Long Gallery.

He wondered if he should mention that he had seen a young woman in white, but instead he remarked:

"Perhaps you would tell me who actually is in the house besides yourself?"

"Only old Betsy, who'll help in the kitchen if necessary, M'Lord," Nattie replied. "Then there's Jacobs, who's an odd-job man and brings in the coals and wood and carries up the bath-water."

The Earl did not speak and Nattie went on:

"There's Abbot in the stables, and his grandson Jem, who'll be riding our horse at the races."

She spoke in a way which told the Earl she was determined not to be intimidated or overpowered by his horses.

There was a faint smile on his lips as he replied:

"And perhaps now you will tell me your name and your position in the household?"

"I was Nurse to Master Gerard, M'Lord, and ever since he was a baby he's called me 'Nattie' because he couldn't say 'Nurse,' and the name's stuck."

"Then Miss Nattie it must be," the Earl said.

"Thank you, M'Lord. This is the room in which we thought you'd be most comfortable. It's the Master's Room, but Sir Gerard still prefers to be where he slept as a boy."

The Earl, despite what Demelza had anticipated, appreciated the big four-poster with its faded velvet curtains and cover, the beautifully carved panelling and the vase of pink roses which stood on the dressing-table.

"The flowers all over the house are delightful, Miss Nattie," he said. "Do I thank you for the arrangement?"

There was just a moment's hesitation before Nattie replied:

"I do them when I've the time, M'Lord."

"Then let us hope you will find time while I am here," the Earl said.

Nattie told him where he would find the stables and he went downstairs to discover that Abbot had already shown Jem where to put the team.

The Earl inspected the rest of the stables.

They were surprisingly spacious, far better than he had expected to find, except in one of the great houses in this particular vicinity.

While he was in the stables his horses arrived.

By the time he had watched them bedded down and found that Crusader was in splendid shape, his staff were at the Manor and the Major-Domo was directing operations like a General in command of an Army.

Because there was nothing to do until his guests arrived the Earl walked into the garden to stand looking at the rhododendrons, the flowering shrubs, and the laburnum trees, which as a child he had called "golden rain."

It seemed to him as he moved towards them that he stepped back into the past and was in a land peopled by gnomes and fairies, dragons and Knights.

As a small boy he had always imagined that fire-breathing dragons lurked in the forests and there were elves burrowing under the mountains or hiding in the trunks of great trees.

He had not thought of such things for years, but now this mysteri-

ous house with its overgrown garden seemed hardly to belong to the
modern world in which he lived.

It certainly had nothing to do with the men and women of the
Beau Monde who would be converging on Ascot to spend a week
not only racing but at parties, Balls, and, as far as the menfolk were
concerned, riotous drinking and gambling.

But here there was only the sound of the wood-pigeons in the
trees and the rustle of small animals moving beneath the shrubs.

The fragrance of the flowers was very different from the exotic
perfumes used by Sydel and Charis and all the other women he
knew.

The Earl walked a long way into the wood before finally he turned
back.

Then when he came again in sight of the house, the same feeling
of mystery and magic he had felt when he first saw it from the other
side swept over him.

Absurdly, for one moment he wished that he could be alone there.

Then he laughed at himself and walked on quickly, feeling certain
that by this time his friends would have arrived.

They were in fact waiting for him in the Drawing-Room, sprawl-
ing comfortably in chairs, glasses in their hands, which were being
continuously replenished from the bottles of champagne that stood in
the ice-coolers on one of the side-tables.

"We were told you were here!" Lord Chirn exclaimed as the Earl
entered through one of the windows, "but nobody knew where you
had gone."

"I have been inspecting the property," the Earl replied. "Nice to
see you, Ramsgill, and you, Ralph! How are you, Wigdon?"

He spoke last to Sir Francis Wigdon, a man he had not known for
long but found amusing and who was with the cards as expert as he
was himself.

"You have certainly found a very attractive house," Sir Francis
replied, "and, in my opinion, far preferable to the Crown and
Feathers!"

"We all agree on that," the Honourable Ralph Mear cried. "It is
so like you, Trevarnon, to find something so unique and comfortable,
when anyone else who had been burnt out in the same circumstances
would be having to put up a tent on the Heath."

"Thank God we are saved from that!" the Earl replied, before
pouring himself a glass of champagne. "I imagine the crowds will be
worse this year than ever!"

"They increase year by year," Lord Ramsgill said, "and my

grooms tell me there has been the usual number of accidents on the way here."

Accidents on the road were commonplace and during Ascot week when drivers poured gallons of beer down their throats to sweep away the choking dust there were always deaths through careless driving or merely because the congestion made them inevitable.

Twice the Royal Carriages returning from Windsor after the racing had been involved in fatal accidents. The first was a postilion who was unseated and the wheel of the carriage ran over him and killed him.

In the second case, a Member of the Household in attendance on the King had knocked over and killed a pedestrian.

It was something that had to be expected, but unfortunately it did not make those who drove any more careful the following year.

"What tips have you got for us, apart, of course, from recommending your own horses?" Lord Chirn asked the Earl.

"I think really you should be asking the Duke of York," he replied. "He told me the night before last that he means to make a killing this Ascot, and I cannot think of anyone likely to stop him."

"That means," Lord Ramsgill said, "that you and he will be backing the colt Cardenio, which he has entered for his own Selling Plate, and Moses."

"Most certainly Moses!" the Earl said. "Nothing short of breaking the Tablets of the Ten Commandments over his head is likely to stop him from walking off with the Albany Stakes."

They all laughed and the Earl sat down with his glass in his hand.

* * *

Upstairs in the Priests'-Room, Demelza wondered how she could have been so stupid as to have been nearly caught unawares by the Earl.

The sound of his footsteps entering the Gallery had alerted her.

She had one quick glance at a man who was handsome, tall, broadshouldered, and extremely elegant, before with a swiftness born of fear she had slipped back through the panel and shut the secret door soundlessly behind her.

She had had no idea that he was expected so early and she had in fact only just finished arranging the flowers.

She had then gone to the Long Gallery to collect the book she had left there when Gerard had called her on the previous day.

She had already moved everything else she wanted up the twisting narrow stairs. Fortunately, her own bed-room was not required for any of the guests, so there was no need to hide her special treasures away.

Gerard had come back last night and left again early this morning with last-minute instructions that no-one was to be aware of her very existence.

"Why should anyone suspect me of having a sister when they have never seen her in London?" he asked.

To Nattie he said:

"You and Betsy look after me here, and when I come home I am alone with you. Is that clear?"

"Quite clear, Master Gerard," Nattie replied, "and I think you're absolutely right. I don't want Miss Demelza mixed up with any of those raffish friends of yours."

"How do you know they are raffish, Nattie?" Gerard asked.

"I've heard enough of the goings-on in London to know what I think!" Nattie replied.

Gerard laughed and called her a prude, but as he said good-bye to Demelza he said:

"Now obey me or I will be very angry. I will not have you meeting Trevarnon or anyone else who is staying in the house!"

"It seems to me that if these friends of yours are so wicked, you might find a few better ones!" Demelza remarked.

"They are all jolly fine fellows and excellent sportsmen," Gerard said quickly.

She had known he would spring to the defence of his friends, and she replied:

"I am only teasing, dearest, but do not drink too much. You know it is bad for you, and Mama always hated men who were hard drinkers."

"Trevarnon is not a hard drinker," Gerard said reflectively. "He is far too keen a pugilist for that, besides being the Champion Fencer at the moment."

It was not surprising, Demelza felt as he rode away, that he left her curious about the Earl.

There was apparently nothing at which His Lordship did not excel, besides being the owner of the most magnificent horse in the whole of Great Britain.

"Is Crusader better than Moses?" she asked Abbot.

"They've not run against each other yet, Miss Demelza," Abbot replied, "but if they do I'd bet me money on Crusader."

"Who is he competing against in the Gold Cup?"

"Sir Huldibrand. That's 'is only real challenge," Abbot answered.

"The horse belongs to Mr. Ramsbottom," Demelza remarked. "I do hope he does not win!"

"He's a good horse," Abbot said, "and Buckle's riding 'im."

Frank Buckle was one of the greatest jockeys of the time, and Demelza, who had seen him ride at other Ascot meetings, knew that he rode at only eight-stone-seven without wasting.

He had in fact been one of her heroes for many years, and she had heard someone say: "There is nothing big about Frank Buckle except his heart and his nose!"

His integrity was famous as well as his last spurt at the finish of a race.

Gerard had told her there was a couplet written about him:

> A Buckle large was formerly the rage
> A Buckle small now fills the Sporting Page.

Demelza had laughed and remembered it.

Now he was getting older, and although she felt it was disloyal she did want Crusader, because he was staying in their own stables, to win the Gold Cup.

As she walked back to the house she admitted that she was not only thinking of Crusader but also of his owner.

Everything Gerard had told her about the Earl had, despite his warnings, intrigued her.

"I have to see him!" she exclaimed, and remembered it would be easy to do so secretly at any time she wished.

Now she recalled that she had nearly met him face to face and was aware how furious Gerard would have been with her!

'This is a warning,' she thought. 'I must never take such risks again and must always be on my guard.'

At the same time, drawn irresistibly towards the man she longed to see, she crept very quietly down the twisting staircase until the sound of laughter told her that, as she had expected, the gentlemen were all congregated in the Drawing-Room.

She had spent as long as she could tidying it, dusting, and arranging the flowers.

She stood for a moment in the darkness, listening to the different sounds of the gentlemen's voices and trying to guess which one belonged to the names which Gerard had given her.

Her brother was not yet back. That meant that there were five men in the Drawing-Room.

She put out her hand to find one of the tiny peep-holes which the Monks or the Priests had made in the panelling so that they could look into every room.

It had been placed at eye-level for a man, which meant that Demelza had to stand on tip-toe in order to look through it.

It was so small, and concealed in the ornamentation in the centre of a flower, that it was quite impossible for anyone in the room to notice it. In fact Demelza had often found it difficult to remember where it was when she was in the Drawing-Room.

She put her eye to the minute hole and the first face she lighted on was that of a man of about thirty-five years of age.

He was not in the least good-looking, but had a benign appearance and was laughing uproariously at something which had been said.

She guessed, although she was not certain, that this was Lord Chirn.

Next to him was sitting a man with small dark eyes, a pointed nose, and a slightly exaggerated cravat.

As she looked at him someone remarked:

"I am sure you think so too, Francis." When he replied, she knew he was Sir Francis Wigdon.

There was something about him she did not like, but she was not certain what it was. She only thought that while his lips smiled his eyes did not do so.

Then she looked a little towards the centre of the group and knew at once that she was looking at the Earl of Trevarnon.

He was exactly as she had imagined him before she saw him in the Long Gallery. Exceedingly handsome, with a broad, intelligent forehead, square chin, and firm mouth, he had two deep lines of cynicism running from his nose to the corners of his lips.

It was a raffish face, cynical, and had a faint resemblance, Demelza thought, to the picture of Charles II which hung on the wall by the stairs.

One of his friends said something which amused him, but he did not smile; he just twisted his lips, but at the same time there was a twinkle in his eyes.

"He is magnificent!" Demelza told herself. "And whatever Gerard may say . . . I like him!"

CHAPTER THREE

As soon as Demelza knew that the gentlemen had gone in to dinner, she slipped down the secret passage to the ground floor and let herself out through a panelled wall into a passage which led to the garden door.

She had taken the precaution of putting a dark cloak over her gown just in case anyone should see her moving through the garden.

It would be unlikely, but, as all her gowns were white, she knew that she stood out against the dark green leaves of the shrubs.

Nattie, who made all her gowns, had found that the cheapest material to be found in the small shops at Ascot or in Windsor was white muslin.

She had fashioned them in very much the same shape for the last five years: falling from a high waist, they not only became Demelza but because she was very slender gave her an ethereal look which had an indescribable grace.

Shutting the garden door behind her but making sure that it was unlatched for her return, she moved through the bushes towards the stables.

She was quite certain that at this time of night the grooms, jockeys, and apprentices, having put the horses to bed, would all have hurried off to the Heath.

There, the booths would be bright with lights and doing a roaring business before the races started the following day.

She expected, however, that Abbot would stay in the stables, feeling sure that she would seize the first available opportunity of seeing the Earl's horses.

Abbot had been told that she was in hiding and he was on no account to mention to anyone her name or that the Manor was her home.

Abbot could be trusted in the same way that Betsy and Jacobs could, and Demelza was certain that where he was concerned there would be no gossip such as might be expected to take place in other houses.

She reached the stables, where all was very quiet. Then as she moved over the cobbled yard Abbot appeared, carrying a lantern in his hand.

"Oi thought ye'd not be long in coming, Miss Demelza," he said with the affectionate familiarity of an old servant.

"You knew I would want to see Crusader," Demelza answered.

"We be right proud t' have such a fine piece of horse-flesh 'ere," Abbot said.

There was a note in his voice which told Demelza, who knew him so well, that he was extremely impressed with the Earl's famous horses.

Abbot went ahead of her and led her inside the stable, where the stalls all opened onto a long passage running the whole length of it.

He opened the barred gate of the first stall he came to and Demelza saw the horse she had longed to see.

Jet black, with a star on his forehead and two white fetlocks, he was a magnificent animal!

She knew he was directly descended from Godolphin Arabia, the Arabian horse which had come to England in 1732 after many strange and unhappy adventures.

He had finally become the property of Lord Godolphin, son-in-law of Sarah, the famous Duchess of Marlborough.

Secretly, the Bedouin who was his constant companion allowed Godolphin Arabian to serve Roxana, a great mare, from whose foals had descended many of the celebrated Thoroughbreds on the Turf.

Demelza patted Crusader's arched neck, and as he nuzzled his nose at her she saw the muscles rippling under the polished shine of his dark coat.

"He is wonderful!" she said in an awe-struck voice.

"Oi'd an idea as ye'd think so, Miss Demelza," Abbot said, "an' Oi admits Oi've never seen a finer stallion in all me born days."

"He will win the Gold Cup . . . I am sure of it!" Demelza exclaimed.

It was hard, after the magnificence of Crusader, to appreciate the merits of the Earl's other horses, but she knew that all of them were exceptional.

When finally they reached Firebird she felt ashamed that she could see so many faults in him.

She put her arms round his neck.

"We may admire our visitors, Firebird," she said in her soft voice, "but we love you! You belong to us and are part of the family."

"That's true," Abbot said, "and ye mark me words, Miss Demelza, Jem'll bring Firebird first past th' winning-post on Saturday."

"I am sure he will," Demelza replied, "and perhaps the Earl will see Jem win and offer him a ride on one of his horses."

"Ye can be sure that's what Jem's a-dreaming, Miss," Abbot said with a grin.

"Is there a horse of any importance in the race in which you have entered Firebird?" Demelza asked.

Abbot scratched his head.

"The Bard might be a danger, Miss, but 'e's a-getting on in years and Oi don't much fancy th' jockey as is a-riding 'im."

Demelza hugged Firebird again.

"I know you will win!" she whispered, and felt as if he responded to her confidence in him.

She had to go back again to Crusader's stall before she left the stable, but before that she looked at the Earl's magnificently matched team of bays with which he had arrived at the Manor.

"One does not often see four horses so identical," she said as she inspected them.

" 'Is Lordship's groom was a-telling me that th' chestnuts with which they started out from London be so exceptional that 'is Lordship's refused twice and three times their value."

"Who would not rather have horses than money?" Demelza laughed.

At the same time, she thought that Gerard could do with both, and she could understand how frustrating it was for him to be with friends who had so much while he had but one horse and had to count every penny.

She talked to Abbot for a long time about the next day's racing, then hurried back to the house in case any of His Lordship's grooms should return early from the Heath.

It was not as late as she had anticipated, and when she started to climb the secret staircase she passed a connecting one which led to the Dining-Room, and she heard laughter.

She knew then that she could not resist looking at the Earl again, and she let herself out onto the Minstrels' Gallery overlooking one end of the great Dining-Hall which had once been the Refectory used by the Monks.

The Minstrels' Gallery had been added after the Restoration, when with the return of the "Merrie Monarch" Charles II everyone had wished to dance and enjoy themselves.

It had been elaborately carved by the great craftsmen of the day and it would have been impossible for someone seated at the dining-table below to know that anyone was hidden beyond it.

Looking through the screen, Demelza saw that because he was

host at the party the Earl was at the top of the table in the chair that had always been occupied by her father.

High-backed and upholstered in velvet, it seemed a fitting background for the man who was now sitting there.

Never had she imagined that any gentleman could look so magnificent or so elegant in evening-clothes.

She had always admired her father when he had been dressed for some formal occasion, but the Earl would, she thought, be outstanding even at a Royal Party at Windsor Castle.

As she looked down at him he was laughing and for the moment it made him look younger and eased away the cynical lines that were otherwise so prominent on his face.

The servants had left the room and the gentlemen were talking over their port. Some of them were cracking walnuts, which filled two of the Crown Derby dishes which had been among her mother's most treasured possessions.

They were seldom used and Demelza thought she must remember to tell Nattie to remind the visiting servants to be especially careful of them.

The candelabra which had belonged to her grandfather had been brought from the safe and now lit the table, but the huge hot-house peaches certainly did not come from what remained of the broken greenhouses. Nor did the large bunches of muscat grapes.

Demelza was less concerned with what the gentlemen were eating than with the man who sat at the head of the table.

She found it difficult to take her eyes from him, and at first the conversation was just a burr of words to which she did not listen, until with a little start she heard the Earl ask:

"Have you any ghosts in this house, Gerard?"

"Dozens of them!" her brother replied. "But personally I have never seen one."

"What are they?" the Earl persisted.

"There is a Monk who is supposed to have hanged himself for the expiation of his sins," Gerard replied. "And there is a child who was burnt at the stake with his parents, by Queen Mary's Inquisition, and of course the White Lady."

"The White Lady?" the Earl asked sharply.

"She is undoubtedly, according to legend and local superstitions, our most famous ghost," Gerard said with a smile.

"Tell me about her."

Gerard told the story of the White Lady searching for her lost lover, and Demelza, seeing the Earl listening attentively, was sure he had in fact seen her in the Long Gallery, which would account for his interest.

She wondered if he would admit to having done so, but when Gerard finished the tale the Earl merely asked:

"To those who see the White Lady does it mean good fortune—or bad?"

"It means," Lord Ramsgill interrupted before Gerard could reply, "that they who see her will seek endlessly for love, which will always elude them."

He laughed.

"That is something which will never happen to you, Valient."

"It would do you good to be the hunter instead of the hunted for a change!" the Honourable Ralph Mear interposed.

"A hope that is as unlikely to be fulfilled as that Crusader will not win the Gold Cup," Lord Ramsgill remarked.

"I suppose you have all backed him?" the Earl asked.

"Of course we have," Lord Chirn said, "despite the fact that we got damned rotten odds! The trouble is, Valient, the book-markers are afraid of your unparalleled success and are not really anxious to take any bets on him."

Looking round the table, Demelza noticed that Sir Francis Wigdon had said very little.

He had the habit of sticking forward his lower lip which gave him a sinister, rather sardonic expression.

'I do not like him!' she thought again. 'There is something about him which is unpleasant.'

She thought him a contrast to the Earl's other guests, who seemed to be decent, sporting types such as her father's friends had been.

She was sure that Gerard would come to no harm with any of them except perhaps Sir Francis.

She did not know why she had taken such a dislike to him, but, perhaps because she spent so much time alone, she was very perceptive about people.

It was as if she could feel the auras that emanated from them and at times to be almost aware of what they were thinking.

"I am sure," she told herself now, "that while Sir Francis pretends to be his friend, he is jealous of the Earl. There is no warmth about him."

Then she told herself that it was time she went upstairs to bed, and she knew that as soon as the servants sat down to supper Nattie would bring her something to eat.

With one last look at the Earl, thinking again how authoritative and imposing he was, she slipped through the secret panel and found her way, with the surety of one moving in a familiar place, to the top of the house.

Nattie was there before Demelza arrived.

"Where have you been, Miss Demelza?" she asked in the severe tone that she always assumed when she was frightened.

"I have been to see the horses, Nattie, and Crusader is wonderful! The most magnificent horse you have ever seen!"

"You've no right to be walking about when you know what Master Gerard said to you."

"I was quite safe," Demelza answered. "There was only Abbot in the stables. Everyone else had gone to the Heath, and I knew the gentlemen were at dinner."

"When they are in the house you are to stay here in this room," Nattie said firmly.

"Stop worrying about me, dear Nattie," Demelza smiled, "and tell me what you have brought me to eat, for I am exceedingly hungry!"

"I thought you would be, and I managed to bring you a little of three of the many dishes they had for dinner."

Demelza lifted the silver lids which covered the dishes and gave a cry of delight.

"They look delicious! Do find out how to make them, Nattie, and we can try them out next time Gerard comes to stay."

"That's exactly what I thought," Nattie replied. "And now I'd better be going back."

"No, wait and talk to me for a moment," Demelza begged. "I am longing to hear everything that has happened. It will save you coming back a second time for the tray."

She knew by the way that Nattie set herself down on the rush-bottomed chair that she was only too willing to be encouraged to talk.

"I have to admit, Miss Demelza," she began, "that His Lordship's servants are helpful and exceedingly polite."

It was what might have been expected, Demelza thought.

As she ate, she listened attentively as Nattie told her about Mr. Hunt, the Major-Domo, the footmen who had told her they would help her with the beds, and the Chef, who had been with the Earl for many years and was undoubtedly a culinary genius.

"There's only one man I don't care for," Nattie chattered on, "and that's Mr. Hayes, the Under-Butler."

"The Under-Butler?" Demelza asked. "You mean to say there are two of them?"

"Apparently the old Butler, Mr. Dean, who was with His Lordship's father, suffers from the heat, and the Major-Domo brought his assistant with him. But there's something about him I don't care for, though I can't put my finger on it. He's polite enough."

Demelza thought with a smile that Nattie had the same instinct about the Under-Butler that she had about Sir Francis Wigdon.

Doubtless, if anyone heard them saying such things, they would think she and Nattie were being spooky because they lived in such an old house.

'We will turn into a pair of witches, if we are not careful,' Demelza thought to herself, but aloud she said:

"I expect he is efficient at his job and knows what wines suit His Lordship."

"Certainly enough bottles have arrived!" Nattie exclaimed. "The cellar's almost full, and that's the truth!"

"Papa always said that racing was thirsty work," Demelza laughed, "and you and I will be thirsty tomorrow, if the dust is as bad as it usually is on the Heath."

"I was just thinking, Miss Demelza, it'd be a mistake for you to go to the races . . ." Nattie began.

"Not go to the races?" Demelza interrupted. "You must be crazy, Nattie! Of course we are going! We have always gone, and certainly nothing would stop me this year, when I want to see Crusader run . . . and of course Firebird."

"It's taking a risk," Nattie murmured.

"How could it be?" Demelza asked. "We shall be on the course and everyone who is staying in the house will be in the Royal Box with His Majesty."

That was so undeniably true that Nattie had nothing more to say.

"As soon as the gentlemen have left the house and the footmen have finished helping you make the beds," Demelza said, "we will slip down to the stables."

Her voice was excited as she went on:

"Abbot has promised to take us in the gig and he will park it well beyond the stands. In the crowds, I promise you, it would be a miracle if anyone paid any particular attention to us."

"I suppose you are right," Nattie admitted a little grudgingly. "I'll bring up a fresh gown in the morning, and you go to bed now straight away."

"I have every intention of doing so," Demelza answered. "I want to dream about Crusader."

"Horses, horses! That's all you think of!" Nattie said. "It's time at your age you had something else to dream about."

Demelza did not answer.

She heard these words so often before from Nattie, and she knew that her old Nurse deeply regretted the fact that they were unable to entertain what she thought of as "the right sort of people."

It was quite impossible, living alone at the Manor without a Chaperon, for her to meet girls of her own age or go to the Balls which occasionally took place in the countryside.

Most of the great houses, it was true, were full only during race-week, or when there was some important entertainment at Windsor Castle.

Even so, if Lady Langston had been alive there would have been parties in which Demelza could have taken part.

But their mother had died when Demelza was sixteen and still in the School-Room, and when Gerard had gone off to London it was impossible for Demelza alone to make any overtures to the people who lived round them.

In fact she did not even know who they were, since many of the houses had changed hands since her father had died.

Actually she had no desire to do anything other than live quietly at the Manor and ride Gerard's horses.

When he occasionally came home because he was unable to afford the expense of London, she was blissfully happy to ride with him over the Heath and in the forest and to listen eagerly while he told her stories of the gaiety of his life amongst the *Beau Monde*.

Sometimes she wondered to herself what would happen if Gerard got married.

Then she knew that that was something he would certainly be unable to afford at the moment, in fact at any time, unless he married a rich wife.

She saw the expression on Nattie's face now, and as she kissed her good-night she said:

"Stop worrying, Nattie. I am happy. You know how happy I am."

"It's an unnatural way of living—that's all I can say, Miss Demelza!" Nattie said sharply.

Without waiting for an answer she went down the stairs to let herself out through the first secret door she came to, because, as she had often said: "Them secret passages give me the creeps!"

Alone, Demelza laughed fondly to herself because she loved Nattie, who gave her heart and soul to her "babies' interests."

Quickly her thoughts returned first to Crusader, then to his owner.

As she knelt to say her prayers she prayed that the great horse would win, but somehow as she conjured him up in her mind, the Earl stood beside him and the two seemed inseparable.

* * *

The next morning the Manor was full of bustle and excitement.

It was always the same the first day of race-week. Everyone was eager to be off and a dozen things seemed to have been overlooked at the last moment.

The Earl with his guests was lunching in the Jockey Club, while owing to the sunny weather the Heath would be covered with people of all classes having picnics.

The coaches which had been crowding in since first thing in the morning had huge hampers of venison, fish, and sweet-meats piled upon their roofs.

The tents and booths were stocked with food, and, because of the heat, casks of spruce-beer had begun to flow very early in the morning.

By the time Demelza and Nattie reached the course, the noise was deafening not only from the punters, the book-markers, and the "tic-tac men," but also from the entertainers.

Outside a Show Booth where a wide variety of freaks were to be seen, the public was being invited to enter for the expenditure of one penny.

They passed "the Bohemian," who balanced coachwheels on his chin, and saw a number of women dancing on stilts eight feet high.

They not only made money by exercising their skill, but also, Demelza thought, they had the advantage of seeing the races over the heads of everyone else.

She was particularly interested to see the new Royal Box when it was filled with spectators, the most important of course being the King.

It had been started in May and had only just been finished last week in time for the races.

The King had employed as his architect the famous John Nash, who was responsible for the improvements to Buckingham Palace, the design of Regent Street, and what were called the "Nash Terraces" in Regent's Park.

Immediately opposite the winning-post, the Royal Box was built in imitation of a Greek portico with fluted pilasters supporting the roof.

It had two storeys, of which the upper part was used only by the

King. During its construction Demelza had visited it and had seen that it had been divided into two rooms, which at the last moment had been fitted out with white muslin curtains.

Today it would have been impossible for her to get in, for round the Royal Stand there was a small enclosure guarded by Police Officers and gate-men and only those invited by the King were admitted.

On either side of the Royal Box were nine other stands of various sizes and they appeared already to be crammed to bursting. Demelza and Nattie looked at them with interest as they drove along the other side of the course.

"Oi thinks we'd be best off 'ere, Miss," Abbot said, drawing the gig to a standstill beyond a number of other carriages, coaches, and wagons.

"I thinks so too," Nattie said before Demelza could speak. "If we cross to the other side we'll not be able to get away quickly, and it's important we leave before the last race."

Demelza knew Nattie was worrying about getting home before the Earl and his party returned.

So she accepted that they should stay where they were, although she knew she might not be able to see the saddling, in which she had always been so interested in the past.

They were no sooner in place than there were cheers at the other end of the course, which they knew announced the arrival of the King.

Abbot had heard earlier in the week that His Majesty might not appear as he was suffering from a "severe and dangerous attack of gout."

However, he had undoubtedly arrived, but did not drive along the course as his father had always done. Instead he proceeded along the rear of the booths.

Demelza could hear the cheers all the way to the Royal Box, then the King appeared at the window and the gentlemen in the enclosure below all raised their hats to him.

He stood for some moments acknowledging the cheers, which were not very effusive, and Demelza could see that he was clad in the Windsor uniform with a single diamond star on his breast.

She wondered if the Earl was with him.

Nattie, who had always shown an intense interest in the Royal Party, recognised the Duke of York and the Duke of Wellington.

"Who is the lady beside the King?" Demelza asked.

"Lady Conyngham," Nattie replied in a repressed voice which told Demelza she did not approve of Her Ladyship.

As soon as the King arrived the first race was run, after which racing was interrupted by a one-hour interval for luncheon.

Nattie produced sandwiches, but Demelza looked rather longingly at the magnificent picnics which were laid out either in the carriages or on the grass.

There were cold brands of every sort, and bottles of hock and champagne were being opened on every side.

It was very hot, but the roar of cheers which went up as Trance, as was expected, won the Grafton Sweep was full-throated and uninhibited.

"That's three hundred guineas for His Royal Highness's pocket," Abbot remarked.

He had previously told Demelza that the Duke of York had backed Trance in the Sweep against a horse called The Duke.

Abbot had left Demelza and Nattie alone in the gig for some time before the race, and Demelza was quite certain that he also had backed Trance.

After one of the Earl's horses had won the third race of the day, Nattie insisted on their leaving, although Demelza longed to stay for the fourth and last race.

She tried to protest, but Nattie said firmly:

"Five days of racing's enough for anyone, and we're taking no risks. Come along, Miss Demelza, there's work for me to do at home, as you well know."

Because no-one else was leaving so early and the roads were clear, they got back to the Manor far more quickly than might have been expected.

"Thank you, Abbot," Demelza said as they drove into the yard. "It was very exciting and I loved every moment of it!"

"We'll see some fine racing tomorrow and Thursday," Abbott answered, "an' if Moses don't win the Albany Stakes—Oi'll eat me hat!"

"I am sure he will," Demelza said with a smile.

Then she was hurried by Nattie round the side of the house to the garden door.

In the passage she opened the secret panel while Nattie went off towards the kitchen-quarters.

It had all been very exciting, Demelza thought, as she began to climb the narrow staircase, but she was hot from the burning sun and stopped for a moment to take off her bonnet.

As she did so, to her surprise she heard a woman's voice say:

"As His Lordship is not at home, I would like to leave a note for him."

"Of course, M'Lady. There's a writing-desk in here," a servant answered.

Astonished that anyone should expect to find the Earl at home at such an hour in the afternoon before the racing was finished, Demelza moved a few steps until by using the peep-hole she could see into the Drawing-Room.

Moving into the room from the hall she saw the most beautiful woman she had ever seen in her life.

Wearing a gown of periwinkle blue which matched the colour of her eyes, her golden hair framed by a high-crowned bonnet covered in blue ostrich feathers, she was breathtaking.

There were diamonds round her neck and over the short gloves that covered her wrists.

She moved with a sinuous grace that struck Demelza as having something almost feline about it.

She reached the centre of the room, where Demelza could see her clearly. Then as the servant following her shut the door, she turned round to say in a different tone:

"Have you anything to report to me, Hayes?"

Demelza remembered that Hayes was the Under-Butler of whom Nattie had spoken.

"No, M'Lady, we only arrived yesterday and there're only gentlemen here. No ladies of any sort."

"Not living in the house?"

"No, M'Lady, only an old Nurse and another servant."

"Lady Plymworth has not called?"

"No, M'Lady."

The elegant visitor stood for a moment, her gloved finger against her chin, as if she was thinking, then she said:

"His Lordship is dining out this evening?"

"So I believe, M'Lady."

"Is it with Lord Dysart?"

"I heard His Lordship's valet mention that name, M'Lady."

"That is what I thought," the visitor murmured almost beneath her breath.

Then to the Under-Butler she said in a commanding tone:

"Now listen to me carefully, Hayes. His Lordship always has a glass of wine when he is dressing for dinner. I wish you to decant a bottle yourself and put into it before you take it upstairs the contents of this."

As she spoke, she drew from her reticule a small bottle about three inches high and held it out to the Under-Butler.

He hesitated.

"I wouldn't wish, M'Lady, to do anything . . ."

"It will not hurt him badly, you fool!" the lady said firmly. "His Lordship will just be unable to attend the party this evening and doubtless will have a head-ache in the morning."

She looked at the expression on Hayes's face and laughed.

"Do not worry yourself. You will not swing on Tyburn, that I promise you!"

"I'm—afraid, M'Lady! Suppose the wine was drunk by the wrong person?"

"If it is, you will suffer for it!" the lady snapped. "I got you this position and I have paid you well. You can expect further recompense if what you do is successful."

"Thank you, M'Lady. It's only that I like the post and don't want to leave it."

"You will leave it when it suits me!" the lady retorted. "Now, you understand exactly what you have to do?"

"Yes, M'Lady."

"So carry out your orders."

"I'll do my best, M'Lady."

"You had better do so!"

The visitor walked towards the door and as Hayes opened it she said:

"On second thought, as I may see His Lordship tonight I will not leave a note for him. What I have to tell him will be a surprise, so please do not inform him that I was here."

Demelza realised that these words were intended for the ears of the footmen on duty in the hall.

The lady went from the Drawing-Room and Hayes followed her, leaving the door open behind him.

Demelza waited.

After a little while she heard the sound of wheels and knew that a carriage was driving away from the front door.

She drew in her breath with a gasp, realising that she had held her breath for most of the time she had been listening.

How was it possible? How could such an exceedingly beautiful person as the lady intend to harm the Earl? And in order to do so, she was intriguing with one of his own servants against him!

Dazed and bewildered, Demelza climbed up the stairs to the Priests'-Room and sat down on the bed to think.

It was nothing new, she remembered, for women to use drugs or medicines of some sort to hurt someone they either disliked or . . . loved.

It struck Demelza that that was the explanation why the beautiful lady who had come to the Manor wished to prevent the Earl from dining this evening with Lord Dysart—she loved him.

That was why she was jealous of Lady Plymworth of whom she had spoken.

But to drug the Earl! That was surely carrying jealousy to extremes!

Demelza could remember hearing her father discussing—years ago —the behaviour of Lady Jersey when Princess Caroline of Brunswick married the Prince of Wales.

Lady Jersey, who had apparently been in love with the Prince, had been one of the people he sent to meet his bride when she arrived in England.

Everybody knew later that Lady Jersey had put a strong emetic in the Princess's food to spoil the first night of the honeymoon.

Although Demelza had not yet been born at the time this had happened, she always felt it was what Gerard would call a "dirty trick." In fact she herself had felt that it was despicable and beneath the dignity of any woman who called herself a lady to sink to such tactics.

And yet here was someone, so beautiful that Demelza felt any man who saw her must be infatuated with such a lovely face, behaving in very much the same way towards the Earl.

Demelza felt she could not bear to think of the Earl's suffering or of him lying unconscious on his bed.

He was so strong, so athletic, and as Gerard had said, "a Corinthian of Corinthians," that it would be like seeing the fall of a great oak tree to see him prostrate through the treacherous hand of a woman.

What was more she had said that it might give him a head-ache tomorrow.

Suppose he was too ill to see Moses run? Or, more important, his own horse who was entered for another race?

"It must not happen," Demelza said to herself positively. "I must stop it! I must!"

Her first thought was that she must tell Gerard, but this would present a number of difficulties.

First was that Gerard's bed-room was one of the few rooms in the house where there was not a secret entrance.

This was because one of the previous owners of the Manor had removed the oak panelling and had instead papered the walls with a very attractive rice-paper which he had brought back from China.

It was certainly very effective; at the same time, it prevented Demelza from being able to reach her brother unless she entered his room from the passage, which would be unthinkable.

Apart from that, she had a feeling that Gerard would not wish to be involved in such an explosive situation which centred round a beautiful lady who loved the Earl and had bribed one of his chief servants.

'No, I cannot tell Gerard,' Demelza decided.

But what else could she do?

She sat thinking for a long time, and finally made a decision.

*　*　*

The Earl came back from the races in extremely good humour.

He had enjoyed an excellent luncheon with the other members of the Jockey Club and had been entrusted by the King with the placing of his bets.

This had resulted in his handing over to His Majesty a quite considerable sum at the end of the day, while the Earl himself had backed three winners out of the four, which was certainly a good percentage.

He was also looking forward to the dinner-party tonight, when he would see Charis Plymworth again.

They had met in the Royal Box and she had intimated very clearly that she was as anxious to be with him as he was with her.

She was looking extremely beautiful, and the slant of her green eyes intrigued him as did the Sphinx-like smile which curved her red lips.

He had known as they talked together that he was being watched by Sydel, but it was difficult for her to make a scene in the King's presence, as the Earl was quite certain she wanted to do.

"Jealous women are a damned bore!" he said to Lord Chirn as they drove away from the race-course.

"All women are jealous," his friend answered, "but some more so than others!"

The Earl did not reply and Lord Chirn went on:

"Beware of Sydel Blackford! It is rumoured that she practises

Black Magic and murmurs incantations over a dead cockerel—or whatever it is they do!"

The Earl laughed.

"That might have been possible in the Middle Ages, but I cannot believe any woman would go as far as that these days."

Lord Chirn smiled. He did not bother to tell the Earl that he himself had had a short but fiery affair with Lady Sydel and knew she was capable of anything and everything to gain her own ends.

He thought, as so many of the Earl's friends had thought before, that it was a pity he could not settle down and have a family.

Most men wanted an heir, and the Earl had so many possessions that it seemed a crime against nature that he should not have a son to inherit them.

Whatever Lord Chirn thought, however, he was not prepared to voice such sentiments aloud, and when they reached the Manor House they were talking about the racing.

There was champagne and sandwiches waiting in the Drawing-Room, but the Earl had already drunk enough in the Royal Box. After talking to his friends for a short time he went upstairs to dress.

He knew that his valet, Dawson, would have a bath ready for him. He was looking forward to cooling off after the heat of the day and getting rid of the dust, which, as he had anticipated, had been worse than usual owing to the long spell of dry weather.

His valet helped him out of his tight-fitting and well-cut coat which had been the envy of the King.

"I cannot think why Weston cuts so well for you and so badly for me!" he had grumbled.

The real answer, the Earl knew, was that the King had grown so extraordinarily fat in the last few years that it was impossible for any tailor to give him the elegant figure he craved. But aloud he said:

"I thought how admirably your uniform became you today, Sire."

His Majesty had smiled and preened himself.

"A good day's racing, Dawson," the Earl remarked now as he untied his cravat.

"Excellent, M'Lord!"

The Earl threw his discarded cravat down on the dressing-table and as he did so he saw a very small note propped against his gold-backed hair-brushes.

It was addressed to him and marked *Urgent!* in a hand-writing he had never seen before.

"Who left this, Dawson?" he enquired.

The valet turned to look at what he held in his hand.

"I've no idea, M'Lord. I've not seen it before."

"It was here—on my dressing-table!"

"No-one's brought it in while I've been 'ere, M'Lord."

The Earl opened the note.

There were only a few lines written in the same elegant but unfamiliar writing:

"Do not drink the wine you will be offered while dressing for dinner. It will make you ill."

The Earl stared at what he had read and as he did so there was a knock on the door.

Dawson went to it.

He came back carrying a salver on which was a cut-glass decanter and a single glass.

"Will you have some wine before or after your bath, M'Lord?" he enquired.

The Earl looked at the wine.

"I wish to speak to Hunt," he said. "Before he comes upstairs, ask him to find out who called here today and who left a note for me."

Dawson looked surprised, but, setting down the silver salver, he obediently left the room.

The Earl picked up the decanter and sniffed the wine. There appeared to be nothing unusual about it. Perhaps, he thought, the note was a joke, a trick played on him by one of his friends.

But he was sure the hand-writing did not resemble that of anyone staying in the house.

He was almost certain it had been inscribed by a woman.

Even as he thought that, he was conscious of a subtle fragrance he had noticed before.

He held the note to his nose and found that it smelt very faintly of some flower to which he could not put a name.

Now it struck him that he had been aware of the same perfume in his bed-room and in other parts of the house.

He had thought that it came from the bowls and vases of flowers that were arranged in every room, but there were only pink roses here in his bed-room and the fragrance on the note was not that of a rose.

It was all rather intriguing and he felt in some way that it was a part of the mystery that was exemplified by the house itself.

There was a knock on the door and the Major-Domo stood there.

"You sent for me, M'Lord?"

"I wish to know who called here today, and who left a note for me."

"I've learnt, M'Lord, that Lady Sydel Blackford called late this afternoon, but at her request this was not reported to me until I made enquiries a few seconds ago."

Lady Sydel Blackford!

"And she left a note for me?"

"No, M'Lord. She expressly said that she wouldn't leave a note because she'd a surprise for Your Lordship this evening and didn't wish to spoil it."

"It seems to me extraordinary that her visit was not reported to you, Hunt."

"It was sheer incompetence, M'Lord, and I've already spoken to Hayes."

"The Under-Butler?"

"Yes, M'Lord. Apparently 'twas Hayes who let Her Ladyship in."

"And who decanted the wine that was brought to my room this evening?"

The Major-Domo looked surprised, but he answered:

"I'm afraid I've no idea, M'Lord, but I'll find out."

"Do that," the Earl said sharply.

Again there was a wait. The Earl had undressed and had his bath, revelling in the cold water and getting Dawson to pour over him the last can before he stepped out to wrap himself in a towel.

He was still drying himself when the Major-Domo returned.

"I apologise, M'Lord, for taking so long," he said, "but it was with some difficulty that I discovered that the bottle of wine in question was decanted by Hayes and also was brought upstairs by him. He then handed the salver to Robert, who's on duty on this floor and who brought it to Your Lordship's room and handed it in."

"What do you know about Hayes?" the Earl asked.

"He came with excellent references, M'Lord, after Your Lordship thought with so much entertaining in the Season it was too much for Dean."

"What references did you take up on him?"

"Two, M'Lord. One from the Duke of Newcastle, which was excellent, and the second from Lady Sydel Blackford."

The expression on the Earl's face was that of a stalker who gets the stag he has been following within range of his rifle.

"Lady Sydel Blackford!" he exclaimed. "And it was she who spoke to Hayes this afternoon! Send the man up to me in five minutes!"

It was not difficult for the Earl to extort from Hayes all the information he required.

He then sent for the Major-Domo and told him to dismiss the Under-Butler immediately, without a reference.

Looking as magnificent in his evening-clothes as Demelza had thought him to be last night, the Earl drove off towards Lord Dysart's house with a feeling of triumph.

He had found the culprit and he would take care in the future that no-one recommended by Sydel Blackford should cross the threshold of any house he possessed.

But one thing remained unsolved.

Who had written the warning note? Who had put it on his dressing-table? And who used the tantalising perfume to which he still could not put a name?

He found himself puzzling over the answer to these three questions the whole evening.

Somehow in consequence he found the enigmatic expression in Charis Plymworth's slanting eyes less mysterious and intriguing than he had expected.

CHAPTER FOUR

Returning from the races on Wednesday, Demelza felt it was one of the most exciting days she had ever spent.

She had not only seen the most superb horses, but she had also been thrilled in a manner that she had never known before by the knowledge that she had saved the Earl.

She could see him in the small enclosure outside the Royal Box and occasionally caught a glimpse of him in the window beside the King.

She watched him in the saddling enclosure after she had persuaded Nattie, much against her will, to cross the course with her.

"What'll Master Gerard say?" Nattie questioned.

"If he notices us, which is very unlikely, he will understand that I cannot bear not to see the horses at close quarters."

She particularly wanted to see a horse called Cardenio race against Mr. Green's horse, Trance.

She also knew that the breeding of both the horses was favoured against the colt entered by the Duke of York for his own fifty-pound plate.

It was run over two and a half miles, and the colt His Royal Highness had, which won, was a three-year-old bay by Election out of a Sorcerer mare.

Boyce, an apprentice whom Abbot had picked out as likely to be a well-known jockey in the future, rode extremely well.

When that excitement was over there was the Albany Stakes to watch, where again the Duke of York was victorious with his Derby winner, Moses.

Moses had been bred by him and was a bay. But although it was a superb animal and Demelza had been looking forward to seeing him, she decided he did not really measure up to Crusader.

She was sure the Earl was winning his bets, and when she saw him talking to Gerard she hoped that her brother was taking advantage of his superior knowledge of the Turf before he expended their precious money with the bookies.

Nattie took her to the far end of the saddling enclosure, as far away as possible from the social viewers who were crowded at the other end nearest to the stands.

The gentlemen who attended the King looked exceedingly smart and wore their high-crowned hats at a rakish angle that was fashionable.

But Demelza felt that not one of them could equal not only the elegance of the Earl but his air of consequence, which seemed an inescapable part of him.

Again Nattie insisted they should leave immediately after the third race, and although Demelza longed to plead for them to stay a little longer, she knew in fact that it was prudent not to take any risks.

She had not spoken to Gerard since the Earl and his party had arrived at the Manor and she knew that her brother was deliberately pretending to himself that she was not in the house.

She could not help wondering why he was making such a fuss, for the Earl's guests behaved in the most decorous manner.

There was no hard drinking, which Demelza had been told was traditional among the Bucks of St. James's.

What was more, there were no riotous parties, which, she had heard, invariably took place in most other houses in race-week.

Last night the Earl had been out to dinner, but tonight he was dining at home and Demelza wondered if his guests would include any beautiful ladies.

Of one thing she was quite certain: the lady who had ordered the Under-Butler to drug his wine would not be present.

Nattie had told her that Hayes had left the house yesterday evening under a cloud.

"I saved him!" Demelza said triumphantly to herself.

She wondered if the Earl was curious as to who had written the note. He would never know, and she found the knowledge somewhat dispiriting.

They arrived back at the Manor and Demelza entered as usual by the garden door so that she should not be seen by any of the Earl's servants who were on duty.

As she went up the secret stairway she could not resist looking into the rooms to see if the flowers she had arranged first thing in the morning before anyone was awake were still looking lovely.

She had cut them from her own garden, which, enclosed by red brick Elizabethan walls, was out of sight of any of the windows of the house.

It was here that her mother had planted an herb-garden, and Demelza took immense trouble in cultivating the same herbs, besides the flowers she loved best.

These included the pink roses she always put in her late father's room.

Climbing over a little arbour at the end of the garden was a riot of honeysuckle intermingled with white roses, which sweetly scented, had been her mother's favourite.

Because she thought the Earl might appreciate them, her bowls of roses in the Drawing-Room were larger than usual and there was hardly a side-table that did not hold them.

She had also changed the roses in his bed-room and thought that they made a perfect splash of colour against the dark panelling.

Then she told herself that as the Earl undoubtedly had so many priceless treasures in his possession he could hardly be expected to concern himself with flowers.

Nevertheless, she took a great deal of trouble over the arrangement on the desk in the Library, where she had realized he wrote his letters and sometimes sat alone first thing in the morning.

She was sure it would be wrong and impolite to spy on him and she had deliberately restricted herself to looking at him in the Dining-Room and of course on the race-course.

There, she could not feel she was intruding, and it was hard to take her eyes from him to the horses.

She kept asking herself why Gerard had said the Earl was so

wicked where women were concerned. Perhaps it was because he
was so handsome that he excited them to behave as did the lady who
had tried to drug him.

She longed to know if he had loved her very much and found herself wondering what happened when a man like the Earl made love
to anyone so beautiful.

They would of course kiss each other, and Demelza could not help
thinking that that would be a wonderful experience. Yet perhaps she
herself would never be kissed.

Nattie was always murmuring that she ought to meet "the right
people," and Demelza was well aware that she really meant she
should meet eligible bachelors from whom to choose a husband.

"Maybe I shall never marry," she told herself, and thought again
how terrible it must be for the Earl to have a wife who was insane.

It gave her almost a physical ache in her heart to think what he
must have suffered, and she prayed that such a tragedy would never
happen to Gerard.

Walking up the twisting staircase to the Priests'-Room, Demelza
decided she would lie down on her bed and read one of the books
that she had brought with her into hiding.

The room was so well constructed that it was in fact quite light,
although the slit-like windows were close against the low ceiling and
hidden under the eaves of the house.

Demelza had cleaned them and the light in the room was diffused
and gave the place an air of coolness after the heat of the sun at the
races.

She picked up her book but found it hard to concentrate on anything but the races—and the Earl.

He was everything, she thought, that she had always envisaged a
man should be: sporting, fond of horses, and, she was quite certain,
a magnificent rider.

He seemed to embody all her childhood dreams of St. George, Sir
Galahad, and the heroes in Sir Walter Scott's novels, which her father had bought for her each time one was published.

"I never thought then," she whispered, "that I would see the hero
of them in real life!"

*　*　*

Demelza must have fallen asleep, because she awoke with a start
to find that there was very little light in the room, which made her
think the sun had already set.

At that moment she heard Nattie coming clumsily up the stairs with her evening meal.

Demelza sat up on the bed.

"I have been asleep, Nattie," she said. "What time is it?"

"Nearly ten o'clock," Nattie answered, "and the servants are starting their supper."

Demelza almost cried out aloud her disappointment.

She had meant to watch the Earl tonight in the Dining-Hall. Now it would be too late, and by the time she had eaten her own food, she was quite certain, they would have moved into the Drawing-Room.

"There was a party tonight," Nattie said almost as if she knew what Demelza was thinking.

"Were there any ladies present?"

"No, only gentlemen. I expect the conversation was of nothing but the racing. No-one can think of anything else in this place!"

"And no-one will talk of anything else tomorrow," Demelza said with a smile, "when Crusader wins the Gold Cup."

"*If* he wins!" Nattie said sharply.

"He will!" Demelza replied. "How could the greatest horse fail to win the greatest race?"

The Ascot Gold Cup had been introduced into the races in 1807.

The first time it was run it was over two miles, but it was increased by half a mile the following year.

Demelza had been told that the Queen and the Princesses had watched the race in a special Pavilion erected at the arm of the course. Another box had been completed opposite the judges for the Prince of Wales.

"Do you remember, Nattie, the very first race for the Gold Cup?" Demelza asked.

"Of course I remember it!" Nattie replied. "The Queen and the Princesses were wearing mantles in the Spanish style, with what I would call gypsy-hats."

Demelza laughed.

She always teased Nattie about her interest in the Royal Family.

"And who won the race?" Demelza enquired. "That is far more important!"

There was a silence, then Nattie said:

"Believe it or not, Miss Demelza, it's slipped my memory!"

Demelza laughed again.

"You were watching the Queen instead of Master Jackey!"

"Perhaps I found Her Majesty more interesting," Nattie retorted almost defiantly.

"Well, you can forget the King tomorrow and concentrate on Crusader!" Demelza said. "I do not suppose the prize money of one hundred guineas will be of importance to the Earl. It will be the honour and the glory which count."

She was thinking of how every year owners and jockeys strove to win what had originally been called "the Emperor's Place" because besides the prize-money there was a gift of plate presented by the Tsar of Russia, Nicholas I.

Demelza's father had always been more interested in the Gold Cup than any other race and he had inspired her with his own enthusiasm.

Nattie's mind was, however, still on the Royal Personages she had seen in the past, and she was relating how King George III and his suite used to arrive on horseback, when as if suddenly she realised the time she rose to pick up Demelza's tray, saying:

"Now you go to bed, Miss Demelza. If you're not tired you ought to be!"

"I was tired when I first came home," Demelza admitted, "but now, as I told you, I have been asleep and feel very wakeful."

"Then don't strain your eyes trying to read until all hours of the night," Nattie admonished.

She had always been convinced that candlelight was too dim for reading and Demelza had heard her say the same thing over and over again during the years when she had been growing up.

"Good-night, dearest Nattie," she said, "and do not worry about me. Remember, I want my very best gown to wear tomorrow."

That could only be another white muslin, but it was new, and, unlike Demelza's other gowns, it was trimmed with some pretty ribbons which had seemed both to her and to Nattie a vast expenditure when they had bought them.

Alone, Demelza undressed and put on her nightgown and over it a white dressing-gown also made by Nattie. It fastened close at the neck and had a little flat collar trimmed with lace.

She brushed her hair as her mother had taught her to do until it shone; then, still feeling wide awake, she picked up her book and forced herself to concentrate on it.

Before she did so she lit two candles, which Nattie would have thought, eyes or no eyes, an extravagance.

Then because her book had begun to interest her she forgot everything else until with surprise she heard the stable-clock strike the hour of midnight.

"I certainly must go to sleep now," she told herself, and shut her book to put it away tidily.

Everything in the Priests'-Room had to be put back in place because it was so small.

Then as she stretched her arms above her head, feeling a little cramped after sitting for so long, Demelza had a sudden longing to breathe the fresh air.

One disadvantage of the Priests'-Room was that it was not well ventilated, and for the first time since she had slept there Demelza felt stifled and restricted.

'I will go downstairs and stand at the garden door,' she thought. 'I will breathe deeply, then come up again. Not even Nattie could find fault with that!'

She slipped her feet into her soft satin heel-less slippers and very quietly began to descend the stairs.

She passed the top floor, reached the first, and was just proceeding farther when she heard voices in what was known as the Red Room.

Someone was speaking clearly but in what seemed a deliberately lowered tone and there was something almost sinister about it, as if the words were hissed.

Without actually realising that she would be prying on the occupant's privacy, Demelza stopped and standing on tip-toe looked through the small hole which was incorporated in the Jacobean panelling with which the room was lined.

As she did so she remembered that it was Sir Francis Wigdon who slept there, the man she disliked.

She could see him sitting on the side of the bed. He was still wearing his evening-clothes but had loosened the cravat round his neck.

"You have brought exactly what I told you?" Demelza heard him say in a lowered voice, which made his words seem deliberately secretive.

She moved slightly so that she could see to whom he was speaking and saw to her surprise that there were two other men in the room.

One looked like a valet, wearing a striped waist-coat in what she thought were Sir Francis's colours. The other was a much rougher type, coarse and wearing a red handkerchief round his neck.

He held his cap in his hands, which he was twisting nervously as he said:

"Oi've got it safe, Guv'nor."

"You are sure it is strong enough to be effective?" Sir Francis asked, speaking now to the man who appeared to be his valet.

"I can swear, Sir, that when 'e's taken it Crusader'll not run to-morrow."

"Good!" Sir Francis ejaculated.

Demelza held her breath as if she could not believe what she had heard.

"Then get on with you!" Sir Francis ordered. "But be absolutely certain before you enter the stables that everyone is asleep."

"We'll be cautious, Sir," the valet replied.

Demelza did not wait to hear any more. She knew now what the men intended to do.

There had always been talk of horses being doped before races, and of owners having guards to watch their stables. But she was quite certain it had never crossed the Earl's mind, or Abbot's, that the horses were not safe at the Manor.

Her first thought was that she must wake Gerard, but it was impossible to get directly into his room and she was afraid if she went into the corridor she might encounter the men to whom Sir Francis was speaking, or even Sir Francis himself.

Almost without conscious thought her feet carried her along the side-passage which led to the Master's Room.

Only as she descended the steps which led to the secret panel by the fireplace did she ask herself if she was doing the right thing and she remembered how furious Gerard would be with her.

Then she told herself that nothing mattered but that she should save Crusader.

How could she stand by and do nothing while he was doped and made unfit to race the following day?

It was not only that the Earl would lose face at having to withdraw his horse and that he and Gerard would lose the money they had wagered on him. It was also a humiliation and an ignominy that such things should happen at the Manor of all places.

She put out her hand without even waiting to look through the peep-hole.

The secret door opened and she stepped into the room which had been her father's.

The curtains were drawn back and by the light of the stars and a pale moon that was creeping up the sky she could see clearly enough to realise that the Earl was in bed and asleep.

Drawing a deep breath, Demelza spoke. . . .

* * *

The Earl had enjoyed his dinner when the house-party had been joined by six of his closest friends.

The food had been excellent, the wine superb, and although the conversation had naturally been about the racing, everyone told amusing anecdotes of one sort or another.

They capped one another's jokes with a wit that made the Earl feel sorry that the King was not present.

If there was the one thing that George IV really enjoyed it was witty conversation to which he could contribute with an intelligence that few people except his closest friends credited him with.

"A damned good evening, Valient!" one of the Earl's guests said when he left. "I cannot remember when I have laughed more."

As the Earl went up to bed he thought he had been wise in insisting that everyone should retire early.

Like the King, he hated parties that went on too long and he disliked it if men drank so much that they became incoherent.

Abstemious himself, he found drunkards a bore and he never allowed himself to be bored.

When he got into bed he echoed the sentiments of Lord Chirn, who had said as they walked upstairs together:

"This is the best Ascot I have ever attended, Valient. Not only have I made money, but I have never been more comfortable and I find in the peace and quiet of this house that I sleep like a child."

It was what the Earl had found.

There were no noisy chambermaids or whistling ostlers to wake him in the morning, and the clean air coming in through the windows carried the scent of the pines and flowers.

He fell asleep almost as soon as his head touched the pillow. Then he awoke with an alertness which came from his training as a soldier.

It was almost as if he sensed danger before he heard a very soft voice say:

"Go to Crusader! Go to Crusader!"

He turned towards the sound and incredulously saw the ghost of the White Lady!

It was the same vision he had seen when he arrived in the Long Gallery, and here she was again, standing by the fireplace. He could see her quite clearly in the light from the window.

Then as he moved to sit up she said again:

"Go to Crusader! Go now! It is urgent!"

The Earl sat up completely and as he did so the White Lady vanished!

One moment she was there, the next she was gone and there was only the outline of the mantelpiece against the darkness of the panelling.

"I am dreaming," the Earl told himself.

But he was awake, and because of the urgency in the soft voice he knew he must do what he had been told, if only to make sure that the whole thing was nothing but imagination.

He got out of bed, and pulled on a shirt and a pair of close-fitting pantaloons with a speed which would have annoyed Dawson, who liked to dress his Master slowly.

He shrugged himself into the first coat he took from the wardrobe and tied a cravat loosely round his neck. Then with his feet in a pair of soft-soled slippers he opened the door and walked down the corridor.

The house was in darkness except for one candle which had been left burning in the hall in a silver candlestick.

The Earl picked it up and it lit him along a corridor which led, he knew, towards the stables.

Only when he reached a side-door before the kitchen-quarters did he set the candle down on a table, undo the bolts, and let himself out.

As he felt the coldness of the night air on his face he told himself that he was being a fool to pay any attention to what had undoubtedly been a very vivid dream.

Yet, if, as he expected, he found Crusader safe and undisturbed, he could just make his way back to bed and no-one would know that he had been seeing visions or whatever one might call them.

'I expect the wine was stronger than I thought, and because I was thirsty I drank too much of it,' the Earl decided.

At the same time, the White Lady had seemed very real. If she was a ghost—did ghosts speak?

He decided he was lamentably ignorant on the subject. Then as he rounded the huge overgrown laurels and had his first sight of the stables, he saw something ahead of him move.

Instinctively he stood still.

The movement he had seen was in the shadow at the entrance to the stables. Once again he thought he was imagining things, until the movement occurred again.

Now he realised that it was a hand, and a hand must belong to a person.

He waited.

A few seconds later he discerned two men moving stealthily in a manner which proclaimed all too clearly that they were up to mischief, creeping towards the stable.

They kept in the shadow of the building and the Earl knew that his warning from the White Lady had only just come in time.

He remembered now that his groom had mentioned that the lock to the main stable door at the Manor was broken.

The Earl had hardly listened at the time. It had not seemed to be of any importance.

The grooms would doubtless be sleeping over the stables as they always did, but, apart from anything else, since his plans had been changed at the last moment it was unlikely that any of the unsavoury characters on the race-course would know where he was staying.

One man ahead of the other pulled open the stable door, then as they disappeared inside the Earl moved.

His slippers made no sound on the cobbled yard and when he entered the stable like a whirlwind they were at Crusader's stall, undoing the iron gate.

He caught the first man who turned round to look at him a blow on the chin which lifted his feet off the ground.

The other man, bigger and more aggressive, went for him, but the Earl had learnt the art of boxing from the greatest professional pugilists of his generation, "Gentleman Jackson" and his partner Mendoza.

It was nothing of a fight, for his opponent was laid out and unconscious within a few seconds.

It was then that the Earl shouted and the grooms came running, with them Baxter, his Head Groom, and old Abbot.

They searched the unconscious men and found the drug with which they had intended to dope Crusader, and as Baxter held it out in the palm of his hand towards the Earl he said:

"I apologise, M'Lord. I should've left a guard on th' 'orses, but I thinks we were safe enough 'ere."

"We have learnt a lesson we will not forget in the future, Baxter," the Earl said. "I wonder who paid these thugs."

As he spoke, Abbot, who was holding the lantern over the smaller man, gave an exclamation.

"What is it?" the Earl enquired.

"Oi've seen this man afore, M'Lord. 'E's visited th' stables several times since 'e's been a-staying at th' Manor."

"Staying at the Manor?" the Earl asked sharply.

"Aye, M'Lord. 'E tells Oi 'e were interested in 'orses, especially Crusader."

"Who is he?" the Earl enquired.

"'E says 'e were a valet, M'Lord. And 'e's a-wearing a livery waist-coat."

The Earl looked down. By the light of the lantern he could see the buttons that fastened the striped waist-coat and he recognised the crest on them.

"Tie this vermin up," he said to Baxter. "Lock them up for the night, and I will see they are handed over to the race-course Police in the morning."

"Very good, M'Lord, an' thank ye, M'Lord. I can only say how humiliated I am that this should've occurred."

"Fortunately I was warned in time," the Earl remarked.

"Warned, M'Lord?"

It was a question which, the Earl thought as he walked back to the house, he could not answer.

He walked upstairs and without knocking opened the door of the Red Room.

Sir Francis was half-undressed and not in bed.

The expression on his face as the Earl entered was one both of fear and guilt.

"I give you ten minutes in which to get out of this house!" the Earl said curtly.

"What is . . ." Sir Francis began, only to be silenced as the Earl interrupted:

"If you are wise, you will leave the country. Your accomplices will doubtless betray you to the Police, and a warrant will be issued for your arrest."

Sir Francis was silent.

Just for a moment the Earl was tempted to knock him down, then he decided that it would be beneath his dignity.

"Ten minutes!" he repeated and went from the room closing the door behind him.

As he reached his own bed-room the full force of what had happened made him stare incredulously at the place where he had seen the White Lady speaking to him.

He walked towards it and as he did so was aware of that sweet elusive perfume and knew who it was who had left him the note warning him not to drink the wine.

"First me, then my horse," the Earl said with a twist of his lips.

Ghosts did not write letters even if, incredibly, they were able to speak.

He stood staring at where he had seen the White Lady. Then he put out his hand and began to feel the panelling. . . .

Far away in the depths of his memory he recalled when he was a small boy staying with his parents at a house in Worcestershire.

It had been very old and surrounded by a moat, which had delighted him.

His parents had paid little attention to him and as there were no other children in the house he had attached himself to the Curator.

He had been a kindly man who had shown him the pictures of battles and other dramatic events in history with which the house abounded.

Then, because he had been an intelligent little boy, the Curator had told him the story of the Battle of Worcester and how the fugitive King had hidden in an oak tree to escape those pursuing him.

"Some of his followers hid here in this house," the Curator went on.

He had then shown the Earl the secret passage where the Royalists remained undiscovered by the Cromwellian soldiers.

To reach it, the Earl remembered, there had been a panel which opened in the wall just wide enough to allow a man to pass through it.

He thought that the Curator had pressed a certain spot in the carving and could remember seeing his fingers feeling for it. Then he remembered his excitement when the panelling opened.

Now his own fingers were feeling among the leaves, the scrolls, the exquisitely carved heads of corn, then the flowers.

He was just beginning to believe that his search would prove unsuccessful when he found what he sought!

As he pressed, a door in the panelling opened and he saw surprisingly on the other side of it there were two pairs of riding-boots!

The Earl went back into his bed-room and lit the candle that stood beside his bed in a brass candlestick.

Then, holding it high to light his way, he went through the panelling, feeling that he was starting on a voyage of discovery as exciting as anything he had ever done in his life before.

Very softly and moving slowly so as not to make a noise, the Earl climbed the narrow, twisting staircase.

Occasionally he stopped to look at where it branched off into other passages, but he continued climbing all the time until he saw a light ahead of him and was aware that he had almost reached the top of the house.

A second or two later he found what he sought.

The Priests'-Room was very small and he saw that it contained a couch against one wall and on the other there was a picture of the Madonna encircled with flowers.

Below it jutting out from the wall itself was what was little more than a shelf but had obviously in the past been used as an altar by the hunted Priests to say Mass.

On the narrow altar now were two lighted candles and between them a bowl of white roses.

Kneeling in front of it with her hands pressed palm to palm in the eternal attitude of a woman in prayer was the White Lady.

Her hair, which fell over her shoulders, was so pale in the light from the candles that it seemed almost silver.

The Earl could see that she was little and slender enough to be a child, but the white robe which buttoned down the front revealed the soft curve of her breasts.

She was in profile and her small nose was straight and aristocratic, her lashes dark against her pale cheeks.

It was a long time since the Earl had last seen a woman kneeling in prayer and it certainly was not what he had expected to find as he climbed the stairs.

Then as if she were aware instinctively that she was not alone, the woman he was watching turned her head.

The Earl found himself looking into the largest and strangest eyes he had ever seen, which seemed to fill the whole of her small face.

For a moment she was very still. Then quietly in the voice which had spoken to him in his bed-room she said:

"Crusader?"

It was a question.

"He is safe!" the Earl answered. "I went to him as you told me to do."

She gave a sigh of relief which seemed to come from the very depths of her being.

"You were praying for him?" the Earl asked.

"Yes. I was afraid . . . terribly afraid . . . you would be too . . . late."

"Your prayers were answered."

Then as she rose slowly to her feet the Earl asked:

"Who are you? I thought you were a ghost!"

She smiled and it seemed to transform the expression on her face from one of perfect spirituality to something very human, and yet in its own way equally lovely.

"The White Lady," she said. "That is who I hoped . . . you

would think I was when you . . . saw me in the . . . Long Gallery."

"Why? Why do you have to hide yourself," the Earl asked.

He had a strange feeling that he had walked into another world. Despite her smile and the fact that they were talking to each other, he felt she was not real, but as ethereal as the ghost she had pretended to be.

"What . . . happened to . . . Crusader?" she replied, as if her thoughts were still on the horse.

"There were two men attempting to dope him," the Earl replied. "I knocked them out. They are still unconscious."

"I hoped . . . you would do . . . that."

There was no mistaking the admiration in her strange eyes, which seemed to the Earl to be almost purple, although he was sure he must be mistaken.

She looked down at his hand and gave an exclamation.

"You are bleeding!"

For the first time the Earl realised that he had broken the skin on his knuckles with the force with which he had struck first the valet and then the larger man, who had not gone down at the first punch.

"It is nothing," he said.

"But it is!" Demelza insisted. "It might become septic and would then be very painful."

She opened a cupboard in the wall and took out from it a small china basin and a ewer in the same patterned china.

She set it down on a chair, then brought a linen towel from the cupboard and with it a little box.

The Earl stood watching her, seeming unnaturally large and broad-shouldered in the confines of the small room, until she said:

"I think My Lord, you had better sit down on the bed so that I can treat your hand properly."

The Earl was too intrigued to do anything but obey.

He put his lighted candle down beside the others on the altar and sat down.

Demelza went down on her knees beside him before she poured some water from the ewer into the basin; then, opening the box, she added what the Earl realised were herbs.

"What is your name?" he asked as she stirred the water with her fingers.

"Demelza."

"Cornish!"

"My mother came from Cornwall."

"As I do."

"But of course!" she exclaimed. "I had forgotten that Trevarnon is a Cornish name . . . but I might have . . . guessed."

"Are you Gerard Langston's sister?"

She nodded as she took his hand in both of hers, dipped it into the cold water, and washed it very carefully.

He wondered if any other woman would have touched him so impersonally, but Demelza was completely unselfconscious while he was vividly conscious of her.

"Do you grow the herbs in the small garden which is surrounded by the red brick walls?" he asked.

"It was Mama's herb-garden."

He gave a sudden exclamation.

"Honeysuckle!"

She looked up at him in surprise and he said:

"The scent you use, which has been haunting me—I can smell it now on your hair."

"It is the honeysuckle which grows over the arbour in the herb-garden. Mama taught me how to distill the oil from the flowers in the spring."

"I could not put a name to it," the Earl explained, "although I was conscious of it everywhere in the house and especially on the note you left for me."

"I did not . . . know how else to . . . warn you."

"How did you know that the wine would drug me?"

He saw the flush of colour on Demelza's cheeks, and before she could reply he exclaimed:

"But of course! You can see into the rooms!"

"I only looked . . . occasionally," Demelza said. "I was . . . surprised to hear a lady speaking in the . . . Drawing-Room when I came back from the . . . races, and tonight I was going . . . downstairs because it was so hot in here and I wanted to breathe the . . . fresh air."

"And you heard Sir Francis speaking?" the Earl prompted.

"I heard him speaking in a . . . strange voice that sounded somehow secretive and . . . sinister. I have not . . . listened or looked at other times, except the first night when . . . you were in the . . . Dining-Room."

She glanced up at him, hoping he would understand, and he said slowly:

"You heard me asking your brother about the White Lady?"

"Yes . . . I was in the . . . Minstrels' Gallery."

"Perhaps I was subconsciously aware of your presence there, but I was already intrigued as to how someone could vanish so completely in the Long Gallery unless they were a ghost."

As if the words recalled to Demelza how angry Gerard would be at her having met the Earl, she rose to go once again to the cupboard. She came back with a piece of linen which she tore into strips.

"I am going to put this round your hand to keep it clean for tonight," she said, "and then please . . . will you . . . forget that you . . . have met . . . me?"

"Why?" the Earl asked.

"Because Gerard made me promise that I would not . . . come into the . . . house while . . . you were here. Unless I . . . promised, he said I must go away . . . but I had nowhere to go."

"Have you any idea why your brother was so insistent that we should not meet?" the Earl asked.

He knew the answer by the way Demelza dropped her eyes, and again there was a blush against the fairness of her skin.

"Your brother was quite right," he said. "We will keep our meeting a secret, although I shall find it hard to explain how I managed to save Crusader."

"You might just have felt intuitively that something was wrong," Demelza said quickly. "I would not . . . wish you to . . . lie, but Gerard would be so very . . . angry with . . . me."

"I see he has made me out to be a monster!" the Earl answered in an angry voice.

"Gerard admires you very . . . much, as does . . . everyone else," Demelza said. "It is just . . ."

"Just my unsavoury reputation where women are concerned," the Earl finished.

There was no need for her to confirm that that was the truth.

"Because I am so grateful to you," he said, "for saving me and for saving Crusader, I will keep the fact that you and I have met a secret."

"That is . . . kind of you. I would not . . . wish Gerard to . . . worry, which he . . . will do."

"He shall remain in blissful ignorance of everything that has occurred," the Earl promised.

He rose from the bed and, putting out his unbandaged hand, took Demelza's in his.

"Thank you!" he said. "Thank you, my little White Lady, for all you have done for me. If Crusader wins tomorrow, the victory will be yours."

He kissed her hand.

Picking up his candle, he took one last look at the strange pansy-coloured eyes raised to his. Then slowly he descended the narrow stairs.

CHAPTER FIVE

Sitting at the glittering gold-ornamented table at Windsor Castle, the Earl found it extremely difficult to concentrate on what was being said.

He had received the congratulations of everyone present, and he had in fact felt they were well deserved.

Crusader had won the Gold Cup, beating Sir Huldibrand after one of the finest and closest races ever seen at Ascot.

Sir Huldibrand had made the first running at a brisk rate as far as the dog kennels, then Crusader came in front and made the fastest pace down the hill.

At the turn of the course Crusader and Sir Huldibrand were neck to neck together, and, as the Earl heard someone say beside him: "It is a toss-up who would be the winner."

Then there was a tremendous, slashing struggle between the two magnificent horses, which ended with Crusader passing the winning-post first by a nose.

"I have never seen a better race, Valient!" the King had said to the Earl when it was over. "But we might have guessed that as usual your persistent luck would enable you to carry off the highest trophy of the meeting."

He gave a little sigh because, although it had been expected, his own horse had been unplaced.

But, being genuinely fond of the Earl, he had drunk his health not once but several times during the dinner at which the winner of the Gold Cup was always the Guest of Honour.

The Earl was aware that Lady Sydel was gazing at him across the table with an expression that he could not help thinking had something murderous about it!

Then he laughed to himself for being overly dramatic and was determined that he had no intention, however hard she might manoeuvre, of talking with her alone.

All through the race-meeting he found himself searching the

crowd with his field-glasses for a face with huge pansy-coloured eyes and wearing what he was sure would be a white gown.

But it was impossible to distinguish anyone in the seething mob, which was greater for the Gold Cup than on any other day of the week.

All along the course for nearly a mile were ranged lines of carriages, and in front of them stood the spectators who had been temporarily driven from the track, which they used as a promenade between the races.

In some places the carriages were ten deep and it was almost impossible for those at the back to have any chance of seeing the race.

Because of the fine weather, and perhaps because everyone expected a fighting finish between the two horses on which an enormous amount of money had been wagered, it was more difficult than usual to clear the course.

Originally, the Earl remembered, this was the duty of the Yeoman Pickers, but they had been succeeded by mounted patrols of Police.

The difficulty in getting everything ready for the actual race usually resulted, as it had this afternoon, in their running late.

After he had changed his clothes at the Manor, the Earl had therefore been obliged to travel to the Castle at a speed which made Jem, who accompanied him, occasionally draw in his breath apprehensively.

However, they arrived without mishap, although they learnt later that there had been a number of accidents on the road to London in which at least two people had lost their lives and several horses had been badly injured.

The King, despite his gout, was in good spirits, and the Earl thought whatever the criticism regarding Lady Conyngham, she was an attractive woman and made His Majesty happy.

The Earl found that everyone in the Royal Party and the extra guests invited for the occasion were all close friends.

He had always been extremely fond of the Duke of York, who had enjoyed an excellent Ascot and was also receiving congratulations on his wins.

"It is my best-ever race-meeting," he told the Earl sleepily, "and my horses have won me something handsome in the way of bets!"

The Duke of York was not clever, but he had an understanding of people which enabled him to avoid the errors into which his brothers had fallen, making them both unpopular and contemptible.

He was in fact both respected and loved, and the Earl on many occasions had said confidentially to his friends:

"His Royal Highness is the only one of the Princes who has the feelings and behaviour of an English gentleman."

At dinner the Earl had the attractive Princess Esterhazy on his left, who was only too willing to flirt with him as she had done so often on previous occasions.

But this evening he kept thinking of his strange adventure of the night before, and the picture of Demelza kneeling in the Priests'-Room in front of the altar kept intruding on his mind when he least expected it.

He had a sudden, urgent desire to be back in the quietness and mystery of the Manor and to open once again the secret door in the panelling of his bed-room.

It was so insistent that when the King retired immediately after dinner was over, saying that he was fatigued after the races and his gout was painful, the Earl went with him.

He did not say good-bye to anyone, knowing that if he did so he would be detained for a long time.

Instead he followed the King to the door, and as if His Majesty realised what he was doing he good-humouredly took him by the arm and drew him outside the Salon, leaning on him as they walked down the corridor.

"You cannot really intend to leave so soon, Valient?" he said.

"A party loses its savour when you are not there, Sire," the Earl replied flatteringly.

"What you mean is, there are other attractions elsewhere," the King remarked with a twinkle in his eye.

The Earl did not reply and His Majesty continued:

"Lady Sydel asked me to intercede with you on her behalf. I gather she craves your forgiveness."

"How unfortunate, Sire," the Earl replied, "that you did not have an opportunity to speak intimately with me."

The King chuckled.

"Up to your old tricks, Valient? No woman likes being a 'has-been.'"

The Earl thought that perhaps His Majesty was remembering how bitterly Mrs. Fitzherbert had complained when he discarded her for Lady Hertford. So, aloud he said:

"I know I can always rely on your understanding, Sire, and your vast knowledge of feminine vagaries."

The King was delighted, as the Earl knew he would be.

"I do understand, Valient," he said. "But if you take my advice you will move quickly under cover before the hounds are on your scent."

He laughed at his own joke, clapped the Earl on the back, and went to his private apartments.

This enabled his guest to hurry down the stairs, call his Phaeton, and be away from the Castle before the rest of the party had any idea that he had left.

Driving back to the Manor, the Earl was determined that he would see Demelza again and talk to her.

Everything about her intrigued him and he told himself he had never known a woman with such a spiritual and unusual beauty.

He wondered what she would look like in the daytime and was half-afraid that he might be disappointed.

Could her eyes really be the pansy shade he had thought them to be last night? Had she really a grace that was different from other women?

He remembered the softness of her hands as she had touched his and the manner in which she had bandaged him without being in the least self-conscious that he was sitting on her bed and they were alone.

He did not know any other woman who would have behaved in the same way in such circumstances.

'She is only a child,' he thought to himself.

Yet there had been a budding maturity in the lovely curves of her body, and he thought too that she was intelligent, as he had not expected a young girl to be.

'I must see her,' he vowed, 'although of course on second acquaintance I may be disappointed.'

It was as if he was being cynical merely to safeguard himself.

He knew that it was not only Demelza that he was finding so intriguing but her background: the beauty and mystery of the Manor, the secret staircase, and of course the way she had saved both him and Crusader.

"She will expect me this evening," he said aloud, remembering that he had told her that if Crusader won the Gold Cup the victory was hers.

It was only a little after ten o'clock when he reached the Manor, and because he had no desire to become involved with his guests who he knew were having a party, he drove not to the front door but directly into the stables.

His grooms came running to the horses' head. He stepped down and only pausing to congratulate Baxter once again on a very successful day, entered the house by the side-door he had used the previous night.

When he was in the passage he could hear laughter and voices coming from the Dining-Hall and realised that the party was in full swing and doubtless the port was being passed round the table continuously.

He moved quickly up the secondary staircase which took him to the passage on which his bed-room opened.

He guessed that Dawson, not expecting him home so early, would be downstairs having his meal, and in fact in his bed-room the candles were not yet lit.

There was, however, still a faint glow in the sky from the sun, which had set in a burst of golden glory behind the Manor.

The stars were coming out faintly overhead and there was a pale bit of the moon to be seen, which the Earl knew once it was fully risen would with its silver light make the Manor seem more enchanted than it appeared already.

He stood for a moment in his bed-room, smelling the fragrance of the roses and seeking the scent of honeysuckle.

He thought it would tell him whether Demelza had come through the secret door today, if, as another woman would have done, she had wanted to look at where he slept and touch the things he had used.

But somehow disappointingly the perfume of honeysuckle was not discernible.

Shutting the door into the passage quietly, the Earl walked across the room to grope as he had done the night before amongst the carving for the secret catch which would open the way to the twisting stairs.

He found it, and pressed, but nothing happened!

He thought he must have been mistaken. He pressed again, but still the oak panel remained immobile.

For a moment he wondered if something had gone wrong and the catch had ceased to function. Then he was aware that the door had been barred.

Never, in all the years in which he had pursued women, or rather thay had pursued him, could the Earl remember any other occasion when a door had been closed against him.

In fact usually they were opened before he reached them and the occupant was in his arms without waiting for an invitation.

Perplexed, the Earl stood looking at the panelling as if he could hardly credit that he had in fact been locked out.

Then he told himself that it was a challenge, which was something he had never refused.

At the same time, he wondered helplessly what he could do about it.

He could hardly knock on wood, and even if he did, it was doubtful that Demelza would hear it at the top of the house.

He thought with a sudden feeling of despair that he had no other access to the secret staircase which led to the Priests'-Room.

He remembered that Demelza had said she had watched him from the Minstrel's Gallery. That meant that there was an entrance there, but he could hardly go blundering about in the Gallery with his party sitting beneath him, where they might hear his movements.

The Earl was well aware that he had been fortunate last night in finding the secret catch merely because he had seen Demelza standing in his room.

Whoever had designed the labyrinth of passages and entrances had done so to save men's lives and make the hiding-place almost impregnable unless they were betrayed.

In his bed-room the secret panel opened beside the fireplace, but he was quite certain that in other rooms its position would be very different.

How then could he spend hours, perhaps days or weeks, searching for another entrance in a house in which, he had already noticed, almost every room was panelled?

'What can I do?' he wondered to himself.

Now his desire to see Demelza was increased a thousandfold simply because she was elusive.

"I *have* to see her! I *will* see her!" he said aloud, and swore beneath his breath that he would not be defeated.

Without consciously realising what he was doing, since he was concentrating so completely on the problem which beset him, he opened the door of his bed-room and walked slowly and thoughtfully down the corridor.

He was in fact working out how the house was constructed and trying to guess where the walls were most likely to be wide enough to contain a passage.

At the same time, he wanted to co-ordinate it with the route he had taken last night when he had climbed to the very top of the building.

He had seen Demelza first in the Long Gallery, but that was at an angle to the centre part of the house.

He did not seem to be getting very far with his calculations when at the far end of the passage beyond the main staircase he saw a figure carrying a tray.

He recognised Nattie and knew that she had come up a third staircase from the kitchens which lay beyond the stairs he had used himself.

Nattie turned left and walked away from him. Alert and interested the Earl followed her at a respectful distance keeping to the side of the corridor.

The candles had not yet been lit and the passage was in fact almost in darkness. He was half-afraid that Nattie would disappear and he would lose her as he had lost the White Lady in the Long Gallery.

Then she stopped, and, balancing her tray with one hand, she opened a door with the other.

She disappeared inside and the Earl quickened his pace and walked hurriedly to the door, which Nattie, having passed through, had pushed to with her foot.

But it was not completely closed, and opening it just a fraction so that he could look inside, the Earl had a glimpse of the Nurse disappearing through a panel in the wall on the other side of the room.

The curtains were not drawn over the windows and there was enough light for him to see that the room was not in use. There were holland covers on the bed, the chairs, and over the dressing-table.

The Earl realised that luck was with him, and he held his breath, for he saw that although Nattie had entered the secret passage she had not, because she was encumbered with the tray, shut the panel behind her.

Quickly he entered the room and crossed to the opposite wall.

Hearing Nattie's footsteps moving rather heavily upwards, he waited for a few seconds, then swiftly and silently he entered through the dark aperture. Inside, he moved down the stairs until he thought that he would be out of sight when Nattie returned.

He heard a faint murmur of voices far away; then, leaning against the wall in the darkness, he told himself that once again his winning streak had not failed him.

* * *

"I'm sorry to be late, dearie," Nattie said as she entered the Priests'-Room.

"I expected it," Demelza answered, rising to take the tray from her.

"It's always the same when there's a big party and more courses than usual," Nattie said. "The servants have to wait for their meal and so do you."

"It has given me a good appetite," Demelza said with a smile.

"I chose the dishes I thought you'd like best," Nattie said.

"They look delicious!" Demelza cried. "But whatever they were like I would not be particular."

She had been far too excited at the races to eat the sandwiches and small pasties which Nattie had brought for luncheon or even a delicious mousse which Betsy had purloined from the kitchen when the Chef was not looking.

All Demelza had been able to think about was Crusader and pray that he would not be beaten by Sir Huldibrand even though she knew Mr. Ramsbottom's horse was a worthy rival.

When finally Crusader had passed the winning-post and a great cheer of excitement had gone up, she had felt the tears prick her eyes at the intensity of her joy.

If she had not overheard the plot against him, the horse might have been lying doped and helpless in his stall, and Sir Francis, who would have backed Sir Huldibrand to win, would have been in possession of an illicit fortune.

"There were some strange goings-on last night, Miss Demelza," Nattie had told her early that morning.

"What has happened?" Demelza had asked.

"Two men attempted to drug Crusader," Nattie related, "but His Lordship heard them, and, Abbot said, laid them out like a professional boxer!"

"What a terrible thing to have occurred here in our own stables!" Demelza exclaimed.

"Disgraceful!" Nattie agreed. "The criminals have been taken away by the race-course Police and one of His Lordship's guests has left in a great hurry."

"Who was that?" Demelza asked, knowing she was expected to be curious.

"Sir Francis Wigdon," Nattie answered. "One can hardly believe that a gentleman and a friend of His Lordship's would be mixed up in anything so disreputable."

"No, indeed," Demelza murmured.

On the way to the race-course Abbot could talk of nothing else.

"'Tis my fault, Miss Demelza," he reproached himself. "Oi should've 'ad that lock on th' stable door mended a time ago, but what do we usually keep in 'em which'd attract th' attention of felons?"

"We must be more careful in the future, Abbot," Demelza replied. "Supposing someone tried to prevent Firebird from running on Saturday?"

"Anyone as tries'll do so over me dead body!" Abbot swore.

Then he chuckled.

" 'Tis just like His Lordship's luck to 'ave an instinct which saved Crusader for th' race."

"Was it an instinct?" Demelza enquired.

"That's what Mr. Dawson, his valet, tells Oi it were."

Demelza smiled secretly to herself, thinking that she had suggested that was what the Earl should say.

"His Lordship's certainly a very fortunate man," Nattie interposed.

"Aye, since 'e's been full grown," Abbot replied. "But Mr. Dawson were a-telling Oi that th' old Earl were a regular tyrant an' 'is son, like everyone else, suffered 'cause o' it."

"A tyrant?" Demelza asked with interest. "In what way?"

"Mr. Dawson said everyone in 'is Lordship's employment went in fear of 'is rages and neither 'e nor 'er Ladyship took any interest in their son."

"They neglected him?" Demelza enquired.

"Ignored 'im, more like," Abbot replied. "Ye be lucky, Miss Demelza, in havin' a father and mother what fair doted on ye. A number of th' gentry an' th' nobility 'as no use for their children."

"That's true enough," Nattie agreed. "They put them in the care of ignorant and neglectful servants, and I've heard of cases where the poor little creatures are half-starved!"

Demelza was silent.

It seemed extraordinary that the Earl, who was so wealthy, envied by his contemporaries for his vast possessions, and who appeared to be the most fortunate man alive, should have suffered as a child.

True or not, she was sure that because he had no brothers or sisters, he must often have felt lonely.

Without having loving parents, what would her life have been like? She could hardly visualize it.

At the same time, whatever she might feel about him, however much she might commiserate because he had suffered when he was a child and because of the tragedy of his marriage, she knew that she must not see him again.

The circumstances which had led her first to save him from the vengeance of Lady Sydel and then to protect Crusader were so exceptional that her disobedience of Gerard's orders and her broken promise to him were excusable.

Now, although she longed to talk to the Earl, to watch him as she had done before, she knew she must behave as her mother would have expected her to do.

It was what she herself knew to be right.

Accordingly, when they returned from the races she had put the bolt across the secret door which led to the Earl's bed-room.

She had then gone quickly upstairs, determined that she would not go down them again until the morning, in case she should overhear anything else which was not intended for her ears.

It had, however, been impossible not to think about the Earl.

When she had seen him leading Crusader to the weighing room after the race was over she thought that no other man or horse could equal them in the whole length and breadth of the country.

She had thrilled to hear the cheers that accompanied them.

Although a number of people must have lost a lot of money on the race, as sportsmen they cheered the victor because he had run a brilliant race in the finest traditions of the Turf.

"Thank you for a very good dinner," Demelza said to Nattie now.

She put down her spoon and fork and poured out a little lemonade from the glass jug on the tray.

"I wish I could tell the Chef how much I appreciate his cooking," she went on.

"That's one thing you can't do," Nattie said. "And if you want the truth, Miss Demelza, I'll be glad when you can come out of this stuffy little hole and go back to your own room."

"After His Lordship and his party have left," Demelza said in a low voice.

"That's right!" Nattie agreed. "I feel as if they'd stayed here for a month already!"

"Has it been a great deal of extra work for you?" Demelza asked.

"It's not the work I mind," Nattie replied. "It's all this being on my guard against anyone learning that you're in the house. Old Betsy almost gave the game away this very morning. Then she catches my eye and bites back the words, but I were only just in time."

"Never mind, Nattie. It is only for another two days," Demelza said.

As she spoke she felt as if her own voice sounded dull and dismal at the thought.

When the horses had gone and the Earl with them, how would she ever settle down? How would she ever be content with the quiet, uneventful life she had known before?

"I'll be getting back," Nattie was saying. "Now don't stay up all night reading. If you ask me, you've had enough excitement for one day!"

"It has certainly been exciting!" Demelza agreed. "Good-night, dearest Nattie!"

She kissed her Nurse's cheek and lifted one of the lighted candles so that the old woman could see her way more clearly down the narrow stairway.

She held it until she saw Nattie move through the panelled door and heard it close behind her.

Then she carried the candle to the altar and set it down to stand looking up at the Holy picture she had known ever since she had been a child.

"Thank you, God," she said. "Thank you for letting him win."

She was sure it was her prayers that not only had saved Crusader but had carried him first past the winning-post. Her mother had always said that one should never receive an answer to a prayer without being grateful for it.

"Thank you! Thank you!" Demelza said again.

As her lips moved she was seeing not only Crusader but the Earl walking beside him, with a smile on his lips as he raised his hat in response to the cheers.

The vision of him was so vivid in her mind that somehow as she turned her head instinctively and saw him standing in the doorway she was not startled or surprised. It just seemed inevitable!

They looked at each other for a long moment.

It was as if they found each other after an age-old separation and were reunited.

Then the Earl said automatically, almost as if he was thinking of something else:

"Why did you bar me out?"

"How did you . . . manage to get . . . in?"

"I followed your Nurse and she left the panel ajar."

"She would be . . . horrified if she knew you were . . . here!"

"I want to talk to you. I *have* to talk to you!"

Demelza drew in her breath at the insistence in his voice. As if he felt she was going to refuse his request, he said:

"I understand if you feel it is unconventional that we should talk here, but where else can we go?"

For a moment he realised she did not understand what he was

saying; then, as if it suddenly struck her that the Priests'-Room was also her bed-room, the blood rose in her cheeks and she said a little shyly:

"I . . . had not thought of it . . . before, but there is . . . no-where. . . ."

She paused, then she added:

"I could . . . meet you in the herb-garden. I can reach . . . there without . . . anyone seeing me . . . leave the house."

"No-one knows I have returned," the Earl said, "so I will go there at once."

He looked into her eyes raised to his, and asked:

"You will come? This is not just a trick to be rid of me?"

"No . . . of course not! I will come . . . if you really . . . want me to."

"I want it more than I can possibly say. I have to talk to you."

There was a note of command in his voice and he knew that she responded to it.

"I will come!" she said simply. "But first you must return the way you came."

"Will I find the catch?"

"If you take the candle, it is quite clear from this side of the panel."

She handed him the candle as she spoke and without another word he turned and went down the stairs.

As Demelza had said, the catch, which was so invisible on one side of the door, was easy to find from the staircase.

The Earl set the candle down on one of the stairs, then went into the bed-room, closing the secret panel behind him.

There was still no-one about and he made his way down the secondary staircase and out through the door which led towards the stables. But now he turned in the opposite direction, walking past the front of the house.

In the ever-deepening dusk he found his way to the herb-garden.

He knew that Demelza would expect him to sit in the arbour, and the scent of the honeysuckle which climbed over it made him feel almost as if she were waiting for him there.

He sat down on the wooden seat, thinking that never in his life had he had a love-affair with such a strange beginning or such an intriguing one.

As he waited for Demelza he could hardly believe his own excitement.

It seemed to be rising in him, making his heart beat quickly. He might have been a boy of eighteen meeting his first love rather than a blasé cynic who had, he believed until now, tasted all the joys of love and found that they had grown tedious.

It suddenly struck him that perhaps after all Demelza would not come and never again would he be able to enter the secret passage and find his way to her room.

Then he told himself that no-one could look so pure, so honest at the same time, and lie. If she told him she would come, then she would keep her word.

He thought it was fitting that someone so spiritual, with an aura of Holiness that he had never before found in any woman who had attracted him, should be housed in a room sanctified by those who had received Mass from an ordained Priest.

He was still alone and now he began to be afraid.

Perhaps at the last moment Demelza had thought it too much of a risk to leave her hiding-place.

Perhaps someone had seen her when she emerged from one of the doors which only she could open and no-one else had found.

Then, as his fears and apprehensions seemed to taunt him, he saw her.

She was coming towards him like the ghost he had first thought her to be, moving so silently and so effortlessly over the path between the rows of herbs that it was difficult to believe she was real.

Then at last she was beside him and as he rose to his feet she said:

"I am sorry if I kept you . . . waiting. The bushes had grown so thickly round the secret door into the garden that it was difficult to get . . . through."

"But you are here," he said, "and I want more than I can ever tell you, Demelza, to talk to you again."

"I wanted to tell you how glad I was that Crusader won," she answered, "but I think you would have known that."

"It was entirely due to you," he said, "and both Crusader and I are very grateful!"

"It was the most exciting race I have ever watched."

"That is what I thought," the Earl agreed. "And it was particularly exciting for me because I knew you were watching it too."

It was what Demelza herself had felt and she looked up at him. Then as if she felt shy she looked away again.

"I want to give you something to commemorate our victory," the Earl said. "But it is difficult to know what."

"No!" she replied quickly. "You must not do . . . that!"

"Why not?" he asked.

"Because I would have to . . . explain where the . . . present had come from, and that . . . as you know is . . . something I . . . cannot do."

The Earl was silent. Then he said:

"How long do we have to go on with this pretence? I know, Demelza, and you know too, because of the things we have done together, that we mean more to each other than if we were mere acquaintances."

He waited for her to reply, but she did not do so and he continued:

"Do you really imagine that on Saturday after the races are over, or perhaps on Sunday, I can leave the Manor and forget everything that has happened here?"

Still Demelza did not speak, and after a moment he asked:

"Will you be able to forget me, Demelza, as you know I cannot forget you?"

Now he waited and after a moment she said in a low voice:

"I shall never . . . forget you . . . and I shall . . . pray for you."

"And you imagine that will be enough? I want to see you, I want to be with you, Demelza, and, if I am honest, I want more than my hope of Heaven to hold you in my arms and kiss you."

His voice seemed to vibrate on the air between them. Then he added:

"I cannot remember ever in my life before asking a woman if I could kiss her. But I am afraid of frightening you, afraid that you will disappear, and I will never find my White Lady again."

His voice deepened as he said:

"May I kiss you, my lovely little ghost?"

He put out his arms towards her. Demelza did not move but somehow he stopped before he touched her.

"I think . . . if you kissed me," she whispered, "it would be very wonderful . . . more wonderful than anything I could . . . imagine . . . but it would be . . . wrong."

"Wrong?" the Earl asked.

He waited for an explanation and after a moment Demelza said:

"I . . . heard today how you had suffered as a child . . . and I have thought so . . . often of how you must have suffered because of your . . . m-marriage . . . but . . . although I would wish to do . . . anything you asked of me . . . it would be wrong . . . because you belong to . . . someone else."

"Are you saying that I belong to my wife?" the Earl asked incredulously.

"You are . . . married. You took a . . . sacred vow," Demelza said in a low voice.

"A vow that no human being should be required to keep in the circumstances!" the Earl replied harshly.

"I know . . . I do understand. At the same time . . . I would feel that I was doing . . . wrong . . . and that would spoil the . . . love that . . . otherwise I could . . . give you."

The Earl was very still.

He could hardly believe what he had heard Demelza say, and yet he told himself it was what he might have expected she would think, because she was so very different from any other woman he had ever known before.

Aloud he said:

"What do you know of love? The love you might have given me if you did not think it was prohibited? Tell me!"

It was a command and Demelza clasped her hands together. Then, looking away from him across the garden, she answered:

"I have thought about . . . love, and although you may think me very . . . ignorant and foolish . . . I think it is . . . something you . . . need in your life."

"You really believe," the Earl asked, and there was no mistaking the cynicism in his voice, "that I lack love?"

Demelza made an expressive little gesture with her hands.

"I think, and again you may think it foolish of me, that there are different types of love . . . and the love you have known, which is the . . . sort the beautiful lady who would have drugged your wine gave you, is not the same as . . ."

Demelza's voice died away and the Earl knew she had been about to say "as mine" but was too shy.

"Tell me about your love," he said gently, "the love you would give a man to whom you gave your heart."

"I know," Demelza began very softly, "if I loved someone . . . very much I would never want to . . . hurt them. In fact I would want to protect them against any kind of pain . . . not only in the . . . body but also in the . . . mind."

"In fact—mother love," the Earl murmured beneath his breath.

But he did not wish to interrupt and Demelza continued:

"There would also be my love for the . . . man I . . . married, and . . . that love is . . . I believe . . . a part of . . . God, who . . . created everything which is beautiful, everything which grows and is . . . part of . . . Creation."

She glanced towards him as she spoke, wondering if he was smil-

ing cynically at what she was trying to describe. Then because she
was nervous she went on quickly:

"Lastly . . . I think if I was in love . . . I would want to learn
not only of . . . love but . . . everything a man like . . . yourself
could teach, because you have so much . . . experience and inevita-
bly you would have . . . wider horizons than the . . . woman who
. . . loved you."

There was silence and after a moment the Earl said:

"Would it be possible to find the love of mother, wife, and child
all in one person?"

"If it was . . . real love . . . the love that really . . . matters . . ." Demelza replied, "then I believe it would be possible."

She glanced at him before she went on:

"It would be like . . . seeking for the . . . Golden Fleece . . .
the Holy Grail, and perhaps the . . . Gates of Heaven, but it would
be the love that human beings were originally . . . promised in the
Garden of Eden."

Her voice was very moving and the Earl drew in his breath before
he said:

"And like the angel who stood with the flaming sword in that garden you are keeping me out."

He felt rather than saw the pain in her eyes, and he knew, because
her fingers were linked together tensely, that he had hurt her.

"I have . . . no wish to do that," she cried, "but . . . how can I
. . . help it?"

"How can you be so cruel? How can you deny me what you know
in your heart belongs to me?"

She did not reply.

"Look at me, Demelza!"

Obediently she raised her head. The dusk had turned to night, and
the moon's first rays of silver were on her face.

He looked into her troubled eyes, which held both faith and an innocence in their purple depths.

He lingered on the softness of her parted lips and he knew that
where they were both concerned time had no meaning and this was
what he had been seeking all his life.

He saw the questioning expression on Demelza's face alter.

Now there was a sudden radiance, as if she felt, as he did, that
they had met across eternity and they were no longer separate indi-
viduals but one.

It was not only what they saw, it was there in the joining of their

hearts, and deeper still in the stirring of their souls, reaching out towards what had been lost yet now had been found.

It was so beautiful, so transcendently divine, that they were enveloped in a light which came from within themselves, more vivid
than the moonlight from above.

"You love me!" the Earl said hoarsely. "You love me, my lovely
little ghost, and you belong to me!"

Yet even as he thought she would melt towards him, as he felt the
vibrations of her reaching out towards him, she said:

"Yes, I love you! I love you in . . . every way which I have tried
. . . inadequately . . . to explain . . . but after tonight I can . . .
never see you again."

"Can you really credit that I would allow you to walk out of my
life?" he asked angrily. "Or, rather, to bar yourself away from me?"

She was silent and he continued:

"You know that what has happened to us is something so unique
and perfect that I can hardly believe that it is not a figment of my
imagination—a fantasy conjured up by the mystery of the Manor itself."

"There is . . . nothing else I can . . . do," Demelza murmured.
"Nothing!"

"That is not true," the Earl said, "and I will convince you of my
love for you and yours for me."

He opened his arms resolutely as he spoke, determined to break
the spell which had prevented him, against his will, from touching
her.

As he did so suddenly they were both aware that someone had
come into the garden and was standing at the opening between the
walls, looking round him.

"Gerard!" Demelza whispered beneath her breath.

"Do not move," the Earl said so that only she could hear him.
"Leave this to me."

He rose without hurry from the seat, standing up to his full height,
knowing that Demelza was hidden behind him.

"So there you are, My Lord!" Gerard exclaimed. "The servants
told me that you had returned and they had seen you in the garden. I
wondered why you had not joined us."

The Earl walked towards him.

"I was hot and a little tired of conversation after so much chatter
at the Castle," he replied.

"Then if you want to be alone, I must not . . ." Gerard began.

"No, of course not! I am delighted to see you," the Earl interrupted. "Let us go back to the house together. I have been meaning to speak to you. There are two pictures in the house which, if you are in need of money, I am quite certain would fetch a very large sum in any Sale-Room."

"Do you mean that?" Gerard asked eagerly. "I did not think there was anything worth a penny in the whole place!"

"They are both in need of cleaning," the Earl replied. "I happen to be an expert on Rubens and I would not mind wagering a large sum that the picture at the top of the stairs is one of his early paintings."

"And the other?" Gerard asked.

"In the Library in a dark corner there is, I am certain, a small, authentic Perugino."

"How fantastic!"

Demelza heard the excitement in Gerard's voice as the two men moved away into the other part of the garden.

If what the Earl said was true, she thought, then Gerard could have the horses he wanted, lead the life he enjoyed, and perhaps spend a little money on renovating the Manor.

But she knew this would not alter the position between herself and the Earl.

It was true that she loved him, loved him with her whole heart, and she thought that she would regret all her life not having let him kiss her as he had wanted to do.

She could imagine nothing nearer Heaven than feeling his arms round her and his lips on hers.

But, as she had said, it would have been wrong.

She rose from the seat in the arbour and reaching up picked a piece of honeysuckle.

She would press it in her Bible, and perhaps in the years to come that would be all she would have to remember—the one moment when she had lost her heart and it no longer belonged to her.

She raised the honeysuckle to her lips.

Then she looked in the direction of the house, listening for the Earl's voice. But there was only silence, except from overhead there came the squeak of a bat.

"Good-bye . . . my hero . . . my only . . . love!" she whispered, and her voice broke on the words.

CHAPTER SIX

"You certainly had a good Ascot, My Lord!" Gerard Langston said as the Earl tooled his horses through the traffic outside the entrance to the course.

The Earl did not reply and he went on:

"Three winners, including the Gold Cup, is as much as any race-horse owner could wish for."

There was a note of envy in his voice which made the Earl say consolingly:

"The race in which your horse took part was one of the most exciting of the meeting."

"It would hardly be described as being completely satisfactory," Gerard answered, "considering that it was a dead heat."

He paused to add:

"It means the prize money is halved—also the bets I laid on Firebird."

"You will doubtless do better next year," the Earl said.

He spoke almost automatically, as if his thoughts were elsewhere.

Although he was not aware of it, several of his friends had looked at him in surprise when, after his horse in the first race had passed the winning-post a length and a half in front of the other competitors, he had seemed curiously uninterested.

It had in fact been to the Earl a day of such frustration that he had found it almost impossible to concentrate on anything that anyone was saying to him.

He had not believed that Demelza had meant what she said on Thursday night and that she really intended never to see him again.

The following day the Earl had hurried back from the races with an exciting anticipation he had never known before, being quite certain she would meet in the herb-garden after dinner.

He had therefore insisted, rather to the surprise of his guests, that they should dine early, and had skilfully arranged for everyone but himself to play cards afterwards.

This left him free to wander, with what appeared to be a casual air, into the garden.

Sitting in the arbour covered with honeysuckle, he had waited and waited until finally he realised that Demelza did not intend to join him.

It was then for the first time that he became afraid.

He was quite certain that he would find it impossible, if she was determined to keep him out, to find again a way into the secret passages, and he wondered frantically as he went to bed how he could communicate with her.

He knew that to betray either to her brother or to Nattie the fact that they had met would seem to her an act of treachery, which she would be unlikely to forgive.

And yet what alternative did he have?

On Friday he had found that the crowds made it impossible for him to distinguish any individual among them.

If Demelza wished to hide, it would be like searching for a needle in a hay-stack to discover her in the seething mob pressing round the race-track.

What was more, the number of carriages, wagons, and carts seemed to have increased since the beginning of the week.

"What can I do? What can I do?" he asked himself over and over again.

He thought that for the first time in his life not only his luck had deserted him but also his expertise where women were concerned.

Always before the Earl had found it only too easy to make assignations with any woman who caught his fancy. That one to whom he had declared his affection should actually avoid him was a new and unpleasant experience.

With any other woman he knew that he could woo her and be certain that sooner or later she would succumb, but Demelza was different.

So different, he realised now while he was driving back to the Manor, that he was worried as he had never been worried before that he might be compelled to leave and never see her again.

He had been confident when setting out that morning that the one place he would be sure to find her was in the saddling enclosure before the second race in which Firebird was running.

He had seen Abbot, spoken to the old groom, and had wished Jem, the jockey, luck.

But, looking round at those watching the horses, he could see no-one with large, pansy-coloured eyes in a small, pointed face.

Last night, when Demelza did not come to the arbour as he had expected, he had told himself harshly that he was being a fool.

How could he be sure that he had not been beguiled by the mystery of the Manor, the secret passages as well as her ghost-like appearances, into thinking she was lovelier and more desirable than she actually was?

Then he knew that his doubts betrayed his own heart and that Demelza meant more to him than any other woman had ever done before. If he had to dedicate his whole life to searching for her he would do so.

It was infuriating to know that she was so near and yet so far, just at the top of the house but guarded by the mystery of an impregnable fortress.

To all intents and purposes she might as well have been in the North of Scotland or the wilds of Cornwall.

It was all the more frustrating that she was divided from him only by the twisting steps of a secret stairway.

Finding that even the horses had become of little importance to him, the Earl had decided to leave after the third race.

He knew only too well that, owing to the crowds, the difficulty of clearing the course was always worse on the last day of the race-meeting and the fourth race could often lag on until six o'clock or later.

He had therefore said nothing to his friends but had set off resolutely to where his Phaeton was waiting, feeling that few people would notice his departure.

The King had not attended Ascot since Thursday, but the Royal Box had been at the disposal of those with whom he was closely associated and the champagne had flowed as bountifully as when His Majesty was present.

The Earl, however, had drunk nothing since luncheon, for he had the feeling that he must keep his brain clear so that he could solve what had begun to appear an almost insurmountable problem.

He found his Phaeton and was about to climb into it when Gerard Langston hailed him.

"Surely you are not leaving so soon, My Lord?"

The young man's face was flushed from celebrating the partial victory of Firebird, and it suddenly struck the Earl that Demelza would not wish her brother to indulge further.

Accordingly, with an unusual consideration, he replied:

"Yes, I am leaving to avoid the crowds. Why do you not come with me?"

It was a favour that even an older, more important man would have found difficult to refuse.

It was well known that the Earl was so fastidious about his companions, and especially those who drove or rode with him, that Gerard for a moment found it hard to reply.

Finally, as the Earl climbed into his Phaeton, Gerard managed to stammer:

"I—I should be very honoured, My Lord."

The Earl hardly waited for him to swing himself into the seat beside him before he moved his horses and Jem jumped up behind.

Then they were through the iron gates and out into the road, where country bumpkins in their smocks were rubbing shoulders with sharp-faced tricksters who had come down from London.

Gerard, saluting some of his friends, who stared at him curiously as he and the Earl passed them, was silent until they had turned off the London road onto one which rounded the end of the course.

Then he glanced at the Earl and was struck by the grim expression on his face, and he wondered if anything had annoyed him.

The Earl was in fact considering how it would be possible to approach the subject of Demelza.

It seemed rather late in the day, having stayed at the Manor since Monday, to ask Langston if he had a sister.

It was equally impossible to say: "I have met your sister and would like to meet her again."

But if he said nothing, he knew, he would be expected to leave that evening as his friends were doing, or at the very latest the next morning.

Lord Chirn and Lord Ramsgill were not even returning to the Manor and had said their good-byes that morning before they left for the race-course.

The Honourable Ralph Mear was going to London and would return to the house only to pick up his luggage.

At any moment the Earl expected Gerard Langston to ask him if he too would be departing before dinner, and he did not know what answer he should give.

'I must see Demelza again—I must!' he thought to himself.

And yet he had the unmistakable feeling that even if he betrayed her trust and sent her brother to fetch her from the Priests'-Room, she might refuse to come.

'God, what can I do?' he wondered desperately, and it was in the nature of a prayer.

Suddenly he saw her ahead of them, driving in an old-fashioned gig.

He recognised Nattie first, and there was no mistaking her straight back and the grey cotton gown she always wore with a white collar and cuffs. On her head was a black straw bonnet which concealed her face, but the Earl thought he would have known her anywhere.

And there was a sylph-like figure beside her.

Demelza was in white and her unfashionably small bonnet was trimmed with a wreath of white flowers.

It struck the Earl immediately that this was the opportunity for which he had been waiting. He had only to say to the young man beside him:

"Surely that is your old Nurse ahead of us? Who is the girl with her?"

Once again, the Earl thought with a sudden elation, his luck had not failed him, and the idea seemed to lift him from what had almost been the depths of despair.

It was as if the sun had suddenly come out in the darkness of night, and his fingers tightened on the reins, slowing his horses just in case the road should widen and he should be obliged to pass the gig.

Then everything happened very swiftly.

Round the corner from a side-turning hidden by a high hedge there came a chaise with two horses travelling too fast, driven by a red-faced, middle-aged man who had obviously imbibed too freely.

It was quite impossible for him to pass the gig, which was in the centre of the road at the place where he had met it.

In a desperate effort to avoid an accident he turned his horses, but one of the wheels of his Phaeton locked with a wheel of the gig, which overturned.

Controlling his own animals, the Earl watched with horror as the gig tipped over onto the verge of the road and its occupant in white was thrown from it.

It all happened so quickly that there was no time to cry out a warning or even to exclaim at what had occurred.

With expert driving the Earl pulled his own horses clear of those which had been drawing the chaise at high speed, which were now rearing and plunging, suddenly checked by the locked wheels.

While the driver of the chaise started to shout and bluster, the Earl handed his reins to Gerard Langston.

"Hold them!" he said sharply.

He sprang down from the Phaeton and was running towards the gig before either Gerard or Jem was fully aware what had occurred.

Demelza had fallen from the gig over the rough grass which edged the road and into a dry ditch on the other side of it.

As the Earl bent down and picked her up in his arms, her bonnet fell back to be caught by its ribbons under her chin.

As he looked at her little face, with her lashes dark against her white skin, he thought for one terrified moment that she might be dead.

It was a fear which struck through him with the pain of a dagger. Then he saw the bruise on her forehead and knew she had only been knocked unconscious.

He was down on one knee, cradling her in his arms, when Nattie raised herself from the rough grass into which she had fallen to say:

"Miss Demelza! Oh, my dearie—what's happened to—you?"

"It is all right," the Earl said consolingly. "She must have fallen on a stone, but I do not think any bones are broken."

Nattie, with her black bonnet on one side of her grey-haired head, stood looking bewildered and, perhaps for the first time in her life, unsure of herself.

Behind her, Jem was trying to create some sort of order out of chaos.

Willing hands had appeared seemingly from nowhere to help unlock the wheels of the two vehicles. The red-faced man's groom by now had his horses under control and the ancient horse which had drawn the gig had scrambled to its feet and was quite unconcernedly cropping the grass.

The Earl lifted Demelza up in his arms and carried her towards his Phaeton. Without waiting for instructions, Nattie followed him.

Gerard, holding the Earl's horses steady with some difficulty, leant forward as they reached the Phaeton to ask anxiously:

"Is she hurt? That damned fool had no right to drive so dangerously!"

The Earl did not answer. Instead he said to Nattie:

"Can you climb up behind?"

"I think so, M'Lord."

She managed to get into the seat at the back.

Holding Demelza very carefully, her face against his shoulder, the Earl took the seat previously occupied by her brother.

"She is not badly injured, is she?" Gerard asked.

The Earl did not miss the note of concern in his voice, and he answered:

"I think she is suffering from concussion. As soon as we get back to the Manor we must send for a doctor."

"I would like to tell that idiot what I think of him!" Gerard said between gritted teeth.

The Earl thought the same, but he knew the drunkard's irresponsible driving had solved his personal problem and brought to his

arms the girl who had shut him out because she thought their love
for each other was wrong.

Holding her in his arms as if she were a baby, he looked down at
her and thought she was even more lovely in the daylight than she
had been at night.

Very gently he undid the ribbons at her throat so that he could
throw her bonnet onto the floor in front of them.

Then he held her close against his heart, thinking that her hair, so
pale gold as to be almost silver, was the most beautiful thing he had
ever seen.

"I love you!" he wanted to cry aloud, and then instinctively he
tightened his arms, knowing that never again would he let her go.

Jem had cleared the road ahead, the gig had been pushed farther
onto the verge, and the old horse, released from the shafts, was being
led home by the boy who had been driving it.

The chaise had a buckled wheel, but there was a chance if it was
driven slowly it could reach a village where doubtless there would be
a wheelwright to repair it.

"You can get through now," the Earl said.

Gerard moved the horses forward, thinking that never in his life
had he expected to have the opportunity of tooling such superb animals and hoping that he would not make a fool of himself in doing
so.

It was only a short distance to the Manor and the Earl knew that
Jem would follow them and doubtless take a short-cut through the
trees which they were unable to do.

He was, however, really concerned only with Demelza, knowing
that he was holding her as he had longed to do, and wishing with an
intensity that surprised even himself that he could kiss her lips.

As they passed through the rusty gates he said:

"I suggest that while I carry your sister upstairs you drive immediately to Windsor Castle. You will find that His Majesty's Physician
in Ordinary is staying there. Tell Sir William Knighton I sent you
and ask him to come here as quickly as possible."

Gerard gave the Earl a quick glance.

"You know she is my sister?" he asked.

"I understood you had one," the Earl replied evasively.

There was a note in his voice which made Gerard say quickly:

"She is called Demelza. She was not permitted to appear when
you were giving your bachelor-party."

"Of course not!" the Earl agreed.

Gerard turned the horses to draw up outside the front door.

"You really mean me to drive to Windsor?" he asked in the tone
of a child who has been offered an undreamt-of treat.

"You had better take a groom with you," the Earl replied. "I
should think Jem will have reached the gates by now."

"If not, I will wait for him," Gerard said.

There was a note in his voice which would have amused the Earl
had he not been so concerned with Demelza.

The footmen ran forward to help the Earl from the Phaeton, but
when they would have taken Demelza from him he shook his head.

"Help Miss Nattie," he ordered, and a flunkey hurried to obey.

With Demelza in his arms the Earl walked into the hall.

"Has there been an accident, M'Lord?" the Major-Domo asked.

The Earl did not trouble to answer but waited for Nattie. When
she came to his side, her eyes only for Demelza, he said:

"Show me your Mistress's room."

Without wasting words, Nattie went ahead of him up the stairs.

Following her, the Earl thought that Demelza was so light, so
fragile, that she might in fact with her pale face actually be the ghost
he had originally thought her to be.

He looked down at her, noting that the mark on her forehead,
which must have been made by striking a stone, was deepening on
her white skin, but her body was warm and very soft and he told
himself fiercely that never again would he lose her.

'You are mine! Mine for all time!' he said in his heart.

* * *

If the Earl had spent a miserable Friday, so had Demelza.

She had known when she awoke early in the morning that her
head ached and her eyes were swollen because she had cried herself
to sleep.

It was one thing to do what was right and tell the Earl that she
could never see him again—quite another to walk alone into the
darkness of the secret passage.

As she moved up the twisting staircase to the Priests'-Room she
knew that she was shutting herself away from the world and from the
Earl in particular.

"I love him! I love him!" she cried to the Holy picture over the
altar.

While she knew she was doing what was right in the eyes of God,
her human body cried out for the Earl with an intensity which became more and more painful.

It was with the utmost difficulty that she prevented herself from running down the stairs to unbar the secret panel which led into her father's bed-room.

'If I could only see him once again! If I could let him kiss me good-bye,' she pleaded in her conscience, 'then I should have something to remember, something to hold close in my heart for the rest of my life.'

But she knew that if she once gave in to the impulse which made her want the Earl's arms round her and his lips on hers, it would then be impossible to deny him anything else he asked.

She had never imagined that love could be so fierce or so cruel. She felt as if she was being torn apart by her desire for a love that was forbidden.

How, she wondered, could all this have happened? And yet even with the agony she was suffering she would not have had it different.

The Earl embodied everything that she had ever dreamt a man could be, and although she might never see him again, she knew his image would always be there not only in her heart but before her eyes.

How could there be another man to equal him? How could there ever be another man who could thrill her as he did, so that when he was beside her she became pulsatingly alive in a manner she had never known before?

"This is love!" she told herself.

Then because it was out of reach, because she had deliberately walked away from it, the tears came.

At first they only gathered in her eyes, then ran slowly down her cheeks until suddenly a tempest shook her so that she threw herself down on the bed to cry until her pillow was wet.

Later in the night she tortured herself with the idea that the Earl would easily forget her.

He had so many beautiful women in his life who would be only too ready to console him; women as lovely as Lady Sydel, and Lady Plymworth, of whom Lady Sydel had been so jealous.

It was obvious that in a few weeks, perhaps sooner, he would forget the ghost who had intrigued him for a short while.

"But I shall never forget!" Demelza said as she sobbed. "I am a ghost who has fallen in love and therefore will be haunted for the rest of my life!"

She cried until she fell asleep and her only thought to lighten the darkness was that although he could not see her, she could at least see the Earl.

"If you asks me," Nattie said when she brought Demelza's breakfast, "five days' racing is too much for anybody! You looks washed out, and there's Master Gerard in a state of agitation over Firebird and asking for brandy at breakfast-time. I don't know what your mother would say to hear him—that I don't!"

She had not waited for Demelza to reply but had hurried downstairs to minister to Gerard, who had always been her favourite, while Demelza, because she did not wish Nattie to be concerned, had done her best to wash away the traces of tears.

Whatever she felt about the Earl, it was impossible not to worry about Firebird.

After all, she and Abbot had trained him, taking him round and round the course early in the mornings in all sorts of weather and often finding it difficult to obtain enough money to feed him properly.

"Sir Gerard will take all the credit if he wins," Demelza said once to Abbot, "but the glory will be ours! We have done all the hard work."

"That's true enough, Miss Demelza," Abbot had answered, "and I doubt if Master Gerard'll ever realise how much you've done to bring this 'ere horse to the peak of condition."

"Do you really think he is at his peak?" Demelza asked a week before the meeting.

"If he ain't, it's not your fault or mine, Miss Demelza," Abbot had replied. "But don't you go worryin' about him. With a bit o' luck he'll win."

Demelza remembered his words and had found them comforting as she and Nattie had set out in the gig for the races.

Today, because Abbot was with Firebird, they were being driven by a rather stupid boy who was employed in the stables because he was cheaper than any other lad would have been.

"I don't like leaving you with only Ben t' drive you tomorrow, Miss Demelza," Abbot had said when they drove back from the course on Friday evening.

"Ben will be all right," Demelza answered. "You will have too much to do with Firebird to worry about us."

"Just you tell him to stay with the gig and not go a-wandering off in the crowds," Nattie said sharply. "If he does, he's quite capable of forgetting we're there and leaving us to drive ourselves home."

"I'll see he does as he's told," Abbot promised, and Ben in fact stayed with the gig the whole day.

Because she was sure that the Earl would be looking for her,

Demelza, to Nattie's surprise, had not insisted on going to the saddling enclosure before the race.

"I was sure you'd be wanting to give all sorts of last-minute instructions to Jem," she said.

"Jem is a good jockey and it is too late for words," Demelza
replied.

But even as she spoke she knew that every nerve in her body was
aching to go to the enclosure, not to see Jem or Firebird, but to see
the Earl.

She knew how pleased he would be that one of his own horses had
won the first race. At the same time, she was certain that he would
be watching Firebird and perhaps wishing Gerard good luck.

It was the first time that Gerard's name had appeared on the race-
card as an owner, and she longed to be beside him to share both his
excitement and his pride.

'He will be very proud when Firebird wins,' she thought.

She felt a pang of anxiety in case the horse failed and Gerard was
faced with large gambling debts and no money with which to settle
them.

Then she remembered the thousand guineas which the Earl had
paid for renting the Manor.

There were so many ways they could use it on the Manor, but she
was convinced that Gerard would expend it all too easily on his life in
London.

She gave a little sigh, and Nattie, hearing it, said:

"Now don't you go fretting about that horse, Miss Demelza. It'll
win if it's meant to win; and if it isn't, there's nothing you can do
about it."

Her words forced a faint smile to Demelza's lips.

"You are always such a comfort, Nattie dear," she said.

She thought even as she spoke that she would need all the comfort
her old Nurse could give her in the future.

She saw the Earl moving about the enclosure in front of the Royal
Box. She also saw him walking through the crowds towards the
saddling enclosure.

Only by an exertion of will-power that was more demanding than
any she had ever had to use before did she prevent herself from running across the track and going to his side when he was speaking to
Abbot.

By standing up in the gig she could watch him pat Firebird's neck
and say a word of encouragement to Jem.

Then, for fear he might see her and be drawn to her by her longing for him, she sat down and did not look again until the race began.

It was a disappointment that Firebird was not the winner, but the Bard ran better than expected, and at least, Demelza thought, Gerard would feel it no disgrace that his horse had done so well the first time it had been entered in a race.

Nattie had been even more elated than Demelza was.

"I suppose you're going to say, Miss Demelza, that it's been worth all the times you've come in chilled to the bone from riding in a north wind or looking like a drowned rat after exercising that animal in the pouring rain."

"Yes, it has been worth it," Demelza agreed, "and Gerard will be delighted."

She saw Nattie's eyes light up with pleasure and added:

"At least he should have made money at this meeting if he backed His Lordship's horses as well as Firebird."

"I've told him often enough he shouldn't gamble at all," Nattie said.

But she was not using her scolding voice, which both Demelza and Gerard knew so well.

When Nattie said it was time to leave after the third race, Demelza looked for the Earl. She told herself that this would be the last time she would ever see him.

She was aware, because Nattie had told her, that two of his guests would not be returning to the Manor.

They had both tipped Nattie generously and Demelza knew that when they were alone again and Ascot had relapsed, until next year, into the quiet, empty place it had been before, the money would be spent on food.

Demelza searched the Royal Box and the small enclosure in front of it for a sight of the tall, handsome figure which made her heart beat quicker every time she saw him.

But she could not see the Earl, and although she told herself it was absurd, she felt even more despondent than before.

Ben manoeuvred the gig with some difficulty away from the carriages and wagons lying four deep along the course, and they threaded their way through the booths and gambling-tents across the Heath.

When they reached the road it was crowded but less so than it would be after the last race was run and all the wagons, coaches, and carriages were moving at the same time towards Windsor and London.

It was very hot and Nattie said:

"I'll be glad of a nice cup o' tea as soon as I get home, and I expect, dearie, you'd like a drink of lemonade."

"It would certainly be cooling," Demelza answered.

"I'll put some ice in it," Nattie said. "The Chef had a large block delivered today to cool the champagne for the gentlemen. That's something we don't often see at the Manor."

Demelza was not listening.

She was thinking of the Earl standing in the Drawing-Room for perhaps the last time and remembering how handsome she had thought him when she looked at him first through the peep-hole.

Even then she had loved him, although she had not been aware of it.

In a voice that she had difficulty in making sound casual she asked:

"Is His Lordship . . . leaving this . . . afternoon?"

She never heard the answer to her question, for at that moment the horses drawing the chaise came round the side-turning, and a split second before they reached the gig, while Ben belatedly began to draw his horses to the left, Demelza knew there must be an accident.

She wanted to cry out a warning, but before she could do so there was the shuddering impact of the wheels colliding and she felt the gig tipping over.

Then there was darkness and she knew no more. . . .

* * *

She came back to consciousness moving, she thought, down a long, long tunnel towards a faint light at the far end of it.

She felt weak and somehow disembodied. It was hard to move, and yet something told her she must do so.

Then Nattie was beside her, lifting her head in the manner in which she had done ever since she was a child, holding something to her lips.

"Wh-what has . . . happened?" Demelza tried to ask, but she could not hear herself make a sound.

After a moment, as if she knew what she wanted, Nattie said:

"It's all right. You're safe!"

"There . . . was . . . an . . . accident?"

"Yes, an accident," Nattie agreed, "and you hurt your head on a stone, but the doctor says you've no bones broken and you've just suffered a little concussion."

"I . . . am . . . all right."

It was a statement, but Nattie took it as a question.

"Perfectly all right! His Majesty's own Physician came to see you —not once but twice!"

"Twice."

Demelza repeated the word, then asked:

"How long . . . ago?"

"He came first yesterday when the accident happened, then again today. He said if we wanted him he'd come down from London. A nice expense that'd be!"

Demelza must have looked concerned, because Nattie added quickly:

"No need to worry. We're not paying. His Lordship saw to all that."

"H-His . . . Lordship?"

"Yes. Very kind he was, and wouldn't leave until Sir William had seen you for the second time."

"He has . . . left?"

Nattie patted the pillows and laid Demelza's head gently down on them.

"Yes, he left this morning. There's nothing to keep him here, now that the races are over."

"No . . . nothing," Demelza repeated, and shut her eyes.

* * *

Later in the afternoon Nattie insisted on Demelza eating something, and although it was difficult to do so she felt better afterwards.

"Where is Gerard?" she asked, feeling it strange that he had not come to see her.

"He went back to London with His Lordship, leaving Rollo here," Nattie answered. "And a good thing, if you asks me. That horse needs a rest."

Demelza thought how pleased Gerard would be to travel in the company of the Earl. But they had gone, and although she told herself it was foolish she felt neglected.

"Master Gerard spoke of coming back one day next week," Nattie said, "so you'd best be getting yourself well. And Abbot wants to see you. Real concerned he's been, in case it was Ben's fault the accident happened."

"You told him Ben could not help it?"

"That boy should have been more on the left," Nattie said, as if she could not help criticising. "At the same time, the gentleman in the chaise was a-driving like a maniac! What I always says is . . ."

Nattie chattered on but Demelza ceased to listen. She was thinking of the Earl and Gerard returning to London and that now the house would be very quiet.

There would be no laughter coming from the Dining-Room, and her late father's bed-room would be empty. There would be no need to bar the secret panel by the fireplace.

She thought of how she had saved the Earl from the lovely lady who had tried to drug him and how she had saved Crusader from the same fate.

Those were the ghosts, she thought, who would haunt her, and most of all, when she went to the arbour covered in honeysuckle she would think of the Earl waiting for her there.

She remembered how she had felt something live within her, thrilling and exciting, reaching out towards him so that although they had never touched each other they were very close.

She felt the tears prick her eyes, then she knew she was past crying. It was all over and the future was dull and lifeless.

* * *

Demelza walked down the stairs rather carefully because if she moved quickly she still felt a little dizzy. If Nattie had had her way, she would have stayed in bed.

"Why're you in such a hurry to get up?" Nattie asked in her scolding voice. "There's nothing to get up for."

That was the truth, Demelza agreed. At the same time, it was somehow worse to stay in bed, with nothing to do but think, than to move about.

She had therefore insisted, after she had eaten the luncheon that Nattie had brought her in bed, on getting up and dressing.

She put on one of her white gowns and arranged her hair, seeing as she looked in the mirror that she was very pale and her eyes seemed almost unnaturally large and dark.

"Now don't you go doing too much," Nattie was saying. "I'll be busy in the kitchen, but I'll bring you a cup of tea at about four o'clock. Then you'll go back to bed."

She did not wait for Demelza to reply, but bustled away, intent on scrubbing and cleaning now that the visitors had gone, even though there was no urgency for it.

Demelza reached the hall and noted that the roses on the table at the bottom of the stairs were shedding their petals and the bowl needed replenishing.

The flowers in the Drawing-Room were also a little overblown but their fragrance was still in the air, and she walked to the window wondering if she was strong enough to reach the arbour.

Then she knew she could not face it so soon and the intensity of the feeling it would evoke.

She would have to steel herself to become strong. Then she could conjure up and remember the magic that had happened there and the pulsating wonder of the Earl's voice when he told her that he loved her.

Her memories were going to be agony to live with, Demelza thought, but what else could she do?

She stood at the window looking out at the garden, at the sun shining on the rhododendrons, the beauty of them in some way a solace for her aching heart.

She heard the door of the Drawing-Room open but did not turn her head, waiting to hear Nattie scolding her because she was not sitting down and putting her feet up as she had been told to do.

Then, as there was only silence, which was very unlike Nattie, she turned, and suddenly her heart seemed to leap in her breast and it was impossible to breathe.

It was the Earl who stood there and he was looking as overpowering, elegant, and handsome as he had in her thoughts ever since she had regained consciousness.

She looked at him wide-eyed, thinking it could not be true.

Only as he reached her side did she feel as if a paralysis which had held her speechless dissolved and she could tremble.

"You are better?"

His voice was deep and she felt herself vibrate to the tone of it.

"I . . . I am . . . well."

"I have been desperately worried about you."

"Why . . . why are you . . . here?"

He smiled.

"I have brought Gerard back with me and an Art Dealer. They are at the moment inspecting the pictures in the Gallery where I first saw you."

"That was . . . kind of you."

The words seemed to come fitfully through her lips.

It was so hard to speak when he was looking at her in the way he was doing now.

"Come and sit down," the Earl said. "I want to talk to you."

She looked at him enquiringly and because something about him compelled her she moved from the window to sit down on the sofa by the fireplace.

"There is a lot we have to say to each other," the Earl said, "but first—and most important of all—is, how soon will you marry me, my darling?"

Demelza looked at him in astonishment. Then, because he was waiting for an answer, she managed to stammer:

"I . . . I . . . thought . . . I . . . understood . . ."

"That is one of the things I have to explain," the Earl said, "and in a way to ask your forgiveness."

"My . . . forgiveness?"

He was sitting beside her but he rose to stand with his back to the fireplace. Then he said in a grave voice which she had not heard before:

"I have in fact deceived you, although I did not mean it to be like that. My wife has been dead for over five years!"

Demelza's eyes were on his, but she could not speak.

She only felt as if the mists of misery which had held her were dissolving and the clouds were parting and a long, golden ray of sunshine was seeping through them.

"I am not going to tell you what I suffered," the Earl continued, "when shortly after my marriage, which had been arranged by my parents some years before it happened, my wife went mad. Suffice to say that when finally I was obliged to send her to an asylum I swore that never again would I allow myself to be humiliated in similar circumstances."

He drew in his breath as if he remembered the horrors which he had never before spoken of to anyone but which had left scars which he believed would never heal.

"But I found," the Earl went on, "when I entered the Social World alone, ostensibly as a bachelor, that not only could I forget but that my peculiar position could be turned to advantage."

He did not need to elaborate, because Demelza understood that while women found him irresistibly attractive, there was no question of having a permanent position in his life or of expecting a legal alliance.

"There is no need for me to tell you," the Earl said, "that, having discovered there was some compensation in being a married man without ties, I kept my wife's death, when it happened, a secret even from my closest friends."

He looked at Demelza as he spoke. Then he said quietly:

"I vowed that I would never marry again, and even when I met you, my darling, I had no wish to tie myself."

"I can . . . understand that," Demelza said in a low voice.

"But when you sent me away I knew that I could not live without you."

There was silence for a moment before the Earl said:

"I was determined, whatever the obstacles you put in my way, to see you, to be with you. But when I saw you thrown out of the gig in front of me, I knew that if you died I had no wish to go on living."

He spoke so quietly that for a moment the full impact of what he was saying was not clear to Demelza.

Then, as she understood, she moved for the first time since he had been speaking and clasped her hands together tightly.

"That is why I have come back," the Earl said, "to explain what I should have explained before, and to ask you to be my wife."

Their eyes met but he did not move towards her. Instead, they looked at each other for a long time.

Then, even as he had done, Demelza rose to her feet to walk not towards him but to the window.

She stood for a moment looking out, then she said:

"I love . . . you! I love you so much that I could not . . . bear you ever to have any . . . regrets."

The Earl's eyes were on her face but he did not speak, and after a moment she said hesitatingly, as if she was feeling for words:

"Now that you are free . . . now it would not be . . . wrong from . . . God's point of view . . . and there would be . . . no-one to disapprove . . . except Gerard and Nattie. . . . I will do anything you . . . ask of me . . . but you need not make me . . . your wife."

Her voice died away and now for the first time since she had risen she turned to look at him.

She saw an expression on his face which for a moment she did not understand, then he walked towards her and took her very gently in his arms.

Her head fell back against his shoulder and he looked down at her with a tenderness which seemed for the moment to change him so completely that he might have been a stranger.

His voice was very deep and moved as he said:

"Do you really think that is what I want, my precious, my darling, my adorable little ghost? I want you as my wife. I want you because

you already belong to me, because we are part of each other, and
never again will I lose you."

He held her a little close before he said:

"I intend to tie you to me by every chain and vow that exists, but
I believe actually we are bound to each other already and no Marriage Lines could make us any closer."

She raised her head and he saw by the sudden radiance in her eyes
that this was what she wanted to hear.

For a long moment they looked at each other, then the Earl's lips
sought hers.

It seemed to Demelza as if everything she had longed for was
there in his kiss. At the touch of his lips the pain she had suffered
vanished and instead there was a wonder and a glory which came
from Heaven itself.

This was what she knew love would be like—the love of God,
which was so perfect, so divine, that it was not of this world.

And yet, the closeness of the Earl and the demand which she
knew lay behind the gentleness of his kiss made her feel as if her
whole being was invaded by a splendour that was blinding in its intensity, and so it was so insistently marvellous that it was almost a
physical pain.

She felt the pressure of his lips increase, his arms tightened, and
then he was kissing her more passionately, more masterfully, more
possessively.

"I love . . . you!" she wanted to cry.

But there were no words in which to express the fact that they had
found each other and now, as they had been since the beginning,
they were not two people but one.

CHAPTER SEVEN

The sun, which had been shining warmly all day, was suddenly
eclipsed by clouds which brought a scud of rain.

It was not a cold rain but warm, and almost like a drink for the
thirsty earth, which had been baked dry all through the summer.

The Earl, driving his team of horses, did not slacken their pace
and they moved swiftly along the narrow country roads which
twisted towards the sea.

There was a hill rising slowly from a verdant valley and when they reached its summit the Earl could look down and see the vivid blue of the Atlantic and below him nestling amongst the trees the chimneys and roofs of a long, low-built house.

It was then for the first time that he pressed his horses with urgency, and there was an expression on his face which gave him a look of almost youthful eagerness.

There was still some way to go before finally he reached the house and saw it in front of him, its gardens still vivid with the colours of autumn.

Originally built as a Priory, Trevarnon House, which had been in the Earl's family for over five hundred years, was not only beautiful but had a mellow warmth about it which made everyone who approached it seem welcome.

The rain had ceased as unexpectedly as it had begun, and now the sun was brilliant again and shone on the many-paned windows, turning them to glittering gold as if they were lit from the inside.

The Earl drew his team, sweating a little with the speed at which they had travelled, to a standstill in front of the porticoed front door.

As grooms came running from the stables he threw down the reins and walked into the hall.

There was only an ancient Butler and a young footman in attendance, who took his hat and gloves. Then, as he would have moved past them, Dawson appeared and said:

"Her Ladyship asked me to see that you changed your coat, M'Lord, for what you're wearing'll be damp."

"There was very little rain," the Earl replied.

But Dawson stood waiting, and impatiently the Earl pulled off his tight-fitting grey whip-cord riding-coat and unbuttoned the waistcoat beneath it.

Dawson took them from him and helped him into a slightly more comfortable coat that he usually wore at home. Then the Earl saw that the valet also held in his hand a fresh muslin cravat.

"Really, Dawson," he exclaimed, "this is quite unnecessary!"

"Her Ladyship's afraid you might get a stiff neck, M'Lord."

"Have you ever known me to have such a thing?" the Earl asked.

"There's always a first time, M'Lord."

The Earl pulled his cravat from his neck and as he took the crisp muslin which Dawson held out to him he said:

"I have a suspicion, Dawson, that I am being simultaneously mollycoddled and bullied!"

The valet grinned.

"Yes, M'Lord, but we wouldn't wish Her Ladyship to worry."

The Earl smiled.

"No, Dawson, we would not wish her to worry."

He tied his fresh cravat with skilful fingers, then walked away from the hall and down the long corridor off which opened the gracious rooms filled with family treasures which, until they came to Cornwall, he had not seen for many years.

He knew that Demelza would be in the Orangery, which had been converted by his grandfather in his old age into a Sitting-Room that was half a Conservatory and half a look-out over the gardens.

It always seemed to be filled with sunshine and now as he opened the door the fragrance of the flowers hit him almost like a wave from the sea.

There were not only the ancient orange trees which had been brought from Spain two centuries ago, there were also orchids, exotic lilies, flowering cactuses and small dwarf azaleas which had once flowered in the foothills of the Himalayas.

At the far end of the room, reclining on a *chaise-longue* by a window, was Demelza.

She had not heard the Earl's approach, and he saw in profile her face tilted upwards, her eyes raised to the skies, as if she was praying as she had been when he first saw her in the Priests'-Room.

Two brown and white spaniels who were beside her couch heard him first and as they sprang towards him Demelza rose too and it seemed as if her eyes held the sunshine in their violet depths.

"Valient! You are back!"

It was a cry of sheer joy. She ran across the room and the Earl put his arms round her to hold her against him.

"You are . . . all right? You are . . . safe?" she questioned, but the words did not seem to matter.

It was the expression on her face that held his attention and the knowledge that because they were touching each other nothing else was of any consequence.

"You have missed me?"

His voice was deep.

"It has been a very . . . very . . . long day."

"That is what I found."

"I was afraid the . . . rain would slow you down. Did you get . . . wet?"

"There was only a little rain," he answered, "and, as you see, I have changed."

"That is what I . . . wanted you to . . . do."

"You are making me soft," he complained.

She laughed gently.

"Nothing could do that, but even for someone as . . . strong as . . . you, there is no point in taking . . . risks."

As she spoke she slipped her hands under his coat, saying:

"Your shirt is not damp?"

His arms tightened as he felt her hands on his back, caressing the strong, athletic muscles beneath the soft linen, and there was a touch of fire in his eyes.

He bent his head and found her lips and they were locked in a kiss which swept away every thought except that they were together.

The kiss lasted a long time, and when finally the Earl released Demelza her face was radiant and her lips soft and parted from the insistence of his.

"Darling, I have . . . so much to . . . tell you," she said in a voice that trembled a little, "but first you must have something to eat and drink. You have been on the road for a long time."

She took him by the hand and pulled him to where at the side of the Orangery there was a table on which there were several covered silver dishes, heated underneath by lighted candles.

There was also a wine-cooler filled with ice, in which reposed an open bottle of champagne.

"Cornish pasties made just as you like them," Demelza said, "and crabs that were caught this morning in the bay."

"I am hungry," the Earl admitted, "but I do not wish to spoil my dinner."

"There is still two hours before we dine," she replied. "I made it late in case you were delayed."

The Earl took a Cornish pasty from the silver dish and poured himself out a glass of champagne.

Then, with his eyes on his wife, he sat down in a comfortable chair while she resumed her position on the wide *chaise-longue* which was covered with satin cushions.

"Now, tell me what you have done," she said eagerly.

"I bought two exceptional mares in Penzance," the Earl replied, "which I am sure will improve our stock and should be just the right age for Crusader when we put him to stud, after he has won the Derby."

"You are very confident of doing that?" Demelza teased.

"How could I think otherwise when he is your horse and mine?" the Earl answered.

"I am glad that your journey was so . . . fruitful," she said. "I was afraid you might have gone all that way only to be . . . disappointed."

"I knew Cardew had some good horses," the Earl replied, "but these are exceptional."

"I also have some . . . news for . . . you," Demelza said.

The Earl waited, his eyes on her face, one hand absent-mindedly caressing the ear of one of the spaniels, which was trying to gain his attention.

"The jumps were finished today."

It was obviously an announcement of some significance.

"Finished?" the Earl exclaimed. "Did Dawson tell you that?"

"He wanted to surprise you," Demelza said, "and so did I. They are exactly the same as those that are erected on the Grand National Course."

She paused to add:

"You now have a chance of winning both the Grand National and the Derby."

"It is certainly a challenge," the Earl said, "but I am new to steeplechasing and it may prove more difficult than training Crusader for the flat."

"It will give you another interest."

He glanced at her sharply before he asked:

"Are you suggesting I need one?"

She looked at him in a way which expressed more clearly than words her inner feelings.

"I am always . . . afraid," she said softly, "that you will begin to be . . . bored, without parties . . . without all the amusing, witty . . . people who have always . . . surrounded you."

The Earl smiled as if something secretly amused him, then he said:

"Do you really think I would miss them when I have something here with you that I have never before had in my whole life?"

He saw the question in Demelza's eyes, but before she could ask it he said:

"A home! That is what all my money has never been able to buy. The home I did not have as a child but which I have found here."

"Oh, Valient, is that . . . true? It is what I have prayed I might give you."

The Earl put down his glass of champagne and rose to his feet to stand at the window looking at the exquisite view which ended in a distant horizon.

"London seems very far away," he said after a moment's silence.

"People will soon be . . . returning . . . there for the winter . . . season."

"Are you tempting me?" the Earl asked, and there was a hint of amusement in his voice.

"It is something I have no . . . wish to do," Demelza answered. "You know that for me, being here with you is like . . . being in Heaven. I have never been so happy."

He walked towards her and sat down on the edge of the *chaise-longue,* facing her.

"Have I really made you happy?" he asked.

He knew the answer before she said, with a depth of intensity in her voice that was very moving:

"Every day I think it is impossible to be happier or to love you more. Then every . . . night I find I was mistaken, and you give me an . . . ecstatic new love which I did not know . . . existed."

The Earl did not reply but just sat looking at her, and after a moment she asked a little anxiously:

"What are you . . . thinking?"

"I am wondering what it is about you that holds me spellbound every time I see you. I think really you are not a ghost but a witch."

Demelza laughed.

"I am certainly no longer a ghost," she said. "I am the one who is . . . haunted, as I have been ever since the first . . . moment I saw . . . you."

"Do you suppose I am not haunted too?" the Earl asked in a deep voice. "Haunted not only by your eyes, your lips, and your exquisite body, my darling, but by your heart, and most of all by your love. That is something from which I wish never to escape."

"Would you . . . want to?" Demelza asked.

"Do you expect me to answer such a foolish question?" he enquired. "If you are happy, how do you suppose I feel, knowing you are mine, knowing we have everything in the world that really matters!"

"Oh, Valient!"

Demelza put out her arms towards him, but he still sat, looking down at her, searching her face as if it was so precious, so perfect, that he must commit every line of it to his memory.

"I have something else to tell you," she said. "I received a letter today from Gerard."

"I expected you would hear from him soon."

"He is so thrilled that you have allowed him to keep his new race-horses in your stables at Newmarket. That was very . . . kind."

"There was plenty of room," the Earl replied carelessly, "now that we have so many of those that matter here."

"And Gerard feels so well off now that he has obtained so much money from the sale of the paintings, which only you recognised as being valuable."

She looked at the Earl from under her eye-lashes as she went on:

"I think, if you are truthful, you . . . forced the Art Dealer into paying more money for them than he would . . . otherwise have . . . done."

"I certainly made him pay what I considered was their true value, and refused to allow him to treat Gerard as a greenhorn as regards Art, which actually he is."

"It has made him very happy," Demelza said with a smile.

"I am more concerned with the feelings of his sister," the Earl replied.

"Do you want me to tell you how . . . grateful I am?"

"I like it when you are grateful," the Earl said, "but my interest in your brother was really entirely selfish. I do not wish you to worry about him, but only about me."

Demelza laughed.

"You are very . . . possessive."

"Not only possessive," the Earl replied, "but fanatically jealous. I cannot bear, and this is the truth, Demelza, that you should think of anyone or anything except myself. I want to possess every particle of you."

His voice deepened as he went on passionately:

"I want to possess you as a woman. I want you to be mine from the top of your head to the soles of your tiny feet, but I want too your mind, your heart, and your soul."

His lips touched her cheek.

"I warn you, my darling, as I have warned you before, that I am jealous even of the air you breathe!"

"Oh, Valient, you know already that I . . . belong to you in every . . . possible way. I am part of you and I know that if you . . . died or grew . . . tired of me I should really become the ghost you once . . . thought me to be."

"That I should grow tired of you is a possibility we need not even contemplate," the Earl said, "and I intend, God willing, that we should both live until we are very old."

"It can never be long enough for me," Demelza murmured, "but you must try, my darling husband, not to be too . . . jealous."

"Why should I try to be anything but what I am?" the Earl asked.

"Jealousy is a new emotion where I am concerned, and although I find it painful, there are compensations in knowing that I must fight and strive to possess you as completely as I wish to do."

"Fight?" she questioned.

"Sometimes I feel that there is something elusive about you," the Earl answered, "some secret within you that is not wholly mine."

"Why . . . should you . . . think that?"

Now her eyes were veiled and her lashes were dark against the translucence of her white skin.

"There is something," the Earl said almost as if he spoke to himself. "At night when you are lying in my arms after we have touched the wings of ecstasy, I feel that we are so close, so completely one, that our hearts beat in unison and we have no life apart from each other. Then, when the day comes—"

"What . . . happens . . . then?"

"I feel you have escaped me," the Earl replied, "just as I feel now there is something—but what it can be I have no idea—that you are hiding."

He reached out suddenly and put his hands on her shoulders.

"What is it?" he questioned. "What are you withholding from someone who would possess you utterly—the man who worships you, but at the same time is your conqueror?"

Demelza was very soft and yielding beneath the grip of his hands and the almost violent note in his voice.

"Perhaps it is . . . because we are so . . . close, my darling," she said after a moment, "that we know not only every . . . inflection in the other's voice, but also every secret . . . every stirring of our . . . souls, which are so linked that we think with a . . . single thought."

"You have not answered my question," the Earl said. "You have a secret! I know it! I know it instinctively! I felt last night that there was something, and when I came into this room today I was sure of it!"

The grip of his hands tightened.

"You will not keep me in ignorance!" he stormed. "Tell me what I do not know—for I will not allow you to play with me."

"I am not . . . playing with you, my beloved husband," Demelza answered. "It is only that I am . . . afraid."

"Of me?"

She shook her head.

"I could never be . . . afraid of you . . . but perhaps a . . . little of your . . . jealousy."

There was a frown between the Earl's eyes.

"What could you do that would make me jealous?"

Demelza did not answer and after a pause he said:

"What are you trying to tell me?"

Demelza glanced at him, then looked away again, and he saw the faint colour rising up her face.

"Only," she said in a whisper, "that perhaps I will not be . . . able to . . . watch you . . . win the Grand National."

For a moment the Earl did not understand, then as he took his hands from her shoulders he asked:

"Are you saying, my darling one—is it possible—so soon?"

"It is . . . soon," Demelza whispered, "but, like you, I am . . . sure it is a . . . certainty!"

The Earl put his arms round her and held her close.

"Why did you not tell me?"

"I wanted to be . . . sure."

"And you were also afraid that I might be jealous?"

"After . . . what you have . . . just said . . . very afraid!"

"I shall be jealous if you love our children more than you love me," he said. "But I know one thing—they will never suffer as I did from neglect and indifference, or from lack of love."

"They will never do that," Demelza agreed. "And, my wonderful . . . marvellous husband . . . we must both give them love, but you will always be first . . . a very easy first . . . you know . . . that."

There was a throb of passion in her voice, which brought the fire back into the Earl's eyes, but as if to hold his desires within bounds he said jokingly:

"Is it possible for a ghost to have a baby?"

"I am not a ghost," Demelza protested. "You have made me a woman . . . a woman who loves you so . . . much and so . . . overwhelmingly that she can imagine nothing more . . . perfect than to have a tiny replica of . . . you."

"If I am going to give you a son," the Earl said, "I must insist on a daughter as well, who will look like you, my darling, and whom I too can love."

"The house is big enough for any number of . . . children," Demelza answered, "and the garden is so lovely and the sea is so near . . . but perhaps . . ."

She stopped suddenly, and the Earl, who was touching the softness of her cheek with his lips, raised his head to ask:

"Perhaps what?"

"Perhaps by the time they are . . . old enough to enjoy such . . .

things, you will want to leave Cornwall for one of your other . . . houses."

He smiled at her.

"I know exactly what you are doing, my precious. You are trying to safe-guard yourself against being hurt, by thinking you must not count too much on my constancy."

He saw by the flicker in Demelza's eyes that he had guessed the truth, and after a moment he said:

"Do you want me to swear that we will stay here for the rest of our lives?"

"No, of course not!" she cried. "You know that from the moment you asked me to be your . . . wife, I have tried to . . . leave you free. I do not want to constrain and confine you as other . . . women have wished to do. I want you always to do . . . exactly what you . . . wish."

The Earl did not speak and after a moment she said a little shyly:

"This is what I believe real love is. To give, not to demand; to ask not for promises or reassurances except for . . . those which . . . come spontaneously from . . . the heart."

She looked at him before she added:

"Wherever you . . . go, as long as you . . . take me with . . . you I shall be happy and content. I do not wish you to feel tied to any . . . place that might become a . . . burden or an . . . encumbrance. All I want is your . . . happiness."

The Earl's expression was very tender.

Even after being married to Demelza for three months she could still surprise him by the depth of her feelings and by an intuition that was so attuned to his that she always said the right thing.

Was there any other woman in the world, he wondered, who would not seek to hold on to him and bind him, to make him in some way her prisoner?

He knew that because Demelza left him free he was utterly and completely her captive. Everything she said and everything she did made him want her all the more.

She was what he had sought in his imagination and never found; she was in fact what he had believed to be impossible—mother, wife, and child in one small, ethereal person.

Only occasionally did he protest at the way she cosseted him and cared for him, for he knew it was what he had always missed in his own mother.

As a wife she gave him everything that a woman deeply in love could give, and so much more besides.

He found her innocence so exciting, so fascinating, that when he taught her about love she aroused him spiritually as well as physically, as no other woman had ever been able to do.

He thought that although he would be a little jealous of his children because they would command much of her attention, he would be proud of them in the same way that he was proud of his horses and his other possessions.

But they would mean more and be more absorbing because they were an actual part of himself and of her.

In loving Demelza so wholeheartedly and in fighting to own her completely, as he had said himself, in body, mind, and soul, he had not until now given any thought to the fact that their union would result in children.

Now he knew it would complete her as a woman; a woman he would love in an even deeper and perhaps more passionate manner than he had loved the innocent and elusive girl.

Demelza was watching him with just a touch of anxiety in her eyes.

"You are . . . pleased? You are . . . really pleased, Valient, that we are to have . . . a baby?"

"I am pleased, my precious one," the Earl answered, "but you must take great care of yourself. I will not have anyone, not even my own child, upsetting you or forcing you to take any risks."

"You must not . . . mollycoddle me!"

"That is what I say to you, but you never listen."

"All I want is for . . . you to love . . . me," Demelza said, "even when I am not as . . . pretty as you think me . . . now."

"You will always be the most beautiful person I have ever seen," the Earl said positively.

He thought as he spoke that there was nothing more beautiful than a rose in full bloom.

But Demelza did not smell of roses but of honeysuckle, and he knew that because the fragrance was always with him it was impossible for him not to think of her every moment, even when they were apart as they had been today.

She knew he was waiting to say more and now he rose to pull off his coat. He threw it on the floor and sat beside Demelza on the *chaise-longue,* putting up his legs in his shining Hessian boots and pulling her against him.

She laid her head on his shoulder and put her arm round him to feel with her long, sensitive fingers the muscles in his back as she had done before.

"Have you any more surprises for me?" he asked, his mouth on her hair.

"I think it is . . . enough for one day," she answered, "except that I want to . . . tell you that I . . . love you!"

"That is strange," the Earl remarked, "because it is exactly what I was going to say to you!"

He felt her lips kiss him through the soft lawn shirt and the little quiver that went through her.

The fire within flamed as he asked:

"What are you feeling, my darling?"

"Very . . . thrilled . . . and excited . . . because I am close to you."

He put his hand under her chin and turned her face up to his.

The love in her eyes and the invitation on her lips made him turn round until, as her head sank against the soft cushions, he was looking down at her while their bodies were very close.

"There has not been a moment today when I have not been thinking of you," he said, "and yet, in some strange way, you were with me."

"I feel . . . that too," Demelza said, "but I . . . wanted you! I wanted you . . . desperately . . . as you are . . . now."

His hand moved over the curved line of her hip, then rose towards the softness of her breasts.

"You tell me I am free, my lively one," he said, "but I could never be free, even if I wished to be."

With the little gesture he loved, she raised her mouth.

Just for a moment he hesitated, as if he had more to say, and then words were unnecessary.

His lips came down on hers and he knew that beneath the softness of them there was a leaping flame which echoed the burning sensation within himself.

His heart was frantically beating against Demelza's as he drew her closer and still closer.

Then there was the fragrance of honeysuckle and the haunting mystery and inescapable wonder of love, which was as free as the wind, as deep as the ocean, and as high as the sky.

The Chieftain
Without a Heart

AUTHOR'S NOTE

The word "tartan" is derived from the French *tertaine*, and the first written reference to Highland dress occurs in the "Saga of Magnus Barefoot" in 1093.

In 1538 James V ordered himself the first Highland suit ever worn by a member of the Royal Family. Until the nineteenth century it was the custom of the women of the house to weave whatever tartan was required by the family.

When the Dress Act of 1746 made it illegal for Highlanders to wear a kilt or a tartan, to play the pipes or to carry arms in place of swords, they carried sticks, and, as a substitute for the dirk, a shorter knife was adopted, called a "skean dhu." This was small enough to be concealed in a pocket or stuck in the top of a stocking.

When in 1822 King George IV decided to visit his mother's Kingdom, a journey no crowned King had made since Charles I, he wore full Highland regalia, the Royal Stewart tartan.

All the details of his Reception and engagements in Edinburgh are correct and come from *A Historical Account of His Majesty's Visit to Scotland,* published in 1822.

CHAPTER ONE

1822

"Thank God we are in calm waters!"

Lord Hinchley poured himself a glass of brandy and drank it in one draught.

"You have been fortunate," his companion replied. "I have known the sea to be far worse than it has been on this voyage."

"Then the Lord knows that I will not come to this outlandish spot again! As it is, I am fully prepared to believe it is the Devil's country, peopled only by barbarians!"

"A popular English misconception about Scotland!" the Duke of Strathnarn said cynically.

Lord Hinchley threw himself down in a chair which was no longer swinging from side to side in the comfortable Saloon of the ship in which they had been buffeted about in an unpleasantly rough North Sea for the last seven days.

"If you ask me," he said confidentially, "you were extremely wise when you shook the soil of Scotland from your feet and came South. You have made a mistake, as I have told you before, Taran, in returning."

The Duke's face darkened and he went to the porthole to stare out at the tree-covered land past which the ship was sailing on its way up the Firth of Tay.

He had no intention of explaining, even to his closest friend, that every instinct in his body rebelled at the thought of coming back to the land he had left in a fury twelve years earlier.

He had been only sixteen at the time, and the cruelty of his father, which had not only bruised his body but humiliated his pride, had made him swear that for the rest of his life he would never have anything to do with Scotland or its people.

He remembered how he had crept aboard the first available ship in Perth harbour, and, unable to afford more than the poorest passage, had suffered intolerably in the airless, stinking hold below decks.

But his late mother's relatives in London had welcomed him with open arms.

They had sent him to a famous Public School and afterwards to

Oxford University; and as the Marquis of Narn, sponsored by his grandfather who had been in attendance on the Prince Regent, he had found life both civilised and enjoyable.

He had in fact almost forgotten that Scotland even existed.

When his grandfather died he left him a large estate and a great deal of money. Basking in the friendship of the Regent, who by now was King George IV, he found in London everything he wanted and everything he enjoyed.

It had come like a bomb-shell three months ago to hear that his father was dead and he was now not only the Duke of Strathnarn but also Chieftain of the Clan McNarn.

Somehow he had always believed his father to be indestructible.

When he thought of him, which was seldom, he had seemed ageless and terrifying, like one of the ancient giants described in the ballads sung by the Bard which he had listened to when he was a child.

He was silent for so long that Lord Hinchley, rising to pour himself another brandy, said:

"You look depressed, Taran, and that glowering expression on your face is grim enough to frighten your Clansmen, or whatever you call them."

"And a good thing if they are frightened," the Duke replied, "because in that case they are more likely to obey me."

Even as he spoke he knew he was libelling the McNarns, for the Clansmen invariably obeyed their Chiefs. In fact, he remembered his father saying once:

"A Chief stands halfway between his own people and God."

Then he told himself almost by way of reassurance that the days of such servitude were over, and now that a Chief no longer had the power of life and death over his people their feelings for him would obviously not be the same.

"Well, all I can say," Lord Hinchley remarked as he sipped his brandy, "is that if I have to travel back in the *Royal George* with His Majesty I shall lie down in my cabin and drink myself insensible until we reach Tilbury."

"It will be calmer on your return," the Duke said automatically, as if he was thinking of something else, "and as the King is a good sailor he will expect you to be on your feet, telling him how much the Scots appreciated his visit."

"The question is—will they?" Lord Hinchley asked. "I blame Walter Scott for inspiring the Monarch with this urgent desire to come to Edinburgh. If the Scots have any sense they will cut him down with their claymores and stick their dirks into him!"

The Duke did not speak and Lord Hinchley continued:

"My grandfather served in the Cumberland Army which took part in the Battle of Culloden. His description of the manner in which the Scots were massacred and the cruelties inflicted on the survivors afterwards should make any Englishman think twice before he braves the vengeance which is undoubtedly still seething in their breasts."

"It was a long time ago," the Duke remarked.

"I would not mind betting you they have not forgotten," Lord Hinchley replied.

"I think you are right about that."

"Of course I am right!" Lord Hinchley said positively. "All barbaric people have their feuds, their vendettas, their curses, which are carried on from generation to generation."

"You are very voluble on the subject," the Duke remarked.

"When His Majesty told me I was to come here as an advance guard and see that he was properly received when he arrives in Edinburgh, I took the trouble to mug up some of the facts about Scotland and the Scots."

Lord Hinchley paused before he added:

"I do not mind telling you, Taran, that the English behaved damned badly to the wretched people they conquered, entirely because they were better organised and carried muskets."

The Duke did not reply and after a moment Lord Hinchley said:

"My grandfather used to relate to me when I was a small boy how the Clans were mowed down at Culloden as they marched, hungry and wet after a night in the open, across a bad terrain, their Chiefs leading them straight into the gun-fire."

The Duke rose to his feet with what was an angry gesture.

"For God's sake, William, stop trying to make my flesh creep about battles that happened long before we were born. We have both been pressured into coming on this cursed voyage and the quicker we do what we have to do and return home the better!"

There was so much anger in the Duke's voice that his friend looked at him curiously. Then he said:

"I had the idea that this, in fact, is your home."

He saw the Duke's fingers clench as if he had touched him on the raw. Then because he was extremely fond of his friend he said in a soothing tone:

"Have another drink. There is nothing like good French brandy to make the world seem a pleasanter place."

The Duke filled his glass from the crystal decanter, which had a broad flat bottom so that it would not fall off the table with the roll of the ship.

As he felt the fiery liquid seeping through his body, he knew that instead of soothing him and bringing him some comfort it merely accentuated his anger and apprehension at what lay ahead.

He had had no intention when his father died of returning to Scotland. He had cut himself off from the McNarns when he had run away with his back crossed and bleeding from the weals inflicted by his father's whip.

If they liked to think of him as a renegade they could do so. He did not intend to concern himself with anyone's feelings but his own.

After he left University he had found that with plenty of money to spend, and with looks which made women gravitate towards him like moths to a lighted candle, he had no time to think of anything but his own pleasure.

The Prince Regent liked to have young Bucks and Beaux round him, encouraging them in the extravagances of dress that he affected himself.

It was a fashion that had been set by his friend Beau Brummell, to which he still adhered even after they had quarrelled and Brummell had died in exile.

It was with the keen excitement of a child going to his first party that the King was planning now to appear in Scotland in full Highland regalia.

He had ordered those who were to be in attendance on him in Edinburgh to wear their tartans and finally to lead their Clans at an enormous review that was to take place on the Portobello Sands on Friday, August 23.

The Duke had not thought for a moment that he would be expected to be present, but the King had made it quite clear that he must be there, and although he wished to refuse he had found it impossible to find a plausible excuse.

But His Majesty's command, for it was little else, only came after he was in fact already considering whether or not he should return to Scotland, having received an urgent request to do so from his Comptroller, Mr. Robert Dunblane.

The communication had been brought to him as speedily as possible, though that meant that even by sea it had taken an inordinately long time for it to reach him.

Robert Dunblane had been Comptroller to his father, and the

Duke remembered him as being almost the only human person to whom he could talk when he was a boy.

It was Dunblane who had informed him three months earlier of his father's death and had made it clear in his letter that he assumed the Duke would be coming to Scotland as soon as it was possible.

His Clan, his Castle, and the land he owned could rot as far as he was concerned!

He was prepared to use the title that was now his, but otherwise the less he heard of the North the better, and he had in fact dismissed Robert Dunblane's letter from his mind.

The second letter was different and not only his eyes but his whole expression darkened as he read what it contained.

Finally he swore aloud:

"Fool! That damned young fool! How could he do anything so crazy?"

He could only remember his nephew, Torquil McNarn, as a crying baby who had been born in 1806, four years before he left home, but he remembered his sister Janet with nothing but love and affection.

She had been much older than he and had taken the place of his mother, who had died when he was very young.

She had married a cousin, also by the name of McNarn, and had unfortunately left the Castle and him to the merciless tyranny of their father.

The only happy memories the Duke had of Scotland were of Janet, and when six years ago she too had died he thought his last link had been severed forever with those whom he was forced, however much he loathed them, to call his kith and kin.

Robert Dunblane's letter had aroused, even if reluctantly, a sense of responsibility towards Janet's son and had made it quite clear to the Duke what he was expected to do.

"Torquil McNarn is not only Your Grace's nephew," he had written, "but also the *Dighre* [heir] both to the title and your position as Chief until you have a son."

The Duke had forgotten that Scottish inheritance could be in the female as well as in the male line.

He found himself wondering what Janet's son was like and if in fact he would make a better Chieftain of the Clan than he was himself.

Then he told himself cynically that if the boy was counting on that it would be a mistake. He supposed that sooner or later he would marry, although he had no inclination to do so at the moment.

There were too many alluring women to keep him amused when he was not involved with sport for him to think it necessary to choose one as a permanent companion.

He was convinced that if he did so he would soon find her a dead bore.

Women were amusing, the Duke had found, as long as they were elusive, as long as they could be pursued and hunted as if they were an animal or a bird, or a trophy to be won.

As soon as they were conquered and there was no more mystery about them, both his interest and his desire faded.

Then he was off again after another prey, and there was, in his opinion, nothing more time-wasting than a love-affair which had lost its dash and its spirit.

Even the King had remonstrated with him over what the women he left broken-hearted called his "callousness and cruelty."

"What is the matter with you, Taran?" His Majesty asked. "You have more love-affairs in a year than I have horses in my stable."

"Like you, Sire, I am looking for a winner," the Duke had replied.

The King had chuckled, admitting that he himself was invariably beguiled by a new and pretty face.

"At the same time, Taran," he went on, "you must remember that these frail creatures have feelings, and in my opinion you leave too many of them weeping."

"A woman only weeps when she cannot get what she wants," the Duke replied cynically. "They must learn to accept the inevitable, Sire: I am unobtainable."

The King had laughed, but nevertheless the Duke had been scowling when he had related the story to his friend William.

"What does he expect me to do?" he had asked. "Marry every woman to whom I make love?"

"No, of course not," Lord Hinchley replied, "but you are savage with them, Taran. Surely one of them must touch your heart?"

"I have no heart," the Duke said positively.

Lord Hinchley smiled.

"That is a challenge to Fate. One day you will fall in love, and then you will understand how agonising it can be to see someone you adore looking over your shoulder to find someone better than yourself."

The Duke smiled cynically, and his friend exclaimed:

"Dammit, Taran, you are too conceited. You are thinking that it is an impossibility because you are the best. All right, go on until retribution catches up with you!"

"And if it does, which is very unlikely," the Duke replied, "I shall still have had a good run for my money!"

Lord Hinchley broke in on the Duke's thoughts now by asking:

"What happens when we arrive?"

"I have not the slightest idea," the Duke replied. "I sent word to my Comptroller telling him the name of the ship on which we are sailing and the approximate date on which we should dock in Perth. I presume he will make arrangements to convey us to the Castle. If not, you may have to walk!"

Lord Hinchley gave a groan of anguish and the Duke said:

"It is no more than twenty miles! But the mountains are very steep for those who are not used to them."

"I know you are roasting me," Lord Hinchley said. "At the same time, in this benighted land fiction might become an unpleasant fact. For God's sake, Taran, let us hope for the best even if we have to expect the worst."

The Duke, however, was pleasantly surprised when after the ship had docked Robert Dunblane came on board.

A tall, good-looking man of over fifty, he certainly looked impressive in a kilt, his bonnet on the side of his greying head and a plaid clasped with a huge cairngorm brooch over his shoulder.

The Duke held out his hand.

"I should have known you anywhere, Dunblane!"

"Unfortunately, Your Grace, I cannot return the compliment," Robert Dunblane replied.

There was however a smile on his lips which told the Duke that he was delighted by his appearance.

It must certainly have been hard for him to recognise the thin boy with wild, defiant eyes, whom he had last seen fighting back his tears, in the tall, incredibly handsome man of the world who now stood in front of him.

The tight-fitting hose-pipe pantaloons, the cut-away coat with its long tails, and the crisp whiteness of an intricately tied cravat did nothing to detract from the Duke's broad shoulders and his athletic figure, tapering down to narrow hips.

Robert Dunblane also noted the McNarn characteristics: the straight, aristocratic nose and the firm, authoritative mouth which could set in a sharp line.

"I suppose," the Duke said after the first courteous pleasantries had been exchanged, "that you have some way of conveying Lord Hinchley and me to the Castle?"

Robert Dunblane smiled.

"There are horses, Your Grace, waiting for you, or, if you prefer, a carriage. But may I suggest, in case you have forgotten, that the roads are very dusty at this time of the year and by far the quickest way is as the crow flies across the moors."

"Then we will ride," the Duke said. "If that suits you, William?"

"I am prepared to accept any mode of travel," Lord Hinchley replied, "except that which involves me in going by sea!"

"You have had a rough journey, My Lord?" Robert Dunblane asked solicitously.

"Damnably rough!" Lord Hinchley replied. "If I had not been able to drown my sorrows in the traditional manner I should have undoubtedly ended up in a watery grave!"

The Duke laughed.

"His Lordship exaggerates!" he said. "It was rather choppy at times, but fortunately the wind was behind us—otherwise it might have been far worse!"

"Impossible!" Lord Hinchley exclaimed, and they all laughed.

It was a sunny day with enough wind to sweep the midges away as they set off on the horses which Mr. Dunblane had provided for them.

Leaving the "Fair City" of Perth, they travelled North, passing the Royal Palace of Scone where the Duke remembered many Coronations had taken place.

He wondered if Lord Hinchley would be interested in knowing that Parliaments and General Councils had been convened at Scone between the accession of Alexander I, who had been born in 1078 and the death of Robert III in 1406.

But he told himself with a wry smile that the English were not impressed by Scottish history and had done their best to stamp out anything that appertained to the prestige or importance of what was to all intents and purposes a conquered Colony.

Then he realised with a start that he was thinking of himself as Scottish and resenting perhaps for the first time in years the English habit of disparaging the Scots and looking on them as uncouth savages.

He believed that a great deal of their hostility and indifference as well as their cruelty was due to fear.

There was some reason for this, for it was only thirty years ago that the troops at Register House in Edinburgh, inflamed by seditious propaganda, had shouted: "Damn the King!"

He remembered too that throughout the country when the news arrived of the victories of the French under Napoleon, the Scots had planted green fir trees, symbolic of liberty.

But this was over now. George IV was coming to Scotland and everyone had been told it was a gesture of friendship.

"I do not know whether His Grace has told you," Lord Hinchley was saying to Robert Dunblane as they rode along, "but I have to leave for Edinburgh in a day or so to prepare for His Majesty's visit."

"I imagine, My Lord, you would prefer to go by road," Mr. Dunblane replied.

"Most certainly!" Lord Hinchley answered. "I shall not be able to look at the sea for a long time without a shudder."

"I hope one of His Grace's carriages will prove more comfortable," Mr. Dunblane said courteously.

The Duke was thinking that if his friend had any sense he would ride.

It was very pleasant to feel a horse between his knees as they climbed above the city with its wide silver river to see the moors purple with heather and above them far in the distance the great heights of the Grampian Mountains.

Silhouetted against the sky, with small pockets of snow still dazzlingly white against their peaks, they were very beautiful.

A covey of grouse rose at the Duke's feet, the old cock with its warning "caw-caw" swinging them away to safety in the valley.

They were climbing all the time until finally at the top of the moor Mr. Dunblane drew his horse to a standstill and they knew that he wanted them to look back at the magnificent vista that lay behind them.

The Firth was a brilliant blue in the sunshine, the spires and roofs of Perth sprawled beside the river, and there was in the wildness of the heather a feeling of freedom.

Surveying it, the Duke felt as if he had escaped from the confines of what had been almost like prison, and it was a sensation for which he could not find an explanation.

He was remembering the expressions on the faces of the servants who had been waiting for them when they left the ship.

Mr. Dunblane had introduced to him the man who was in charge, a huge, rough Scot whose eyes when they met the Duke's had an expression of devotion that was inescapable.

'After all these years, can I still mean something to those who bear the same name as myself?' the Duke wondered to himself.

He would have liked to question Robert Dunblane about it but told himself he would feel embarrassed because Lord Hinchley would undoubtedly laugh at his curiosity.

He recalled how vehemently he had complained about coming on the journey in the first place and how often he had reiterated how much he hated Scotland.

"If you hate it so much, why are you going back?" William Hinchley had asked one evening at dinner.

"Family reasons," the Duke replied briefly.

Because he knew it would be intruding on his privacy, Lord Hinchley had not questioned his friend further.

He had, however, thought to himself that Taran was a strangely unpredictable creature.

He had a warm affection for him and it was impossible not to admire him as a sportsman, but at the same time he thought there were deep reserves in the Scot which he had found in no other man of his acquaintance.

He had thought, as they were close friends, that there would be nothing they could not discuss, nothing which would be a "taboo" subject.

And yet he found that where the McNarns were concerned the Duke was not prepared to talk.

Now, riding across the top of the moors, they could move more swiftly and found as they descended a hill that the horses achieved quite a considerable pace.

Both the Duke and Lord Hinchley were used to spending long hours in the saddle. They also drove to Newmarket Races without finding it fatiguing, and they had raced against each other and the King's record often enough to Brighton.

Yet Lord Hinchley was in fact relieved when two hours later Mr. Dunblane said:

"We have only a short distance to go now and we shall see the Castle in five minutes."

The Duke had seen it often enough in boyhood, and yet when they rounded a crag and saw it ahead it was impossible not to feel that it was larger, more impressive, and more overpowering even than he remembered.

A great grey stone edifice of towers and turrets, with ancient arrow-slits and seventeenth-century additions, Narn Castle was one of the most outstanding and certainly the most magnificent of the Castles in the whole of the Highlands.

Lord Hinchley gasped and stared at it with undisguised admiration.

"Good God, Taran!" he said. "You never told me that you owned anything as fine as, if not finer than, Windsor Castle!"

"I am glad it impresses you," the Duke said dryly.

He could not, however, help a faint stirring of pride within himself.

He had hated the Castle. It had stood like a dark shadow across his childhood, to become so menacing, so oppressive, that when he had fled from it in the middle of the night he never thought that he would go back.

Yet, with the sunshine on its windows, with its flag flying in the breeze above the highest tower, with its command over the surrounding countryside, he knew it was a fitting background for the Chief of the McNarns.

He glanced back to see if the grooms who had been following them were still in sight.

The luggage was to travel by road, but they had also been escorted by six men on horse-back and now the Duke realised they were drawing closer and not keeping their distance as they had during the long ride.

He turned his head to go forward again and Robert Dunblane said quietly:

"They will be waiting outside the Castle to greet Your Grace."

"They?" the Duke questioned. "Who?"

"The Clansmen. Only those of course who live in the immediate neighbourhood. The others will be coming in from the hills tomorrow or the day after."

The Duke was silent for a moment, then he asked:

"What for?"

It was a sharp question and he knew there was a touch of apprehension in it.

Mr. Dunblane glanced at him swiftly from under his dark eyebrows.

"To welcome a new Chieftain there is always a traditional ceremonial and they have been waiting eagerly for your return."

The Duke did not reply.

It was impossible for him to say to Mr. Dunblane that until his second letter he had had no intention of returning.

Vaguely he remembered his father holding meetings of the Clan, to which he had not been invited, and festivities at Christmas, to which he had.

Now he was recalling how important a Chief was to his people, and though he had reassured himself in London that such things were out-of-date he knew that he had been mistaken.

He wished he had made it clear to Dunblane in the letter which announced his arrival that he wanted no fuss, no special greetings, no Clansmen paying him homage.

Then he thought that even if he had said so, it was very unlikely that anyone would have paid any attention.

A Chieftain was the father of his Clan, and as previously he had had the right of life and death over his people he had been equally responsible for their welfare.

What was it he had read in some book when he had been at Oxford? It had been explaining the position of the Chieftains before the Rebellions in 1715 and 1745 and stated:

As landlord, father-figure, judge, and general, his power was great and absolute, but on occasions he would debate major issues with the members of his family and leading members of his Clan.

One thing was quite certain, the Duke thought sharply—he had no immediate family or plans to debate.

His father was dead, thank God, and so unfortunately was his sister Janet.

That left Torquil, and it was that foolish young man, his heir presumptive, who had brought him back to Scotland from the comfort and the amusements of London.

And yet he supposed there were other relatives, whom he had not remembered, and in a voice deliberately casual he asked Robert Dunblane:

"Is there anyone staying at the Castle?"

"Only Jamie, Your Grace."

The Duke looked puzzled.

"Jamie?"

"Lady Janet's younger son."

"Of course!"

The Duke remembered now, but he had not recalled the name.

It was due to her second son that she had died in childbirth.

"He is a very amusing little boy," Mr. Dunblane was saying. "Brave, adventurous, and a true McNarn in every way."

"Being adventurous is not a quality I am particularly looking for in my nephews at the moment!" the Duke said shortly.

It was a rebuke and Mr. Dunblane looked anxious for a moment, but he said nothing.

Then, so unexpectedly that it made both Lord Hinchley and the Duke start, men appeared from the concealment of the heather and came hurrying round them.

Their arms were raised in greeting and at the same time their mouths opened to give a war-like cry which the Duke recognised as the slogan of the McNarns.

It was a wild, savage exaltation, either as a reminder of the heroic past or as an invitation to slaughter the enemy.

The Duke remembered that it was part of the Clan's identity, as was the badge of heather, gale, ling, or myrtle, which the men wore in their bonnets.

The slogan was yelled and yelled again. Then there was the high sweet note of the pipes and the Clansmen fell in beside the horses and marched with them towards the Castle.

Almost before he was aware of it the Duke found himself riding alone ahead, while Mr. Dunblane and Lord Hinchley rode behind him, with the escort of six horsemen which had joined them.

It was a procession, and a moment later the noise of the pipes was drowned with a cry from hundreds of throats and he saw the Clansmen waiting for him along the drive that led to the Castle.

They looked strange, rough, and poor, yet there was a pride in their bearing, a width to their shoulders, and a strength to their arms which told the Duke that they were men to be reckoned with.

The uproar was tremendous and there was no question of his speaking to any individual or making any response, except a gesture with his hand and a bow of his head.

Then as he reached the Castle door the noise and the voices ceased suddenly, as did the music of the pipes.

The Clansmen watched him in silence and as they clustered round him the Duke could see their wives and children beyond them, taking no part, but peeping from behind the shrubs and over the brow of the heather.

He had meant to walk straight into the Castle, but something stronger than his own desire, some instinct to do what was right, which he could not ignore, made him stand facing the men who had welcomed him.

"Thank you," he said in a voice that carried. "Thank you, and may good fortune attend us all."

It was a greeting which came to his mind from the past, but the strange thing was that he had said it in Gaelic, the language he had not spoken or thought of for twelve years!

As a great cheer went up, spontaneous and whole-hearted, the Duke raised his arm as if in salute and, turning, walked into the Castle.

* * *

"Now tell me what my nephew has done," the Duke said.

They had finished dinner and Lord Hinchley had retired to another room while the Duke had taken Dunblane into the Library, where his father had always sat.

As he crossed the threshold his eyes expected to see the dark shadow of the man he had always hated at the desk by the window which overlooked the Glen below.

The Duke had always thought his father was like a gargoyle staring balefully and menacingly out over the land he owned.

Strangely enough, the room was far from the dark cavern of misery and despair that he remembered.

The magnificently appointed Library had been designed by William Adam with a symmetry and a beauty that was indescribable.

The Duke stood looking round him, thinking it was impossible that the room had been like this when he was a boy and he had not realised its perfection.

Now the colourful leather-bound books seemed to exude a benign influence and the shadow of his father receded.

Without really thinking about it, the Duke sat down automatically in the chair his father had always occupied and invited Dunblane to sit opposite him.

"I gathered from your letter that the situation is desperate, but I can hardly believe that to be the truth," the Duke went on.

"It is certainly very serious, Your Grace."

"In what way?"

"Torquil is a prisoner of the Kilcraigs."

"A prisoner? Surely they cannot intend to incarcerate him in a dungeon or lock him up in a cellar indefinitely?"

The Duke spoke lightly.

"I imagine his quarters, whatever they may be, are none too comfortable," Mr. Dunblane replied, "but the alternative, I understand, is to send him to Edinburgh to stand trial."

"To stand trial?"

There was no doubt that the Duke was startled. "On what charge?"

"The charge of cattle-stealing, Your Grace!"

"Good God!"

There was no doubt now that the Duke was astonished.

"I have seen The Kilcraig, Your Grace, and he informs me that, while he will wait to discuss it with you on your arrival, there is no doubt in his mind that Torquil and his associates, if they are taken before the Justices, will be severely punished—in fact very likely transported!"

The Duke was stunned into silence.

He was well aware that cattle-stealing was frowned upon by the authorities and very severe sentences were passed on those who committed such crimes.

The growth of the beef trade in the Lowlands and in England had increased cattle-thieving and what was known as "blackmail." The levying of blackmail was an old Border and Highland custom.

"Mails" were the rents paid in money and in kind on Scottish estates, and "blackmail" was the tribute paid by law-abiding men to freebooters or raiding Clansmen in return for a promise that their stock would not be lifted or their steadings burnt.

Offenders were no longer hanged as had been usual in the past, but the Justices had no compunction in transporting a convicted man to the Colonies or sending him to prison for a long sentence.

"Why the devil did you allow the boy to do anything so inane?" the Duke asked angrily.

Mr. Dunblane sighed.

"I had discussed Torquil's position with your father for many years, Your Grace. I told him that he had not enough to do, and, as was inevitable, he got into mischief."

Mr. Dunblane's voice had a pleading note in it as he went on:

"I believe, quite frankly, that it was just a boyish prank. The Kilcraigs have always been our avowed enemies, and it amused him to slip across the border at night to steal away a calf or, if possible, a prime animal and bring it home in triumph."

The Duke could understand all too clearly what Mr. Dunblane was saying. It would have been a triumph because the McNarns through age-long feuds had always hated the Kilcraigs, just as the Kilcraigs hated the McNarns.

They had warred between themselves for as long as anyone could remember, and the fact that the Kilcraigs had herds of good cattle would be an enticement in itself.

Aloud the Duke asked briefly:

"How was he caught?"

"Apparently it is not the first time he has played this sort of prank," Mr. Dunblane replied, "although unfortunately I had not heard of it until The Kilcraig informed me that Torquil and the three boys with him had been taken prisoner."

"The herdsmen had lain in wait for them, I suppose?"

Mr. Dunblane nodded.

"I imagine," the Duke went on, "that they were foolish enough to go by the same route to the same place as they had done before."

"It was the nearest to the border," Mr. Dunblane said briefly.

"I cannot imagine anything more irresponsible or more infuriating!" the Duke exclaimed. "I suppose The Kilcraig will see reason if I talk to him?"

"He said he would negotiate with no-one but yourself, Your Grace."

The Duke sighed.

"Then I suppose I shall have to see him. I do not mind telling you, Dunblane, that I am extremely angry about the whole thing."

"I was afraid you would be, Your Grace. At the same time, it would have been reasonable to send Torquil to school and later to a University."

"But my father would not listen to reason," the Duke said cynically. "How old is Torquil now?"

"He will be seventeen on his next birthday, Your Grace—he is the same age as you were when you ran away."

The information, the Duke knew, was given to make him realise that Torquil had felt just as he himself had: rebellious, angry, and determined to do something about it.

"Has he been educated at all?" he asked.

"Yes, Your Grace. Your father engaged several excellent Tutors for him, but unfortunately he found them boring."

"I am not surprised at that," the Duke said, "knowing the type of men my father would engage."

"He needs, Your Grace, to play games with boys of his own age and his own class."

"And those who were captured with him?"

"Crofters' sons, decent boys, but of course, Your Grace, uneducated."

"The whole thing is out-of-date! Ridiculous! It should never have been allowed to happen!" the Duke stormed.

Even as he spoke he knew that he was being unfair.

Dunblane had surely done the best he could for Torquil, just as he had done the best he could for himself; but, against his father's obstinacy and supreme authority, anything he could have suggested would have proved hopeless from the start.

"Well, what are we going to do?" he asked more quietly.

"I have arranged tentatively for you to call and see The Kilcraig tomorrow. He will not come here."

"Do you mean that I have to go to him?"

"It may seem a loss of face. At the same time, he holds the trump card, Your Grace."

"Torquil!" the Duke murmured.

"Exactly!"

"Very well. But I warn you, Dunblane, that if The Kilcraig makes it too difficult I shall tell young Torquil he can go to the Devil!"

The Duke spoke violently, but even as he did so he knew he was shadow-boxing.

It would be quite impossible for him to allow his nephew and heir presumptive to go up for trial in the Edinburgh Courts like a common felon.

What was more, it would not be Torquil who would be humiliated and punished, but the whole Clan. They all bore the same name, and they all believed themselves to be part of the same stock.

He knew that every Clansman on his lands would fight to the death for his own family and his honour, just as he would fight any battle into which his Chief might lead him.

"The sooner we get this over the better!" the Duke said sharply. "Send a message to The Kilcraig that I will call on him at noon tomorrow. I presume you will come with me?"

"If you are going into Kilcraig country, Your Grace, you must travel as befits your position. Not to do so would be looked upon as a sign of weakness."

The Duke looked at his Comptroller in surprise.

"What does that imply?"

"You will go with your immediate henchmen, Bard, Piper, and gillies, as your forefathers travelled before you."

"God in Heaven! In this day and age, is this necessary?" the Duke asked.

"As I have said already, if you do anything else it will be looked on as a sign of weakness, and at the moment, as Your Grace knows full well, you have no good cards in your hand."

The Duke thumped his clenched fist on the arm of his chair.

"This is intolerable! What is more, I feel, Dunblane, as if I have stepped back into the past. In England, noblemen do not hold each other's children as prisoners. Duelling is almost out-of-date, and arguments are conducted in a gentlemanly manner over a glass of port!"

"Unfortunately, Your Grace, The Kilcraig is very like your father, who would always rather have used a claymore than had a sensible argument."

"Very well," the Duke said harshly. "Have it your own way! I will leave everything to you, Dunblane, and I only hope we can retain some vestige of pride out of all this tomfoolery!"

He walked towards the door, and only as he reached it did he turn back to say:

"Do you expect me to get myself up in fancy-dress?"

"If you mean should you wear the tartan, Your Grace, you must meet The Kilcraig as a Chieftain—the Chief of the McNarns."

The Duke did not reply but went out of the Library, slamming the door behind him.

CHAPTER TWO

The Duke was in an extremely bad temper.

He had in fact got up with what his Highland Nurse would have called "a wee black devil" on his shoulder.

His valet had laid out for him, obviously on Mr. Dunblane's instructions, the Highland dress that he had brought from London.

He had taken very little interest in it and had merely given the order to his tailor to make what was necessary.

He was to realise later that the tailor was in fact a conscientious man who had taken immense trouble in finding out what was the correct regalia for a Chieftain.

After he had finished his bath, the Duke saw lying on the chair trews of skin-tight tartan, which a Chief would wear when he preferred to ride rather than walk.

There was also a tartan jacket, a tartan waist-coat, and the plaid that would be clasped with a silver-and-cairngorm brooch on his left shoulder.

He had seen his father often enough wearing the same traditional garments, but quite suddenly he revolted.

"Take them away!" he said harshly. "I will wear the clothes of the gentleman which I am and which I hope to remain!"

When he went down to breakfast he thought that the kilted servants attending him glanced at him with a question in their eyes.

It made him even more determined than ever that he would not pander to the ridiculous nonsense of ancient customs which were "as dead as a door-nail."

Deliberately, so as to avoid mention of the ordeal that lay ahead of him, he said in a conversational tone to Lord Hinchley:

"What do you intend to do with yourself today, William?"

"Something that will make you extremely envious," Lord Hinchley replied. "I am going fishing."

The Duke did not reply and he went on:

"Dunblane tells me there are plenty of salmon in your river, and tomorrow, if you can spare the time, Taran, I should like to have a shot at your grouse."

The fact that his friend intended to do some things he would have liked to do himself did not improve the Duke's temper.

He merely concerned himself with breakfast, which he found, despite a desire to find fault, extremely appetising.

As he was finishing the excellent dish of sea-trout, his nephew Jamie came into the room.

He had had only a brief glance at the boy the evening before, when he arrived, and now he appraised him more critically, noticing that he had red hair and blue eyes.

He found that surprising until he remembered that it was characteristic of the Campbells—the Race of Diamid—and that Jamie's grandmother on his father's side had belonged to that Clan.

As he had obviously been instructed to do, Jamie bowed first to him, then to Lord Hinchley.

"Good-morning, Jamie!" the Duke said perfunctorily.

"It is not a good morning!" Jamie replied hotly. "Jeannie says I should be coming with you today to fight the Kilcraigs, but Mr. Dunblane will not let me."

"I am not going to fight the Kilcraigs," the Duke replied, "so Jeannie, whoever she may be, has been misinformed."

"They are our enemies and we hate them!" Jamie insisted. "You must battle with them as Chief of the McNarns, and I should be with you."

The Duke sighed impatiently.

It seemed that even the child was inoculated with these barbaric customs, for he was well aware that if a Chieftain went into battle his

kinsmen accompanied him, besides all the other henchmen whom
Dunblane had mentioned last night.

"Now let me make this quite clear," he said firmly. "I am not
fighting the Kilcraigs, nor do I intend to do so. Those feuds and
hatreds are out-of-date. They are our neighbours and we must learn
to live in peace with them."

"In peace with the Kilcraigs?" Jamie exclaimed. "And also the
MacAuads?"

"With both!" the Duke said firmly, and concentrated on his breakfast.

He knew that his small nephew was staring at him in surprise and
also with what he thought was an expression perilously near contempt.

It was an impertinence, he told himself, that should be severely
corrected, but not this morning, not when he had so many other
troubles on his hands.

Jamie had, however, started off a train of thought which returned
to his mind when he was wending his way up the moors.

Behind the Duke came, as Mr. Dunblane had predicted, a procession of mounted Clansmen, although the Duke knew that in the past
they would have walked, with the Piper playing a battle-tune to stir
their senses and accelerate their progress.

As it was over a two-hour ride to Kilcraig Castle the Duke was
grateful that at least he was permitted to travel there on horse-back,
and he guessed that his entourage had been reduced in size to fit the
availability of horses to mount them.

Nevertheless, he told himself sourly, there were quite enough, and
by the expression on his henchmen's faces they were all as ready as
Jamie had been for a fight with their traditional enemy.

The Duke, however, had no intention of doing anything but rescue
Torquil, and he hoped to create a new spirit between the Clans
which would prevent this sort of thing from happening in the future.

With the MacAuads it was a different cup of tea altogether.

The lands of the McNarns stretched eastwards for many miles and
the Clans between them and the sea were either too small to be of
any importance or were united by marriage with what amounted to
blood ties.

But all through the centuries the MacAuads, a wild, uncouth, and
savage Clan, had been an hereditary enemy whom every other Clan
hated and feared.

They shared the western border of the McNarn lands with the
Kilcraigs, and while the latter were in some ways almost a respected

enemy, the MacAuads' deeds had put them beyond the pale of any emotion save that of utter loathing.

"Touch a snake and ye'll find a MacAuad!" was a current phrase amongst the Clansmen; another said even more forcefully: "If ye go down to Hell, ye'll find the Devil is MacAuad."

Not having heard of the MacAuads since he was a boy, the Duke wondered if they were still so ferocious.

He imagined that if there was any cattle-stealing in this part of the world it would be done by the MacAuads, not as a boyish prank but deliberately to enrich themselves at another Clan's expense.

It was a clear day with just a touch of wind, the heather smelt fragrant, and the purple of it was more vivid than the Duke remembered.

There was enough water still left in the burns to make him feel sure that Lord Hinchley would catch several salmon.

It was unfortunate that he could not join his friend but instead was forced to expend his time and energy in visiting a man he had never seen, and in the uncomfortable position of a supplicant.

Then the Duke told himself that The Kilcraig would surely listen to reason.

He supposed that if he paid the full price for the cattle which Torquil had stolen, and perhaps made it more generous than the animals were worth, the whole confrontation would die down.

"Why Dunblane could not have settled the matter for me God only knows!" the Duke muttered beneath his breath.

Then he knew that that was impossible because only a Chief speaking to a Chief could negotiate problems which concerned a Clan, and Dunblane would have no authority despite his long connection with the McNarns.

The Duke's thoughts were back to his position as a Chieftain.

It had been impossible not to notice the solicitousness, which was almost an act of reverence, with which he had been helped onto the saddle of his horse and the way in which the henchmen saluted him.

The women who had been waiting at the gates to the Castle to see him leave had curtseyed while the Clansmen amongst them had lifted their bonnets and waved them at his approach.

The Duke now remembered when he was a small boy, about the same age as Jamie, saying to his father:

"Why do they love you, Papa?"

His father's answer had been simple:

"I am their Chief."

"What does Chief mean?" the little boy had insisted.

His father, speaking solemnly, almost as if he was thinking aloud, had replied:

"The Highlanders esteem it a most sublime degree of virtue to love their Chief and ply him with a blood obedience, although it be opposition to the Government and the law of the Kingdom, or even the law of God. He is their idol and they know no King but him."

The Duke repeated the words now to himself and he wondered if it was possible to find anywhere else in the world this unquestioning subservience that was not only for the Chief himself but for what he stood for in his followers' imagination.

God knows his father had not deserved such devotion, and yet he had received it just because he was invested with the aura of authority which had been handed down through the centuries.

It was somehow embarrassing, as if one looked into another man's heart and soul.

'The sooner I get back to sanity,' the Duke thought savagely, 'the better!'

He had decided before he left London that he would return South with the King on the *Royal George*.

He knew that His Majesty would be only too pleased to have him and he was quite sure that it would be an amusing voyage. They would all be able to laugh over the incidents that invariably occurred on such occasions.

The King, the Duke knew, was taking his visit very seriously.

Ever since he had decided to go to Scotland he had talked about it with an enthusiasm which surprised those in attendance, who were quite sure that he would be disappointed at what he found in the most northern part of his Kingdom.

But when George IV made up his mind to do something there were few people brave enough to dissuade him and the arrangements had gone ahead.

The Duke supposed that by this time Edinburgh was in a fervour of excitement and anticipation and he certainly had no wish to be there.

He was, however, hot and thirsty by the time they had ridden for over two hours and had the first sight of Kilcraig Castle.

The Duke had never seen it before and he realised that it was a very different building from his own.

From its vantage point on the side of the hill it would have been impossible for an enemy to approach through the valley without being seen and there was something weird and eerie about its high walls with few windows.

Vaguely at the back of his mind the Duke remembered when he

was young hearing that the Kilcraigs had ghosts and evil spirits besides ancestors who were cruel monsters, one of them having kid-
napped children to use as sacrifices in his sorceries.

The Duke had not believed such stories even when he was a boy,
and yet now, looking at the Castle in the distance, he could understand how they had arisen.

There was something about it which stirred the imagination and
would, he was quite certain, arouse to wild flights of fancy the superstitions of a primitive people who had been brought up to believe in
such things.

The Duke had long ago laughed to scorn the Celtic mythology of
giants, witches, unconquerable swordsmen, loch-monsters, precogni-
tions, stones which spoke with the voices of men, and singing trees.

In the South, while few people he knew were concerned with anything but their own amusements, even religion was spoken of with a
faint air of mockery.

While the King was obliged to attend Divine Service on Sundays,
the Duke and his contemporaries spent their Sundays like any other
day, in sport and gaming.

They were within a mile of the Castle when Mr. Dunblane moved
his horse beside the Duke's.

"From here, Your Grace," he said in a low voice, "we will all
leave our horses, with the exception of yourself."

"Why?" the Duke enquired.

"The Kilcraig, as was your father, is a stickler for custom."

The Duke was about to reply that The Kilcraig could go to Hell,
then he told himself that the purpose of the meeting was to be conciliatory, and to anger the old man before it had even started would be
foolish.

"Arrange things as you wish, Dunblane," he said curtly and rode
on.

He was, however, well aware that the horses were being left in the
charge of henchmen and a procession had formed behind him on
foot.

First came Dunblane as his immediate body-guard and with him
should have been his kinsmen, if Torquil had not been a prisoner of
the Kilcraigs and Jamie too young.

Then came the Bard, an old man whom the Duke remembered
since his father's time.

Barding was hereditary and carried with it a grant of land. The
Highlands had no written history and a man's reputation and the
memory of it could mount or fall on the tongue of the Bard.

The Duke wondered wryly what would be said of him when he was dead, and thought it unlikely that his behaviour would inspire an epic poem.

Behind the Bard came the Piper, who now was playing the marching-tune of the McNarns—a tune which led them into battle and accompanied them on their last journey to the cemetery of their forefathers.

Behind the Piper should have been the *Bladier,* the Chief spokesman, a golden-voiced man of debate and argument who knew every precedent in every quarrel.

If he was there he was unnecessary, for the Duke had every intention of speaking for himself and certainly allowing no-one else to interview on his behalf.

Behind these there should have been a gillie to carry his broadsword and buckler and several others who in the past would have been swordsmen, axemen, bowmen, or musket-men.

It was compulsory for a Clan which was visited by the Chief of another to bed and feed these wild, often savage men without protest.

Except in the case of a Clan like the MacAuads, once having accepted a Clan's hospitality and eaten their salt, there would be no more fighting until they had left the land.

As they drew nearer to Kilcraig Castle the Duke saw the Clansmen waiting for him.

He was surprised to see so many of them wearing the tartan. He had been told in the South that after the ban on it had been lifted in 1799, many of the Scots, after years of persecution by the English, had been too lethargic to reintroduce their own tartan.

Instead they had kept to the anonymous, dark-dyed garments they had worn during the persecution.

The Duke now realised he had made a mistake in not listening to Mr. Dunblane and coming attired in the regalia of a Chieftain.

Then he thought angrily that it did not matter in the least what The Kilcraig or anyone else thought.

They would accept him as he was or be damned to them!

He was received with courtesy but otherwise in silence, and when he dismounted at the door of the Castle he was led by a man resplendent in kilt, badger sporran, and silver-buttoned jacket up a narrow uncarpeted stone staircase to the first floor.

The Duke knew he was being taken to the Chief's Room.

His own Chief's Room, having been redecorated and improved by

William Adam, was one of the most impressive and magnificent rooms in the whole building.

He saw at a glance as he entered the Chief's Room of the Kilcraigs that it could be very little changed since the Clansmen had first plotted how to harass and kill their enemies, and bowmen had been on the alert on the Castle turrets to watch for them.

The floor was covered only with fur rugs, and the furniture, of heavy, unpolished oak, would doubtless, if it could talk, have told strange tales.

The windows were narrow so that the sunlight seemed to be excluded, and the great claymores hanging on the walls and the flags and banners captured in battle gave the place a sinister air.

It was easy to believe many of the unpleasant and frightening legends which had grown and multiplied about the Castle down the centuries.

At the far end of the room, in front of a high-backed chair which was almost like a throne, stood The Kilcraig.

The Duke saw that banked on either side of him were his kinsmen, all wearing the Kilcraig tartan.

Again the Duke wished he could rival their splendour and again admitted to himself that he had made a mistake.

Because he resented the show that had been put on to impress if not to intimidate him, he walked languidly down the long room, looking round him with a supercilious air.

He was followed only by Robert Dunblane, the rest of those who accompanied him having been left outside the front door.

He reached The Kilcraig and was annoyed to find that his host stood on a dais which made him half a foot taller than he was in reality.

The Duke was, however, determined to take the initiative and before The Kilcraig could speak he held out his hand.

"We have never had the chance of meeting before, Kilcraig," he said. "May I say that I am delighted to make your acquaintance?"

It was almost with an air of reluctance that The Kilcraig took the Duke's proffered hand.

He was a man of seventy or over, with dead white hair and a beard. He carried his shoulders like a soldier and exuded pride in every inch of his bearing.

"Nay, we've not met before, My Lord Duke," he said, speaking with a broad Scottish accent. "But I welcome you to my Castle."

He released the Duke's hand and introduced him to his sons, his nephews, and then his grandsons.

The Duke knew instinctively that they had no wish to shake his hand, but regarded him warily. He thought too that they were somewhat bewildered by his appearance, looking at him as if he were a strange animal of which they had heard but never seen.

The Kilcraig indicated a chair on the right of his own, and as the Duke sat down servants brought whisky and set on the table a haggis, bannocks, girdle scones, and other Scottish dishes.

This, the Duke knew, was not luncheon but merely the sort of food that would be offered to a traveller to abate the exhaustion of a long journey.

He drank a little of the whisky and waved away the food. Then, determined once again to take the initiative, he said:

"I think, Kilcraig, we could serve our interests better if we spoke alone on the matter which concerns my visit."

The Chief's heavy white eye-brows shot up.

"Alone?" he queried.

"Why not?" the Duke enquired. "I have the unfair disadvantage of having no kinsmen, while there are so many reinforcements on your side of the table that the odds are heavily against me."

He spoke lightly, with a note of amusement in his voice, and he knew that he surprised The Kilcraig.

"Alone!" the old man repeated under his breath.

"I think between us we can see that justice is done," the Duke said.

The Kilcraig snapped his fingers and without comment his kinsmen filed slowly down the long room and out through the door.

The Duke leant back at his ease.

"That is better!" he said. "And now we can talk as man to man. Shall I start by apologising for the mischievous and very tiresome behaviour of my nephew who, I understand, is somewhat wild and out-of-hand?"

The Kilcraig did not speak but stared at the Duke in a penetrating manner as if he would look beneath the surface of his casual air.

The Duke again sipped his whisky. It was unpleasant, but he was thirsty.

"Torquil McNarn was captured by my men in the act of stealing a valuable animal," The Kilcraig said at length.

"So I have been told," the Duke answered. "It was extremely reprehensible, but no more than a boyish prank."

"It has happened before. Several of the crofters on the borders of my land have complained in the past few months."

"Of losing cattle?"

"In one instance several sheep."

"They must of course be recompensed," the Duke said. "But I am sure you will agree with me that adolescent boys get up to mischief when they have nothing to do, and that is something I intend to remedy in the future."

"What sort of recompense did you have in mind?" The Kilcraig asked.

The Duke made a gesture with his hand.

"Anything you consider adequate for those who have lost their animals."

"My sons insist that Torquil McNarn be sent to Edinburgh and punished by the Courts."

"Surely that is making rather heavy weather over what is nothing very serious?" the Duke questioned. "The days of feuding and the demand for vengeance by our Clans are over."

"Do you think that is possible?" The Kilcraig asked.

"Of course!" the Duke replied. "The world has become more enlightened. The feuds of the past are as out-of-date as the Dodo!"

"It is a pity you cannot say that to the MacAuads!"

The Duke wondered why the MacAuads had been introduced into the conversation.

"I remember that years ago they were always up to some devilment," he said reflectively. "They have not changed in any way?"

"If anything they are worse!" the Kilcraig answered. "I am prepared to admit there was no question of the McNarns as a Clan conniving with your nephew, but where the MacAuads are concerned they attack your Clan and mine, not in isolated instances, but continuously, viciously, and with premeditated violence!"

"I can hardly believe that!" the Duke exclaimed.

"It is true," The Kilcraig said, "and that is why, Duke, I have a proposition to put to you."

"A proposition?" the Duke questioned.

"I have been thinking over this for some time," The Kilcraig said slowly, "and the behaviour of Torquil McNarn has only accelerated a decision I have come to reluctantly but of necessity."

"And what is that?" the Duke enquired.

"It is that if we are to withstand the assaults of the MacAuads, then your Clan and mine should become affiliated by the oath of friendship."

The Duke looked at the old man in sheer astonishment.

In his wildest imagination he had never expected that such a proposition would have come from The Kilcraig.

All his boyhood he had been brought up to consider him a natural enemy, not in the same category as the MacAuads, but nevertheless an enemy.

He had hoped to create a better relationship between the Clans but nothing as sweeping as this.

There was silence until he managed to say:

"Do you really believe such a solution is possible?"

"I think it is not only possible but imperative!" The Kilcraig answered. "We cannot go on as we are. Your nephew has taken some cattle from us, but that is nothing to what is happening on our borders which march with the MacAuads."

His voice deepened with anger as he went on:

"Some of our more prosperous farmers have even paid blackmail, but the MacAuads in their treachery not only took the mail but waited for a moonlit night and took the animals as well!"

He struck the table and continued:

"Only by guarding every mile of our land can I protect my own people, but the burden is growing too heavy. The marauding thieves get through, however much we try to stop them."

"And you think the McNarns would help you?" the Duke asked.

"Look at the map," The Kilcraig answered. "If we combine we will be twice the size, if not more, of the MacAuads."

"I suppose that is true," the Duke murmured.

"They are not only thieves and bullies, treacherous and without honour, they are also leaderless," The Kilcraig answered. "Their Chief prefers the soft living of the South, like many others who have deserted those who trust them."

The old man paused, then said:

"A Clan without a Chief is like a ship without a rudder."

The Duke was silent. After a moment The Kilcraig asked:

"Will you listen to my proposition, My Lord Duke?"

"I am very willing to do so," the Duke answered.

"It is this," The Kilcraig said. "I will release Torquil McNarn and the three youths with him. I will give you my sacred oath on the dirk that the Kilcraigs will live in peace with the McNarns, and you will give me yours. To make sure that all those who follow us know that the hand of friendship wipes out the blood that has been shed between us, you will marry my daughter!"

For a moment the Duke felt he could not have heard The Kilcraig aright.

It was with an effort that he prevented his mouth from dropping open in sheer surprise.

Then in a voice which sounded strange even to himself he asked: "Did you say that I should—marry your daughter?"

"She is of marriageable age, but I have not yet found a husband for her," The Kilcraig said. "As the Duchess of Strathnarn she will be respected by both our own people and yours. There will be no problems between us in the future and we can concentrate on repressing the MacAuads."

It all sounded extremely reasonable, the Duke thought, as set forth in the deep, slow voice of The Kilcraig.

Then he told himself he had no intention of marrying anyone, least of all a raw, uncivilised Scottish girl, who as far as he was concerned was as remote from his chosen way of life as an Aborigine from Australia.

Aloud he said:

"I certainly agree to your idea of uniting our Clans to our mutual benefit, but I am sure you will understand that I have no intention of marrying anyone, preferring for the time being at any rate to remain a bachelor."

The Kilcraig pushed back his chair.

"In which case, Your Grace, there is no point in continuing this conversation. Torquil McNarn will go to trial and doubtless the Judges in Edinburgh will not be overly hard on him."

The Duke did not rise. He merely sat still, his eyes on the old Chief, trying to think of a way out of this impasse.

"Surely," he said in a conciliatory tone, "the fact that I am prepared to agree to the oath of friendship is a step forward that does not need my private involvement to the extent of marriage."

The Kilcraig did not move. He merely said:

"First, I doubt if your Clan or mine will accept that things are greatly changed without a physical sign that we are affiliated closer than can be shown by words."

The Duke had to acknowledge that this was very likely the truth. What was more, as the majority of the Highlanders could not read, there would be some difficulty in making them understand exactly what was involved unless they had a wedding, or some equally sensational ceremony in which to take part.

"Secondly," The Kilcraig went on, "what is to stop you, once Torquil McNarn has been handed over to you, from repudiating our arrangement?"

"Would you doubt my word of honour?" the Duke asked sharply.

The Kilcraig smiled cynically—it was little more than raising the corners of his thin lips.

"It has happened in the past. You will remember that in 1423 your ancestor made a bargain with mine not to invade the northern approaches to our land."

This was a piece of history that the Duke had forgotten, if he had ever heard of it.

"The Kilcraigs were relaxed and at their ease," the old Chief went on, "and the McNarns, creeping through the heather, took them by surprise. They killed fifty of our Clansmen, raped their women, and carried off their cattle."

There was a note in the Chief's voice which told the Duke that the act of treachery was as vivid and real to him as if it had happened yesterday.

"I have therefore made up my mind," The Kilcraig continued, "that only by a marriage between you and my daughter will peace come to our troubled people."

"Are you seriously telling me," the Duke asked, "that if I do not agree fully to what you suggest you will send my nephew to Edinburgh?"

"My men are waiting to escort him there," The Kilcraig said, "and my eldest son will lay his crime before the Justices."

The Duke was still.

He knew that if he abandoned Torquil and those with him to their fate he would not only find it impossible to face his Clansmen but his own name would be dragged through the dust.

He imagined how quickly the Press in Edinburgh would become aware of the fact that the Duke of Strathnarn's nephew and heir was in the dock as a common thief.

The publicity would doubtless coincide with the visit of the King, and the Duke thought he would be a laughing-stock not only to all the other Scottish noblemen but to his English friends who were to accompany His Majesty to Edinburgh.

He felt like a cornered rat and it seemed to him there was no possible escape.

To play for time he asked rather feebly:

"Is your daughter in agreement with this proposition?"

"My daughter does as she is told, as do all my family," The Kilcraig answered. "She will serve you with the same obedience and loyalty she has given to me."

The Duke thought that if he was in his right senses he would rise to his feet and tell The Kilcraig that this was blackmail of the worst type and he had no intention of submitting to it.

Then he knew that the old man was as obstinate and determined as his father would have been and that nothing would budge him once he had made up his mind.

It was part of the spirit of the Scots, who would die rather than surrender, who would fight to their last breath rather than admit defeat.

For a moment the Duke wondered if he was dreaming and would wake to find himself in his house in London with no more important decision to make than in which style he should tie his cravat.

He wanted to play for time, to discuss his predicament with someone cleverer than himself.

Then he knew without asking that The Kilcraig would not wait. He had already said that the Clansmen were ready to escort Torquil to Edinburgh, and the Duke was sure he had not lied.

He looked at the rugged countenance of the Chief and saw a granite-like hardness that recalled the past.

It was how his father had looked when he was determined to beat him into submission, when he gave orders that he was forced to obey because he had not the strength to fight him.

Almost as if it came to him from a far distance he heard his own voice saying:

"If I agree to your suggestion, Kilcraig, will you allow me to take back with me my nephew and those whom you hold?"

The Kilcraig made no movement; only his voice, quiet yet authoritative, replied:

"Torquil McNarn will come to your wedding, which I suggest should be held at the same time as you receive the homage not only of your own Clan but also of mine."

"But that, I believe, is scheduled to take place in the next day or so," the Duke protested.

He remembered that Mr. Dunblane had intimated that the McNarns were gathering from all parts of his land and he had known without being told what this would entail.

"Exactly!" The Kilcraig said. "And because yours is the older Clan, Clola will be married at your Castle, and you will present her to both our people at the same time."

It was a clever idea, the Duke thought, and he knew The Kilcraig must have been cogitating over it and thinking out every detail for a long time.

The ghastly thing was, he could think of no possible way to prevent it from taking place.

There must be something he could say, some loophole, some escape, he told himself, and felt his mind turning over and over in an effort to free himself from a noose which seemed to be tightening round his throat.

"I suppose . . ." he began.

The Kilcraig moved impatiently.

"Will you eat with us, Duke?" he asked. "Or would you be on your way home?"

It was an ultimatum and the Duke had the feeling that whichever way he decided there would be no appeal, no second chance, no possible way in which he could extricate himself.

He longed as he had never longed in his life before to hurl defiance at The Kilcraig and tell him to do his worst.

Then he knew it was impossible—impossible to betray his own blood, impossible to wash his hands of the inevitable consequences.

Slowly and with dignity he rose to his feet.

"I am extremely hungry, Kilcraig," he replied.

*   *   *

Afterwards as they rode home the Duke could remember only the expression of sheer astonishment on Robert Dunblane's face when after their meal was finished The Kilcraig announced to his kinsmen who had sat at the table with them the decision which had been reached.

If Mr. Dunblane was surprised, so were they.

"Join with the McNarns?" one of The Kilcraig's older sons enquired.

Although he spoke quietly it might have been a yell of savage protest.

"This is our only chance to control the MacAuads," The Kilcraig replied.

The men did not mention their sister Clola, but the Duke knew by their uneasy glances that they were thinking of her.

Finally The Kilcraig toasted the Duke and the Duke was forced to toast him in return.

"May our hearts be as closely united as our hands and our tongues," The Kilcraig said finally in Gaelic.

With an effort the Duke managed to answer in the same language:

"May your wish come true."

He was bemused, bewildered, and only as he rode away from Kilcraig Castle, followed by his procession with the bag-pipes swirling out, did he remember that he had not in fact seen his future bride.

For a moment he tightened the reins and brought his horse to a standstill.

Surely it was an omission that was not only fantastic from his own point of view but also an insult to the woman he was to marry.

Then he told himself that if The Kilcraig had meant them to meet, he would have suggested it.

The old Chief had been, the Duke thought furiously, in complete command of the whole situation from the very beginning.

He had had everything planned in his mind, he had been determined to have his own way, and he had succeeded without any opposition.

"I am weak, feeble, puerile!" the Duke flayed himself.

But he still found it was impossible to think of any means by which he could have refused The Kilcraig without sacrificing not only Torquil but his own pride and honour.

Once or twice already there had been various scurrilous reports written about him in the newspapers in London, and a cartoon had depicted one of his amatory adventures in a manner which had made him grind his teeth.

It had been nothing half as bad as what was said about the King, who paid the cartoonists "hushmoney."

At the same time, something savage and unrestrained in the Duke had made him feel as if he was prepared to run his sword through the body of the artist who had lampooned him or blow his brains out with a bullet from his duelling-pistol.

He had in fact taken part in quite a number of duels, and, although he had never killed a man, he had come perilously near to it in one instance.

He thought now as he rode across the heather that it would give him great pleasure to be present at The Kilcraig's funeral, however much the old man might enjoy himself at his wedding.

He wanted to swear aloud to relieve his furious conviction that he had been out-manoeuvred by a very clever antagonist.

Although he might be The Kilcraig's superior as a Chieftain, he was certainly his inferior when it came to brain-power.

Could it be possible that this uncivilised savage, Chief of a Clan of which South of the border nobody had ever heard, was shrewd enough to humiliate the dashing, much-admired sportsman who was a friend of the King?

He knew that he held a position amongst the other Bucks and Dandies of St. James's that was almost unique.

He was aware that he was sought out by Statesmen and older men because of the wit and intelligence of his conversation, and certainly as far as women were concerned for his other attractions.

Yet within twenty-four hours of landing in Scotland he had been out-witted, out-manoeuvred, and treated as a pawn in the hand of a man who he was quite certain had never travelled South of Edinburgh.

It was impossible for the Duke to speak to Mr. Dunblane of what he was suffering.

When he arrived back at the Castle to find Lord Hinchley delighted with himself for having caught three salmon, he told him briefly what had occurred.

"You have to marry this woman?" Lord Hinchley ejaculated. "I do not believe you!"

"It is true!"

"Good God! I would not have believed that such a thing was possible if you had not told me so with your own lips."

"You must see that I have no alternative!"

"It is inhuman! Barbaric! Just what I should have expected of these savages!"

"What could I do?" the Duke asked.

"I do realise that it was impossible for you to abandon the boy, but to have to marry a woman you have never seen. . . !"

"It would make it no better if I had," the Duke said gloomily.

He sounded so depressed that Lord Hinchley rose from where he was sitting to pour out a glass of brandy and hand it to the Duke.

"There is only one consolation," he said slowly as he did so.

"What is that?" the Duke asked, with not a flicker of hope in his voice.

"You will have to marry her—I see that," Lord Hinchley replied. "Then get her with child and leave her. Come South and forget the whole incident."

He paused before he added in a more cheerful voice:

"After all, the fact that you are married should certainly not restrict your activities in London. The last dozen women with whom you amused yourself all had husbands."

"I suppose that is true," the Duke admitted.

"Then why worry?" Lord Hinchley asked. "Married or unmarried, they will still find you the best-looking and most amusing man in London, and Scotland will be very far away."

"As you say, William, Scotland will be very far away," the Duke repeated.

He raised his glass.

"I shall be able to drink not to absent friends but to my absent wife—and may she never come South!"

CHAPTER THREE

Clola Kilcraig stared at herself in the mirror and thought it was impossible that this should be her wedding-day.

Ever since her father had told her she was to marry the Duke of Strathnarn she had felt that she was living in a dream and would wake to find that it was all a figment of her imagination, which her family had often threatened would get her into trouble.

She had been a dreamer all her life, and to her the superstitions and legends not only of the Kilcraigs but also of the other Clans were part of the mountains, the glens, the burns, and the moors that she loved.

She had listened when she was small to the stories her Nurse had told her of snow-maidens, elves, and ghosts, and thought she heard and saw them.

When she grew older she had sat at the feet of the Bard while he recited long poems which bored her brothers but which she found entrancing and stimulating to her thoughts and feelings.

There were books at the Castle that had accumulated over the years, but no-one read them or was even aware of their existence, except for Clola.

Only when she went to Edinburgh to stay with her grandmother had she found in literature all that she vaguely sensed within herself but had not been able to put into words.

Her visits to Edinburgh had, she realised, altered her whole life in a way she could never explain to her brothers without hurting their pride and their belief that the whole world began and ended on their own lands.

They had been to school and Edinburgh University but they had hated every moment of it and had lived only to return to their farming and to obeying their father implicitly because he had not only bred them but was also their Chieftain.

Clola had visited Edinburgh first with her mother when she was twelve.

It had been difficult for Lady Janet Kilcraig to see much of her family, whose lands lay South of Edinburgh and were therefore inaccessible at many times of the year, owing to the roughness of the roads.

But the Countess of Borrabul had written, saying that she was ill, and even The Kilcraig could not forbid his wife to visit her mother, who might be near to death.

Lady Janet had therefore taken her youngest daughter with her and set off on the long and arduous drive to Edinburgh, the roads being at times a morass of mud and at other times under water from swollen burns and flooded lochs.

But they had reached the city safely, and Clola would never forget how impressed she had been with the thousand-year-old Castle standing on a great rock, the wide, busy streets, the Palace with its memories of Mary, Queen of Scots, and the elegance of the people she met.

The Countess, who seemed in surprisingly good health considering that she had written so dramatically to demand her daughter's presence, had exclaimed in horror when she saw her clothes and the rough garments worn by Clola.

"They are suitable enough, Mama, for the life we lead," Lady Janet Kilcraig had protested.

But the Countess had ordered dressmakers, furriers, milliners, and shoe- and glove-makers to call, and had made long lists of what they would require.

Clola and her mother had been fitted out in beautiful, expensive gowns, which they knew would be quite useless when they returned home.

In Edinburgh for the first time Clola had heard music that was not played on the bag-pipes, and she listened to intelligent people who talked about things other than feuds, vengeance, and the price of cattle.

She had cried when she was obliged to return home, and her grandmother when kissing her good-bye had said over her head:

"This child must be properly educated. She will be a beauty when she grows up, but who is going to see her but grouse and stags if you keep her shut up in that gloomy, ghost-ridden Castle of yours?"

Her mother had laughed, but when three years later she died, the Countess of Borrabul, by using the excuse that she might not live long, had persuaded The Kilcraig to send Clola to Edinburgh.

For nearly three years Clola had lived a life that was so completely different from everything she had known previously that it had a special magic of its own.

Not the magic of the mountains and the moors, but a magic never-theless, in that she could feel her mind expanding and broadening as she learnt the subjects which before had been incomprehensible.

Most important of all, she could listen to the Concerts that were given at the Theatre in Edinburgh and even occasionally hear an Opera.

She was not, however, allowed to go to school; for that, the Countess had told her, was not correct for daughters of the nobility, wherever their brothers might be sent.

But she had had teachers for every subject and she thought there was so much history round her that it was almost unnecessary to open the books on it.

When she was eighteen and had been launched into Society the previous winter, the tragedy her grandmother had so often used as a pretext to get her own way happened, and the Countess died, leaving Clola to return home.

She had not forgotten what the Castle meant in her life. She had not ceased to love her brothers and even her father, although she was afraid of him. But she knew, when she was honest with herself, that life at home was going to be restrictive.

She would not feel as she had felt in Edinburgh that her mind, like her imagination, had wings which would carry her up into the sky.

She found, however, that her years in the city had given her a deeper appreciation of the beauty of the mountains and wild moors that had been so much a part of her childhood.

Sitting in the heather, she could look out over the glen beneath her and hear music on the breeze and feel that it carried a special mes-sage to her heart, as even the great orchestras she had listened to in Edinburgh had been unable to do.

Apart from her imagination and a certain perception which her old Nurse had told her made her "fey," Clola had a practical side.

On arrival at the Castle she put away her silken gowns and al-lowed her sisters-in-law and the servants to weave for her home-spun garments in which she could climb the hills or ford a burn without their coming to any harm.

She had also been intelligent enough to assimilate herself quickly into the family circle, keeping her newfound knowledge to herself and listening to her brothers with an attention which both pleased and flattered them.

She felt at times that her father sensed she was not as complaisant as he required, and although she had never defied him she knew per-ceptively that he expected her sometime to do so.

In fact, the first time during the three months since her return home that she had been involved in an argument with him was after the Duke had left.

Like everyone else in the Castle, Clola had been excited at the thought of his visit. She had been told when Torquil McNarn was captured what a score it was over their enemies the McNarns.

Having heard noises the previous night and wondered what was occurring, she was actually surprised and horrified when she learnt the following morning at breakfast what had occurred.

It was her elder brother Andrew who told her that they had waited in the darkness on the border of their land to capture Torquil McNarn and three other lads in the very act of thieving.

"Thieving?" Clola had questioned.

"Not for the first time," Andrew replied. "But now he'll pay the penalty. I have always hoped to catch a man in the act, but I did not expect such a prize prisoner as the Duke's nephew!"

"Surely the McNarns will be very angry?" Clola said.

"Undoubtedly," Andrew replied. "And now we will wait to see what they do about it."

Clola had clasped her hands together in horror.

She hated the thought of fighting, violence, and bloodshed. There had been far too much of it in their history.

But she knew that if she objected, her brothers would merely despise her for her weakness and, what was more, would ignore any protest she might make.

To them, a woman's place was in the home, looking after her babies and superintending the kitchen and the Still-Room. If she had time on her hands she would weave and spin as the Scottish womenfolk had done since the beginning of time.

But at least Torquil's capture had given them something different to talk about and had brought new visitors to the Castle.

First had come Mr. Dunblane and the fathers of the three boys who had been captured at the same time as Torquil McNarn.

Clola had not been allowed to be present at their meeting with her father, but she had watched them arrive and had peeped at them as they ascended the stairs to the Chief's Room.

She had thought Mr. Dunblane looked charming and very like some of the interesting, intelligent men she had met in Edinburgh.

The Clansmen with him had stared at The Kilcraig, who had glared back, and Clola was sure it was only by the greatest exertion of self-control that they were not at one another's throats.

She had almost forgotten in Edinburgh how violent the feuds between the neighbouring Clans could be and how the hatred that had been engendered could easily make a man into a murderer.

When Mr. Dunblane had ridden away she had learnt that her father had refused to negotiate with anyone but the Chieftain of the McNarns, the Duke of Strathnarn.

She had heard him spoken of when she was in Edinburgh.

She knew that he had run away from home when he was sixteen because he could not tolerate his father's discipline and that he now lived in the South.

Her father had the utmost contempt for the Duke's maternal grandfather, who, although he was a Scot, was a Lowlander and had not taken part in the Jacobite Rebellion. Instead, he had accepted the favours of the English and was welcomed at the Court of St. James.

"A renegade! A traitor! A man who has betrayed his own people!" were just some of the insults hurled by The Kilcraig at him and all Scots like him.

But in Edinburgh Clola had begun to understand why so many Chieftains found the life of the Highlands too hard and too restrictive for them.

In the previous centuries the Chiefs had been men of contradictions, civilised savages whose interests and experiences were often wider than most Englishmen's.

Many of them could speak Gaelic, English, and French, as well as Greek and Latin, and they had sent their sons to be educated at Universities in Glasgow, Edinburgh, Paris, and Rome.

They had come back wearing lace at their throats, with a liking for French claret, and able to dance the Highland reels as well as the minuets of the South.

To the French and indeed to the English, the Chieftains had been attractive and rather picturesque foreigners.

When they were with their Clans they were Kings, but of very small Kingdoms and with few amusements other than shooting and fishing, Bardic poems and wild pipe-music.

For the earlier Chieftains, in the sixteenth century, there had been continuous Clan battles and cattle-raids to occupy them.

There had also been hunting on the high mountains where in those days stags, wolves, and cats abounded. Deer-hunts with cross-bows and broadswords were a spectacle which the Bards would re-create in the long, dark winter evenings when there was nothing to do but sit round the great peat fires.

But the Chieftains who had travelled were beginning to find it a bore to return to their own country.

In one way Clola could sympathise with them, but she knew that a Clan without its Chieftain was helpless and, like the MacAuads, deteriorated until the words "savage" and "barbarian" were an apt description.

When she thought of this Clola began to be afraid that the soothsayers' predictions of the curse that would come upon the Highlands and the suffering and misery which would ensue from it would come true.

It would be called, she had been told, *Bliadhna Nan Caorach*— "The Years of the Sheep."

When she was in Edinburgh she had learnt that successful sheepfarming in the far North had resulted first in large-scale emigration to Canada, and how when other Highlanders refused to emigrate they were evicted.

News travelled slowly.

In Edinburgh the public had not been alerted to what was happening in Sutherland until after Clola had come to live with her grandmother.

Then people talked of little else and every day brought further tales of crofts being burnt over defenceless heads, of cruelties which lost nothing in the telling, and the determination of many Highland Chiefs to follow the lead set by the Marquis of Stafford in Sutherland.

Riots followed the evictions in Ross, and the more people talked, the more Clola's heart began to be wrung with the thought of those who had been forgotten and betrayed by their Chieftains.

They lived, she was told, in caves by the seashore or were forced aboard the ships which carried them, defenceless and half-starved, to the other side of the world.

She began to understand as she never had before what her father meant to the Clansmen who followed him, and she knew that for him to betray his own people in such a manner would be unthinkable.

She was sure that when her father died Andrew would take his place and be the guide and leader of the Kilcraigs in exactly the same way.

But she could not help wondering whether the Marquis of Narn, whom she had heard spoken of in Edinburgh, would return from the South to take the place of his father, the Duke of Strathnarn.

Several of the gentlemen whom her grandmother entertained had met the Marquis in London.

They spoke of his success on the Turf, of his expertise at driving a Phaeton drawn by six horses, and also of his attraction for women.

The latter was of course not spoken of openly in Clola's presence. Their voices would be lowered when they discussed such things with her grandmother, who delighted in learning of the scandals and the *affaires de coeur* which took place at Carlton House.

Yet, invariably when such whispered conversations took place, Clola heard the name Narn repeated and rerepeated.

When Mr. Dunblane had left and The Kilcraig had told his family that he would not negotiate the release of Torquil McNarn except with the Chief of his Clan, Clola had asked:

"Now that the old Duke is dead, the Chief will be the Marquis of Narn?"

"That is right," The Kilcraig agreed.

"But he is in the South. Will he come North?"

She thought there was a faint twinkle in her father's eye as he replied confidently:

"He will come!"

"How can you be sure?" she persisted. "Supposing like other Chieftains he prefers the South?"

"He will come!" The Kilcraig repeated.

"You really think this incident of cattle-stealing will force him to return to his own people?" Andrew questioned.

Clola had been surprised that her brother appreciated the situation, because she thought from all she had heard it was very unlikely that the Marquis had any interest in Scotland or Scottish affairs.

"Blood is thicker than water," The Kilcraig said. "The Chieftain of the McNarns will come home!"

He had been right, and it had been exciting!

Long before the Duke's ship had docked in Perth, the Kilcraigs as well as his own Clan were aware that he was on his way.

Clola was not surprised, as visitors to Scotland were, that somehow without newspapers everyone always knew what was happening in other Clans, even though they hated one another and did not speak.

Her father knew the very hour that the Duke would arrive; and when the day after his arrival a messenger from Narn Castle came with a letter, Clola sensed an atmosphere of triumph in the very air.

With the other women in the Castle she watched the Duke's approach.

The others were scandalised by the fact that he was not wearing the customary kilt.

"A Chieftain dressed like a Sassenach!" they scoffed. "Does he mean to insult us?"

They speculated amongst themselves as to whether The Kilcraig would refuse to see him, but to Clola the Duke seemed very elegant and exactly as she had expected him to look.

She had known he would be handsome and as tall as, if not taller than, her brothers. She had been sure he would also have an air of authority and consequence that they had never achieved.

There had been many handsome Scots in Edinburgh who moved with a pride and assurance which was somehow different from that of those who came from the South. But the Duke surpassed them all.

When Clola watched him walk from the Chief's Room at her father's side she had thought that the McNarns were fortunate in having a Chieftain worthy of their long history and the deeds of valour which had been attributed to their forefathers.

As the Duke rode away she had watched from an upper window until she saw the procession behind him mount their horses. Then with a little sigh she went down the twisting stone stairs to be told that her father wished to speak to her.

Because he had summoned her to the Chief's Room she expected that what he had to say might be of significance, but his actual words had rung in her ears like the firing of a cannon.

"In three days' time you are to marry the Chief of the McNarns," The Kilcraig announced briefly.

For a moment Clola was speechless. Then she asked:

"D'do you . . . mean the . . . Duke of Strathnarn? B-but . . . why?"

Her father then told her the terms he had imposed for the release of Torquil McNarn.

Clola drew in her breath.

"How could you . . . ask such a thing of him?" she enquired. "And how, indeed, can he . . . agree?"

"If he had not agreed, his nephew and your brother Andrew would be setting out for Edinburgh at this moment with those who would give evidence against him."

"But, Father, I cannot . . . marry like that. It is . . . wrong. It is not a . . . civilised way of doing such a thing."

Her father looked at her from under his eye-brows in the searching manner which had always made her afraid as a child.

"Are you challenging my decision, Clola?" he enquired.

"You know, Father, that I am always prepared to do as you wish," Clola answered. "At the same time, surely this is too precipitate. Could any marriage succeed in such circumstances? I have not even met the Duke."

"There will be plenty of time after you are married to get to know each other," The Kilcraig said, "and it would be difficult to gather the Clansmen together for a second time when they are engaged on the harvest."

Clola knew that this was true. To show their allegiance to their new leader, the McNarns would be coming now from all over their territory.

For many it would be a long and tiring journey, and they would be forced to leave their wives to look after their cattle and to bring in what harvest was ready.

They would certainly resent, if they did not find it impossible, having to leave home a second time for the marriage of their Chieftain in the months before the winter made it difficult for them to travel.

She could appreciate the practicality of what her father had decided. At the same time, her instinct told her that from her personal point of view and from that of the Duke it was intolerable.

"Please . . . Father, I do not . . . wish to be . . . married in such haste," she pleaded.

"You will obey me," The Kilcraig replied, and she knew that nothing she could say, nothing she could do, would have any influence on him.

What was more, as the Duke had agreed to what her father had asked, she knew that the joining of the Clans was a victory that nothing would make him forgo.

"Unfortunately, there will be no time for a trousseau," Andrew's wife had said almost gleefully. "But you have enough already to last you for a dozen years or more."

She was usually a placid woman and made Andrew a good wife, but it would have been impossible for any woman not to feel envious of the great trunkloads of clothes which Clola had brought home with her from Edinburgh.

Her grandmother's one great extravagance had been clothes: she loved the new fashions, which thrilled her in the same way that her granddaughter was thrilled by music; and a new style of the hair would bring a light to her eyes even when she was ill.

When she was almost on her death-bed she had said to Clola:

"Do not waste the things in my wardrobe. Take them with you when you return home. You can easily refashion the gowns, and the wraps trimmed with fur will keep you warm."

There was a faintly sarcastic note in her voice, as if she remem-

bered the bleakness of the Castle where her granddaughter would
live after her death, and because she only wished to please her
grandmother Clola had done as she had asked.

She had thought as she travelled northwards that she would give
her sister-in-law anything she desired from her plenteous wardrobe.

But on arrival she found that her own gowns were far too small
for her, as were those that had belonged to her grandmother, who
had grown thin in her old age.

What was more, Clola realised that she would consider it an insult
to be offered clothes that had been worn by somebody else.

Her ball-gowns, and the silks, satins, and muslins which she had
worn in the afternoons, were therefore left in the trunks, ready now,
she thought, to be carried just as they were over the moors to Narn
Castle.

Fortunately, and it would have been surprising if she had not, she
had a dress that would be very appropriate as a wedding-gown.

Her grandmother had bought it for her with a number of others, a
few weeks before her death, because she had learnt of the likelihood
of George IV coming to Edinburgh.

The date had not been settled but the rumour had spread like
wildfire, and at the first mention of such a tremendously important
occasion her grandmother had had the dressmakers come round and
had ordered gowns for herself and for Clola.

She was too weak at the time to do anything but superintend the
fitting from her bed.

Although her Doctors had shaken their heads and said it was too
much excitement, Clola knew it gave her great pleasure, and she
stood for hours, fitting the gowns, enduring endless amendments, additions, and alterations.

She could not help feeling when her grandmother died that it was
desperately sad that she should not have had the pleasure of being in
Edinburgh for all the festivities that were planned to welcome the
King.

No-one would have enjoyed them more; no lady, she felt, would
have been more outstanding. But by the time the date for the King's
arrival was fixed, her grandmother was already buried and Clola was
back at home at Kilcraig.

Now she looked at the gown lying on the bed in the small room
that she occupied in one of the towers.

Two storeys above her was Torquil McNarn's prison. He had been
confined there in solitude since the night he had been brought to the
Castle.

Clola had suggested that she might visit him, but her brother Andrew had been horrified and had said harshly:

"We will not have you talking to a McNarn!"

"He is only a boy," Clola protested, "and it must be very lonely for him up there."

"He will fare far worse in a prison in Edinburgh," Andrew answered savagely, and the others laughed.

Hamish, however, who was Clola's youngest brother, and about the same age as Torquil McNarn, had whispered to her later:

"Don't worry about our prisoner, Clola. He's all right."

"How do you know?" she asked.

"I've seen him!"

"You have done that? I thought Andrew kept the key to his room."

"I know where he hides it," Hamish said with a grin. "So I've talked to Torquil McNarn and I took him one or two things to make him more comfortable."

"That was kind of you."

"He was unlucky," Hamish answered. "I've got away with what he did half a dozen times!"

"You mean you have stolen from the McNarns?"

Hamish grinned at her.

"Of course! It's a fine sport as long as one isn't caught."

"Oh, Hamish, how could you do anything so dangerous?" Clola exclaimed. "If Father knew, he would be furious!"

"I bet he does know," Hamish answered. "But he wouldn't stop me getting the better of the McNarns. It's the MacAuads he's afraid of."

"Afraid?" Clola questioned.

Hamish looked over his shoulder as if he was scared that someone might be listening.

"They broke a man's back last week and killed two of our Clansmen last year."

Clola gave a little cry.

"Father told us not to speak of it, but you can understand why he hates them."

"I can indeed. But I am sorry for Torquil McNarn; he must be afraid of what is going to happen to him."

"Yes, he's afraid all right. He doesn't think his uncle will come to his rescue. He says they all know how much he loathes Scotland."

"I have always been told that the Duke's father was cruel to him," Clola said.

"He beat him until he ran away," Hamish agreed. "One thing about Father, he doesn't often beat us."

It was true, Clola thought, that The Kilcraig's authority rested not on his physical strength, but on his personality, which dominated his family and his Clan.

He had only to look at one of his sons or his henchmen in disapproval and they shook in their shoes.

She could understand, if the new Duke had been as proud as her brothers were, how much he would have resented the humiliation of being beaten.

Hamish then told her of Torquil's reaction to the news that the Clans were to be united and she was to marry his uncle.

"He didn't believe me at first," he related. "Then he said scornfully, 'My uncle would never marry a Kilcraig!'

" 'You don't suppose my sister wants to marry a stuck-up polecat of a McNarn?' I answered."

Clola gave a little cry.

"Oh, Hamish, you did not say that! If he repeats it to his uncle it will make things more difficult for me than they are already."

"How do you know they'll be difficult?" Hamish asked. "You've not met him yet."

"How would you like to be told to marry one of the McNarn women whether you liked it or not?"

"I would slit my throat first," Hamish answered.

Clola laughed.

"I promise you that is something which will never happen."

"You never know," her brother said gloomily. "Only father could have thought of anything so fantastic as our being united with the McNarns after all the years we have fought them and all the things we have said about them."

"I expect they feel the same," Clola answered philosophically. "And what we have to do, you included, Hamish, is to see that the bargain works. You know as well as I do that the fights between the two Clans and the stealing of each other's cattle means only misery and worse poverty than there is already."

"Those McNarns won't change any more than a wild-cat can change his stripes," Hamish grumbled.

Clola had laughed and kissed him because he was too young to understand the deeper issues as she was trying to do.

Only now did she realise that in a few moments she would be leaving her family and the Castle in which she had been born, and she felt desperately afraid of what the future held.

She could understand that her father's plan would be for the benefit of both Clans and would certainly safe-guard those who lived on the border where their lands joined.

But what he had forgotten, she thought, was the human element, and she wondered how long it would be before the McNarns could accept the Kilcraigs as brothers-in-arms and vice versa.

Over her relationship with the Duke was a question-mark which made her tremble to think of it.

With a sigh she put on an attractive summer habit in which she would ride across the moor.

She had some difficulty in making her father realise that it would be impossible for her to ride a horse for two hours in her wedding-gown without arriving hot and dishevelled at the Castle where she was to be married.

He might have planned everything else to his satisfaction, but she was well aware that he had not thought of her as a woman but merely as a weapon in his hands to force the Duke into accepting the terms he had suggested.

Now as a woman she protested volubly.

"I will not, Father, I repeat *not,* whatever you may say, arrive with my gown creased, my slippers dirty, and my hair blown about my face!"

"Women! Women!" The Kilcraig exclaimed in disgust.

But he gave in and finally sent a messenger to Mr. Dunblane to ask where Clola could change and where the Kilcraig Clansmen could assemble.

To gather them together a fiery cross had been sent across-country. This consisted of two burnt or burning sticks to which was tied a strip of linen, traditionally stained with blood.

This item was omitted on this occasion, but the cross was still passed from hand to hand as if by runners in a relay.

Clola knew that one of the last occasions on which the fiery cross had been sent was when Lord Glenorchy rallied his father's people against the Jacobites in 1745.

Then it had travelled thirty-two miles round Loch Tay in three hours.

She was aware that a Clan that had been gathered by the cross was moved by deep and ancient superstitions.

A stag, fox, hare, or any beast or game that was seen by the runners and not killed promised evil.

If a bare-foot woman crossed the road before the marching men rallied by the fiery cross, she was seized and blood was drawn from her forehead by the point of a knife.

When Clola learnt that her father intended to send the fiery cross, knowing that no Clansman would refuse to obey its message, she had with her own hands overhauled the strip of linen which held the sticks together, changing it to a bow of white satin ribbon in which she fixed two pieces of white heather.

The men might scoff at it but she knew it would interest and excite the women.

It would be a bitter blow that for most of them it would be impossible to leave their children and the harvest to join their husbands as they rallied to their Chieftain.

Mr. Dunblane's reply to what Clola had thought of as a cry for help had been to say that the Manse was at her disposal and the Kilcraig Clansmen could also gather there the night before or as early in the morning as they wished.

Clola was to ride across the moors, while the long journey involving nearly four hours by road was to be undertaken by her sister-in-law and her small children in a carriage.

"You would be more comfortable with us," she suggested, but Clola shook her head.

"It is far quicker on horse-back," she said, "and besides, if your carriage should get stuck in the mud or held up by a sudden spate, what do you think would happen at Narn?"

Her sister-in-law laughed.

"A wedding without a bride would certainly be as dismal as a wake, but perhaps the Duke would find a pretty crofter's daughter to satisfy him!"

She was being unpleasant, Clola realised, because she had not yet adjusted herself to the thought that they were to have a family relationship with the McNarns.

She was sure her sister-in-law's attitude was typical of that of many other women, whose enmity was often deeper and more violent than that of their menfolk.

Her father and brothers were waiting for her when she came downstairs, and then she saw with them a young man she had not seen before and knew that he was Torquil McNarn.

He was standing apart from her family and when she looked towards him she saw the hate in his eyes and knew that here was one of the McNarns who would not accept her so easily.

Deliberately she walked across to him.

"I regret that you and I have been unable to meet until now," she said in her soft voice, "but I hope that the poor hospitality my family have been able to offer you will not weigh against me in the future."

He was embarrassed by her attitude.

Because she had taken him by surprise, he was only able to mutter something incoherent. Then Clola turned towards her father.

"We had better get started," she said, "for I warn you, Father, I shall need quite a long time to wash and change before I set out for the Castle."

"Women!" The Kilcraig growled.

But she knew he was in too good a mood today to be disagreeable or forbidding, as he might have been on another occasion.

The warm weather, which had appeared at the beginning of July after a wet and dismal June, was unshadowed.

The sun shone out of a clear blue sky, the bees were busy in the heather, and coveys of grouse rose ahead of them as they set off from the Castle.

"We are wasting a good shooting day," one of Clola's brothers said.

"Grouse, or men?" Hamish asked irrepressibly.

They had been riding for a little over two hours when the Castle came in sight.

Clola had peeped at it often enough from the high hills on the Kilcraig land, but she had never seen it close to. Now she thought it was everything a Castle should be, an idealised structure that might have stepped out of a fairy-story.

The glen beneath it was verdant and had more trees than any glen in the Kilcraig country.

This was due to the river which ran down the centre of it, fed by burns which cascaded down the sides of the rocks.

Clola was aware that her brothers were envious, as they had no equivalent river on their land, and she wondered with a faint smile how often they had been daring enough to poach salmon here at night.

Certainly she could remember salmon on the menu when she had been a little girl, and although there would always be tales that they were brought in by one of the gillies as a tribute to their Chieftain, Clola now had her doubts.

As they drew nearer she saw crowds of men making their way up the drive which led to the Castle, and there were great numbers of what were obviously McNarn Clansmen on the skyline, blocking the road, and climbing down the sides of the cascades.

The Manse stood alone just beyond a small cluster of cottages.

Beside it was the white-washed Kirk, but Clola knew that her marriage would take place in the Castle itself.

As they rode towards the Manse, the women and men who stared
at them blankly and without greeting were obviously McNarns, and
it was with a sense of relief that they saw how many hundreds of
Kilcraigs were gathered ahead of them.

They were reclining on the ground, some sleeping or eating, while
the old men were smoking their white-clay pipes.

As Clola appeared, riding beside her father, a great cry went up.
Then as the Clansmen scrambled to their feet there came the roaring
yell of the Kilcraig slogan.

Loud and shrill, it seemed to echo towards the Castle as they
repeated it again and again.

Then in response the slogan of the McNarns came back, roar after
roar. It sounded defiant, a war-cry—an exhortation to battle.

For one moment Clola looked apprehensively at her father.

Supposing instead of the peace he had envisaged the McNarns and
the Kilcraigs began to fight each other in the way they had done for
generations?

If this happened, if their fiery temperaments were aroused, then
even their Chieftains would find it impossible to pull them apart.

But Clola had reckoned without her father's resourcefulness. He
made a sign to his Piper who rode behind him, and instantly the
pipes shrilled out and the noise of the slogans died away.

It was a marriage-tune he played, a tune known to every Piper
and composed, it was always said, by the McCrimmonses, who were
the greatest of all Pipers in Scotland.

The Kilcraig's Piper had no sooner started than he was joined by a
dozen other Pipers amongst the Kilcraigs and finally by those belonging to the McNarns.

The glen swelled with their music and the hills seemed to throw
back the sound so that the whole world was filled with it.

"That was clever of you, Father," Clola said as their horses came
to a standstill outside the Manse door.

He smiled at her and for a moment she thought that however
handsome the Duke might be, it would be impossible to admire any
man more than her father for his strength, his wisdom, and his command.

The Manse door was opened and she walked inside.

The Minister's wife, a nervous, middle-aged woman, curtseyed po-
litely and offered her food and drink before she led her upstairs to
the best bed-room.

It was poorly furnished but spotlessly clean and the roses growing up the Manse wall gave the room a welcome fragrance.

The Minister's wife brought up the wedding-gown, which had been carried carefully wrapped across the back of a pony. When Clola shook it out and hung it on the outside of the wardrobe she exclaimed at the beauty of it.

Alone, Clola without hurrying took off her riding-habit, washed at the washing-stand in the corner of the room, and arranged her hair in front of the mirror.

"How are you going to dress yourself?" her sister-in-law had asked.

"I will manage," Clola replied. "I expect there will be someone who will button my gown."

"But supposing they have all gone to the Castle for the wedding?" enquired her sister-in-law, who was always ready to make difficulties.

Clola laughed.

"In that case, Father will have to do it up for me, or Hamish."

Her sister-in-law had been shocked.

"Really, Clola, you do say the most preposterous things since you have been in Edinburgh. As though any man could understand the niceties of a lady's attire!"

Clola doubted if Andrew and her younger brothers, with their preoccupation with the land, would notice if she appeared naked or wearing a sack.

But she was sure that after associating with the great beauties of London, and the women who, if rumour was to be believed, spent astronomical sums on their gowns and jewels, the Duke would be critical.

She was glad that whatever he might think of her looks, he would find it difficult to disparage her gown.

Then she wondered what he would expect her to look like.

She was aware that there would not have been time for him to learn much about her from her father, and perhaps he had not been curious.

It would have come as an overwhelming shock, she was quite certain, as it had been to her, to be forced into marrying a Kilcraig with such speed and without even a brief acquaintanceship.

"Perhaps he will be pleasantly surprised," she told herself optimistically.

Then she felt that fear, which had beset her in the night ever since she had learnt what was to happen, flow over her insidiously—fear of the unknown, fear of the man she had never met, fear of the Chief of the McNarns.

The Minister's wife came timidly back into the room to fasten her gown at the back, and exclaimed over and over again with genuine admiration at her appearance.

"Ye looks real lovely, Mistress Kilcraig," she said. "Th' bonniest bride I've ever seen! A fitting mate for th' Laird."

"Thank you," Clola replied.

"I wish ye every happiness," the elderly woman went on, and suddenly there were tears in her eyes. "Ye're so young. So young, lovely as an angel, and ye bring with ye peace te our people. God will bless ye, I know it!"

"Thank you," Clola said again.

Then on an impulse she bent and kissed the Minister's wife.

"That is to bring you luck," she said. "And thank you for your kindness."

With the tears still on her cheeks the Minister's wife escorted Clola downstairs.

Outside the Manse door was a carriage drawn by two horses.

The hood was down and as Clola stepped in she saw that behind her the procession that was to escort her to the Castle was in place.

Her brothers, with Torquil McNarn, rode behind her carriage. After them came the Bard, the Piper, The Kilcraig's special body-guard, and the senior members of the Clan, each a Chieftain in his own right on his own land.

It was impressive, but Clola had the feeling that anything they could produce would be overshadowed by the Castle and the McNarns.

The Manse was not far from the Castle drive and the road was lined with people of every age, the children holding bunches of heather in their hands, some white, some purple.

From under the fine veil of Brussels lace which covered her face Clola could look about her with curiosity, but those they passed did not cheer and anyway it would have been hard to make themselves heard above the noise of the pipes.

Now behind her father's Piper there were twelve others, all walk-ing with a swing, wearing black cock's-tail feathers in their bonnets and blowing with crimson faces through their bone flutes.

They played two tunes before they reached the drive which led to the Castle, the carriage and horses moving slowly, at the walking pace of the procession.

Then, as they ascended the incline which led up to the Castle it-self, the pipes played the march of the Kilcraigs.

It was a tune which had led them into battle for centuries, a tune which had been a challenge to the McNarns since the beginning of time.

All the way up the drive the McNarn Clansmen had stood silent and immobile as they passed. There was something a little frighten-ing about them, and almost despite herself Clola put out her hand and slipped it into her father's.

His fingers closed over hers and she knew that whatever anyone else was feeling, he was elated at the thought that the two Clans would live in peace and the MacAuads would get their just deserts.

'I doubt if he even gave me personally a second thought,' Clola thought to herself.

She was sure of it as they reached the great iron-studded door of the Castle and there was no response from him as she relinquished his hand.

Servants in kilts sprang forward to help her alight. Then she saw waiting to receive her the tall figure of Mr. Dunblane, whom she had peeped at when he visited her father, and beside him was a small boy.

It was Jamie who came forward to say in his high, childish voice:

"Welcome on behalf of my uncle and the McNarns, Sir."

He spoke to The Kilcraig first, bowed, then bowed his small red head in Clola's direction.

"Welcome," he said.

The Kilcraig nodded perfunctorily and put out his hand to Mr. Dunblane.

Clola bent down so that her face was on a level with the boy's.

"What is your name?" she asked.

"Jamie."

"Then thank you, Jamie, for the nice way you have greeted us. I hope you and I will be friends."

"Have you brought Torquil with you?" he asked.

"He is outside."

Jamie gave a whoop of excitement.

"May I go to him?"

"Yes, I am sure you may," she answered.

He ran out through the front door and they heard him cry ex-citedly:

"Torquil! Torquil! You're back!"

Clola smiled at Mr. Dunblane.

"He is excited to see his brother," she said, "and it must be a relief to have Torquil home."

As she spoke, Torquil McNarn, followed by Jamie, came in through the front door.

"I ought to have been here to greet the bride," he said furiously, "but instead they brought me here tied to their chariot-wheels."

He was being angry and provocative, Clola thought, but she could understand his feelings in that he had not been allowed to go to the Castle until The Kilcraig went with him.

It was in fact insulting that her father should be afraid that the Duke would go back on his word and refuse to marry her.

Her father paid no attention to Torquil's outburst. He continued to talk to Mr. Dunblane as if nothing had happened.

"I am sorry," Clola said to Torquil in a quiet voice, "but now that you are here, will you tell us what we are to do?"

Because she seemed to need his help, the angry expression on the boy's face softened.

Assuming an air of authority, he said to Mr. Dunblane:

"Should we not get on with the ceremony? I am sure my uncle is waiting upstairs."

"Yes, of course," Mr. Dunblane replied. "Will you and Jamie lead The Kilcraig and the bride to the Chief's Room? But first you would wish to present her bouquet."

Both Torquil and Clola looked round and a servant came forward with a small bouquet of white heather tied with long satin ribbons resting on a silver salver.

Torquil took it from him and handed it to Clola with an awkward little bow.

Her father offered her his arm and they started to climb the wide, carpeted stairway which led to the first floor.

Now there was the skirl of the pipes, this time playing a wedding-march, and to the music of it Clola and The Kilcraig entered the Chief's Room.

She had a quick glimpse of an enormous and magnificent room, filled, it seemed, with men in the McNarn tartan.

Then as she moved slowly between them, peeping from beneath her long eye-lashes, she saw that the Duke was waiting for her at the far end and so was the Minister in his black robes.

After one quick glance to see if he was there, she felt too shy to raise her eyes again.

Then as her father drew her nearer and nearer she was aware of her sister-in-law and her children on the left side of the room and beside them her brothers and the senior members of the Clan.

But her eyes were drawn irresistibly to the Duke.

He looked even more splendid and more impressive wearing his rightful regalia than he did dressed as an Englishman, and she felt her heart beating with shyness and at the same time a strange excitement.

This was the man she was to marry. This was the Chieftain of a Clan larger than her father's, and a Duke who was admired for his sportsmanship even by the English.

He was to be her husband and she was to be his wife and there would be no dividing them, for they were to be joined by God.

Now she was at the Duke's side and she looked up at him, wondering if he would be looking at her.

Then she saw that he was staring straight ahead of him at the Minister, waiting for the marriage-ceremony to begin, and there was a dark, glowering scowl on his handsome face and his lips were set in a hard, sharp line.

CHAPTER FOUR

The Duke had awakened to feel as if some menacing shadow lay over him, and his depression was not lightened as he heard the sounds of the Clansmen outside the Castle and the music from half-a-dozen different Pipers.

He realised that for his people it would be a day of excitement and rejoicing, even though they might resent their affiliation with the Kilcraigs.

But for himself, he thought, it was a day when he would walk into a trap, and there was no manner in which he could extricate himself.

He could not prevent himself from continually thinking of the woman whom he was to marry.

If ever he had visualised himself as married, it had always been to some sophisticated and beautiful creature who moved in the same world as he did. As his wife she would be admired, and even more would he be envied for his possession of her.

To know that he had no choice but to be linked with a woman of the Kilcraig family, with whom he would have nothing in common, was a horror which seemed to deepen with every second that passed.

He was quite certain that she would be barely educated, if she had had any learning at all, and would doubtless be thick-hipped and have the sturdy appearance of her menfolk.

What was more, he was afraid that his own revulsion at being forced into marriage might make it impossible to do as Lord Hinchley had suggested: give her a child and leave her as soon as possible.

Almost as if he were being taunted, he remembered all too clearly that the English always averred that it was impossible to cross the border unless one held a scented handkerchief to one's nose!

The Duke recalled how George IV when he was Prince of Wales had found that his bride, Princess Caroline, smelt unpleasant.

He had accordingly told one of her ladies-in-waiting that she was to "wash all over," but that had not prevented him from being excessively drunk on his wedding-night, which caused the marriage to founder almost before it was consummated.

The Duke was extremely fastidious where women were concerned.

He had, unlike his contemporaries, never been interested in the expensive and alluring Cyprians or "bits o' muslin" with which the Bucks of St. James's spent a great deal of their time.

Instead, his love-affairs had always been with experienced and beautiful ladies of the Beau Monde and he found it impossible to remember an instance when he had been to bed with a woman who attracted him only physically.

There had always been something else about the association that had intrigued him—her wit, her sense of humour, or perhaps only a fascinating mannerism.

Whatever it was, it raised their association from the carnal to something different.

Admittedly, such allurements palled rather quickly, while the lady in question invariably fell deeply in love with him, finding him an ardent lover with other qualities which set him apart from the usual run of men.

This, although the Duke did not realise it, was the imagination and idealism of his Celtic blood, which was an indivisible part of his make-up.

Yet, now, by a bitter blow of fate, he was to be married to a woman he had never seen, a woman who, he was instinctively convinced, would wound not only his pride and his self-esteem but also his friends' estimation of him.

One thing the Duke swore to himself as he dressed reluctantly and with gritted teeth in the full Highland regalia that was required: he would never take his wife into Society, where his choice could be criticised.

Worse still, the marriage could be laughed at by those who at the moment respected him not only for his position and his achievements but for his good taste.

He sat down at the breakfast-table in the small Dining-Room, which was used when there was only the family present, and saw lying by his place a programme of the day's events.

He pushed it to one side, feeling that if he read it before he ate, the food would undoubtedly choke him.

Yet, when he did try to eat, he found that he was not hungry, and he ordered a glass of brandy, which was very unusual.

The Duke was far too much of an athlete to indulge in alcohol. He drank if the occasion demanded it, but even then sparingly, and his choice in his own house in the South was invariably champagne or good French claret.

He had not brought these North with him, relying on his father's cellars, but he had included in his luggage some kegs of excellent brandy.

He thought as he sipped it slowly that it would steady his nerves and make it easier to face the ordeal that lay ahead.

It was early, and the marriage-ceremony was the first item on the agenda. This was to be completed as quickly as possible because so much time would be taken up in accepting the allegiance of the Clansmen.

The Duke was just about to rise from the breakfast-table when Lord Hinchley joined him, saying:

"The noise outside, which sounds like Bartholomew Fair, makes it impossible for me to sleep, Taran, so I have risen at this unearthly hour."

He looked at the expression on the Duke's face and added:

"Perhaps it is a good thing, because now I am here to cheer you up."

"Nothing could do that," the Duke replied.

"Quite frankly, I am very sorry for you," Lord Hinchley answered, "but, as there is nothing you can do to avoid it, you must make the best of a bad job."

Lord Hinchley sat down at the breakfast-table, and when the servants, having helped him, had left the room, he said:

"Take my advice. Cut your losses and come to Edinburgh as quickly as possible. I must leave here the day after tomorrow."

"So soon?" the Duke murmured automatically.

"Soon?" Lord Hinchley exclaimed. "I have stayed, at your special request, for your wedding for longer than I had intended, but I thought we might have one more day's shooting. I have never known grouse to be more plentiful. But then I really must be about my duties."

"I do realise it would be impossible for you to arrive after the King," the Duke joked, and Lord Hinchley gave an exclamation of horror.

"God forbid! I should be shot at dawn, incarcerated in the Tower, or, worse still, confined in the dungeons of Edinburgh Castle!"

"That, I admit, would be the ultimate punishment," the Duke said sourly.

"Then join me in Edinburgh. I presume you will be going by sea?"

"It is quicker," the Duke replied, "and I believe Dunblane has already sent off our Clansmen who are to represent the McNarn Yeomen at the Review on Portobello Sands, but they, of course, are riding to Edinburgh."

"I see you are really becoming a Scot," Lord Hinchley said. "At least in appearance."

The Duke gave a sigh that was curiously like a groan, and because his friend was really sorry for the predicament in which he found himself he changed the subject.

All too soon, it seemed to the Duke, it was time for them both to repair to the Chief's Room, where the marriage-ceremony was to take place.

As space was naturally limited, only relatives and the most important personages of the two Clans were invited inside the Castle.

The Duke and Lord Hinchley entered the Chief's Room when everyone else including the Minister was already there.

In the few minutes that the Duke had to wait he had time to notice The Kilcraig's relations and recognise his eldest son, Andrew, and beside him his wife.

One look at her told him all too clearly the type of woman he was being forced to marry.

Mrs. Andrew Kilcraig had a pleasant face but had lost her figure bearing three children.

Dressed plainly in a manner which made the Duke think that if he had seen her in London he would have mistaken her for a servant-girl, her skin was tanned by the sun and her hair was the pale sandy shade of red that had nothing to recommend it as a feminine adornment.

The Duke looked at her and then looked away.

He had always disliked red hair, whether it was the red portrayed by Titian and so much admired on the Continent or was the more flamboyant red associated with many Scottish women.

Once again he felt everything that was fastidious in him recoil in horror at what lay ahead.

He thought of what the Prince of Wales had had to put up with through Princess Caroline's unclean habits.

The Duke modelled himself, as soon as he had been old enough, on the strict principle of cleanliness which had been laid down for the Beaux and Dandies by Beau Brummell.

Brummell had been so obsessed that he had even had the soles of his shoes polished, and had sent his linen to be washed in Hampstead, which, he averred, made it smell of sweet country air.

Frenchmen who worked to copy his elegance had their own dirty linen sent across the Channel to be washed by English laundresses and laid out in the sun on Hampstead Heath.

The Prince of Wales had in fact at the beginning of the century swept away the uncleanliness of the generation before him.

Only a few of his older associates, like Charles James Fox and the Duke of Norfolk, wore dirty linen and apparently washed as infrequently as possible.

The Duke insisted on a cleanliness in his own houses which echoed that of Carlton House, and, when the Regent succeeded to the Monarchy, of Buckingham Palace and Windsor Castle.

Now he thought that if his wife was dirty as well as unprepossessing it would be impossible to follow Lord Hinchley's advice or even to touch her.

'She can stay here,' he thought savagely to himself, 'and rot, for all I care!'

He heard the swirl of the bag-pipes and knew that the moment was upon him. Then, as he was aware that The Kilcraig was coming down the centre of the room with the bride on his arm, he knew he could not look.

It was not only cowardice, it was a feeling of being unable to come face to face with the destruction of his pride and the foundation on which he believed his life was built.

He therefore stood staring ahead, and as the Minister in his broad Scottish accent started the Service he found it impossible to listen to the words, conscious only of his own feelings of rebellion and anger.

For the first time, it struck him that his father had won.

He had imagined when he ran away that he had escaped him and was free not only of the brutality of the parent he had loathed but of all the hide-bound customs and superstitions that were embodied in the Castle.

It had been to him a place of torment, while the people who lived there were his natural enemies, because they gave their loyalty to his father.

Now that he had come back, his father had recaptured him and he had become a prisoner of everything from which he believed he had escaped.

The Minister's voice droned on, then the Duke was aware that Lord Hinchley was handing him a wedding-ring.

He put it onto a finger that seemed to appear from out of a white mist and steeled himself against revulsion at his first contact with the woman who was now his wife.

Then the Minister said the last prayer over them and it was with a sense of relief that the Duke could move. Although he had given his arm to his Duchess, he did not look at her.

It had been arranged by Mr. Dunblane that they should all repair to the large Dining-Hall for a wedding-breakfast.

This would entail, the Duke was aware, a meal of gigantic proportions, consisting mostly of a profusion of meats which had been in preparation since the day they had left Kilcraig Castle with no choice but to accept the ultimatum.

Everyone who had attended the ceremony in the Chief's Room could be seated in the Baronial Dining-Hall, which had been added to the Castle by William Adam and was a magnificent example of that great architect's work.

The carved ceiling, painted and gilded, was a treasure in itself, and the huge mantelpiece, of Italian stone carved by craftsmen who had been brought especially to Scotland by his grandfather, was unique.

The furniture was as outstanding as the paintings.

To the Duke it was all very familiar, but to Clola it was a surprise and a delight that she had not expected.

She thought that the Castle would be fine but she had not thought to find it filled with treasures that she had learnt and read about in Edinburgh but never expected to see in her own land.

Vaguely at the back of her mind she remembered hearing that the Duke's grandfather had been a great traveller.

It must have been he, she thought, who had brought so many fine foreign paintings to the Castle and perhaps too the French furniture, which she had noted in the corridors as they moved through them.

Sitting next to the Duke at the top of the long table at which were seated many of the kinfolk of the Kilcraigs as well as those of the McNarns, Clola was glad that the Duke did not speak to her.

She knew that if he did so it would cost him a tremendous effort, for she had felt his anger emanating from him as they had stood side by side before the Minister. She had known even more intimately what he was feeling when his fingers had touched hers in the giving of the ring.

'He hates me!' she had thought.

While it frightened and perturbed her, she thought that perhaps if they could talk alone together it would be easier than if he faced her with enmity in public.

She therefore bent her head so that the lace veil which had been flung back after the wedding-ceremony fell like a curtain on either side of her face.

She knew that such a gesture would be attributed to the shyness which was expected of a bride, and no-one was likely to comment on it.

She, like the Duke, could force herself to eat only very little of the many dishes that were laid before them, and she was glad too that because of the strenuousness of the afternoon ahead there were to be no speeches.

The toast to their health was proposed by The Kilcraig in just a few short words.

She was not aware that the Duke had said to Mr. Dunblane when he had wished to discuss the details of the wedding:

"Arrange anything you like. If I have to be a performer in this circus I will do what is expected of me and no more!"

Finally he had said to his Comptroller:

"What is more, I will not make a speech, nor will I listen to any. Make any excuse you like, or tell the truth. I have been blackmailed into this marriage and I shall not pretend to enjoy it!"

"I will try to make everything as painless as possible, Your Grace," Mr. Dunblane promised.

"Dammit, Dunblane! How could this have happened to me?" the Duke asked.

For a moment Mr. Dunblane thought it was the same cry that he had heard from the Duke twelve years ago when as a boy he had said in almost the same voice:

"How can I endure this any longer? It is impossible!"

Young Taran had in fact broken under the strain and run away to freedom. But he had come back to find himself embroiled, through no fault of his own, in a situation about which anyone must feel sympathetic.

And yet, Mr. Dunblane thought philosophically, good might come out of evil.

He had, although he would not admit it to the Duke, an enormous respect for The Kilcraig.

He was a great Chieftain, the old-fashioned type who had made the Clans at one time small armies within themselves, following a code of honour and an integrity that if it had been known universally would have been admired by the entire world.

The word "Clan" means "Children." The Kilcraig and his like considered themselves the fathers of their families, loved and feared, benevolent at their best and exercising their terrifying power of "pit and gallows" at their worst.

The Kilcraig Clan's excessive pride came from a belief in a common ancestry and an exclusive identity that placed them above other races and especially the men of the South.

It was this pride which made them fight with a courage and a valour that was the terror of other armies and was to earn them later the name of "The Devils in Petticoats."

In Gaelic terms, Mr. Dunblane knew, killing and death was always heroic and grief was its shining laurel for the slain.

Somewhere between the vision and the reality there were men like The Kilcraig, struggling to lead his people and to do what was best for them.

'If the Duke will only stay with us, he too will be a great Chieftain!' Mr. Dunblane thought, but he was well aware that there was a very large question-mark over the Duke's immediate plans.

At last, when the Duke had begun to think that time was standing still, the meal came to an end and in traditional manner the Piper played round the table, stopping beside the Duke's chair to receive a word of appreciation and a small silver cup filled with whisky.

He said the Gaelic word *Slainte,* which means "Health," drank it in one draught, and was then ready to lead the Duke from the Banqueting-Hall along the corridors and out through the front door to the front of the Castle.

Again without looking at her the Duke offered his arm to Clola, and as they appeared on the steps of the Castle a great cry went up which seemed to shake the very turrets.

It was the slogan of the Kilcraigs and that of the McNarns yelled at the same time by hundreds of men, deafeningly explosive, and yet at the same time evoking in those who heard it a pride that was unmistakable.

Without pausing, his Piper leading the way, the Duke and Duchess walked from the door of the Castle towards the place where all the Chieftains of the McNarn Clan had in the past accepted the homage of their Clansmen.

There were stories of how the Kings of Scotland had met there and tales, believed by the Clansmen, that the Kings' ghosts could still be seen and their places sometimes taken by the giants and monsters who lived high in the mountains.

But today there was only one chair, which had been fashioned from the antlers of stags, every one of them a Royal.

The chair had been made for the first Earl of Strathnarn, whose title had been created after a battle in which his Clansmen had distinguished themselves with conspicuous gallantry.

The Duke stood in front of the chair, The Kilcraig standing beside him, and Mr. Dunblane handed him a dirk.

First The Kilcraig kissed the metal of which it was fashioned, then said in a voice which rang out so that all the Clansmen who were listening could hear:

"On this drawn dirk I take my oath to extend the hand of friendship to the Chief of the McNarns. The feuds of the past are forgotten and we will face the future as brothers, commanding all those who follow us to do likewise. On this I swear, and if I ever prove perjured may I be stabbed with this same weapon for having betrayed my trust."

He kissed the blade again and handed it to the Duke, who repeated the same oath before handing the dirk back to Mr. Dunblane.

Then the two Chieftains clasped their hands together and bowed to each other. Another chair was set with that of the Duke's and he and The Kilcraig sat down side by side.

Then The Kilcraig said in a loud voice:

"The Oath of Allegiance will be given by our followers to us both, but first, My Lord Duke, your wife—my daughter—will swear allegiance to you."

The Duke drew in his breath.

Now he knew he would have to look at the woman he had married, touch her hand, and kiss her cheeks.

It was the Oath of Allegiance that had always been given in the past to the Kings of Scotland, and he wondered if any King had ever been as reluctant as he was to accept it.

Then as she moved in front of him the first thing he noticed was that her gown was not only in the height of fashion but very elegant, and that she moved with a grace that he had not expected.

For the first time since the wedding-ceremony Clola held her head high on her long neck in a way that had commanded a great deal of admiration in Edinburgh.

For a moment she stood facing the Duke and he saw in astonishment not the homely Scottish woman he had expected but someone so beautiful, and yet so unusual, that he thought he must have imagined her.

There was no doubt that Clola was lovely, and her dark hair was in contrast to her white skin, which had the texture of a magnolia.

Her eyes were dark but with touches of gold in them like the sunlight on a stream, framed by a fringe of lashes that curled back like a child's.

They seemed to hold in their depths a mystery which was part of the Castle towering above them and the high mountains in the distance.

For the first time it struck the Duke that her voice when she repeated the marriage-vows had been very soft and musical, and he knew before he touched them that her hands too would be soft and sensitive.

For a moment they stared at each other as if they had forgotten they were being watched by hundreds of curious eyes. Then with the grace of a swan Clola went down on her knees in front of the Duke.

Slowly and distinctly she said the ancient words of the Oath of Allegiance:

"So may God help me as I shall support Thee. I swear and hold up my hand to obey, defend, and serve Thee as long as my life lasts and if needs to be die for Thee."

Her hands were outstretched in front of her, palms together, pointing upwards in an attitude of prayer.

The Duke covered them with his own and accepted her allegiance, then bent his head formally and kissed her first on one cheek, then the other.

As he did so he felt her fingers tremble in his and there was a faint fragrance of a French perfume that he did not recognise, and then the ceremony was over.

He rose and helped Clola to her feet, then as he looked round as if to find a chair for her she shook her head and moved as she had been told to stand beside his chair.

It seemed discourteous but the Duke suspected that by custom only he and The Kilcraig as head of the Clans could sit in this traditional place.

Then he had no time to think of anything else, for the Chiefs came forward one after another to kneel on one knee in front of him and The Kilcraig and swear their allegiance.

Clola had taken the oath in English, while the Clansmen spoke in Gaelic.

The Duke was not aware that Clola, after watching and listening to the Clansmen for some time, had been taken back to the Castle by Mr. Dunblane.

"You must be tired, Your Grace," he said as he drew her away and they walked side by side over the grass towards the front door.

"I am, a little," Clola admitted. "I think it is because I found it difficult to sleep last night, and we rose very early to reach here."

"I do not need to tell you," Mr. Dunblane said, "that you are the most beautiful bride anyone could hope to see, whatever their Clan might be."

"I am more afraid of the criticism of the McNarns than the admiration of the Kilcraigs!" Clola laughed.

"I do not think you need be afraid of anything," Mr. Dunblane replied.

He had in fact been astounded by Clola's beauty as she came into the Chief's Room on the arm of her father.

Then he thought that perhaps when her veil was raised there would be flaws in the face beneath it. But instead he knew, watching her in the Banqueting-Hall, that she was in fact the loveliest person he had ever seen.

How could The Kilcraig have bred anything so exquisite and kept it a secret? he wondered.

He was curious but delighted in a manner he had never expected— for here was the answer to the question of whether the Duke would stay in Scotland.

Only Mr. Dunblane was aware of how important to the McNarns was their Chieftain for the life of the Clan.

He had thought when the old Duke died that it would be impossible for anyone to take his place or to keep up the high standard of behaviour that had been shown by the McNarns during his lifetime.

And yet when he saw the new Duke he had known that here was another man in whom the Clansmen would be able to put their trust.

Mr. Dunblane, who was very intelligent, was a Scot who loved his country with a passion that made it agonising for him to know how

Clans bereft of their Chieftain deteriorated and to learn the tragedy of what was happening in Sutherland.

But while he was a patriot he was also an extremely practical man.

He had friends who had told him a great deal about the activities of the Marquis of Narn.

He knew about his sporting achievements, his friendship with the King, and his position as leader amongst the Courtiers and those who were admitted to the Royal Circle.

This was the life in which the new Duke had won for himself the most distinguished place, but there was another one waiting for him: one in which if he liked he could be King, not Courtier—first, not second.

Mr. Dunblane looked at Clola now and thought she embodied all the legends sung or recited of snow-maidens and wild nymphs, and he wondered if the Duke would think the same.

They reached the Castle and he took her up the staircase and into a very elegant Drawing-Room where the walls were of blue brocade, the furniture was French, and there were huge vases of flowers on many of the polished tables.

"This is always known as the Duchess's Room," Mr. Dunblane explained, "and I thought perhaps you would wish to say good-bye to your family here before they return home."

"Perhaps you would tell my sister-in-law where I am, and she could join me," Clola suggested.

"I will do that," Mr. Dunblane said, "but I thought first I would show you your bed-room, which is on this floor."

He led Clola down a long corridor and she could see that the walls were of great thickness and this part of the Castle had been built as an impregnable stronghold against enemies.

Mr. Dunblane opened a door and Clola followed him into a room which looked out on the other side of the Castle.

Here was a more magnificent view than she had expected, over the moorlands to where there was a great loch fringed by high hills.

The room had a painted ceiling rioting with gods and goddesses and cupids, and there was a huge four-poster bed hung with satin curtains. The furniture was French, as was the carpet.

"I never expected to find anything to lovely!" Clola exclaimed.

"This has been the Duchess's bed-room for centuries," Mr. Dunblane explained. "It is in the old part of the Castle but was redecorated by the last Duke, as was the Chieftain's Room next door."

A faint flush came to Clola's cheeks and Mr. Dunblane said quickly:

"I will find your sister-in-law and bring her to the Duchess's Room."

"Thank you, you have been very kind," Clola said. "When I watched you behind the curtains of the window arriving at my home, I did hope that one day I would meet you."

"I pray, Duchess, that we shall be friends and that I can help you if you need help."

"I am quite sure that I shall need not only help but also a friend," Clola replied.

She held out her hand as she spoke and Mr. Dunblane took it in his, then raised it to his lips.

"It is difficult for me to find words," he said, "in which to tell you how glad I am that you are here."

There was a ring of sincerity in his voice which warmed Clola, and when she was alone she stood for a moment looking at the door through which he had passed, then at the furnishings of the bedroom.

"There is so much to see," she murmured to herself.

She would have liked to take off her wedding-veil, but she did not know if she would be required to appear again, in which case it would be a great mistake to change her appearance.

Perhaps she and the Duke would have to walk amongst the Clansmen and talk to their wives. She did not know, and she wished she had asked Mr. Dunblane before he had left her.

Interested in everything she saw, she moved back to the Duchess's Room and gave a little exclamation of delight as she found that on one wall there was a built-in bookcase containing many books which she knew she would enjoy reading.

She was joined, as Mr. Dunblane had promised, very shortly by her sister-in-law and her children.

One small boy was about the same age as Jamie and almost as soon as they were brought into the room they disappeared together, as Jamie said he had something to show his new friend.

"This is certainly far grander than I expected," Mrs. Andrew Kilcraig said, looking round with an air that told Clola she would like to find fault.

Clola did not answer and after a moment she went on:

"I suppose you realise how lucky you are? You may have been forced into marrying a McNarn, but after all he is very presentable and apparently has plenty of money!"

"I have been told little about my husband," Clola said in her soft voice.

"I expect you will learn all you have to soon enough," her sister-in-law said tartly. "Well, I have only come to say good-bye. As it is we shall be back long after the children's bed-time, and they will be as cross as two sticks, if I know anything about them!"

Clola was not sorry to see her go, and the only delay was that they could not find Jamie and Andrew's son and the servants hunted all over the Castle before finally they were discovered on the roof.

"We had a wonderful view, Mama," the young Kilcraig said.

"View or no view, you had no right to disappear!" his mother snapped. "I shall tell your grandfather how badly you have behaved when we get home!"

Clola thought with a smile that this was the ultimate threat at Kilcraig Castle, but when her sister-in-law and the children had driven off she felt lonely.

Although she was a bride and this was her wedding-day it seemed that no-one wanted her, and she wondered how soon it would be before she and the Duke were alone.

There was in fact no chance of that before dinner-time.

Mr. Dunblane came to tell Clola that the oaths of allegiance were taking far longer than they had anticipated.

"I could not have believed that so many Clansmen would reach here in such a short time," he said, "and I suppose it is my fault for underestimating the number. Anyway, I will take the blame."

"So, what is to happen?" Clola asked.

"I have arranged for dinner at seven o'clock, and your father will eat with you before he starts on the journey home."

"He will be very late," Clola said.

"It will not be dark," Mr. Dunblane replied.

"No, not really dark," Clola agreed.

"Your brothers, of course, will dine at the same time," Mr. Dunblane went on. "I expect you would like to bathe and to change your gown. Your luggage should all have been unpacked for you by now."

"That sounds delightful!" Clola exclaimed with a smile.

"I have arranged for Mrs. Forse, who is quite intelligent, to look after you," Mr. Dunblane said. "Later, of course, we will find you a personal lady's-maid—perhaps a woman from Edinburgh. But Mrs. Forse will, I am sure, be able to do all that you require of her for the moment."

"I am sure she will," Clola answered. "And thank you for all the arrangements you have made for me."

"Let me assure you that it is a very great pleasure!" Mr. Dunblane smiled. "And now may I escort you to your room?"

Clola put down the book she had been reading.

"I can find my own way to my bed-room," she said. "I know how busy you must be."

"Then we will meet at dinner," Mr. Dunblane said, "and I will arrange for everyone to gather here so that it will not seem so formal as in the Chief's Room."

"Thank you," Clola said again.

She felt quite light-hearted as she walked towards her bed-room. After all, with Mr. Dunblane at the Castle it did not seem so frightening as it had at first.

She walked into her room.

A middle-aged woman was arranging Clola's hair-brushes on the dressing-table.

She turned as Clola entered and dropped a curtsey.

"You must be Mrs. Forse," Clola said, moving towards her and holding out her hand.

To her surprise, the woman ignored it.

"That's ma name, Yer Grace."

"Mr. Dunblane tells me that you will look after me until I can obtain a personal maid."

"Them are ma orders, Yer Grace."

She spoke in a quiet, restrained voice which somehow sounded unnatural.

Then, when she raised her eyes, Clola knew why, for she saw an expression of such hatred that she recoiled from it as if she had found a serpent on her path.

Quite unaccountably, she found her heart beating in a manner which told her she was afraid.

'I am being stupid. It is just because I am over-tired,' she thought; and aloud she said:

"Forse is an unusual name. Do you come from this part of the world?"

"I'm a McNarn," the woman replied fiercely. "A McNarn, Yer Grace, born an' bred."

Clola did not say anything, but as if she felt she must give an explanation Mrs. Forse went on:

"Me husband were called Forse. He came from Caithness, an' a great mistake I made in marrying out o' the Clan. He left me wi' a child ta bring up on ma own, so I came back ta ma ain people."

"I am sorry," Clola said.

She felt the woman spoke in a manner which made her sound as though she was slightly unhinged.

It seemed as if, having spoken, Mrs. Forse had nothing more to say.

Almost in silence, except when she had to question Clola as to her choice of dress, she assisted her to undress, poured water into the bath that was arranged in a small room off the bed-room, and buttoned Clola into her evening-gown.

She had chosen one of pale pink which her grandmother had bought for her at the same time as the one which she had worn for her wedding.

It had been very expensive, and her grandmother had envisaged her wearing it, with the addition of a train, at the Reception that was to be held in the Drawing-Room at Holyrood Palace when the King would meet the most distinguished ladies of Scotland.

'It is far more important that I should look attractive tonight,' Clola thought to herself, 'for it is not the King I have to please, but my husband.'

She knew, and it would have been foolish to pretend otherwise, that she was looking her best; in fact, those who had admired her in Edinburgh certainly would have said that she was looking her most beautiful as she left her bed-room to go to the Duchess's Room.

"Thank you, Mrs. Forse," she said as the Scottish woman opened the door for her.

Mrs. Forse did not reply. She only looked at Clola with that expression in her eyes which made her shiver.

Dinner was delicious, with dishes which were cooked with a delicacy that had not been apparent at the Wedding-Breakfast.

Clola realised that everyone was very tired, including her father and the Duke.

It had been a long day, and although The Kilcraig talked of what they had achieved, it was obvious that he was in a hurry to start on his journey home.

She was aware that Lord Hinchley was looking at her in a bemused fashion, but she found it hard to keep her own eyes from the Duke's face.

She felt that he was no longer angry as he had been at the wedding-ceremony, and yet she was not sure.

She only knew that she felt shy and now the fears that had beset her last night and this morning were back.

When dinner was over there were farewells to take of her own family, and as Clola saw them off she was aware of the noise coming from the Clansmen.

She had a suspicion that a great number of them were getting drunk, which was not surprising as she had realised that there had been plenty of ale, provided by the Duke, with which they could celebrate.

There was the smell of roasting oxen, lamb, and stag, and in the dusk there was the light of fires being kindled over the moorlands opposite the Castle and in the valley beneath them.

There was also the skirl of the bag-pipes, the cries of those who were dancing reels, and voices singing and sudden bursts of somewhat intoxicated laughter.

"They are certainly enjoying themselves!" Lord Hinchley said as The Kilcraig rode away and they turned back to enter the Castle.

Clola had noticed that Torquil ran for a little while beside Hamish's pony, obviously unwilling to break off a conversation they were having.

Then he joined them as they all walked up the stairs together.

"That was a jolly good wedding, Uncle Taran!" he said.

The Duke turned to look at him as he said:

"I wish to speak to you, Torquil!"

There was an ominous note in his tone and Clola longed to cry out:

"Not tonight! Do not say it tonight, on top of all the other things that have happened today."

She looked at Torquil's paling face, and then almost pleadingly at Lord Hinchley.

He seemed not to understand that she was appealing to him, and he said to the Duke:

"Shall the Duchess and I wait for you in the Sitting-Room?"

"No!" the Duke replied unexpectedly. "I want her to come with me."

He walked ahead to the Chief's Room and Clola and Torquil followed him. When the door was shut behind them the Duke said:

"Your family took my nephew prisoner, and doubtless they will ask you what punishment I have given him for his behaviour which has resulted in several unforeseen consequences."

Clola winced, as she knew he was referring to their marriage.

Looking at Torquil, the Duke said:

"It is your behaviour which brought me here from the South and because of it I have married a Kilcraig. What may be the result of that is a question that only the future can decide. But now I have to say this. . . ."

He paused for a moment and Clola saw Torquil brace himself as if for a blow.

"As you are aware," the Duke went on, "I am forced to leave for Edinburgh within the next day or so to meet the King when he arrives, and to lead the Clan at a Review which has been commanded by His Majesty."

Torquil nodded, indicating that he was aware of that, and the Duke continued:

"While I am in Edinburgh I intend to arrange for you to go to school there for a year. After that time, if you have learnt enough— and that will certainly mean a great deal of hard work—I will send you to Oxford."

Torquil's eyes widened for a moment in astonishment, then he stammered almost beneath his breath:

"O-Oxford?"

"I hope you will enjoy it as much as I did, and when you are South you will doubtless have the opportunity of going abroad and visiting France, Italy, and perhaps Greece."

Clola could see that Torquil was absolutely stunned, but when he did not speak the Duke continued:

"Those are the plans I have made for you and which Mr. Dunblane agrees would be in your best interests, but I must also give you a warning."

Now the Duke's voice changed and he said sternly:

"If before the beginning of the school term you get into mischief of any sort, if you behave with stupidity and a lack of responsibility, then I shall send you to a school in Glasgow which I understand caters to boys who need restraint and discipline. Do I make myself clear?"

"You do indeed, Uncle Taran!" Torquil cried. "I never thought I had a hope of going to Oxford! Thank you, thank you, Sir!"

"You had better go and thank Mr. Dunblane," the Duke said. "Perhaps we had both better go; I imagine there are quite a lot of things he will want to tell you about your future."

The Duke walked towards the door, but Torquil reached it before him and held it open, and then they both waited for Clola. She smiled at the Duke a little shyly as she passed him. Then, because she thought it was expected of her, she went to the Duchess's Room.

Lord Hinchley, who was looking at a newspaper, rose to his feet.

"You are still in one piece?" he asked. "I thought Taran sounded rather like my School-Master when he was going to beat me!"

"He has been very kind to his nephew," Clola replied, "and Torquil is thrilled at the idea of going to Oxford."

"I've always thought that Taran's bark was worse than his bite!"

Lord Hinchley smiled. "After all, he was the same age as young Torquil when he ran away from home, so he ought to have a kindred feeling for him."

Clola sat down on the sofa and Lord Hinchley stared at her for a moment. Then he said:

"You are very beautiful! How could I imagine that anything so lovely would be languishing here in the Highlands?"

Clola smiled.

This was the second man today who had called her beautiful, and she wondered with a little feeling of excitement if the third would be her husband.

But whatever the Duke had to say to Mr. Dunblane and Torquil, it certainly took a long time.

When the clock on the mantelpiece struck a half-after-ten and the Duke still had not returned, Clola rose to her feet.

"If you will forgive me, I think I will retire," she said to Lord Hinchley. "It has been a long and exciting day."

"I can understand that," Lord Hinchley said, "but I hate to let you go. There is so much more I would like to talk to you about."

Clola smiled.

Lord Hinchley had done all the talking and she realised that he wanted to show off, to tell her what a close friend he was of the Duke's, and to make sure that she too would accept him as a friend.

She gave him her hand, and just as Mr. Dunblane had done, he kissed it, and then she went along to her own bed-room.

She was not certain what her feelings were when she entered the room.

She found Mrs. Forse waiting for her and once again she had an intimation not only of hatred but of evil.

But she was too tired to trouble herself over the woman, and she let her help her to undress in silence.

Then, when she was in her nightgown and just about to get into bed, Mrs. Forse said:

"This is yer weddin'-nicht, Yer Grace, a nicht when we should be wishin' ye great happiness, but I wish ye nothin' o' the kind!"

"Then it would be best if you just said good-night, Mrs. Forse," Clola said with dignity.

"I'll no wish ye guid-nicht. It can be nothing but bad. Bad for His Grace and bad for the McNarns that they should link with the Kilcraigs, who have the stains o' our blood upon their hands!"

The woman spoke with such ferocity that Clola wished she did not feel it difficult to silence her, or to drive her from the room when she was only wearing a thin, diaphanous, lace-trimmed nightgown.

"I do not wish to hear that sort of talk, Mrs. Forse," she managed to say sharply. "My father, as you well know, has sworn the oath of friendship and loyalty to the McNarns and the Duke has sworn the same to the Kilcraigs. There will be no more talk of bloodshed or enmity between us."

"That's what ye may believe, Yer Grace, but the spirits o' the dead will not be appeased by worrds. They cry oot for vengeance!"

Mrs. Forse's voice seemed to echo evilly round the room. Then she walked towards the door.

"It's been a bad day, Yer Grace," she said as she reached it. "A bad day an' an evil day! But retribution will come! Ye can be sure o' that. There'll be retribution, an' 'tis upon yer head that it'll fall!"

As she spoke the last word she closed the door and there was a silence in which Clola could hear her heart beating.

CHAPTER FIVE

Clola stood staring at the door which Mrs. Forse had closed behind her, and as she turned to look towards the great bed she was suddenly afraid.

Afraid of the hatred which the Housekeeper had spat at her, and afraid of the hatred she had felt emanating from the Duke during the wedding-ceremony.

It seemed to be closing in on her and she was aware that in what had always been the enemy's camp she was alone, far from her own family and everything that was familiar.

She had a longing to be with those who bore her name, who were outside celebrating what she felt would be a "mockery of a marriage."

Without really thinking, carried by an impulse that was stronger than thought, she opened the door of her bed-room and crossed the wide corridor, trying to find another room which would look out on the front of the Castle where the Kilcraigs were encamped.

She opened the first door she came to, and, though it was unlit by candles, the light from the windows told her she was seeing the glow from the fires that had been lit below the Castle.

Shutting the door quietly behind her, she crossed the room, feeling that the golden light drew her and she must run to it for safety.

When she reached the window she could see, as she had expected, dozens of small fires round which the Clansmen were sitting and several big ones where she knew they would be roasting meat.

Now the comforting sound of the pipes was in her ears and she stood there wishing desperately that she could be amongst those whom she knew rather than incarcerated in a place where there was nothing but hatred.

She felt panic-stricken at the thought of what lay ahead of her.

It had been strange enough to come home, after three years, from the life she had lived in Edinburgh with her grandmother.

Because she was so acutely sensitive, it had been hard at first to adjust herself and not let her father and brothers know that there was any need for adjustment.

But this step into the unknown aroused a fear that was almost a terror.

How could she live with a man who hated her, and with servants like Mrs. Forse crying out for the vengeance of the dead? And, Clola knew, they believed every word they said.

She had thought it would be difficult to live at her father's Castle, without the intelligent people, the music, and the books which had all been so much a part of her life in Edinburgh.

But at least she had belonged there, at least she was part of a family, while here . . .

She felt herself trembling, and her heart, which had beaten frantically when Mrs. Forse had raged at her, was still thumping in her breast, sounding almost like the beat of doom.

"I cannot . . . bear it! I must go . . . away! I must . . . hide somewhere!" Clola said frantically.

Then in the darkness of the room behind her she was aware of a "presence."

She knew it was not human, yet it was very real.

She sensed it as she had sensed so often things that other people could not see or hear, and yet to her they were present.

She felt it come nearer and yet she was unafraid; she knew it was a Lady, grey and insubstantial, who understood what she was feeling and reached out to her from the World Beyond.

The feeling of the Lady's presence was so vivid that Clola felt she could almost hear the words of comfort she spoke.

"You must be brave and unafraid," the Lady told her.

"How . . . how can . . . I?" Clola asked.

"Fate has sent you. There are things to be done which only you can do."

Like a child who has run to his mother for safety, Clola felt her agitation subsiding. Then, as the violent beating of her heart abated and she no longer trembled, she felt calmer but desperately tired.

Almost as if the Grey Lady beside her took her by the hand, she walked blindly to the bed, seeing its shadowy outline in the light from the window.

It was not made up with sheets, but beneath the velvet cover there were blankets and pillows.

Clola felt that the Grey Lady helped her onto the blankets and pulled the velvet cover over her.

Then as her head touched the pillow she fell asleep to the music of the pipes.

* * *

Clola awoke with a start to find the sunshine coming through two long windows. At first she wondered where she was, and then she remembered.

She sat up, realising that she had slept all night in a bed without sheets, but it had been warm and comfortable under the cover, which had been embroidered by loving hands.

It was quiet and she thought that by now the Clansmen would be dispersing back to their homes and the work which would be waiting for them.

She looked round and saw that the room was panelled and that the curtains and the hangings of the bed were embroidered with seventeenth-century needle-work.

It was an austere room compared with the furnishings in the rest of the Castle, and she thought that as it was in the old part of the building it must have changed very little through the passing centuries, even though it had been redecorated by the late Duke.

She slipped out of bed and went to the window. As she had expected, most of the Clansmen had gone and there was no Kilcraig tartan to be seen amongst those tidying up the debris left from the night before.

She wondered if she had dreamt the presence of the Grey Lady who had come to her aid when she had been so afraid. Then she was sure that the Lady was real, as real as those moving about below, and the other people in the Castle, and even Clola herself.

She was about to turn towards the door when she saw over the mantelpiece a portrait. It was very old, painted on wood, and enclosed in an ancient carved frame.

Looking at it, Clola knew without being told that here was the Lady who had come to her rescue.

She moved nearer and looked at the inscription under the portrait.

Morag, 3rd Countess of Strathnarn
1488–1548

Looking at the portrait, Clola could see a serene face, not beautiful but with something spiritual and wise about it.

Here, then, was her Grey Lady. Here was someone who must in her lifetime have helped those in need and still extended her help beyond the grave.

"Thank you," Clola said quietly, and went to her bed-room.

Because she had no wish to see Mrs. Forse until she had to, she did not ring the bell, but washed in cold water and then dressed herself in one of the attractive gowns which her grandmother had bought for her in Edinburgh.

When she was ready to leave her room she looked rather fearfully at the door which she knew led into the Duke's bed-room.

Had he come to her last night and found her gone? Or had he hated her so violently that the door had remained closed?

She remembered how his eyes had met hers before she made the Oath of Allegiance before him. She had felt then that in some way they spoke to each other without words.

Later she was sure she had been mistaken and he must still have been hating her as he had hated her in the Chief's Room, where they were married.

If he had come to her last night, would he have thought that she was breaking her oath to obey and serve him as she had promised to do?

With a deep sigh Clola thought that while the Grey Lady had brought her peace and rest during the night, the problems were still there.

And yet, because she was rested, they were not so fearful and she felt somehow that she could cope with them.

She looked at the clock and saw that she had taken longer in dressing than she had intended and it was in fact nearly half-after-eight.

'I will go down to breakfast,' she thought, 'and I shall know by the Duke's expression if he is still angry with me or not.'

She walked along the corridor and encountered Mrs. Forse, obviously coming to her room, carrying a tray which held tea-things.

She looked surprised when she saw Clola, who merely inclined her head as she passed, saying: "Good-morning, Mrs. Forse!"

It was too early, she thought, for dramatics, curses, or threats of vengeance, and the less conversation she had with Mrs. Forse the better!

She remembered how Mr. Dunblane had said that she could have a personal maid of her own, and she decided that she would speak to him as soon as possible and ask for one to be provided.

She entered the Dining-Room to find only Jamie, eating alone, and she said:

"Good-morning, Jamie!"

"Good-morning," Jamie replied. "Everyone's gone shooting, but they wouldn't take me."

"Everyone except me!" came a voice from the door.

Torquil came in as he spoke to throw himself down in a chair at the table without greeting Clola.

The servants set a bowl of porridge in front of her and one in front of Torquil.

"It's jolly unfair!" he said, speaking to nobody in particular and not looking at Clola. "I can shoot as well as or better than anyone in the place! But Uncle Taran said he wants to find out if I'm safe before I can join a party on the moors."

Clola thought this was a wise precaution, but aloud she said:

"I am sure there are many other things you can do. What about fishing?"

She thought that Torquil's discontented expression lightened a little.

"I might do that," he muttered ungraciously.

"Can I come with you, please, Torquil? Can I come with you?" Jamie asked.

"I suppose so," he replied, "if Jeannie lets you."

"I'll soon run away from her!" Jamie said.

"My brothers have always envied you your salmon river," Clola said to Torquil.

For a moment she thought he was going to refuse to speak to her directly, but then he said:

"Hamish told me that."

"I am sure he did." Clola smiled. "I am glad that you and he are friends."

Clola wondered if Torquil's reply would be that he could never be friends with a Kilcraig. Then he said:

"He was decent to me when I was imprisoned in your Castle."

He said no more, but Clola thought that he had suddenly had an idea of how he should spend the day.

He ate the rest of his breakfast in silence while Jamie chattered away, and as he finished he said to one of the servants:

"Tell them to bring my pony to the front door. I'm going riding."

The servant went from the room and Jamie said:

"I thought you were going fishing and I could go with you."

"No. I have something else to do this morning," Torquil answered. "I might fish later this afternoon."

"I will tell you what I would like you to do, Jamie," Clola said. "Show me round the Castle."

The small boy seemed attracted by the idea, and when breakfast was over they set out to explore every room and climbed up one of the turrets onto the roof.

The Castle was high, far higher than any other Castle Clola had ever seen, and from the battlements there was a most magnificent view over the whole countryside.

It was easy to realise how impregnable it had been in the past and how difficult it had been for the McNarns' enemies to attack this stronghold.

She was looking out towards the Loch and the mountains behind them, which she had seen last night from her bed-room, when Jamie said:

"You mustn't go near the edge. Jeannie says that some people when they look down get giddy and fall over."

"Jeannie is right," Clola said, "and it is very sensible of you to remind me. I hope you never come up here alone."

"I do sometimes," Jamie confessed, "but you mustn't tell Jeannie."

"I will not do that," Clola promised, "but please be very careful. I do not want to lose my first friend in the Castle."

"Is that what I am?" Jamie asked.

"My very first," Clola said, and she nearly added: "The only one!"

* * *

The Duke, Lord Hinchley, and Mr. Dunblane had an excellent day's sport.

It was early in the season and some of the birds were small, but they were all good enough shots to avoid killing the "Cheepers," as they were called.

As they walked home the Duke felt he had had one of the most satisfying shooting days he had ever enjoyed.

It was only as they neared the Castle that he began to wonder what had happened to Clola the night before.

He had in fact gone to her room, which he felt would be expected of him as a bridegroom, but he had not been as reluctant as he had anticipated or afraid of what he would find.

Watching Clola at dinner, he had been astounded by her beauty and even more by her elegance.

He was far too experienced where women were concerned not to realise that her gown would have graced Buckingham Palace.

In fact, with her dark hair, in which there were blue lights, her white skin, and her strange, mysterious eyes, he knew that his friends and certainly the Monarch would acclaim her a beauty.

He remembered his fears of becoming a laughingstock and his decision never to allow his wife to go South. These were two of the things which no longer perturbed him.

At the same time, he could not dismiss so lightly his resentment at being forced into a marriage he did not want, nor could he overcome his dislike of the Kilcraigs as a Clan.

He was intelligent enough to realise that what was done could not be undone. For better or for worse, Clola was his wife, and the sooner they talked things over together and decided to make the best of a bad job, the better!

Lord Hinchley had said nothing about Clola in the presence of Mr. Dunblane, but the latter moved ahead of them as they neared the Castle.

He excused his haste on the plea that there were innumerable things for him to see to, among them the arrangements for Lord Hinchley's departure early in the morning, and the two friends walked alone.

"Shall I say what you know I am thinking?" Lord Hinchley asked.

The Duke did not pretend ignorance.

"She is certainly not what I feared and expected."

"She is beautiful!" Lord Hinchley said positively. "And she has, if I may say so, the most haunting face I have ever seen."

"Haunting?" the Duke questioned.

"I find myself thinking," Lord Hinchley answered, "that a man would find it difficult to forget her."

The Duke made no comment, but he was listening as his friend went on:

"Perhaps it is her eyes. There is something about them which I cannot put into words. Perhaps it is the way they tip up a little at the corners, or the thickness of her eye-lashes."

He laughed as if at himself and added:

"I am quite certain, Taran, that in the olden days she would either have been burnt as a witch or worshipped as a goddess!"

"If you stay in the North much longer," the Duke said warningly, "you will develop a Celtic imagination, which is something Sassenachs are never supposed to have!"

Lord Hinchley laughed again, but as they entered the Castle he knew without being told that the Duke was in a very different frame of mind from what he had felt before his marriage.

As the Duke went upstairs he decided it would be polite to tell Clola that he was back before he went to his bed-room to bathe and change.

He looked into the Duchess's Room but to his surprise there was no-one there. He thought perhaps Clola was out in the garden or lying down, and went farther along the corridor.

It was then that he heard music, and it was not the music he had ever expected to hear in the Castle.

The Duke was a genuine music-lover.

It was fashionable in London to patronise the Opera. But for most of the *Beau Monde* it was an excuse for the ladies to be seen in their diamonds and for the gentlemen to "quiz" the Opera Dancers, from whose ranks their mistresses were usually chosen.

However, the King liked classical music and so did the Duke, and they both attended performances given by the Royal Philharmonic Society and gave concerts in their own homes, to which only their more musical friends were invited.

The Duke had been largely responsible for persuading the fine violinist Louis Spohr to accept the Philharmonic Society's invitation to visit England, and he considered him the equal of Mozart and Beethoven as a musician.

Now for a moment the Duke could not place the instrument he heard being played.

It had a clear, liquid, melodious sound and he knew the player was gifted, as whatever instrument it was vibrated in her hands.

He realised the sound came from the Red Drawing-Room, which was sometimes called the music room.

It was a room that had hardly even been used in his father's time, but it contained an ancient harpsichord, a viola, and a harp.

The Duke smiled to himself. He had solved the question of what he was hearing.

It was the harp that stood in the Red Drawing-Room being played, and he could not remember ever before hearing it.

Quietly he opened the door.

Just as he had expected, Clola was sitting beside the huge golden harp and her long fingers were plucking from it a melody that the Duke recognised as having been composed by one of the great Masters.

She made a picture which his artistic instincts appreciated. Wearing a gown of yellow silk, her head silhouetted against one of the windows, she seemed to be enveloped in a light from the Heavens themselves.

Her small chin was lifted and her eyes looked ahead, and the Duke thought she was seeing sights that were not visible to him, as the curve of her lips showed that she was happy in a fantasy-world of her own.

Then, as he told himself he was being imaginative, Clola turned her head and saw him standing there.

As if he had taken her by surprise, her fingers faltered and then fell in silence.

The Duke walked across the room towards her.

"I had no idea you were a musician," he said. "I do not recall ever hearing that harp played before."

"It wanted tuning," she said, "and one or two of its strings need . . . replacing, but it is a very . . . fine one."

She spoke shyly, in a way which told the Duke she was nervous in his presence.

"We must see if we can find you something more modern than these instruments," he said with a gesture towards the harpsichord.

"That would be . . . delightful."

She looked up at him, then glanced away, her long, curved eyelashes hiding her eyes.

"What were you playing?" he asked.

She hesitated a second or so before she replied:

"It was . . . something I . . . composed myself . . . but I admit it was . . . inspired by Mozart."

"Can you play a pianoforte?"

"Yes."

"Then we had better buy one of the new ones made by John Broadwood."

Clola clasped her hands together and he saw the light in her eyes.

He did not know how much she had missed at Kilcraig Castle the pianoforte she had played at her grandmother's house in Edinburgh.

They were both silent and somehow words were not necessary.

Then as if she was compelled to break some strange spell which had rendered them speechless, Clola asked:

"Did you have a good shoot?"

"Very good!" the Duke replied in an absentminded way, as if his thoughts were elsewhere.

"I am . . . glad."

"I hope you have not found it lonely today?"

"Jamie was kind enough to show me round the Castle. I found it very . . . interesting."

It suddenly struck the Duke that it was something he would have liked to do himself. Then he thought that perhaps Jamie knew more about it than he did.

"I hope you were impressed," he said lightly.

"How could I . . . fail to . . . be?" Clola answered. "It is so . . . magnificent, and larger than I . . . expected."

"My grandfather, as you must realise, was extremely extravagant," the Duke said.

"You should be grateful that he was. Now you have a . . . treasure-house in the Highlands of which anyone would be . . . proud."

"I am not certain that where I am concerned 'proud' is the right word," the Duke said. "I expect you know I ran away to forget not only the Castle and everyone in it but also Scotland?"

He spoke as if he was being deliberately provocative. Clola looked at him with her strange eyes and said quietly:

"I have thought of how you must have . . . suffered. That is why Torquil and Jamie must . . . never feel the . . . same."

There was a note in her voice which told the Duke that she really cared about his nephews, and it surprised him.

"I can see you are always ready to champion the underdog," he said with a smile.

They exchanged a few more words before the Duke went to his own room and Clola went to hers.

As she changed for dinner she found herself thinking so intently about the tall, handsome man who was her husband that she was able to ignore the baleful looks given her by Mrs. Forse.

They were sitting at the dining-table when there was the first sound of thunder in the distance and a sudden gust of wind came through the open windows to stir the curtains.

"I thought that would happen," Mr. Dunblane remarked.

"A thunder-storm?" the Duke enquired.

"It was far too hot today for the weather not to break," Mr. Dunblane replied.

"It was certainly hot," Lord Hinchley interjected. "I do not think I have ever before felt such intense heat when I was shooting."

"It will be cool enough in a short while," Mr. Dunblane said, and signalled to one of the servants to close the windows.

"I suppose it is going to rain," Lord Hinchley remarked. "A good thing this did not happen last night!"

Clola was thinking the same thing.

She knew that when there was a thunder-storm over the mountains it would gradually move to cover the whole countryside and after the thunder and lightning there would come torrential rain which would put the burns in spate and swell the rivers.

She hoped that all her Clansmen were home by now and she wondered too if Torquil was back in the Castle.

She had not seen him since breakfast-time and she was not surprised, as he had said he was going riding, that he did not appear for luncheon.

Last night he had not been at dinner and she supposed the Duke had thought him still too young to dine with the grown-ups.

Her brothers when they were past fifteen always dined with their father, and she thought it was a mistake that Torquil was not being treated as an adult.

As soon as she had any say in what took place in what was now her home, she decided, this was one of the things she would change.

It was hard to think that this enormous, magnificent building was "home," but because she was practical in many ways Clola was determined to assume her rightful responsibility as soon as everyone became used to her presence.

She was well aware that a "new broom that sweeps clean" was never popular.

"I must not make suggestions, or alterations, until they have accepted me," she told herself.

She was sure that where Mrs. Forse was concerned that would never happen, and she had yet to find out how many other servants there were who would feel the same.

The Duke and Lord Hinchley were telling Mr. Dunblane of the large shoots they had attended in the South, the number of partridges and pheasants they had bagged, and obviously they did not expect her to join in the conversation.

She therefore watched the Duke as he sat at the head of the table, looking, she thought, more handsome than any man she had ever met before.

His air of authority and importance was, she was sure, exactly what a Chieftain should have, and doubtless it impressed not only his followers but also the Kilcraigs.

She would like to have an opportunity, she thought, to talk to him alone, and she hoped that that would be possible tomorrow when Lord Hinchley had left, or perhaps later tonight. . . .

At the thought of that there was a faint flush on her cheeks, and the Duke, looking at her suddenly, wondered what it was that was making her look shy.

At the same time, as Lord Hinchley noticed, there was a mysterious expression in her eyes.

When dinner was over and the pipes had been played round the table, they retired to the Library because Mr. Dunblane had mentioned that there were some sporting prints in one of the books there which would interest the Duke and Lord Hinchley.

Clola took the opportunity of looking round and found a number of books she wished to read.

Then because she knew it would be expected of her to make the first move, she said good-night.

"I shall doubtless leave before you are up in the morning," Lord Hinchley said. "I have to hurry to reach Edinburgh before His Majesty arrives on the fourteenth, and may I say how much I shall be looking forward to meeting you again."

"Thank you," Clola said.

Lord Hinchley did not release her hand but went on:

"I want too to wish you and Taran every happiness together. You know he is my closest friend, and I am delighted that he should have such a beautiful wife."

"Thank . . . you," Clola said with a smile.

Lord Hinchley kissed her hand as she curtseyed.

As she rose she looked a little uncertainly at the Duke, wondering if he too would kiss her hand.

Then, realising that he had not said good-night, she thought it was intentional. She felt the blood rise in her cheeks, and, withdrawing, she hurried to her own room only to find, as she had feared, that Mrs. Forse was there waiting for her.

Tonight, because she was determined not to be upset again, Clola did not speak but allowed the woman to undress her in silence.

Only when she was nearly ready for bed did she say:

"That will be all, thank you, Mrs. Forse!"

Without speaking the woman left the room and Clola gave a little sigh of relief.

It was then that a violent clap of thunder made the windows rattle, and she thought again of the Clansmen, knowing that some at any rate would be drenched to the skin and might have to spend the night in the open.

The clap of thunder was followed by another and yet another.

Now the thunder-storm that had been drawing nearer all the evening appeared to be directly overhead and Clola thought that if the curtains were drawn the lightning would be like streaks of fire.

She got into bed, leaving two candles burning beside her, and she had hardly done so when the door opened.

She turned her head, expecting, though it seemed too soon, that it would be the Duke, but instead Jamie stood there, looking very small and lost in his long flannel nightgown.

"I'm alone," he said forlornly.

Clola knew only too well from the sound of his voice that he was frightened, and because she had brothers she said quickly:

"I am so glad you have come to see me. It is a horrible thunder-storm! I would like you to keep me company."

Jamie came into the room and shut the door behind him.

"Would you really?" he asked tremulously.

"Yes, I would," Clola answered.

As she spoke there was another explosion overhead.

With a movement like a small scared animal Jamie clambered onto her bed and slipped in beside her.

She put her arms round him and found that he was trembling.

"Are you—frightened?" he asked in a whisper.

"Not now that you are with me," Clola answered.

"Jeannie says the—giants on the mountains are—angry," Jamie said with a quiver in his voice.

"It is not giants who make the thunder-storms," Clola replied.

"No?"

"It is the naughty angels in the sky who push the clouds round until they run into each other! That's what makes the noise. It is only a game, but you know that if we bang two stones together we can see sparks, and when the clouds do it they make lightning."

"That must be rather fun!"

"I would rather like to push clouds round too," Clola said with a smile.

The idea excited Jamie's imagination and they talked about it for a little while until the small boy's voice became slower and slower and she knew he was falling asleep.

He was very soft and warm and smelt of soap and the lavender in which his nightshirts had obviously been kept.

The thunder moved farther away but Clola could hear the rain pouring down in torrents, as she had expected.

She was listening to it, thinking there was music even in its violence, when the communicating-door between her bed-room and the Duke's opened and he came in.

He had undressed and was wearing a long green velvet robe which nearly touched the floor, and the white frill of his nightshirt showed against his throat.

He did not speak but walked quietly towards her. Only when he reached the bed did he see that she was not alone.

He stood there, staring at her, seeing in the light from the candles her long dark hair falling over her shoulders, and her arms round Jamie with his red head against her breast.

She looked up at him and after a moment said very softly in a whisper:

"He was . . . frightened."

The Duke's eyes were on her face. For a moment he did not answer, then he said with a twist of his lips as if he was amused:

"I suppose it would be a mistake to wake him?"

"He is very young. I am . . . honoured that he should . . . come to me."

"Then—good-night."

He was still speaking in a whisper so that they should not disturb the sleeping child.

"Good-night," Clola answered.

The Duke lingered for a moment and Clola had the feeling that he was looking for something in her eyes, but she was not certain what it was.

Then abruptly he turned and went back to the door through which he had entered, and she thought that her heart beneath the heaviness of Jamie's head was beating in a strange manner.

* * *

It must have been two hours later when Clola awoke to hear a knock on the door.

In his sleep Jamie had moved away from her, turning over to sleep on the other side of the bed, with his back towards her.

She herself had not fallen asleep at once but had lain awake thinking about the Duke and wondering what they would have said to each other, or what might have happened, if the little boy had not been with her.

She felt that he was not hating her as he had done before.

At the same time, there were still barriers between them, barriers she could sense rather than to which she could put a name.

Now as she was startled to wakefulness she thought she had dreamt the knock at the door, until it came again.

She rose quickly from the bed, and picking up a wrap which lay over one of the chairs she put it on, slipping her feet as she did so into a pair of soft slippers.

As she opened the door she saw that an old man stood there with a lantern and she guessed he was the night-watchman.

"I'm real sorry te disturb Yer Grace," he said, "but there's a young gent'man at th' door an askin' for ye."

"A gentleman?" Clola repeated in surprise.

"He says he's yer brother, Yer Grace."

Clola was astonished and she said:

"I will come with you and speak to him."

She went out into the passage and shut the door behind her and they walked side by side towards the stairs, the light from the lantern guiding their steps.

"I didn'a know what te do, Yer Grace, when he comes an askin' for ye," the night-watchman said, "but most insistent he was he should speak te ye."

"You were quite right to wake me," Clola assured him. "It must be something very urgent!"

As she spoke, her thoughts were busy over what could have occurred. Had there been an accident involving her father on his way home?

It must, she thought, be something desperate for them to send for her in the middle of the night.

Then as she reached the top of the stairs, by the light of the candles in the sconces she could see her brother Hamish standing in the Hall below.

She hurried down to him, saying as she reached him:

"Hamish . . . what has happened? Why have you come here?"

"I have to speak to you. I have to tell you something," Hamish replied.

She thought he looked wild, his kilt covered in mud, his bare legs stained and very dirty.

She drew him to one side, out of earshot of the night-watchman, who tactfully removed himself to the outer Hall.

"What is it?" she asked.

"It's Torquil," Hamish answered. "The MacAuads have taken him prisoner!"

Clola stared at him in horror.

"What do you mean? What are you telling me?"

"We planned together that we should have a go at them just to teach them a lesson," Hamish said. "But while we were driving a calf over at the border, two men appeared from nowhere and caught hold of Torquil."

"Oh, Hamish, how could you do anything so stupid, so wrong, at this particular moment!" Clola cried.

"We planned it when Torquil was in prison," Hamish said, "and it seemed quite safe."

"Where is Torquil now?"

"That's what I came to tell you. I ran away before the men could catch me, but I watched them, hidden in the heather, and they've put Torquil in the watch-tower and have gone to get help."

"The watch-tower!" Clola exclaimed.

"They dragged him up the cliff and I expect locked him in. I have never been there so I didn't try to reach him. I thought it'd be best to get help."

He paused to say tentatively:

"Perhaps we could rescue him—before they come back."

Clola thought quickly.

"I will help you," she said, "but no-one must know about this. It would be terrible if the Duke learnt that Torquil had disobeyed him."

"How can you help?" Hamish asked.

"I will tell you when we get there," Clola said. "Go to the stables . . . no, wait a minute . . . I will give the order."

She went to find the night-watchman.

"My brother has brought me some bad news," she said to the old man. "A great friend is very ill. Will you please order two ponies for us? We will come to the stables, for I do not wish to disturb any-one."

The night-watchman looked surprised, but he was obviously used to obeying orders.

"I'll go te th' stables, Yer Grace, right awa'," he said.

"You go with him, Hamish," Clola said. "I will join you as soon as I have put on some clothes."

Then to her brother she said in a low voice so that only he could hear:

"Stick to my story about illness. Take care not to mention to anybody what has really occurred."

"No, of course not," Hamish said, indignant that she should think him so stupid.

Almost before she had finished speaking Clola was running up the stairs to her bed-room.

She pulled open the wardrobe, searched for a plain dress which had luckily been included among her many elaborate gowns, slipped it on with the warm jacket that went with it, and then tied a scarf over her head.

She put on the short boots she wore for walking on the moors, which she found in the bottom of her wardrobe.

It took her only a few minutes to dress, and while she did so Jamie never moved but slept peacefully in the big bed.

Clola left the candles burning just in case he should wake and feel frightened; then, picking up a pair of leather gloves, she ran down the stairs and out through the front door, going towards the stables.

By the time she reached them a sleepy groom had been roused by the night-watchman and had saddled two ponies.

Hamish was already in the saddle, and as they started to move away from the Castle, Clola said to her brother:

"You have your skean dhu with you?"

"One in each stocking," Hamish answered.

Another time Clola would have laughed at the idea of wearing two of the short Scottish knives at the same time, but she knew the reason he wore two was to equip him for cutting loose an animal they were going to steal.

They moved with all possible speed over the moors towards the border. Clola in fact knew the Look-out well because it had always been one of the deep bones of contention between her Clan and the MacAuads.

Originally a Pictish Fort, the stones had been utilised by the MacAuads for building what they called a Look-out on a rocky cliff overlooking both the Kilcraig and the McNarn country.

As it was on the border of MacAuad land, Clola felt that it had been put there more as an act of defiance than for any serious use.

But it had in fact infuriated her brothers that the MacAuads if they wished could climb into their Look-out, which stood about twenty feet high, and stare over Kilcraig land, while they were in the unfortunate position of not being able to overlook the MacAuads' land.

Clola must have been eleven when her second brother, Malcom, had taken her with him to explore the Look-out, and, greatly daring, they had climbed the cliff.

It had been easier than Clola had expected and when they reached the top they had found their way into the Look-out itself.

It had a heavy studded oak door and Clola now remembered that there had been no lock. It was fastened by twine, which Malcolm had cut with his skean dhu, and they had gone inside to find a dark and smelly hole with only a wooden ladder up which those who wished to reach the top could climb.

Malcolm had been disgusted.

"I thought it was something better than this!"

"It looks more impressive outside than in," Clola had agreed.

"The MacAuads can keep it!" Malcolm said in disgust. "But we must leave them something to show we have been here."

They had nailed a rather dirty handkerchief to the door and tied Clola's hair-ribbon to the wooden steps inside.

It was not a very effective gesture but it had given Malcolm pleasure to think that he had braved and defied the MacAuads. But they had been far too frightened to tell Andrew what they had done, and certainly not their father.

Clola was thinking now that it was very unlikely that a lock had been added to the Look-out since she had last been there.

If she knew anything about the MacAuads it was that they were far too slap-dash to bother to exert themselves, unless it meant money in their pockets.

The rain had ceased, but the drive when the ponies trotted down it was swimming with water and the heather was very wet.

Now the storm had almost died away in the distance and there was only an occasional rumble far in the East.

The moon, which had been full the night before, came out from between the clouds.

Clola and Hamish might have been able to find the Look-out without its assistance, but it was certainly easier when the light showed them the sheep-tracks running between the thick heather.

They were also able to avoid the gullies and, most important of all, the swollen burns.

Nevertheless, they had to cross one or two, and the ponies, being used to them, splashed through without difficulty where a horse from Edinburgh and certainly one from the South might have been afraid.

At last after they had been riding for a little over half-an-hour the Look-out came in sight.

"Did Torquil spend the day with you?" Clola asked.

"We met this morning," Hamish answered, "as we had arranged to do, and caught a salmon at the top of the river."

Clola had thought that perhaps that was what they were doing.

"What did you do with your ponies?"

"When we arrived here we tied them up over there," Hamish replied, pointing with his finger. "I was afraid to ride away in case the MacAuads heard me. I crawled through the heather, then ran all the way to the Castle."

Clola thought it was not surprising that he looked so dirty. But now it was dangerous to talk any more and she rode ahead, taking her pony as near to the bottom of the cliff as she dared.

Then she dismounted and Hamish did the same.

The ponies they had been given from the stables were tough, strong, and used to long journeys over the moors without suffering from any fatigue.

The moment they were free they put their heads down, seeking the grass between the heather, and Clola was certain that they would not wander away.

"Follow me," she whispered to Hamish, and they went to the base of the cliff and looked up.

It was actually a rough gorge which started high up the hillside, going deeper on the MacAuad side until it ended at the Look-out.

There was quite a lot of water in the bottom of it, but Clola and Hamish splashed across regardless of wet feet and started to climb.

Frantically Clola tried to remember how she and Malcolm had managed all those years ago.

Fortunately, the moonlight was full on the cliff, so they could avoid the great bare rocks on which their feet slipped and keep to what footholds there were between them.

Clola found it hard to hold on because the rocks were wet, but somehow she managed to keep going, and she knew that gradually as they kept moving higher and higher she was nearly at the top.

As she pulled herself over the edge she was breathless and at the same time was listening intently just in case Hamish had been mistaken and one of the MacAuads had remained behind as a guard.

Nothing could be a worse disaster, she knew, than that not only Torquil but she too should become a prisoner of the MacAuads.

Then she saw the Look-out towering above her and there was no-one there, no sight or sound of the MacAuads.

She got to her feet and Hamish joined her.

They went to the door, which, as Clola had expected, was tied with thick twine, and there was no lock.

Without being told, Hamish drew his skean dhu from his stocking, cut the twine, and pulled the door open.

For a moment it was difficult to see what was inside because they themselves blocked the moonlight.

Then Clola realised that Torquil was lying on the floor, bound by a rope which tied his hands at his back, and that his mouth was covered with a piece of cloth, which gagged him.

First she pulled the gag from his mouth.

Then she took Hamish's other skean dhu and they hacked away. They got him free in a few minutes, and shaking the rope from his legs Torquil stood up.

Still without speaking, they slithered down the cliff and splashed across the burn to run towards the ponies.

Only as they reached them did Torquil say:

"We must collect the ponies Hamish and I rode here."

"Yes, of course," Clola agreed. "Ride behind Hamish—and we must hurry!"

The other ponies were only about a hundred yards away and as soon as they reached them Clola said:

"Hamish, go home! Get on your own pony and go at once. Torquil, you will have to lead the other one."

"I expect he'll follow us anyway," Torquil answered, but he took hold of the bridle, which meant, however, that they could not move so quickly.

Hamish left them, and Clola, looking back as she and Torquil rode ahead, asked:

"How could you do anything so crazy after what your uncle said to you?"

"I had promised Hamish. I couldn't go back on my word," Torquil said.

It was the perfect answer! Clola knew that for any Scot to break his word was bad enough, but for a McNarn to break it to a Kilcraig would be unthinkable!

They rode on. Then Torquil asked anxiously:

"Does Uncle Taran know you came to save me?"

"No, of course not," Clola replied. "No-one knows and no-one must ever know. Do you understand?"

She thought for a moment, then added:

"We will have to persuade the night-watchman and the groom not to talk. I think his name is Hector."

"He'll not talk," Torquil said.

"You must make sure of it," Clola said earnestly. "You know as well as I do what your uncle threatened if you got into mischief."

Torquil was silent. Then he said:

"It was jolly sporting of you to save me. How did you know how to reach the Look-out?"

Clola thought perhaps it was a mistake to say that she had been there with her brother Malcolm.

"We were lucky," she said. "Hamish had the sense to come and tell me what happened, and there was almost a full moon."

"We just had bad luck in being seen."

"It was not bad luck but crass stupidity to go at all!" Clola said crossly. "You have to promise me, Torquil, promise me on your word of honour, that you will never do such a thing again."

He did not answer and she pulled up her pony.

"Promise me," she said sharply, "or I might betray you to your uncle!"

"I promise!"

Torquil's tone was surly for a moment, then he changed it.

"I'm grateful to you too. Those MacAuads are rough and spiteful. They even hit me after tying me up."

Clola felt inclined to say: "It serves you right!"

But now they were getting nearer to the Castle and could ride side by side, and she could see that there was a mark on Torquil's cheek which she was certain would be a great purple bruise on the morrow. There was also a cut on his forehead.

She saw that his jacket-sleeve had been torn from the shoulder, presumably when fighting with the MacAuads, and his bare knees were bleeding from cuts and bruises.

She felt that he had had a lesson he would not forget.

Now they had reached the Castle drive and Clola thought with relief that it could not yet be four o'clock in the morning.

They could both go back to bed, she thought, and no-one would be any the wiser about the adventure in which they had taken part.

They reached the stables to find there was no-one about and the groom who had saddled their horses had obviously gone back to bed.

They put all three ponies into their stables, pulled off their bridles and saddles, and shut the doors quietly.

"I'll see you in the morning," Torquil whispered. "Shall we go in by the side door?"

"No, the night-watchman will be waiting for us at the front," Clola answered.

They hurried from the stables to the front of the Castle.

As Clola had expected, the door was unbolted. As they pushed it open the old man who had been waiting for them rose from a chair in the outer Hall, where he had been sitting with his lantern beside him.

"Ye're back, Yer Grace!" he exclaimed with an obvious note of relief in his voice.

"Yes, we are back," Clola answered, "and thank you for waiting for us."

She moved softly towards the stairs while Torquil hung back for a moment, and she knew he was telling the night-watchman to say nothing about the night's events.

Then as she started to climb the stairway he joined her.

"He'll be all right," he said.

She turned her head to smile at him and saw by the light of the candles how dishevelled he looked and thought she must look very much the same.

There was a turn on the staircase, the last six steps taking them onto the landing of the first floor, when Clola's heart gave a sudden leap.

Standing waiting for them, illuminated by the candles which had been lit since she left, was the Duke!

He was wearing the long green robe in which he had come to her bed-room and there was an expression on his face which made her and Torquil stop in their tracks.

He did not speak until Clola with Torquil just behind her had reached the last step of the stairs and was standing in front of him.

Then he asked:

"May I enquire where you have been at this time of the night?"

Clola heard Torquil draw in his breath, and quickly, having no time to think and therefore saying the first words that came into her mind, she replied:

"I had to . . . go and . . . meet someone . . . unexpectedly . . . and because I got into a little . . . trouble, Torquil came and . . . rescued me."

"Had to meet someone?" the Duke repeated. "And who might that be?"

"A . . . friend. Someone . . . who wished to . . . see me, and it was impossible to . . . wait until . . . morning."

"A friend!" the Duke exclaimed, and there was no mistaking the disbelief and contempt in his voice. "By 'friend' I presume you mean 'lover'!"

Clola gasped and as she did so it seemed as if the Duke grew taller, larger, and more overwhelming. Then he said in a voice which cut her like a knife:

"I knew that I was marrying a Kilcraig, but I did not realise she was also a harlot!"

His voice seemed to ring out. Then he turned and walked away, disappearing into the shadows of the corridor.

Torquil took a step forward but Clola put out her hand and laid it on his arm.

"No," she said. "Not now . . . not at this . . . moment, when he is so . . . angry. Wait, we . . . will think of . . . something to-morrow."

But she thought almost despairingly that there would be nothing she could say then, no explanation she could make which the Duke would understand or forgive.

CHAPTER SIX

Clola awoke and realised it was late in the day.

Jamie must have slipped out without waking her and she knew that she had in fact been utterly exhausted when finally she fell asleep.

It had taken a long time because she had been deeply perturbed by the manner in which the Duke had spoken to her, and she had got back into bed feeling a despair that was worse than anything she had ever known before.

For a long time she had turned over and over in her mind what explanation she could give him other than the one that had come spontaneously to her lips when she had found him standing at the top of the stairs.

It seemed to her that there was no way in which she could excuse herself without involving Torquil.

Though she felt it was extremely reprehensible of him, after all that had been said, to go with Hamish into the MacAuad country, she was aware that it would have been almost impossible for him to admit to a Kilcraig that he was afraid of the consequences.

She thought despairingly that the Duke would never understand because he had lived too long in the South, where men would break their word far more easily and lightly than a Scot would ever do.

"What can I do? What can I do?" she asked herself over and over again.

Although mentally she was in a high state of tension, eventually, because climbing the cliff had been physically fatiguing, she fell asleep.

On waking she realised that she was stiff and she thought too she might have caught a cold.

But nothing was of any importance except to try by some means, though she had no idea how, to make the Duke believe that she had not, as he had inferred, been meeting a lover.

She turned a dozen different explanations over in her mind, only to find that they all sounded unconvincing and untruthful.

She rang the bell and after some delay Mrs. Forse came into the room to say in her hostile voice:

"Ye were asleep, an' I left ye."

"I was tired," Clola said simply. "But now I must get up."

Mrs. Forse had crossed the room and was pulling back the curtains.

"There's nae hurry for Yer Grace," she said. "The gentlemen have all gone awa' and there's only the children and yerself left in the Castle."

"The gentlemen have left?" Clola questioned.

"Aye. His Grace and His Lordship were awa' firrst thing."

"And Mr. Dunblane?" Clola asked.

She thought that it was Mr. Dunblane to whom she must turn in her difficulties.

It was he who had persuaded the Duke to send Torquil to school and to Oxford; and she was certain that if she confided in him he would be sympathetic and understanding.

"Mr. Dunblane has also gone te Edinburgh," Mrs. Forse said.

There was something almost triumphant in her tone, as if she was glad that Clola was left behind.

Clola got out of bed, wincing as she did so because her knee was scratched and bruised from climbing the cliff.

She had also broken the nails on her fingers and she felt as if the pain of it all added to the unhappiness in her mind.

"Ye're stiff," Mrs. Forse said, as if it had suddenly struck her that Clola was moving more slowly than usual. "I'll awa' and fetch ye sommat te ease it."

"Please do not bother. I shall be all right," Clola replied. "I think perhaps I have caught a cold."

"It's nae trouble," Mrs. Forse said, and went from the room.

Because she felt so low, Clola was almost grateful that the woman who had been so hostile was now being more amenable.

It was unreasonable, but she felt as if the Duke had deserted her by leaving for Edinburgh sooner than she had expected.

She had meant when she could talk to him to tell him how well she knew Edinburgh and all the people in it.

She had hoped when she explained how long she had lived there with her grandmother that he would suggest taking her with him to meet the King.

Now she thought she had been foolish in not explaining how she had only recently come North.

Yet there had been no opportunity at the table when the men were talking of sport, and the first night she was sure that the Duke had deliberately left her out of the conversation.

Last night had been the only time, and she had actually thought of telling him after dinner a little about her life.

But Lord Hinchley had been there and somehow it seemed egotistical to talk about herself at all intimately with a stranger present.

She had imagined that there would be plenty of time, but now it was too late and the Duke was gone.

Although she longed to join him she knew it would be impossible to travel alone and without Mr. Dunblane's assistance in making all the arrangements.

Clola was nearly dressed when Mrs. Forse returned. In her hands she carried a tray on which reposed a glass of warm milk.

"I've put some herrbs in it," the woman said. "It'll tak' awa' th' stiffness an' prevent a cold."

"It is very kind of you."

Actually Clola disliked warm milk but she had no wish to hurt Mrs. Forse's feelings by refusing the drink she had taken so much trouble to bring her.

She took a sip and found there was honey mixed with the milk and it therefore was not unpleasant.

"You are knowledgeable about herbs?" she asked. "My old Nurse used to know a great deal about them and as children we were always given herbs when we were ill."

"There's been a herrb-garden at th' Castle fer at least twa centuries," Mrs. Forse said, "and the people all come te me wi' their ailments."

"You must tell me sometime which herbs are efficacious," Clola said with a smile.

She finished the milk, thanked Mrs. Forse, and when her gown was buttoned she walked towards the Duchess's Room.

There was no-one about and she guessed that because it was already afternoon the boys would have had their luncheon and gone out into the sunshine.

It was a bright day after the storm last night and she thought she would like to walk down and see what undoubtedly would be a spate in the river.

When she appeared, the Butler came into the room to ask if she would like anything to eat.

"I have just had some milk, thank you," Clola said, "and I will wait until tea-time. I am sure you have cleared away everything by now."

"It'd be nae trouble to bring Your Grace something fresh," the Butler said. "I wouldn't like te see Your Grace hungry."

He seemed a kindly man, and Clola replied:

"Thank you, but I will wait until tea-time. I suppose Mr. Torquil and Master Jamie have gone out?"

"That's right, Your Grace."

Clola walked to the Music Room.

Whenever she felt perturbed, worried, or unhappy, it was always music that could bring her solace, and she would forget everything else when she played.

She remembered how the Duke had promised her a pianoforte, but she thought now that he would bring her back nothing but a renewal of his hatred for her and the rest of the Kilcraigs.

Because the thought was so depressing she felt the tears prick her eyes; then, fighting her emotions, she sat down at the harp and started to play.

A composition by Mozart came to her mind and her fingers, but after she had played for only a few minutes she suddenly felt very tired.

She was in fact so sleepy that she left the harp to sit down on the sofa. . . .

The next thing she knew was that the Butler and the footman were bringing in the tea-things and she must have been asleep for nearly two hours.

Her head felt heavy and it was hard to open her eyes to see that they had brought her all sorts of delicious scones, griddle cakes, and shortbread. But while she found it hard to eat more than a mouthful, she drank the fragrant tea thirstily.

After she had finished, Clola sat on the sofa feeling it too much of an effort to move or even to think.

She had meant to ask Torquil if he would like to dine with her, but when she went along to her own room to change for dinner Mrs. Forse said:

"Ye're looking real played oot, Yer Grace. Why do ye no get inta bed, and I'll bring ye yer dinner?"

"I am sure I must be getting a cold," Clola said, "and I do feel very tired."

"Then just ye do as I suggest, Yer Grace, and I'll fetch ye another drink o' my herrbs, and that'll soon put ye on yer feet again."

Clola leant back against her pillows, with her eyes closed, thinking it was strange that she should feel so exhausted.

It must be due, she thought, to the softness of her life in Edinburgh.

She remembered how before leaving home she could have walked all day on the moors and then stayed up half the night without it having any more effect on her than it had on her brothers.

Mrs. Forse brought her the same honey-sweetened milk and she drank it quickly, ready to take anything which would make her feel better.

"Yer dinner'll be a-coming in a wee while," Mrs. Forse said.

If it came Clola was not aware of it, for she had fallen asleep while planning that as soon as she was well enough she would ride over to Kilcraig Castle to see her family.

The following morning she felt worse, and because she told herself it was sensible to eat she forced herself to consume some of the breakfast which Mrs. Forse brought to her, but was persuaded to stay in bed.

Luncheon came and with it another glass of milk. Clola drank only a little of it, feeling that it was too sweet to take at the same time as the Chef's delicious food.

She felt stronger in the afternoon and decided that her illness was passing and tomorrow she would be up again.

"Ye didn'a drink yer milk at luncheon, Yer Grace," Mrs. Forse complained.

"I know, but there were so many other nice things," Clola said in a conciliatory tone, feeling that the woman had taken a lot of trouble.

"Tonicht, I've ordered some special soup te put strength intae ye," Mrs. Forse said, "an' there's chicken with cream sauce which th' Chef'll be disappointed if ye dinna eat."

"I will do my best," Clola promised. "It is ridiculous to feel so weak and lie about when there are so many things I want to do."

Because she had felt better after luncheon, when her dinner came she made a great effort to eat a little of every dish.

The soup was certainly delicious and so was the chicken with a thick sauce poured over it.

There were other dishes from which she could choose but she sent them away, thinking she had had enough.

An hour later Mrs. Forse came in with what she called her "herbal night-cap."

"I've made it from herrbs which I plucked only this morning, Yer Grace," she said. "Fresh and sweet they are, they'd put heart intae a dying man!"

"Thank you, but I will drink it later," Clola said.

"Drink it the noo, while it's just th' right temperature," Mrs. Forse insisted. "I must get Yer Grace well—otherwise, what'll His Grace have te say when he returrns?"

Clola thought that she would certainly need her strength to face the Duke again.

Because she felt too weak to argue with Mrs. Forse she drank the herbal drink, finding it a trifle unpleasant, but she was too polite to say so.

She went to sleep, then awoke in the darkness to find herself gripped with almost intolerable pains in the stomach.

It was so excruciating that after enduring it for some minutes she rang the bell because she was frightened at the violence of it.

Mrs. Forse came hurrying into the room.

"Ye rang, Yer Grace?"

"Yes, Mrs. Forse. I am in pain. Terrible pain. I cannot think what it is."

"It's going too long wi'oot proper food, Yer Grace, an' a chill in the stomach often results in th' cramps."

"Yes, of course, that must be it," Clola agreed. "I must see a Doctor in the morning, but is there something you can give me in the meantime to make it more endurable?"

"That's what I thought ye'd ask," Mrs. Forse said, "an' I've brought sommat with me."

She gave Clola a milky white liquid in a small glass.

She drank it off and almost immediately the pain ceased, but once again she felt intolerably sleepy and knew nothing more. . . .

* * *

Clola awoke, heard a clock chime and realised it was midnight.

She remembered it had been the early hours of the morning when she had rung for Mrs. Forse.

A sudden thought struck her, so extraordinary that she could hardly credit it, and yet what other explanation was there?

She had missed a whole day!

With an effort she forced her brain to think back, remembering the pain that had gripped her, the milky drink that Mrs. Forse had brought with her and which had sent her to sleep.

Why had Mrs. Forse brought the drink into the room with her?

It was strange, very strange, Clola thought, and now suddenly, unaccountably, something else came back to her.

She had been aroused from sleep to drink again, but why was it so indistinct, just the memory of something trickling down her throat, not once but twice. Perhaps more.

She thought she was in a nightmare and perhaps had a fever and she would raise her hand to her forehead.

But when she tried to do so it was impossible. Her hands seemed to be made of lead and she could not move them from her sides.

The shock of it seemed to make her think a little more clearly: now she knew what was happening and was possessed by the terror of the knowledge.

Then she became aware that someone was near her, someone she had known before, calming her, protecting her—it was the Grey Lady!

She was so real that Clola spoke to her in her mind even though it was impossible for her lips to move.

"What has happened to . . . me? Why am I . . . like . . . this?"

The Grey Lady gave her the answer:

"You are being poisoned!"

Clola gave a little cry.

Poisoned by Mrs. Forse . . . and she was helpless . . . unable to move.

She desperately wanted to close her eyes and go to sleep again, but with a superhuman effort she made herself think back.

Now she was certain that not one day but perhaps several had passed while she was unconscious.

"Help me! Help me!" she cried to the Grey Lady.

It was as if she drew nearer and Clola could feel her hand on her forehead, soothing and calming her.

"What can I . . . do? I do not . . . want to die!"

It was a cry in her heart, and yet still her lips did not move. She felt her whole body was numb and . . . paralysed.

"Help will come!"

She could hear the words spoken.

"Help will . . . come?" she asked. "But how . . . and from . . . where?"

"You must be brave, you must fight."

Again the words were in her mind, just as if they had been spoken aloud.

Clola tried to raise her hand and again found it impossible, but it seemed as if the very effort made her breathe more easily.

'That is what I must do,' she thought to herself, 'breathe deeply. Try to clear my mind so that I can think.'

She breathed and went on breathing steadily in the darkness, until she saw the first streak of light at the sides of the curtains.

It was another day, perhaps a day which would bring her death, the death she could not avoid.

"Help me! Help me!" she cried again to the Grey Lady, and thought that the Lady had gone and she was alone.

For a moment sheer panic swept over Clola, but she told herself she had to fight and being afraid would not help.

She went on breathing deeply and watching the light creeping in between the curtains.

It suddenly struck her that it was coming from only one window instead of three; then, as it grew brighter, the outline of the four-poster bed in which she had slept in the Duchess's Room was not there.

Incredulously, as more light came in from the only window, Clola found that she was in a room she had never seen before.

It was small, so very much smaller than the room in which she had slept when she came to the Castle.

Then she realised that the room was round and she knew where she was—in one of the turrets!

For a moment it seemed so incredible that she thought she must be mad or, as she had thought at first, delirious.

Then she was aware of the furniture.

It was plain, sparse, and there was a small hearth in the curve of the wall and a second door which she knew would lead out onto the battlements.

How could she have been brought here without being aware of it— and for what reason?

It flashed through her mind that she was a prisoner as Torquil had been—but not the prisoner of the Duke, who was away.

No . . . a prisoner of Mrs. Forse!

Clola remembered the hatred in her eyes and the way she had spoken on her wedding-night.

She knew now that she should have asked Mr. Dunblane that very first evening if he would find another woman to act as her lady's-maid.

But it had seemed impossible to cause trouble the moment she arrived in the Castle.

Yet now she was in Mrs. Forse's power and it seemed unlikely that she would survive the poison that was being poured into her.

'I will take no more of the food and drink she brings," Clola decided.

Then she knew that as she could not move her hands it would be impossible to prevent Mrs. Forse from pouring her pernicious herbs down her throat as she must have done when she was too drugged to know what was happening to her.

She would die!

Die by the hand of a woman who hated her because she was a Kilcraig, and there was no-one to rescue her from this turret where Mrs. Forse must have had her conveyed.

It was all so terrifying that Clola closed her eyes at the sheer horror of it, but, afraid that she might fall once again into a drugged sleep, she forced them open and went on breathing deeply, as she had before, trying to get more oxygen to her heart and to her brain.

As the light grew brighter and brighter she could now see everything in the room clearly and thought it was a condemned cell from which she could never escape!

She tried to move her hands again and this time succeeded in raising them an inch or so off the mattress.

But her legs still felt as if they did not belong to her, and it was impossible to sit up.

"Help me! Help me!" Clola cried to the Grey Lady, thinking that if only she could move she might open the door and somehow get downstairs to find someone to help her.

Then she heard a sound and stiffened.

It would be Mrs. Forse, she thought, coming with more of her evil herbs.

She wanted to scream but knew that even if she could do so it would be impossible for anyone to hear from the very top of the great Castle.

Then as she waited, so frightened that even her breath seemed to have stopped, a door opened slowly and creakily, and it was the door onto the battlements.

A small face appeared round it and she saw that it was Jamie.

"Jamie!" Clola called his name but it was only a croak which came from her lips.

He opened the door a little farther and came into the room.

"Mrs. Forse said we weren't to come near you as you had a fever," he said, "but I came over the roofs to tell you I was sorry."

Clola forced herself to speak.

"Jamie!" she said in a croaking whisper. "Fetch . . . Torquil to . . . help me . . . fetch him . . . quickly!"

"You want Torquil?" Jamie asked. "You look ill—very ill!"

"I am ill . . . tell . . . Torquil to come . . . quickly . . . quickly . . . and do not . . . let anyone . . . hear you. . . ."

It was terribly hard to say the words, but she saw that Jamie understood.

As if he was frightened by her appearance and her croaking voice, he turned and ran back through the door onto the battlements, shutting it behind him.

Clola closed her eyes.

To speak, she thought, had been the greatest effort she had ever made in her life.

Her mind drifted away for a moment into the darkness and she was sinking, sinking lower and lower until she was aware of someone leaning over her.

She knew who it was before she opened her eyes to look, knew it by the unmistakable sense of evil.

Then she felt Mrs. Forse's arms go round her.

"Come along, Yer Grace," she said in a voice that was almost mesmeric. "Come for a walk, then ye'll nae longer feel ill."

She pulled Clola up into a sitting position.

"Leave . . . me . . . alone," Clola tried to say, but the words did not sound very coherent.

"I'm a-doing what's best for ye an' best for the McNarns," Mrs. Forse said.

She was speaking in a low voice as if she were talking partly to herself and partly to a child.

"Come along the noo, then ye'll know nothin' more—nothin' at all!"

By this time she had lifted Clola's legs onto the floor, and now putting her arm round her waist she pulled her onto her feet, except that they would not hold her.

She would have sagged and fallen if Mrs. Forse had not held her up.

"Let . . . me . . . go!" Clola managed to articulate.

"Noo, ye're a-goin' te die!" Mrs. Forse said. "Ye're going te die by th' hand o' a McNarn—an' there's justice in that!"

She suddenly chuckled in an evil way which made Clola realise through a haze of horror that she was insane.

She wanted to fight the woman and push her away, but she could not move her hands and Mrs. Forse was carrying her bodily across the small room to where Clola could see the open turret door.

"No! No!" she cried. "You cannot . . . do this!"

"Ye'll die!" Mrs. Forse ejaculated. "Ye'll die an' for th' vengeance o' ma ancestors I'll thank th' Lawd."

She paused a moment to push the heavy door a little farther open. Then she said:

"Ma son Euan'll avenge those who died by th' hand o' th' English when he shoots doon their King, who dares te set his blood-stained feet on th' soil o' Scotland."

As she spoke out, she dragged Clola onto the battlements.

There was a sharp wind and the coolness of it on her face seemed to revive a little of Clola's strength.

She managed to put out her hands to hold on to the high point of a crenellated battlement.

"No!" she managed to cry. "No!"

"Look doon an' see how far ye'll fall," Mrs. Forse said. "Ye'll die when ye reach the ground, an' they'll say: 'Puir lady, she walked from her room in her fever, an' fell!' "

She laughed and it was a horrible sound.

"An' who'll mourn a Kilcraig?"

Clola could feel the rough stone of the battlement beneath her fingers, then Mrs. Forse started to pull her along to the lower part, where the wall only reached to her knees.

Her arms were strong and Clola knew despairingly that it was only a question of seconds before she would no longer be able to hold on but must fall as Mrs. Forse intended.

"Die!" Mrs. Forse cried, and her voice seemed to ring out. "Die, an' may th' Devil take yer black soul down inta Hell!"

She pulled with all her strength as she spoke and Clola felt herself about to fall.

She looked down, and the ground far away beneath her was swimming before her eyes. Then there was a sudden yell and the sound of heavy footsteps coming over the roof.

Mrs. Forse had almost pulled her free of the higher battlements to which she was clinging when Clola felt strong arms go round her to pull her back to safety.

"Let her die, Master Torquil!" Mrs. Forse screamed. "Her's a Kilcraig an' she has te die!"

"Let go of her, you wicked woman!" Torquil shouted.

He had one arm round Clola, but Mrs. Forse was still pulling at her and Torquil struck out.

He hardly touched Mrs. Forse but she stepped back to avoid the blow and her feet slipped on the damp lead of the roof.

As she did so, she released her hold on Clola and overbalanced and fell through the opening in the crenellation where she had meant to push her victim.

She screamed and Clola saw her face contort, her eyes wide with terror and her mouth open, before she disappeared from view.

Clola gave a sob which was the only sound she could make as Torquil dragged her back through the door into the turret.

With his arms round her—for otherwise she would have fallen to the ground—he stood looking at the small bed and the partially furnished room.

"You can't stay here," he muttered.

Then as he realised that she was too weak to do anything for herself, he picked her up in his arms and carried her very carefully down the stairs.

He was tall and strong for his age and Clola was very light and weak from all she had been through.

It was not difficult for him to take her down the twisting turret staircase, then to descend the wider one which led from the top floor of the house down to the first, where the Duchess's bed-room was situated.

He was halfway down the second flight of stairs when Jamie came running from behind him.

"You've saved her! Oh, Torquil, you've saved her!" the little boy cried.

"Go and fetch Jeannie," Torquil said. "Tell her to come quickly."

It was the voice of command and Jamie ran past him to obey.

They had almost reached the Duchess's bed-room when Clola remembered.

Her brain felt as if it was packed with cotton-wool, so that it was too great an effort to speak and she felt too weak to attempt it.

All she could see behind her closed eyes was Mrs. Forse's open mouth and wide-eyed terror.

Then she made herself remember what the woman had said.

"Tor-quil!" Clola forced the name between her lips.

"It's all right," Torquil replied. "You are safe. She's dead. She can't hurt you any more."

"Her . . . son!" Clola gasped. "Her son . . . Euan . . . means to . . . kill the . . . King!"

She felt Torquil's arms stiffen in astonishment and a moment later Clola felt him put her down on the bed.

She thought he might go away and tried to reach out her hand to prevent him.

"You . . . must . . . tell . . . the Duke," she murmured faintly. "Go . . . to Edinburgh . . . warn him!"

She knew that Torquil was staring at her as if he thought she had taken leave of her senses, and she said:

"Think of the . . . Clan. . . . For a . . . McNarn to . . . kill the King . . . it . . . would be . . ."

There was no need to say any more.

"I understand," Torquil interrupted. "I'll go at once. I'll take two men with me and if it's possible we'll get there in time."

"Hurry . . . hurry!" Clola insisted.

She heard Torquil's feet running down the corridor, and she shut her eyes.

Vaguely, as she drifted into unconsciousness, she remembered the Grey Lady saying:

"Fate has sent you. There are things that only you can do!"

* * *

The Duke had travelled to Edinburgh in a black rage and there was nothing Lord Hinchley could say to disperse it.

Because of the delay caused by the Duke's wedding and Lord

Hinchley's desire to shoot, they all travelled by sea, which was quicker.

Mr. Dunblane had chartered a ship which was large and comparatively comfortable, and the sea being calm, the voyage only took a day.

So Lord Hinchley was spared two days of jolting over bad roads which he would otherwise have been forced to endure.

The Duke found the whole of Edinburgh *en fête* and it seemed extraordinary that such elaborate preparations should have been made to welcome the King from England.

There was no doubt that the Scots for the moment had put aside their hatred and their resentment of the past, and the gaily decorated city and the obvious excitement in the air seemed to forecast a better relationship in the future.

The Duke found on arrival that His Majesty was to stay with the sixteen-year-old Earl of Dalkeith at Dalkeith Palace.

He was also informed that every house in Edinburgh was packed from floor to ceiling with the nobility who had poured in from every part of Scotland for this auspicious occasion.

He had however been for many years a friend of the Duke of Hamilton, and he knew that if it was possible the Duke would entertain him at Holyrood Palace.

The Duke of Hamilton was hereditary Keeper of the ancient Palace, which had been burnt by the soldiers of Cromwell.

It was however later repaired and enlarged, and the Young Pretender, Prince Charles Stuart, had resided there for some time during the Rebellion of 1745.

The Duke knew that a great part of the building was now uninhabited, but the Duke of Hamilton had lodgings within it when he came to Edinburgh, as had several others of the Scottish nobility.

The Duke of Hamilton welcomed the Duke with open arms and assured him that there was plenty of room in his part of the building for both himself and Mr. Dunblane.

Lord Hinchley had arranged before he left England that he would stay at Dalkeith Palace with the King.

The first night the Duke arrived he was able to dine quietly with the Duke of Hamilton and a few friends, because although the *Royal George* had dropped anchor, His Majesty was not due to land at Leith until the following day.

The Duke of Hamilton discussed with the Duke the arrangements that had been made especially concerning the Cavalry Review on Portobello Sands.

Then as the port was passed round the table he said:

"There is a rumour, which may be entirely untrue, that you are married, Strathnarn."

The Duke's eyes darkened for a moment, but because there was nothing else he could say he replied:

"Yes, that is true."

"This is most unexpected," the Duke of Hamilton said, "but we must certainly congratulate you and give you all our good wishes. There is only one thing I cannot understand."

"What is that?" the Duke enquired.

"Why you have not brought your beautiful Duchess with you."

The Duke looked surprised but the Duke of Hamilton smiled.

"I have known Clola since she first came to Edinburgh when she was fifteen. She was lovely then, but I can assure you, Strathnarn, that last winter at least half the eligible bachelors of Scotland laid their hearts at her feet."

"That is true," another man interposed, "but she would have none of us. I always suspected that her grandmother was keeping her for someone as grand as Strathnarn."

The Duke was too astonished to make any reply, but, as he seemed reluctant to talk of his new wife, the Duke of Hamilton did not refer to her again.

When the party broke up, Lord Brora, who was an old friend and often stayed in London, accompanied the Duke to his rooms.

The moment they were alone Lord Brora said fiercely:

"When did you marry Clola, and why was I not told about it?"

"We were married only a few days ago," the Duke said coldly.

"It is intolerable! Absolutely intolerable that you should sweep her off in this manner!" Lord Brora exclaimed in a strange tone. "If I had any guts I would blow a piece of lead through you!"

"What the devil are you talking about?" the Duke enquired. "Do you know my wife?"

"Know her?" Lord Brora's voice was raw. "I have asked her to marry me a thousand times and the answer was always the same— no!"

He walked across the room, his kilt swinging from his hips as if it expressed the anger he was feeling.

"Have you not enough women in the South," he asked, "that you should come North to carry off the most desirable woman in all Scotland under our noses?"

"Are you telling me that Clola lived in Edinburgh?" the Duke asked.

"Of course, she has lived in Edinburgh for the last three years," Lord Brora replied. "She was brought up here by her grandmother, one of the most outstanding and certainly the most intelligent women North of the Tweed."

The Duke was silent and Lord Brora went on:

"Surely Clola must have told you that she was acclaimed, fêted and loved by everyone—especially by me?"

"She has certainly never mentioned you," the Duke said truthfully.

"It would be like her not to boast of her conquests," Lord Brora said, and his voice softened. "But I am asking myself, Strathnarn, how I can live without her."

There was a note in his voice which told the Duke that the man who had been his friend for some years was suffering. But he did not know what he could do about it.

"How did you persuade her into accepting you?" Lord Brora went on after a moment. Then he gave an exclamation. "I know what it is! You are both musical! How could I compete with that when I cannot tell one note from another?"

"Clola is musical?" the Duke asked tentatively.

"Of course she is musical. She plays like an angel and sings like one too. If she had not been a lady and wealthy she could have made a fortune as a professional!"

The Duke was stunned into silence.

Vaguely at the back of his mind he remembered assuming he was marrying someone uncivilised and uneducated.

"Well, I am going to bed!" Lord Brora said sharply.

This told the Duke that he felt too upset at what had occurred to stay talking to him, but as he reached the door Lord Brora added:

"What I cannot understand is why you did not bring Clola with you."

He gave a short laugh.

"I suppose the answer is that you are too jealous to let any of her old friends near her."

He left the room and the Duke rose to stand at the diamond-paned window, looking out at the courtyard of the Palace.

He did not see the moonlight on the roofs and chimneys. Instead, he saw two mysterious eyes with flecks of gold in them and he heard a soft voice repeating the Oath of Allegiance.

The Duke did not sleep well that night, nor the next.

*   *   *

The King arrived and was delighted with his Reception and with the large number of the nobility who were in attendance upon him.

His own Suite consisted of many of the Duke's more personal friends.

Like Lord Brora, as soon as they heard that he was married they bombarded him with questions, many of which he found impossible to answer.

The King's eyes were twinkling when he congratulated him.

"Caught at last, eh, Taran?" he said. "And from all reports, the Duchess is so lovely and so attractive that I cannot understand why you are hiding her from me."

"She was unable, Sire, to come to Edinburgh so soon after our marriage."

It was the excuse that the Duke had given to all the other enquirers, but he could not help his voice from becoming more stiff and more reserved each time he had to repeat it.

"Bring her South, my boy," the King said. "Bring her to London as soon as possible. I am determined to make the acquaintance of this paragon of beauty and virtue, so do not try my curiosity too high!"

The Duke bowed his acceptance, remembering his decision to leave his wife, whom he had been forced into marrying, alone in Scotland.

His Majesty held a Levee at Holyrood Palace on August 17, at which the Duke was in attendance.

Besides the Chieftains of the Clans, many noblemen and gentlemen appeared in Highland dress, among whom, together with the Duke, were the Dukes of Hamilton and Argyll and the Earl of Breadalbane.

After the Levee, His Majesty held a Privy Council, and on Monday a Court and closed audience, also at Holyrood Palace.

The following day a Drawing-Room Reception was attended by all the most important ladies in Edinburgh, and there again the Duke was bombarded with questions as to why Clola was not with him.

"At least she will not eclipse us all as she did at the Balls last winter!" the Marchioness of Queensbury exclaimed.

While the Countess of Elgin added:

"But she was so sweet and unspoilt by her success that it was impossible to be jealous of her."

After this, there were processions, meetings, inspections, and a special Banquet given in Parliament House by the Lord Provost, so the Duke hardly had time to think.

Finally, everyone was looking forward to the Cavalry Review that was to take place on Portobello Sands.

The Duke was surprised to learn that fifty thousand spectators were expected and the whole Corps of Volunteer Troops numbered over three thousand.

He learnt that Mr. Dunblane had arranged for fifty of the McNarn Yeomanry, in which his father had taken a special interest, to represent the Clan.

Each Clan had its own Standard, Badge, and Piper, and when the Duke saw the McNarns rehearsing the day before the Review, he had been very impressed by their appearance.

They were just as smart as, if not smarter than, those under the command of the Earl of Breadalbane, who wore yellow plumes in their bonnets and crests on their right arms.

The Duke of Argyll was to lead the Celtic Society, a body of one hundred Highlanders, all superbly dressed, each in his own Clan tartan with a belted plaid.

Sir Euan McGregor, carrying the same broadsword which his grandfather had used at the Battle of Prestonpass, led the Clan Gregor. He wore an outstanding red tartan and each of the Clansmen had a branch of fir in his bonnet.

The Marchioness of Stafford had sent fifty Highlanders from Dunrobin, and Lady Gwydir had sent a gallant band of Drummonds, their Badge a holly bough.

There was a great deal of rivalry and a certain amount of jealousy amongst the Clansmen, but the Duke felt that the McNarns would hold their own and he found himself feeling extremely proud of their appearance.

Just before he left the parade Mr. Dunblane said to him:

"There are several men who would like a word with Your Grace, if you can spare the time."

"What about?" the Duke enquired.

"Their problems," Mr. Dunblane replied.

"Their problems?" the Duke queried.

There was a faint smile on Mr. Dunblane's face as he said:

"It is traditional, as you will appreciate, that they may bring their problems to their Chieftain as in ancient days. It is in fact a compliment."

"Do you really expect me to solve the problems of these men?" the Duke asked. "What do I know of their lives when I have lived in the South for so long?"

"They trust you, they believe in you, and they will do what you say," Mr. Dunblane said.

The Duke thought for a moment.

"Very well," he replied. "I will speak to them, but God knows if the advice I give them will be any good."

"I think you underestimate your sympathy with your own people," Mr. Dunblane said quietly.

Before the Duke could think of a reply, Mr. Dunblane went to fetch the men who wished to see him.

To his own surprise, the Duke found himself giving decisions on problems covering land, cattle, family difficulties, and even in one instance whether a man was too young to take a wife.

As he rode back to Holyrood Palace with Mr. Dunblane beside him he said:

"I suppose this is another way in which you are trying to trap me into assuming my responsibilities and staying in the North?"

"I am not trying to trap you," Mr. Dunblane replied. "It is perhaps your heart that will do that."

"I have no heart!" the Duke said harshly.

He thought as he spoke that he had put too much emphasis on the word.

They reached the Palace and rode in through the great gates. As they drew their horses to a standstill outside the door which led to the private apartments, the Duke saw a young figure come racing towards him and stared in disbelief.

"Torquil!" he exclaimed.

Then his nephew was at his side, his words tumbling over themselves in his anxiety to make the Duke understand the urgency of what he had come to tell him.

CHAPTER SEVEN

"Now try an' rest, Your Grace, and, if ye can, have a quiet nap," Jeannie admonished. "I'm taking Master Jamie away to th' river and we won't be back 'til it's nearly his bed-time."

Jeannie spoke in the kind but firm way that Clola remembered her own Nanny speaking and she found herself responding to it as if she were a child.

Jeannie, who had looked after her when Torquil left for Edinburgh, was a middle-aged, sweet-faced woman who had devoted her life to other people's children. First Torquil, and then Jamie, had been "her baby."

She fussed over Clola like a mother-hen, and gradually the poison had gone from Clola's body and she felt herself coming back to life as if she had been on a long, dark journey into the unknown.

"I never trusted that Mistress Forse," Jeannie said over and over again. "I sensed her wickedness even while she were wi' us but couldna' put ma finger on it."

Clola shrank from asking who had found Mrs. Forse when she had fallen from the battlements and what had happened.

It all seemed in retrospect like a horrible, evil dream, but she could not think of how near she had been to death without shuddering.

"I saved you, didn't I?" Jamie asked her when she was well enough to talk to him. "I ran for Torquil as you told me to and he came over the roofs so quickly I couldn't keep up with him."

"Yes, you saved me, dearest," Clola agreed.

"Jeannie says I'm to look after you until Uncle Taran comes back."

"You are doing that very well," Clola said with a smile.

When Jamie had left her bed-side she had lain worrying ceaselessly as to whether Torquil would be in time and if the Duke would believe him.

She could understand how hard it would be for him to realise the violence of the hatred for the English which still possessed many of the Clansmen.

She could not help feeling frantically afraid in case he should dismiss Torquil's message as a lot of nonsense and that Euan Forse would assassinate the King.

Even if an unsuccessful attempt was made, she knew it would be a terrible blow to the pride of the McNarns, and, worse still, it would reverberate throughout the whole of Great Britain.

Living in Edinburgh amongst intelligent people, Clola had learnt how desperately the Scots were trying to establish their position.

There was intellect, invention, and industry in Scotland, ready to enrich the growth of an Imperial Britain if only the South could realise it.

But the English still behaved as if the Scots had to be kept down, and there were many unjust restrictions which affected an already impoverished economy.

Clola felt that if only there were more men of influence as well as intelligence, like the Duke, the Scottish cause could be heard and public opinion would swing in their country's favour.

But would the Duke be prepared to use his influence?

That was the real question in her mind and she wondered how she could make him understand how desperately needed he was in the Highlands.

If he would listen to the call of his blood, then there would be a chance of the Golden Age of which the Bards had sung and the Soothsayers had prophesied but which never seemed to come to fruition.

"I must talk to him," she told herself.

Then she wondered despairingly if he would listen, seeing that he had believed her to be unfaithful to him within forty-eight hours of their marriage.

How could he think such a thing? How could he believe it?

She recalled in all justice that he knew nothing about her and she was in fact at fault for not having told him of her life before she became his wife.

It all seemed to be a hopeless, imponderable problem, which kept Clola awake all night and retarded her recovery in a way which distressed and puzzled Jeannie.

Sitting now on the sofa in the Music Room, which she had made a special place of her own, Clola longed to tell the Duke not only about Scotland and his responsibilities but also about her love of music and what it meant to her.

As the evil of what had happened faded from her mind and body, she began to hear melodies carried on the breeze outside the Castle.

When she was well enough to stand at her window, looking out towards the loch, tunes came to her mind that she longed to translate into composition and song.

"If only I could explain to him," she whispered to herself, "perhaps he would . . . understand."

She remembered how they had looked into each other's eyes as she stood in front of him before she knelt for the Oath of Allegiance.

She had felt then as if they reached each other across time and there was no need for words.

Then she told herself it was just an illusion; nevertheless, when his hands touched hers she had felt herself vibrate in a way she had never done before.

Clola was very sensitive to the vibrations of other people, and she had known at the touch of the Duke that she felt a strangeness which was spiritual.

There had also been something magic about it.

Because the thought of him disturbed her and yet at the same time she longed to see him, she started to calculate, as she had done a dozen times already, how soon he would return to the Castle.

If indeed he did return!

She had a feeling that though nothing had been said in her presence, the Duke might leave Scotland and go South with the King.

The idea hurt her so excessively that it was like a physical pain.

But she tried to tell herself it was because she was so desperately anxious to know if Euan Forse had been apprehended.

Had he been prevented from committing a ghastly murder on the instigation of his fanatical mother?

It was intended, Clola knew, that the King should sail in the *Royal George* on August 29, embarking from Port Edgar, near Kingsferry, after a visit to the Earl of Hopetoun.

Clola was sure that the Duke would stay at Hopetoun House with His Majesty, and that meant there would be no chance of his returning before August 31.

She guessed that Euan Forse would have planned to assassinate the King at the Cavalry Review on Portobello Sands.

And she felt now as if the long-drawn-out delay before she could have any news was unbearable.

Perhaps Torquil would return to tell her what had happened, and yet she doubted it! Supposing he had not been in time, or that Euan Forse had evaded them?

Bad news would not travel faster than good.

The complexity of it all made Clola so restless that, disobeying Jeannie's instructions, she rose from the sofa to walk across the room to the harp.

She had grown very much more proficient at playing the ancient instrument these past days since she had been well enough to leave her bed-room and walk, at first very unsteadily, into the other rooms of the Castle.

The day before yesterday she had been allowed to sit outside in the sunshine, warmly wrapped in one of her grandmother's beautiful sable stoles.

The feel of the sun on her face and the fresh air from the moors swept away not only the last lingering effect of Mrs. Forse's poison from Clola's body but also the terrors from her mind.

The next morning, despite Jeannie's protests when she had insisted on rising after breakfast, she had gone across the passage and entered the room of the Grey Lady.

The sunshine coming through the window dissipated the eeriness Clola had expected.

Instead, she felt that only a calm serenity pervaded the room, and looking up at the painting of the Countess Morag, she knew that the message she had received from her had in fact saved her life.

If she had not remembered that she must fight and struggle against Mrs. Forse's hold over her, she might have been too weak and too bemused by the drug to send for Torquil and to hold on to the battlements for those vital seconds before he came to save her.

Looking up at the portrait on the wall, Clola knew that she had not been mistaken on the night of her marriage when she had felt that the Grey Lady was with her.

She had been real, more real than many people she had known, and she knew that she would always be there in the future if her help was needed.

"Thank you," she said softly as she had said once before.

Then she had gone from the room with a smile on her lips and for a little while had ceased to worry about what was happening in Edinburgh.

But it was impossible to escape for long from the anxiety, which, because of her sleeplessness, was making soft purple shadows under her eyes.

She had grown much thinner during her illness and her eyes seemed larger and to fill her whole face.

But she had in fact recovered much of her strength, and she had known that that was true when yesterday she had sung, accompanying herself on the harpsichord, one of the ballads that were part of Scottish history.

Her grandmother's friends had loved to listen to her singing these ancient songs after great dinner-parties they enjoyed at her house in Edinburgh.

Because Clola knew now that only music would soothe her and prevent her from worrying over what was happening miles away, she sat down at the harp and ran her fingers over the strings.

The soft notes, she thought, were like the sound of the burn cascading down the rocks and the wash of the sea against the shore.

She plucked out note by note and now they combined to give form to the melody that had come to her mind when she was still too weak to move from her bed but knew she was safe in Jeannie's capable hands.

It was a song of the mystery of the mountains, of the wildness of the moors, and a song too . . . of love.

Clola's fingers faltered for a moment.

What did she know of love? she asked. Yet it was there in her melody and, if she was truthful, in her heart.

A love so compelling, so inescapable, that it was no use trying to deny it.

It was the love she had sought and never found with any of the gentlemen who had asked for her hand in marriage.

She had refused them because she had known that they could never, however long she knew them, attain the ideal which lay enshrined in the secrecy of her heart.

And yet now, although tremblingly she dared not admit it, that shrine was filled.

As if the wonder of it must be translated into music, Clola played and felt the sound of it envelop her like angels' wings and lift her into the sky, from where her inspiration had come.

Then as she knew an ecstasy that came from within herself as her fingers on the strings echoed what was Divine, she was suddenly aware that she was not alone.

Something drew her compellingly and she turned her head to find, almost as if she had expected him, the Duke standing inside the door.

How long he had been there Clola had no idea; she only knew that her heart had called to him and he had answered the call.

Her hands dropped from the harp and she rose to her feet, her eyes held by the Duke's and by an expression on his face she had never seen before.

Vaguely, some part of her mind thought he looked even more handsome, more proud, and more imperious.

Then he moved slowly towards her, his eyes still holding hers, and it was impossible to think and almost impossible to breathe.

"You are all right?"

His voice, deep and low, seemed to come from another world.

"Wh-why are you . . . here so . . . soon? What has . . . happened?"

It was difficult for Clola to speak the words and there was a touch of fear behind them.

"I could not stay away any longer," the Duke replied.

Then as he stood in front of her, face to face, looking down into the mystery of her eyes, he said:

"When I first saw you, Clola, you made a vow of allegiance to me. Now I have one to make to you."

As he spoke he went down on one knee in front of her and put his hands together, palm to palm. Then, looking up to her, he said very slowly:

"I swear by Almighty God to protect and serve you for as long as my life lasts, to live or to die for you. I will love you with my whole heart, worship you as my wife, and will strive to give you happiness. May God help me!"

His voice seemed to vibrate through Clola and every word brought a response from her which seemed part of the music she had been playing.

Then because she sensed that he was waiting for her response she put her hands on each side of his.

Shyly, aware that her heart was beating wildly, she bent her head to kiss him as he had kissed her on her cheek.

But somehow instead of his cheek it was his lips she found. Then, holding her captive with his mouth, the Duke's arms were round her.

He rose to pull her close against him as his kiss deepened and became more compelling, more possessive.

Like the music which had carried Clola on angels' wings into the sky, she felt that the Duke was carrying her still higher into the heart of the spheres.

He was carrying her into a glory and a wonder that was so indescribable that she knew there were no words but only the singing of the stars.

The kiss lasted so long that they stepped out of time and only when the Duke raised his head to look down at her did Clola's hands reach out to hold onto him.

"You are mine!" the Duke said, and there was a note of triumph in his voice. "Mine, and no-one shall take you from me!"

Then he was kissing her again, kissing her fiercely, passionately, but she was not afraid.

She only knew that this was not only what she had been seeking, but what she had been made for and the reason why she had been born.

She was his, a part of him as he was a part of her, and the magic enveloping them came from other lives and other knowledge they could only find when they were together. . . .

* * *

When Clola could speak, and it was difficult because of the wild feelings springing inside her, she asked:

"Torquil . . . was in . . . time?"

For a moment it seemed as if the Duke found it hard to think of anything but the softness of her lips. Then he answered:

"As soon as he told me what you had sent him to say, we went in search of Euan Forse. When we found him with a loaded pistol, he fired it indiscriminately in an effort to defend himself."

Clola gave a little cry of horror.

"He . . . might have . . . killed you!"

"I was not meant to die any more than you were, my precious," the Duke answered.

He held her close against him before he went on:

"I think Forse is deranged, like his mother. When we took his pistol from him he burst into an uncontrolled and violent tirade against the English."

The Duke paused for a moment before he went on:

"As far as Dunblane and I could understand, his grandparents had been killed after the Rebellion in forty-five and a cousin had her hands cut off for helping a wounded Highlander."

Clola gave a little murmur of horror and the Duke said gently:

"I do not want to upset you. I have left Euan Forse in the care of a competent Doctor who will see what he can do for him. We need not think of him again, any more than we need think of his mother."

Clola was still for a moment, content because the Duke's arms were round her. Then she asked:

"Why are you . . . here so soon? I was not . . . expecting you until His Majesty left Scotland."

"I told the King that I had very urgent matters to attend to at home," the Duke replied. "They were extremely urgent, because I could stay away from you no longer."

Clola raised her eyes to his and it seemed as if the sunshine was imprisoned in them.

"The King was not . . . angry with you for . . . going away?"

"He understood," the Duke answered, "but I had to promise him that I would take you South to meet him. He had heard so much of your beauty and your brilliance."

Clola blushed and the Duke asked:

"Why did you not tell me how talented you were?"

"I did not . . . think you would be . . . interested," she replied.

"But there are so many . . . things I want to . . . talk to you . . . about."

"We have our whole lives in which to talk to each other," the Duke answered, "but now I only want to kiss you."

He would have sought her lips again, but Clola put up her hands.

"You must be . . . tired. I am sure you have been riding for . . . many hours."

"I rode all through the night."

"To . . . see me?" she asked incredulously.

"To see you!"

"Then you must be both tired and hungry," she said. "I am sure a bath will be waiting for you, and we will dine as soon as you are changed."

"Shall I come and help you dress, as you have no lady's-maid?" the Duke asked with a smile.

Clola blushed.

"No, of course . . . not. The housemaids will . . . help me."

"When we have finished dinner we will send them away and I will look after you as I wish to do."

Clola turned her face against his shoulder to hide her shyness. Then she gave a little laugh.

"Why do you laugh?" the Duke asked.

"My sister-in-law would be so . . . shocked," she explained. "She thinks that a man's . . . work is . . . outside and he has no . . . interest in . . . women's dress."

"I have a great interest in what you wear or do not wear," the Duke said, "and I assure you I am quite experienced in such matters."

"I can . . . believe . . . that," Clola whispered.

He smiled as he lifted her face up to his.

"Are you jealous, my darling?" he asked. "I should be very proud if I thought anything I could do would make you jealous."

She did not answer and he looked down at her face to say hoarsely:

"Could anyone be so beautiful, so perfect, so different in every way?"

His lips took hers captive and he kissed her until the room seemed to whirl round them and the Castle itself seemed to dissolve into the sunlit sky.

Then urgently, because she loved him and because she wanted the night to come so that they could be alone, Clola drew him by the

hand down the passage towards their bed-rooms with their communicating-door.

* * *

Clola stirred against the Duke's shoulder and he kissed her forehead.

"You are not too tired, my darling?"

"How can I be . . . tired when I have never . . . known such
. . . happiness?"

"I have really made you happy?"

She pressed her lips against his chest and he tightened his arms
about her, thinking that the soft warmth of her body was the most
perfect thing he had ever known.

She had not thought it possible for a man to be so passionate and
yet so gentle, so demanding and yet so tender.

The Duke looked up for a moment at the great embroidered can-
opy overhead, just visible in the light from the one candle which still
flickered behind the curtains.

"It is fate that brought you to me," he said quietly.

"That is . . . what the . . . Grey Lady said," Clola murmured.

"The Grey Lady? How do you know about her?"

There was a little pause, then Clola answered:

"If I tell you . . . you might . . . think I am very . . . foolish."

"I would think nothing you said or did was foolish. How could I
when everything you have done for me, for the Clan, and for Torquil,
has been so wise and so completely and absolutely right?"

Clola looked up at him, and although she did not ask the question,
the Duke realised what she wanted to know, and he said:

"Torquil told me, my precious, how you saved him from the
MacAuads. Could anyone else have been so wonderful or so re-
sourceful?"

Clola gave a little sigh of relief and the Duke said:

"Have you forgiven me for what I said to you? I realise now, although I was hardly aware of it at the time, that I was wildly,
furiously jealous!"

"How did you . . . know I had left the . . . Castle?"

"Mrs. Forse told me."

"Mrs. . . . Forse?"

"Yes, that devillish woman through whom I might have lost you."

There was a note of fear in the Duke's voice that was unmistakable.

He turned Clola's face up to his and kissed her first on the lips, then on both her eyes, and finally once again on her lips.

Her response made the fire rise within him.

With an effort Clola moved her mouth from his.

"Go on . . . telling me about . . . Mrs. Forse," she pleaded.

"If only I had known what she was like," the Duke said, "and Dunblane blames himself for not having suspected she was insane."

"What did she . . . say to . . . you?"

"She awakened me to say: 'I'm awfu' worried, Yer Grace.'

" 'Why, what has happened?' I enquired.

" 'Her Grace left th' Castle nigh on two hours ago an' hasna returned.'

" 'Left the Castle?' I exclaimed.

"It seemed so incomprehensible that I sent the woman away and went to your bed-room. Your nightgown was lying on the floor, the wardrobe was open, and I knew that Mrs. Forse had not lied."

"I wonder how she . . . knew I was . . . gone," Clola murmured.

"Doubtless because her bed-room overlooks the front of the house," the Duke answered. "But I was certain that you had some clandestine reason for going out at such an unearthly hour, especially after you had sent me away because Jamie was sleeping in your arms."

He paused for a moment before he said:

"Do you know how beautiful you looked with the child's head on your breast, your hair falling over your shoulders, your eyes wide and a little frightened?"

He pulled her almost roughly against him.

"My adorable little love, supposing you had died and I had never been able to make you mine as you are now?"

"But I am . . . alive," Clola whispered softly, "and I . . . love you!"

"I will make you love me more and more," the Duke promised, "only never again will there be any misunderstanding between us, nor will we ever be separated."

He kissed her forehead, then he said:

"You were telling me about the Grey Lady. I cannot imagine how you knew about her."

"Is she . . . really called the . . . 'Grey Lady'?"

"In all the legends that is how we refer to her."

"I did not . . . know that," Clola said. "But the first night when Mrs. Forse . . . cursed me and said only . . . evil would come of our . . . marriage, I was . . . afraid of her and . . . afraid of you."

"I promise that you will never feel that way again," the Duke said.

"But I knew you . . . hated the idea of . . . marrying me! I felt it . . . when the Minister . . . joined us as . . . man and wife."

"I did not look at you then," the Duke said. "I did not dare to."

"I can understand that . . . but I felt . . . lonely and . . . afraid," Clola explained. "Then I felt that if I watched the Kilcraigs celebrating outside the Castle and . . . listened to the . . . music of the . . . pipes, I would feel . . . better."

The Duke moved his lips over the softness of her skin.

He had been right, he told himself; it had the velvet texture of a magnolia. But, though it moved him, he listened to what she was telling him.

"I went into the bed-room on the other . . . side of the . . . corridor to look out," Clola went on, "and when I was feeling . . . miserable and . . . unhappy, I knew a Grey Lady was standing beside me. She comforted me and gave me . . . courage."

"How did you know that?" he asked, then added quickly: "That is a stupid question. I know what you felt. Go on!"

"She said quite clearly," Clola continued, "that it was . . . fate that had . . . brought me here and there were . . . things for me to do which no-one else . . . could."

"She was right," the Duke said, "and I know that while you were born a Kilcraig you are now irrefutably a McNarn."

He smiled before he continued:

"The Grey Lady, Morag Countess McNarn, lost her husband in the Battle of Flodden. Forever afterwards she wore not black but grey, and she brought up her three sons to be as noble, brave, and just as their father had been. The eldest became one of the greatest Chieftains the McNarns have ever known."

He paused for a moment before he said slowly and impressively:

"Whenever the Chieftain of the Clan is in danger or in real trouble, it is understood that the Grey Lady comes to help and advise him. That she came to you, my darling, is so significant that I know now what I have to do."

"What is . . . that?" Clola asked.

"I think you know the answer," the Duke replied. "Stay here with my people, as I know you would want me to do."

Clola gave a cry of sheer happiness.

"Do you mean . . . that? Do you . . . really mean . . . it?"

"I knew when I led them in the Cavalry Review," the Duke said, "that they meant to me something impossible to ignore. I knew, when they brought me their problems, where my duty lay. And when I thought of you, I realised that my heart, which I never knew I had before, belonged to Scotland."

"Oh, my wonderful . . . magnificent husband, that is what I have . . . prayed you might . . . feel. Our country needs you so . . . desperately. There is so much to . . . do, so much to . . . fight for . . . so much to . . . live for."

Tears came to Clola's eyes with the intensity of her feelings. Then the Duke asked:

"Do you love me enough to help me? I shall need your help and your love, because I cannot live without it."

"I love you!" Clola said passionately. "With my whole . . . heart and . . . soul I am yours, completely and absolutely . . . as you know . . . I am."

"That is what I want," the Duke said. "That is what I must have, and, my darling, whatever the difficulties ahead, I know that our love will surmount them."

His lips were on hers as he spoke the last words.

Then he was kissing her with a passion and fire that seemed to come from the wildness of the moors and the spirit of the mountains.

It was, Clola knew, as beautiful as the music which throbbed within them both and made the desire of their love a rising crescendo of wonder and rapture that carried them away on the wings of ecstasy.

'I love . . . you! I love . . . you!' she thought, as her lips were held captive by his.

Their bodies were entwined, and their souls were closer still.

They had found, as few are privileged to find, the perfection of a love that belongs to the brave and valiant and those who must live as well as die for their faith.

ABOUT THE AUTHOR

BARBARA CARTLAND, the celebrated romantic novelist, historian, playwright, lecturer, political speaker, and television personality, has now written over two hundred books. She has had a number of historical books published and several biographical ones, including a biography of her brother, Major Ronald Cartland, who was the first Member of Parliament to be killed in the war. The book has a preface by Sir Winston Churchill.

In private life Barbara Cartland is a Dame of Grace of St. John of Jerusalem and one of the first women, after a thousand years, to be admitted to the Chapter General.

She has fought for better conditions and salaries for midwives and nurses, and, as President of the Hertfordshire Branch of the Royal College of Midwives, she has been invested with the first Badge of Office ever given in Great Britain, which was subscribed to by the midwives themselves.

Barbara Cartland has also championed the cause of old people and founded the first Romany Gypsy Camp in the world. It was christened "Barbaraville" by the gypsies.

Barbara Cartland is deeply interested in Vitamin Therapy and is President of the National Association for Health.